MW01127987

It truly is "a 70s recipe for a rainy day," these road-tripping adventures with Zimmer and company in Abby, his powder blue VW "Bee-atile." It's a band of flawed friends building family out of improvised meals from whatever ingredients are in the fridge, while the cat, Whomee, looks on. It's a romp, a gallivant, a philosophy, an ode to irresponsibility, because, although we know these marginal folks might be a train wreck waiting to happen, we would dearly miss them if they weren't there, doing what they do—refusing to fit neatly, safely beneath the bell curve.

--R.P. Saffire, author of *Shoe Burnin' Season: A Womanifesto*

The "lumpers" in Joe Formichella's eponymous novel work the night shift at Regency Grocery's Warehouse. They love to gather at Lear's to drink longneck beer. Their second love at Lear's is to kibbutz a soap opera entitled, *Incoming Flights*. "So why do they always have to start with that music and that plane crash?" Zimmer's friend and faithful follower Steph asks. Zimmer knows exactly why: Because all lives start with a crash, don't they? Zimmer has left—some might say run from—upstate New York via Vermont to wind up in Tripoli, Pennsylvania, where he works as a lumper, where he's befriended Steph and a nearly feral cat called Whomee, and where he's quickly become something of a myth to Steph and the other lumpers because of his skills in pick-up basketball, in drinking, in pool, and in all-around camaraderie. Oh yes, he's also a grand baker and cook, who's organized "St. Fill-ups Day" a free-for-all-meal featuring snitched items from Regency's Warehouse. So why shouldn't he run for mayor of Tripoli? Why? Therein lies the rub, for both Zimmer and a handful of others who aren't so certain of the hero-myth surrounding this man named Anthony Zimbarco, aka Zimmer. And beneath that itching rub lies the novel's tragicomic movement as Zimmer fights to overcome the myth assigned him, to find just what it is that itches Anthony Zimbarco so deeply, so perpetually.

--Joe Taylor, *Pineapple,* and *Ghostly Demarcations*

Lumpers, Longnecks, and One-Eyed Jacks: A 70s Recipe for a Rainy Day

Joe Formichella

For brothers.

OTHER BOOKS BY JOE FORMICHELLA

Schopenhauer's Maxim
Waffle House Rules
Scarpete Stories
The Wreck of the Twilight Limited
Whores for Life: Scatolo's, and other stories

NONFICTION

A Condition of Freedom
Murder Creek
Staying Ahead of the Posse

1. BEGINNINGS

BEGINS with a trucker, early one cold November morning in 1979, just outside of Tripoli, Pennsylvania: "Lumpers," he had called them, as he watched the overnight crew at the Regency warehouse unload his truck: Steph, Zimmer, Bruce, and Mickey, all of them under the supervision of the all-seeing Frank Curry. They separated the bundles extracted from the cavernous trailer, redistributed the groceries into other bundles, stored some, loaded others back onto his truck as well as other eighteen wheelers poised at the lip of the warehouse platform. Lumping. Steph both started and finished the progress-less process, guiding his forklift—the nearest he had ever been to owning a vehicle—into and out of the vans. The tractor portions pointed back toward Warehouse Drive, dieseling away, like bronco bulls waiting to be loosed from their pens, away from the noise and the light and the people scurrying around, back into the quiet, dark night.

"You guys are just Lumpers, moving this here, that there. Shit, you got to be out of your minds to do this," he repeated, leaving the crew by themselves under the dock's spotlights, climbing back into his cozy cab to snooze for a while, Willie Nelson ballads serenading him in his slumber from the eight-track tape player.

Big Bruce loved the designation immediately. "Yeah, Lumpers!" he was cheering even before the break was over. In the six years he'd been working at Regency since he'd graduated Tripoli's Central Tech, he'd been called all manner of names and insults.

"Who cares about a name?" he'd ask later, if he decided he didn't like it. There was something scarier, more threatening about Bruce because he was so accommodating, as if all the potential damage he could cause *needed* to be vented once in a while, or the world was in real trouble.

Mickey, smaller, younger, braver, somehow, denied it, challenging the driver, shouting up to his closed cab on their way back to work, "If we're Lumpers, what the hell does that make you?"

Zimmer knew. He cared about names. He held them semi-sacred in his inflexible way. He explained to Steph, for instance, when it came time for him to name the forklift, that everything had its own name, whether he realized it or not, that he'd just have to wait and think and let it come to him, even as Steph defended his choice. "What's wrong with Clementine?"

"What's right with it?"

"I just wanted something I could sing to it."

And Zimmer knew that truckers had a kind of immortal's point of view, from all that time zone changing and marathon hauling—staying awake and driving three, four, five days straight. He knew that their perspective was other-worldly, at least, from the extent to which their chemicals were all screwed up if nothing else; and that their pronouncements, grudgingly bequeathed, were seldom something to take lightly.

He had to think about the name; then had to push it back farther, from any conscious thoughts, letting it cycle through his head, maybe repeating the name as the night wound on, "Lumpers... Luuuumpersss..." as if testing its bouquet, until, once their shift was over, looking back up to the platform, bathed in daylight, busy with dayshifters, looking and seeing the exact same platform that'd been there the night before, looking—thinking about grocery store shelves, the virtual end product of their work, how they do always look the same, maybe prices change, displays get altered, no more—realizing, We really don't do anything, do we?

"Lumpers."

But the name needed even more validation, both by Zimmer's requirements and by the process and procedure of the common man's network where most of the popular lexicon was birthed. It had to be passed around, within their group, throughout the other shifts at the warehouse, passed through the network of drivers, where it would be whispered over truck-stop cafeteria tables, squawked over citizen band radios; until all night-time warehouse workers became Lumpers; until no one could remember who were the first Lumpers; until, weeks later, an icy Thursday morning in December, it came full circle; until the exact same driver, huddled with the overnight Regency crew on nearly the same circle of asphalt out away from the platform, said, "You fucking Lumpers are out of your minds," leaving them his pint bottle of Four Roses, which was supposed to warm them all, leaving them for his heated cab, and the road.

"Fucking Lumpers," they mumbled back, the phrase becoming a curse, a salutation, a cheer, all at the same time, not looking up to the driver as he eased his rig down the drive, but huddling closer now that their windbreak was gone.

"Might as well be numb Lumpers," Bruce said, tilting the Four Roses up against his lips. "Mick?" he asked, passing the bottle. "You got to relax, quit all that shaking."

Mickey tried to drink, but the glass rattled against his teeth. "It's too f-f-fucking c-c-cold."

Mickey couldn't possibly dress warm enough, not with three flannel shirts, no matter how many pairs of socks he wore. He just had that kind of metabolism, Bruce'd diagnosed.

"Needs more carbs. Maybe some roids."

Each winter he froze, and each summer night, after a long sweltering day, the platform, under the thousand watt spotlights, felt like an oven to him and he'd threaten to quit, at regular intervals, like the solstice.

"Are you ever comfortable, Mick?"

"Hardly."

"Carbs."

Steph took the bottle. But he tested his lips, enunciating, "Dumb-ass numb fucking Lumpers," before attempting to drink.

"You know what it feels like out here?" Zimmer asked, though not directly. The rest of them groaned. Zimmer's descriptions were often worse than reality. He had his chin and his mouth buried down into the pulled-up collar of his Air Force fatigue jacket, shivering himself, clenching the cold metal zipper of his coat between his teeth just to keep them from chattering. "You know how the water seeps through the rocks up on the interstate where they cut through? You know how on winter days some places are always in shadow, so that the water never thaws out, just hangs there, a kind of frozen blue waterfall?"

"Ah, Jesus, Zimmer..."

"Ahh!" Bruce hollered, wrapping his arms around Mickey and deadlifting him, up and down, trying to pump some blood into motion.

They heard the squawk box crackle to life up on the platform. From a protected cubicle that he used as an office on cold nights, where a GE space heater glowed lava red, Frank called, "Aw-right LUMPERS..." They groaned, shifted some, knowing what was coming, but staying on their spots until the last possible moment, "...back to work."

Steph took Frankenstein-sized steps back up the drive, crunching the frozen remnants of the first snowfall in the darkness.

"What time is it, Mick?" Zimmer asked, both to be sure Frank wasn't cheating them and to find out how much longer they had to work that night.

"I think my watch stopped," he said, but wouldn't look, wouldn't take his hands out from the folds of his armpits.

"Let's see, let's see," Bruce said, grabbing at one skinny wrist as they mounted the stairs.

"No, NO!"

Up on the platform, Zimmer held one arm, Bruce the other.

"NO!"

"Move it Lumpers," Steph called, breaking up the tussle with the vacant tongs of Clementine, raised to about hip level, speeding toward them at all of two miles an hour.

"Did you see that Frank?" Zimmer yelled, then turned and hurled an asbestos glove at Steph.

Zimmer finished snapping up his ice-box overalls, pulled his blue watch cap all the way down over his ears, retrieved the glove and skulked to the refrigeration unit, stomping across the platform in his white Arctic boots, slapping aside the clear plastic straps that made up the door.

"Aw, Jesus," he said, as the unit's circulating air assaulted him. "These goddamn things don't work," wrapping his arms around his chest, pounding his hands against his ribs. "This is inhuman!" he growled, raising his arms and bellowing like some great polar bear agonizing his captivity.

He broke open a carton of frozen pizzas and heaved one against the wall, laughing, more screaming, "HAH!" at the little bits of frosted dough and pepperoni that shattered, burst through the thin cellophane and fell to the floor where they'd be underfoot for months.

"I saw *that*!" Frank answered him finally, over the intercom.

"Tough shit!" Zimmer said, and broke open a box of cherry popsicles, holding one over his shoulder, at the ready, like a boomerang.

There was no answer from Frank, except static, so Zimmer put aside his weapon, and went back to work on the palette at his feet, lifting cases of the popsicles, dividing, shelving, "Lumping!" in the hopes of escaping the incessant winds of the unit when he was done, just for a few minutes.

But Steph breezed through the doorway, singing, "Oh my darling, O-oh my darling," lowering another full palette wrapped in its silver insulation sheeting on top of the one Zimmer'd just cleared.

It was exactly how Frank wanted them to work: "Finish one, start on another," he'd told them their first night, pacing the platform, showing them the different aspects of the job.

Zimmer wished he hadn't encouraged Steph to name the fork just then, and reached for the popsicles. That systematic approach was too unyielding for him, most nights, once he'd grown tired, or cold, frustrated and fading. He unwrapped one popsicle and launched it at Steph who was backing Clementine out of the unit. It smacked against the raised tongs.

"Hey, watch the wheels, man."

The next splattered against the roll bar. Steph could feel the spray of ice. He huddled down further and ground the pedal of the machine all the way to the floor of the cab. Just before he cleared the straps, Zimmer scored, a popsicle thumping off of Steph's parka, leaving a small wet spot.

"Gotcha!" Zimmer yelled, holding two additional missiles up over his head, one in each hand.

"Zimbarco! Don't forget that any breakage comes out of your pocket."

Zimmer stared at the box up in the corner of the unit, hating Frank suddenly, or at least hating Frank's voice, his deep, throaty, supreme-being managerial voice. Not since the eighth grade, he thought to himself, when Monsignor Horrigan had announced throughout St. James elementary school that President Kennedy had been shot, has Zimmer tolerated any other chickenshit hiding behind a box like that and barking orders, or giving out bad news.

"Asshole," he said, and threw one of his remaining popsicles at the voice.

"I mean it Zimbarco. You'll pay."

"So what, Frank?" He threw the other one. "So fucking what?"

The battle could be heard by the other Lumpers—at least Frank's side of it—if not seen. Frank didn't use the boxes to spy on any one in particular. He kept them all open so that if anyone had a question, all they had to do was yell it out and he'd answer. If a truck was on its way, speeding down Highway 13 and calling ahead, if it had some rush load or pick-up, Frank could alert the crew and they'd give that driver priority.

Frank wasn't necessarily attempting any heavy-handed management techniques nor using any big-brother tactics of control, they all knew. Just as they didn't have to be told that Zimmer was the other combatant. But Zimmer wasn't being personally reactionary to Frank, or Steph, or anyone else. He was just being Zimmer, just being reactionary. He got unruly—uncontrollable, even—about five, maybe as late as six, just an hour or so before they were done for the night.

Frank had asked them their first night, "Have either of you worked shift before?"

"Sure," Zimmer answered quickly.

Steph thought to agree, not wanting to jeopardize the job, but shook his head, "No."

"Where?" Frank asked.

"In the service."

"Uh-huh. I mean *work* shift, not just get paid for shift work."

Zimmer squinted one eye and studied Frank. Later, after three, four days on the job, he figured out the difference. He couldn't get fully used to the schedule somehow. It wasn't like he couldn't stay up all night, couldn't function with the fatigue; he would just start to deteriorate, or his mood would, after five, six hours.

"I mean, what's the point, Steph?" he seemed to need to know before he could finish the shift most nights, which probably stemmed from the realization of what they really were, the name: Lumpers. "What's the point? Why *should* I go the distance? What difference will it make?"

Steph couldn't be dissuaded though, not now, not after enduring all of Zimmer's other speeches and sermons. A month ago he might have wavered, might have doubted. But now, on his own track, he liked the shift, not so much because it made a difference. Because it *was* different. Having his rhythm out of pace with most of the real world was sufficiently contrary to suit his present attitude. It provided immediate, undeniable distinction. And maybe, maybe even gave him the beginnings, the outline of a definition. He could be different.

"It *is* different, Zimmer," he would say, over and over again. "They pay us *differential*."

Otherwise, he couldn't answer for Zimmer, wouldn't respond to his pleading existential questions.

"But what's the fucking point?"

Part of Zimmer stayed at the job just because he was stubborn, willful. Part of him stayed for Steph's benefit, surely, though neither of them would ever admit that. Beyond either of those reasons, the one factor that seemed to keep Zimmer going, through the fatigue, through the cold, through the extra harassment everyone felt obliged to bestow on him—mainly because he provided such an easy target—was leaving, going home in the morning.

"I don't know," he'd try to explain, apologetic to Steph, Bruce, to anyone listening, anyone who'd been witness to his belligerence. He'd duck his head, scratch at his scalp. "I know I should quit, that I'm never going to like this. And just when I get to the point where I'm ready to walk, it's only thirty minutes till we get to leave, and then I think about driving home while everyone else is trying to motivate themselves to get through another day. It tickles the shit out of me."

"Differential," Steph would say, toasting him with a Lumper happy-hour bottle of beer. "That's the point."

That's what Zimmer'd focus on, as the morning wound down, once he was too tired to even think, where, if he didn't concentrate real hard, the items listed on one invoice or another wouldn't make any sense to him, he'd find himself in the produce section looking for a case of tomato sauce, say, screwing everything up. When the clocks around the platform seemed to stop, about four, four-thirty, like they were running out of energy too, Zimmer had to concentrate on seven, had to count hours, and then minutes, had to set his sights on the exact moment of release from the job and use whatever reserves of energy and temperament he had to get him through to that moment in his absolute, flexible/inflexible scheme of things. That's the only way he could manage the shift, timing his cessation of work and departure from Regency to a precision NASA would be proud of, counting, "Three, two, one..." jerking the snaps of his overalls and flinging the thick gloves along with the cadence. And then, on cue, the "habit," as Frank called it, the routine—which, because of Zimmer's manic approach to it, took on larger, life and death significance—was punctuated by Frank's hearty tug on that whistle of deliverance.

"Remember," he'd cautioned them, "we work right up to that last whistle."

Zimmer thought about little else the last hour, hour and a half, and often considered asking Frank to count down with him over the intercom, lest he should be late with the signal and Zimmer should die of something if he were forced to spend one second more on the platform.

Or he thought of asking Frank to give two-minute warnings, to help speed up Steph's transition. It took Steph several weeks to appreciate the depth and desperation of Zimmer's struggle. He wouldn't ever have anticipated the whistle, would've just kept working. Unlike Zimmer, Steph was a lousy gauge of time.

Zimmer, come back to life suddenly, would be loping across the yard for the parking lot, turning around, walking backwards and shouting back up at his roommate, "Hurry up, Steph," adding, "I swear, sometimes you move like goddammed jello!"

Steph hustled off the platform, jumping to the ground instead of fighting the crowd at the stairwells at either end, pulling on his jacket as he trotted to catch Zimmer. He reached the car, snapping the final fastener just under his chin, shivering in that renewed blast of cold that seemed to come along with the sun on winter mornings, and listened as Zimmer tried the ignition.

"Come on, baby, come on," Zimmer urged, but his VW only whined, and then clicked.

"Jesus," Steph said. "Every day we hurry out here for this." He got out, pulling his collar up higher. "Am I the only one who wonders why?"

"We hurry out here," Zimmer answered, still inside Abby, still cranking, "because the faster we get away from here, the better I'll feel. *This* is just a minor nuisance, a necessary evil."

Steph mumbled, "And the sooner we'll have to come back," asking Zimmer, who'd given up the attempt to start the Bee-atile, "Did you ever think of that?" He could feel the cold creeping up his fingers, heading for his ears, the point of his nose.

Zimmer thought, That's stupid, but didn't say it. Mornings, before the transition from work to non-work was well along, were not the best times for either of them to challenge the other, directly. He just reached in to be sure Abby was in neutral, then joined Steph at the rear of the car.

"Don't you think, Zimmer," Steph tried, taking up position beside him, "we can afford a genuinely rebuilt starter, a brand new battery, instead of just raiding the junkyard?"

They leaned against Abby to nudge her from her frozen tracks. In-between surges, Zimmer said, "You kidding?" catching his breath, which, because of the cold, came a little harder. "And waste. All that money."

"Now there's. Logic. For you," Steph answered, as they repeated the routine: heaving the car into motion, Zimmer skipping to the front, leaping in and popping the clutch, only to have Abby gulp and cough and seize.

They braced against the Bee-atile once more, puffing the icy air, blowing great clouds of foggy-breaths in each other's faces. Steph was crouched down low, sprawled with his back to the dead engine compartment, wrapping his long arms around to either wheel well, pushing with his legs. Zimmer stood upright, shoving Abby higher up, around the rear window.

"Typical," Steph grunted with each step, "Zimbarco. Logic," only able to stand from the position and catch his breath, watching Abby roll, turnover, but not start.

"Jesus. Maybe we should forget the whole thing, get a rebuilt car!"

Zimmer stood from the driver's seat.

Steph didn't mean it, of course, though he was tired of Zimmer's badgering him to hurry, hurry, hurry away from the platform only to spend another twenty minutes just to get out of the parking lot. It was a most trying habit they'd developed, and not nearly as necessary as Zimmer wanted to let on.

Zimmer grunted and stepped behind the stalled Bee-atile before Steph could catch up, could take back what he'd said. He pushed Abby into motion himself, placing one large hand on each rear light and sending the car rolling down the slight decline toward Warehouse Drive. He kept pushing, faster and faster, working his way up along the driver's side, slipping and sliding on the ice and the slush, then jumped into the seat, worked the gear shift into second and slammed the clutch wheel into place. Abby coughed and coughed, shuddered, and kicked over.

"Oh, shit," Steph said, and started running after the convulsing car.

Abby, though missing a stroke every cycle or so, was gaining speed, while Zimmer laughed, "Hah!" after each backfire. He floored the accelerator, urging, "Come on, baby, you can do it," bouncing up and down in his seat trying to generate some extra momentum.

"Zimmer! Wait!"

"Come on Abby-gal, dust that asshole."

The Bee-atile spit a cloud of blue-black exhaust—all that pooled oil and gas Zimmer'd been forcing her—and the engine settled into a rhythm, winding past its usual purr, tacking higher and higher, finally sounding like her old self, TAT-A-TAT-TAT-TAT...

"Yeah," Zimmer yelled. "Yeah! Now I got you."

Steph reached the door handle just in time, pulling it open, trying to keep his feet. Abby pulled him a couple of extra yards with each step he made. He managed to get one foot up on the running board, skipped once, twice, and hopped up with the other foot. The rusted through brackets snapped, sending Steph tumbling into the car, across his seat, halfway into Zimmer's lap. Abby veered over the curb toward the tree line before Zimmer could elbow Steph out of the way and right her.

"Whooo-wheee," Zimmer yelled, taking a wide, swerving arc onto the Drive, across the path of another tractor trailer full of groceries—the driver yanking on his air-horn at them. "How's that for an answer to your miserable accusations?"

"Se-sorry, Abby," Steph said, panting, doubled over in the passenger's seat.

"And I thought you knew her," Zimmer said, barely slowing for the stop sign at 13, glancing quick left, right, then left again, gunning the Bee-atile. She skipped once more, kind of hiccoughed as she straddled the mid-line—Steph cowering again, thinking, Oh, great—but revved back up and sped them away

from Regency safely.

2. OTHER HABITS

AT night, going to work, at the *end* of their day, the Lumpers would take the drive southward on dark and abandoned 13 at the most leisurely pace they could manage, having learned exactly what time they needed to leave Lear's and head out for work to arrive at the platform time clock mere seconds before their tardiness window closed. The rest of the world, of course, all those normal people, got up in the morning, beginning their day, with work immediate, probably the second or third thought to run through their awakening minds, right after the bathroom. They rushed to work because they were building momentum for their day. They hustled through their jobs, busy, determined, caught up in the mechanizations of an ever expanding yet ever encroaching world. Then at three, four, five in the afternoon, they breathed sighs of release, ambled out of office buildings, assembly plants, cavernous warehouses, chit-chatting, standing around in parking lots, moving the gatherings to nearby watering holes, having a few drinks, some nuts, pretzels, maybe some little pizza squares, wandering homeward, putting their feet up, eating dinner, maybe watching some television before shuffling off to bed, sleeping, ready to do it all again.

Lumpers were different. Their day began when work ended. And even though their bodies wanted respite, after working all night, their minds—Zimmer's at least—were busy with the day's necessities. That disharmony between body and spirit had to manifest itself somehow. So Zimmer could be counted on to be a little argumentative, until he could superimpose the divergent tracks of his conflicting existences a little better. Steph knew this, but he was suffering a milder version of the disorientation himself. It was not the best of combinations.

Zimmer stroked the dashboard of the Bee-atile, cooing, "That's my girl," and Steph grumbled, "Yeah, but for how long?" Zimmer slammed on the brakes, Abby fish-tailing then spinning all the way around, sliding across those southbound lanes, coming to a rest on the opposite shoulder, but facing north.

Steph stared at him wide-eyed, until Zimmer said, "You want to walk?" through clenched teeth, so that it sounded like, "Gewannawalk?"

"Oh, Jesus, Zimmer. Come on."

"What the hell was that crack supposed to mean?"

"Nothing!"

Zimmer folded his arms and stared.

"Look, all I meant was that Abby's ten years old. The odometer quit how long ago? How much longer can she last? That's all."

Zimmer snorted, and slipped the stick into first, easing back onto 13. Steph could tell he was still agitated, though, the way he slammed through the gears, wound the engine a few hundred revolutions past the point of optimum gear ratio each time, the way he let out the clutch with a thump, jostling Steph around in his seat.

"Nine."

"What?"

"She's only nine years old."

"I don't think--"

"NINE."

"TEN!" Steph finally shouted back.

They rode on some more in a kind of charged silence. The heat of their tempers warmed the interior of the car. Steph knew that these tempers were just the side-effects of their flip-flopping back to normalcy. They were werewolves mutating back to humans, feeling the pangs of autogenesis, nothing more. He knew they had to try to be civil, try to help each other over that threshold.

"Listen, Zimmer," he tried. "Abby's a 1970, right? This is December, 1979. New cars come out in the fall, the year *before* they're dated. Actually, that's something Volkswagen started, isn't it?"

Zimmer remained unyielding.

"Anyway, Abby's ten years old. I'm not trying to insult her, honest. You should know that."

The Bee-atile, Abby, was a 1970, bought on a whim, to commemorate, or mourn, actually, the break up of the Beatles. Zimmer was still six months shy of beginning his Air Force duties, but the car dealer had drawn up the papers on the promise of Zimmer's guaranteed bi-monthly checks from Uncle Sam, knowing he'd have a lot of help finding Zimmer if the young recruit ever defaulted. Zimmer was broke, jobless, eight months out of high school, long-haired and hungover most of the time, but he had a new car all of a sudden, and a couple of weighty contracts.

Now it was 1979. Chronologically, she was ten years old. Unlike her namesake, Zimmer and Abby would always be together, of course, so it didn't really matter. He would never seriously consider getting rid of her. But in Zimmer's inflexibly ordered world, all kinds of logic, even chrono-logic, were equally disregarded, if need be. Abby was nine years old.

They pulled into the Regency retail store farther up 13, arching through the empty parking lot, backing onto the slant cut out of the sidewalk in front of the store that was supposed to be for shopping carts and wheelchairs. Climbing out of the Bee-atile—handicapped, in a lot of ways—Zimmer said, "Nine."

"Jesus," Steph screamed from his side. "Fine. FINE. I don't care. Jesus, you're bone-headed sometimes."

"Aw, now," Zimmer said, entering the store. They both passed silently under the pale green Regency sign glowing above the pneumatic doors that hissed at them.

Steph followed Zimmer into the produce section, but not too closely. They stopped at the grocery most mornings on their way home, out of easy habit, by now, more than necessity. Some days all they did was roam the aisles, without buying anything. By way of explanation, after spending five, ten minutes leading Steph all over the store, Zimmer would turn to him, as they walked through the only check-out lane that was ever open at that time of the day, and say, "This is inspirational. You get the best ideas for cooking from food, the real thing, not some generic description in someone else's book."

Steph didn't understand, or care that much. Zimmer did all the cooking, so he followed him, fondled the same vegetables, "This is a perfect eggplant," sniffed the same spices, even acknowledged the pieces of meat when Zimmer urged him, "Say hello."

They almost always had the store to themselves, as well as the full attention of any early morning employees. Usually that consisted of a shift manager, pacing about in his Regency blazer, who'd discretely follow them around, only stepping out of his surveillance to shake a finger at them when they sampled grapes or disturbed a display; and Angela, a new lone checker on duty. With no one else to ring up, she would stand leaning against the bagging shelf at her register and watch their journey through the store, shaking her head, grinning.

Zimmer stopped in front of the meat coolers along the back wall, turned around and said, "You got to understand, Steph, Abby's not just a car, she's like family."

Steph's heard all this before, of course.

"We should conveniently ignore particulars, numbers, like we don't go around talking about Uncle Ernie being queer, Aunt Sarah tipping the bottle too much. She's family, like you, and Whomee, and Bruce, and Mickey, and Mr. Boyles, even Frank."

Finally, the butcher came out from behind his glassed-in space, asking, "Can I help you?"

"Family packs?" Steph asked.

"Down at the end."

Like an old married couple, they had ways of displaying their irritation or exasperation, all the while still exhibiting a kind of public discretion; kind of. Zimmer stomped off for the beer coolers.

"Alcohol and sex," Zimmer said to Steph when he caught up to him, "those are the only things you can always depend on."

He held up two six-packs.

Steph, understanding that the comment meant he was not to be counted at the moment, asked, "Which one's the sex?"

Zimmer stomped away from him again.

"Jesus," Steph said, reaching for two more six packs.

"Everything else," Zimmer continued, "all other aspects of reality, especially things as nebulous as family and *friends*, you make up as you go."

They set the beer whispering down the conveyor belt of Angela's check-out, Zimmer asking, "Why isn't the beer ever cold?"

Angela stopped the belt. "You shouldn't be drinking at this time of the morning, that's why it's not cold."

"See what I mean?"

"What?"

"Spoken like a true mother."

"Oh, goddammit Zimmer..."

"What does that mean?" she asked Steph.

"Zimmer thinks you can make up your family as you go along."

"She *could* be our mother."

"I could *not*," she snapped, backing away from the register, folding her arms angrily. Their beer sat there getting warmer by the second, suspended in a place where they could easily reach it but couldn't have it. "I'm not nearly old enough to be your mother, even if I wanted to be," she said, punctuating the remark by turning away from them, tossing her outrageous mane of red hair over her shoulder.

"Not that we'd mind," Steph said quickly.

Truth be told, Steph was more than a little enamored by the hair, by Angela's could-get-lost-in blue eyes that might have reminded him of his mother's, though it wasn't familiarity that attracted him.

She just grunted, "Un-huh."

"What a wicked thought you're having," Zimmer said.

Angela turned back around quickly, to see Steph blushing. She resumed the transaction, trying to hide her own glow of embarrassment.

"Wicked, wicked thought," Zimmer repeated, watching Angela squeeze Steph's change into his hand, and they all knew he was speaking to both of them by now.

They got in Abby, pushed her started, opened up a beer each, and continued the trip home, forty-five minutes old already.

"Denial," Zimmer said, catching Steph in mid sip.

"Hmm?" Steph asked, the can frozen in place just before his mouth.

"That's it," Zimmer said. "Every day we get off work and act, even if only subconsciously, like we're supposed to flip back into that daytime existence. But we're Lumpers," he said, moving the beer to his left hand, holding on to it and the steering wheel at the same time, not taking any measure to conceal it.

"Now what are we talking about?"

"I'm still talking about the same thing, asshole, if you'd just pay attention."

"Families?"

"Yes."

"And now, denial."

"Right."

"Tell me, what is all this talk about family all of a sudden? I thought you couldn't care less about that stuff. I thought, *This is now*; thought you hated the warehouse, *and* Frank."

Zimmer stopped again, just inside Dagaton Woods. "I hate the *institution* of Regency, the work, because it's all made up by dayshifting majorities. I'm talking about the people, the Lumpers. We're different, like you said. So why don't we act it? See, this is better than any real family. In a real family, you honor the institution, even if you hate the people."

Steph frowned. But Zimmer wouldn't be discouraged. He grinned, shrugged, convincing himself anyway, and drove on, saying only, "Yeah, that's it."

After a few more minutes, Steph asked, "Zimmer, you hate your family?"

"You guys?" Zimmer answered, turning the radio up a little louder. "Never."

That was the only answer Steph would ever get, even though they both knew what was going on. Things got pretty fuzzy whenever Steph pressed him for personal, historical details. Steph just mumbled, not to be heard over the music, "Nice dodge."

They really did both know what was going on, even enjoyed the game to some extent. Steph knew it wasn't just a dodge—kin to a lie—just to throw him off the track. Zimmer kept all that information inside for some reason. They could even talk about that, his aloofness, on occasion, without any emotional upheaval. He just did it, that's all.

Passing through Dagaton Woods, towards the back entrance, to the Turnpike, and home, the sun was finally creeping high enough over the hills and into the winter sky to look like daylight, daytime. They hurried on in silence, feeling more and more like werewolves, chased by the light back into their holes.

Whomee, their cat, sat coiled on top of his chair inside the door to Fill, ready to pounce on any intruders. Every morning, despite the fact that it was Steph and Zimmer coming up the stairs—who provided for his realm, who fed the damn thing— he would snarl and swipe at them, without the slightest signs of remorse. After a while, a week, a month, everyone began to understand and accept that that's what made Whomee who he was. He was family too, and as long as he was, they'd ignore his habits, which is pretty much what Zimmer had been saying all morning.

Zimmer walked past the cat, offering only, "Morning Whomee," giving him plenty of berth, heading for the kitchen.

Steph tried to be friendlier, tried to pet him, reaching past the flashing claws to rub his head, say, to relax those ears. "Come on, Whomee, be a buddy."

"Forget it," Zimmer said from the kitchen doorway. "Just wait until he smells some food. That'll calm him down." Then, to convince both of the combatants that eating was a far better idea than whatever it was they were doing, offered, "Omelette?"

Steph looked up to see Zimmer standing there holding about seven eggs. "What else?"

"You *want* something else?"

"No, no," Steph said, hurrying away from Whomee, knowing that tone in Zimmer's voice too well. "You're just so fond of those things, that's all."

"We've discussed this," Zimmer said, turning back for his kitchen.

Zimmer set the eggs in a stainless mixing bowl and bent into the refrigerator, repeating himself anyway. "They're leftover reincarnations," as he gathered four, five assorted plastic containers that held remnants of earlier creations, a little lasagna, some chili, fried chicken, salad dressing. "The possibilities are endless," he said, not knowing, nor really caring, if Steph was listening, if he was even in the kitchen.

He stood, carefully, rising above the partition of the icebox door, old margarine tubs and whipped cream containers stacked up to his chin, reciting, "It's a religious exper--" when he saw that Yes, Steph was in the kitchen, standing over in the opposite corner--dancing with Whomee, teasing him with an untied lace of one work boot—mouthing along with the litany, like any good parishioner, though Zimmer knew better, knew he was being mocked.

"...experience. A culinary resurrect--" Steph looked up. "How about a hand with all that?" he said, and rushed to the refrigerator, taking the containers and setting them on the counter. "Can I help?"

"Get out of here. You, who doesn't even appreciate good cooking, you want to help?"

"I appreciate--"

"Look," Zimmer said, spreading the containers out on the counter, like he was preparing for surgery, gently lifting off one cover after another. "These were all wonderful dining at one time, right?"

"Right."

"So why not mix them together some such way and wrap an egg around them?"

Steph hovered behind Zimmer, looking at the possible combos: chicken chili; chicken lasagna; chili lasagna; lasagna chili salad... "I just don't understand, that's all."

"Of course you don't. You don't want to. Get me another beer."

"I just don't see *how* you do it," Steph said, reaching into the refrigerator. "You take this, and that, a little-tiny bit of that," he said, standing again. "You got this tiny little space, one fucking pan, and you shake, and you chop, this, that," he continued, acting it all out next to Zimmer at the counter, "and POOF! Omelette!" He pulled the pop-top of Zimmer's beer. "How?"

"Organization."

"What?"

"I'm telling you, organization's the single most important ingredient to cooking."

"Right," Steph said, retreating to his corner again. "My mother's organized, to the millisecond."

"And? Doesn't she cook?"

"She'd rather not. Says she doesn't like to."

"Doesn't like to?" Zimmer tried to comprehend that, holding a fork poised over the mixing bowl, drooling raw egg.

"Nope. She's pretty busy, though. She resorts to frozen food whenever possible."

"Well, frozen food's not all that... Just because I..."

Zimmer quit trying so hard and went back to work, slap, slapping the egg and pepper and cooking sherry into a blend.

"No, Zimmer, I'm talking frozen dishes. Prepared frozen food. Meals in a pouch. T.V. dinners. Did you know they can even freeze eggs now?"

Zimmer stopped again.

"She's got packages in her freezer that say, I swear, Fresh Frozen Bread."

"What the hell does that mean?"

"Whenever we raid the warehouse and I bring her some fruit, say, or veggies, she always wants to know how to freeze them."

"Stop, STOP!" Zimmer cried, checking the progress of his biscuits, cupping a hand over his left ear, the one closest to Steph—who followed him along the counter, guzzling his beer.

"I don't think she'd know what to do if she had to prepare fresh food every day. She'd probably boil the piss out of it anyway."

"But she's organized?"

"Oh yeah. The federal standard."

"And doesn't cook?"

"Doesn't like to."

"Well..."

"She's got other talents, to be fair. Like her shop. She just never developed a touch for cooking."

"Touch? What touch?"

"For cooking," Steph repeated, irritably. "The touch, the talent."

"It's not a talent. It's a practice."

"Hah! But you won't let me practice? Explain that."

"Maybe it's genetic?"

"It's a talent," Steph said again, watching Zimmer shake a sauce pan, rotate the frying pan so that the egg would spread and cook evenly, glance through the oven door once more, all the while clinging to his beer. "I mean, look at you. You're a wiz."

Zimmer waved the spatula at him. "Don't start that shit."

"It's true, it's true. You can do anything."

Steph had convinced himself, once overcoming his doubts about how chili and lasagna and the rest of it would all blend, that he could live off of the aromas alone that Zimmer coaxed out of the different foods and that ancient stove, of things frying and things baking. "It's truly a talent."

"It's a discipline."

"Then where'd you learn it?"

Zimmer hesitated.

"You really want to know?"

"Jesus. No. No, don't tell me, I already know," Steph said, leaving the kitchen for the dining room table just the other side of the wall. "Somewhere in New York, right?"

"Hah!" Zimmer yelled, and turned up the radio, Steph's cue to drop the subject.

He sat, rubbing the table's grainy surface. He looked underneath, at the legs, the ornate carving that had been so contentious when they bought the thing. He thought, then, not for the first nor last time, that the table, like the Bee-atile, even the puny kitchen on the other side of the wall he was pressed against—listening to Zimmer finish their breakfast with a flourish—together spoke more about Zimmer than he'd ever actually say. If Steph endeavored to keep them all in mind, he might not need bother Zimmer with more direct questions. Wasn't that enough?

Steph at least had witnesses concerning the table.

"Oh yeah, I've been thinking of getting a table for a long time now," Zimmer announced suddenly one day, to everyone, as they sat around the bar at Lear's.

"That's a lie," Steph said. "He's looking for a table because of what happened when my jackass brother came to dinner last week."

"Oh, bullshit..."

"Picture this," Steph said, getting off his stool and standing with his back to the bar in the space between Bruce and Zimmer. "You' guy's have seen Fill. We're standing in the kitchen, leaning against the counter, looking out over Dagaton Woods, eating spaghetti, right," he said, twirling an imaginary fork.

Bruce slurped. "I love pasta."

"It was great too. I mean, thick, garlicky sausage hunks, little bits of actual tomatoes..."

Zimmer lifted a hand. "Steph, do you mind?"

"So there we are, enjoying this sumptuous meal--"

"Sumptuous?" Mickey asked.

"No, Mick," Bruce corrected him. "Suuuumptuous."

"Jesus," Zimmer said, pivoting away from the three of them.

"And we're congratulating Jack on his choice of wine, all that shit, and I'm thinking, This is going well... Didn't you think so?"

Zimmer wouldn't answer.

"Anyway, after dinner, we're playing cards—I don't know, some cut-throat game I think Jack made up, until, of course, asshole Whomee decides he wants to play--"

"Hey, he's lived there longer than any of us."

"So then Jack leaves, but all tolled I thought it was a pretty good evening, I really did."

"Such an exquisite judge," Zimmer mumbled.

"So what happened?" Bruce asked.

"I go home for the usual family lunch the next Sunday afternoon, and it's a little quiet, I'll grant, but I didn't think too much about it."

"Naturally."

"Until Kathy asks, 'Can we sit on the floor?' Then I figure it out. I glare over at Jack and he's sitting next to my mother looking just as smug as he can. And my father grumbles, 'Takes a lotta damn gall to invite someone over for dinner and then ask them to stand at the kitchen window to eat it!' I wanted to answer, 'Well, actually, Dad, he kind of invited himself...'"

"But did he?" Zimmer asked.

"And my mother, in her less than subtle way, asks, 'Stephen, how can you live like that?' digging for a confession or just more dirt, which is about the time I figured the whole thing out."

"Ding."

"...figured Jack was just a mole. So I'm sitting there, chewing on a still frosty crust of Tony's frozen pizza, thinking, How can I not live like that?"

"Did you say that?" Bruce asked.

"No, because he knows she's right," Zimmer answered. "How could we live like that?"

"Mr. Family Counselor."

"We need a table, Steph. It doesn't matter who pointed it out."

"I would've pointed it out, if I'd been invited to dinner," Mickey said.

"Take heart, little buddy," Bruce said. "I've never been invited either."

"See? See how much we need a table?" Zimmer said, finishing his beer, standing. "It's time."

The rest fell in behind him, though it was a short expedition. They walked out the front door, turned right, and at the end of that same block was another of Tripoli's seemingly endless number of second-hand stores—a gutted grocery, where used items of life were hauled in, stuffed into one corner or another. Sometimes there was a price chalked onto the item, sometimes not. There wasn't any apparent scheme of batching or departmentalizing. Old record albums were everywhere, lining the bottom shelves of the racks along either long wall, or propped up in the old meat cooler in the back of the building, or just in cardboard boxes sitting on top of tables and shoved under mattress sets. Clothes were hung from any horizontal pole. And lamps were set on top of any flat surface, of which there were plenty, even if it was difficult to tell which were for sale and which came with the building.

"It's a truer form of shopping," Zimmer had to lecture them before they could start their search in earnest. "It's better than being funneled and programmed along a narrow marketing executive's corridor of manipulation. It's shopping without an overhead, and without corporate profit margin."

Zimmer'd furnished all of Fill, even his wardrobe, shopping in such places, so he had what could be considered a method. The others were a little slower to catch on. To them, every flat plank or slice of aluminum qualified as a suitable eating surface for Fill. Zimmer was hailed from one corner of the store to the next by various cries of, "I found it!" and then had to repeatedly explain, "That's a *banquet* table, Mick. You've seen Fill. How the hell are we supposed to get that thing in there?" Or, "Bruce, put a little weight on that piece of shit. How long do you think it'd last with us?" But with a little time, he found what he was looking for.

"This is it," he called, down on the gritty floor of the shop, all the way against the back wall, poking his head under a table, on his elbows and knees, like a bloodhound sniffing at the base of a tree.

The table wasn't really for sale. It was a large round oaken table that had been scratched up and stained and soiled, with the leaves missing, stuck back there, burdened by piles of boxes of used books.

"But look at those paws," Zimmer'd shouted from beneath it, spooking two bag ladies. "They're beautiful."

The other Lumpers gathered around the table, and the ladies even hovered nearby.

"I think those are claws, Zimmer," Mickey said, joining him on the floor.

"Feet aren't claws. These are feet," Zimmer said, looking around to the others for help. "Right? Paws, right?"

Only the ladies answered, nodding to each other, "That's right."

"They're the table's feet, that's true," Steph tried, "but I think they're carvings of claws. They look like they're holding something, a little beast maybe, something it's just caught, a tiny bunny rabbit."

"A bunny rabbit?"

"Fast table," Bruce said.

The ladies had heard enough.

"They're paws," Zimmer said. "Look, there's a big toe."

"Or a thumb," Mickey said, closer to the carved appendages.

"Who cares," Zimmer finally said, standing. "Call them whatever you want. This is the table I want. And once inside Fill—whatever they may be now—they're paws."

Steph stepped in. "Well, okay, so they're paws. But what about chairs, Zimmer? If it doesn't have any chairs, we're right back where we started."

"It doesn't have any leaves, either," Bruce said, lifting off a few of the boxes.

"No problem," Zimmer said, scouting around the shop, the other tables, piles of wood shelving, even trash from disassembled crates, anything, to find two or three leaves that would fit the table.

Find them, he did; and fit, they did, though just barely. They didn't match. They meshed, which was all they had to do. "We'll just saw off the end that sticks out."

"They're not even the same color!" Mickey said.

"We'll get a table cloth. It's the feet that matter."

"The claws."

"They're *not* claws, you little--" Zimmer started, but Mickey was already scurrying away from him.

They found chairs too, between the four of them, scouring the shop, grabbing anything that fit and didn't look like it belonged with any other set. They finally found eight: some painted, some stained, some with arms, some without. Again, particulars of style and fashion and coordination didn't matter.

"Once everyone's sitting, what difference does it make?"

"But look," Mickey said, sitting next to Bruce, the only time he'd ever been the taller of the two. "They're not even close."

"We can fix that."

The other Lumpers gave up their resistance only when Zimmer was challenged from the outside. "That table ain't really for sale," the woman at the cash register had tried to tell them, out of the side of her mouth, while she kept her eyes on the flickering day time images of a portable black and white television.

Not that it mattered. Zimmer would not be denied.

"I ain't going to clean it off for you," she told him at the end of their negotiations. "And we don't deliver."

"Not to worry," Bruce said.

Together with Zimmer the two of them angled and jockeyed the thing out the front door. Steph had run ahead to Lear's to be sure beer was ready to celebrate the purchase. And Mickey ran back and forth from the shop moving the chairs out and onto the sidewalk near the front entrance of the bar where

Bruce and Zimmer set the thing down again.

At the time, Steph remembered being glad to have volunteered to buy the beer, as he watched the café scene develop outside the window.

Now, he was more than a little embarrassed to have been such a chickenshit.

"Zimmer," he called. "You remember when we got this table?"

"Sure," he said, appearing around the corner of the kitchen with two fresh beers.

"Was that after we'd already started raid night?"

"Goddammit, Steph," Zimmer said, his voice trailing as he reached back into the kitchen for their plates. "How many times do I have to tell you, it *all* started that day. Don't you ever pay attention to anything?"

Steph lifted the edge of his omelette with a fork, just to see the final concoction.

When Randy had stopped Steph, thanks to an open container law in Tripoli, from taking the beer outside, and the Lumpers had to join Mr. Boyles at the bar and settle for just sitting there and looking out at the table, that was the first time any of them really considered how they were going to get it home.

Randy had pushed the issue by saying, "You know, Zimmer, parking on the sidewalk is one thing. Setting up house on it is quite another. Isn't it?" He turned to Mr. Boyles for confirmation.

"Regretably."

"How in the hell are we..." Steph started, looking back and forth from the Bee-atile to the table.

"Not to worry," Bruce said again. "I'm gonna carry it on top of the goat." He had a late model GTO. "I can hold on with one hand, drive with the other. Mick, you handle the passenger's side. Piece of cake."

Between the two cars, Zimmer's Volkswagen and Bruce's

sports coupe, Steph figured they'd need four trips.

"We'll tie four of the chairs to the legs," Bruce suggested.

Steph winced.

"Piece of cake," he insisted.

"Shut up, Bruce," Mickey finally said.

"Uh, Randall?" Mr. Boyles said.

Randy was leaning against the cooler buffing clean beer mugs and storing them along the shelves under the counter. He looked around the bar, spying just two other patrons. "I've got a truck, Zimmer," he said. "You could borrow it, or I'd be glad to help."

"When Randy volunteered his truck," Zimmer said, explaining to Steph, watching him eat. "That's when it all began, that very moment. We were a family then, don't you see? We had that frontier spirit, *compadres* bound by a common cause."

"Well, sure, symbolically, but," Steph said, frowning, "What I don't remember--" pausing, as the separate textures of egg noodle and fried egg played out.

They loaded up Randy's truck, after far too much maneuvering, as the table suddenly took on greater prominence, wedging three of the chairs onto the bed with it-- padded with Bruce's logger shirt. Mr. Boyles whispered to Randy while the Lumpers distributed the remaining chairs between Abby and the Goat. He disappeared inside the closed bar and returned with two cold cases of Iron City, which he slid onto a corner of cargo area left up behind the cab.

Like an Okie caravan they crawled through Dagaton Woods Park, Zimmer in the lead, veering back and forth across the park road, keeping his attention on the scene in his rearview mirror, studying Randy, the table. Bruce and Mickey brought up the rear, giving the shifting load ahead plenty of cushion, the GTO's flashers on, like those jeeps that accompany mobile home trucks.

When they rolled onto the lawn adjacent to Fill, Zimmer

looked up the slope of lawn to the main house, where he saw Donald peering over his cut-away bifocals, through the venetian blinds of his den. Zimmer waved and smiled. Donald only nodded, almost imperceptively, and rolled the slats closed.

"Probably afraid we'd ask him to do some work," Zimmer mumbled.

Bruce was standing at the top of the staircase, measuring the doorway with his arms. "We'll have to take that door off," he said.

The first thing they did was haul the beer up and stock it in the refrigerator, as well as one of the chairs—a tall, swiveling bar stool, not unlike those at Lear's. Mr. Boyles sat inside in a corner, Whomee finding his lap immediately, watching the show.

"Who could forget that day? You should've seen yourself," Steph said, with his head down, picking at the remains of his omelette. "You know," spearing one last kidney bean smeared with ricotta, then looking up. "That was pretty good."

Zimmer frowned.

"Come on, Zimmer. If you picked up a menu somewhere and read, Chicken/chili/lasagna omelette, would you order it?"

"Why not?"

"Jesus."

"What did that other crack mean?"

"About the day we brought the table up here? You were a maniac. Everything had to be just right: A little to the left, no, the right. No, there. No, no, not there. Here. Here! You were driving everyone crazy."

"Not everyone," Zimmer said, sitting back and folding his arms. While Steph was in the kitchen, stacking dishes, he added, "You just don't have any sense of ceremony, that's all."

"Ceremony?" Steph yelled, scraping any remnants into Whomee's dish, to see if he'd eat it. "Furnishing an apartment?"

"We broke bread with our new family that day."

Steph poked his head back into the big room. "We broke onion rings."

"We baptized our new family, and now you're mocking it."

"There you go again, talking about family," Steph said over running water, rinsing the dishes. "What are you, homesick?"

He didn't hear any answer, pulled two final beers from the refrigerator. "Do you miss your family?" he asked.

"No."

"Really?"

"That's not what this is about," Zimmer said, sitting forward, propping his elbows on the table's edge, staring over at Steph through half closed eyes.

Their tiredness, and the beer, was catching up to them. Steph sat back in his chair, his beer propped on his stomach. He knew this would be the last one of the morning, the one he'd wake and find still three-quarters full; the one he'd wonder, Why the hell did I open that one for?

"I got all the family I need right here; just enough to keep me from feeling temporary. I mean," Zimmer said, looking across at Steph, who was slouched down in his chair, his head lolling back, looking through the narrowest of gaps, just fuzzy slits where his eyelashes met, "starting over doesn't necessarily mean impermanence."

"Permanence is but a word of degrees," Steph said. "Emerson."

"Maybe we should save this."

"No, no, I'm listening," Steph promised, lifting his head with some sincerity, kind of tilting it forward, using as few muscles as possible. "That's what this is about? Not starting, but starting over?"

"I don't know. I just need rituals, I guess. Traditions, something to celebrate, so I don't get lost, habitual, or too comfortable. If I can just establish some kind of tradition, where every day is kind of like a prelude to the next, so that I'm anticipative, not just trying to survive..." Zimmer trailed off, his left hand flexing, flailing in front of his face, trying to form and then hold on to the idea, the words that eluded him.

Steph said, "You mean like dinner day?"

"Right, RIGHT. I can do that stuff. Cooking, for the Lumpers, everybody coming over here. That's what I mean. And that's not such a big deal, really."

Steph raised his head, tried his best Zimbarco eyebrow imitation. "It's not?"

"I don't know. Yeah, in a way, it is. Maybe it's too important."

"Even onion rings?"

"That was just the first time, Steph, come on. What's important is that it happened, just like that," Zimmer said, and even his fingers slurred when he tried to snap them. "We all got together and lumped this fucking table up here," pounding it, "and it was a good time! Forget about particulars."

"Forget about a jillion greasy onion rings, and forget about a whole bottle of catsup. Forget all that beer, and the Mick puking? Those particulars?"

"Jesus." Zimmer was pretty sure—if he could be sure of anything at the moment—that it wasn't such a good sign that they took on each other's traits when they were drunk.

Steph sat up and pounded the table himself. "I'm not trying to give you a hard time. I'm just trying to get all this tradition stuff straight. Just tell me, when was raid night?"

"All right, all right. It's tonight."

"What?"

"Raid night: it's Thursday night. Tonight. Thurs-raid night. Why the hell can't you remember this stuff?"

"Tonight?"

"Jesus. Go to bed, Steph. You're delirious."

Obediently, Steph stood and crossed the room, falling onto the cot they'd borrowed from Lear's. "Really?" he said, unlacing his boots.

Zimmer knew that he wouldn't get them all the way off, knew Steph would be mostly asleep halfway through the word, well before he leaned back onto his pillow. He was amazed, as always, at what a champion sleeper Steph was.

Raid nights started after Frank joined them on dinner days. After that first haphazard gathering, Zimmer instituted official dinner days, the Saturday afternoon after payday, every other week. "I've decided," he'd said at Lear's when he told everyone about it. "It'll be like Thanksgiving 26 times a year."

"Thanksgiving in February?" Mickey asked.

"Yeah, in February, in March. August. Every two weeks. Who can remember what they're supposed to be thankful for after a whole year anyway?"

Steph had looked at Zimmer that day, as he spoke further, in that chest-thumping, Zimbarco style, about appreciating the present, the immediate—a "this is now" variant—about not taking any chances that the good times won't be around for another ten months so that they could toast them with turkey and giblets and mashed potatoes and pumpkin pie only when the rest of the world said they could, shaking his head, not unlike he had that first night in Lear's, listening to him rage and froth about pool, and gentlemen, and guppies, but for different reasons now. It was because he'd witnessed that earlier speech that Steph knew, as maybe only Mr. Boyles knew too, that Zimmer wasn't suggesting anything. He was stating, simply, his case. He had decided, what amounted to an inflexible absolute.

Every other Saturday since they'd moved the table into Fill became dinner day. After the second or third edition they'd asked Frank to join them, because, Zimmer'd said, "This is a Lumper holiday, and Frank's a Lumper too."

"Frank doesn't ever do anything but squawk at us," Mickey said, unafraid of correcting Zimmer.

"He's Lumper alumnus, Mick," Bruce tried.

Frank was not, precisely, a Lumper any longer. As their supervisor, he was a Lumper mother, at best. But he used to work the platform, used to be one. Zimmer reminded everyone, "Once a Lumper, always a Lumper," standing in the permanent dusk of Lear's, holding a sanctimonious left index finger in the air, declaring, inflexibly, "Once a Lumper, always a Lumper."

With Frank, seven of the eight chairs they'd picked out were filled for Lumper dinner days—Fill-Up Day, St. Fill-up's Day, whatever they chose to label the holiday. Whomee would hop up into the eighth from time to time, to check on progress, scouting for scraps pushed onto the plate they always set for the cat, or to just aggravate Bruce, who would always be seated next to unoccupied stools, to round out the collection.

Then it got complicated, bogged down. Once it lost its spontaneity, when everyone started feeling responsible in one way or another, it became routine. What happened was that the others started letting their consciences get in the way of a good feast. Who wouldn't, confronted with Zimmer's heroic efforts at the multi-coursed meals, with fresh bread, and Randy's liquid contribution? The rest of them wanted to know how *they* could help.

"Help? In my kitchen?" Zimmer would answer, panicked.

And not just on the dinner day, either. All week, they'd badger Zimmer with questions. "What can I bring?"

"Mickey, what *would* you bring besides a package of doughnuts or something?"

When Frank, who had the busiest conscience of all, tried to pay once, "Left a fucking twenty-dollar bill in the fucking mailbox!" Zimmer'd threatened to call the whole thing off.

He sat at Lear's and sulked the very next payday Thursday night, after threatening to call in sick all week, "I might just quit," after not even allowing them to mention dinner day, just mumbling every so often, "Goddamn twenty-dollar bill, like I'm some kind of hooker or something."

They all sat there trying to commiserate, trying to bring Zimmer back from his funk, and not trying to piss him off too much, a difficult mission, at best. First Mickey said they'd all quit. Then Bruce offered to cook that week, something that at least got a laugh out of Zimmer. Then Steph started talking some gibberish about staging a protest, all of them calling in sick, just to remind Frank of something or other. "At least to impress upon him that the human element is sometimes overwhelmed by the natural one: if the temperature falls below Zero, say, plus or minus two degrees, we walk. Are you with me?" he asked, though no one was really listening.

"I got it," Zimmer said finally, about ten minutes before it would've been time to leave, or not. "We won't quit. We'll get fired. Come on, Steph."

"But the temp?" he said, lamely, waving at the television, the silent weathercast.

"No time," Zimmer answered, wrapping himself up in his fatigue jacket, pulling Steph through the door moments before the present conditions were displayed on the screen.

Mr. Boyles saluted their departure, raising his tumbler with one hand. But if he actually offered, "Greetings," it was lost, muffled, by the collar of his sweater, as he tugged it up around his chin when they'd slipped through the door.

At Regency, it was an acknowledged if not entirely condoned practice for the workers to help themselves to samples. They pilfered, a little. All the cameras and loudspeakers and such had been measures taken by the district management to ward off such things. But the local management, the night management, Frank, didn't have any hopes of quashing the practice. Really, he didn't need to bother trying, so long as it didn't get out of hand. Frank knew, but would never, ever admit, that at times, a little flexibility was the least of evils, if he couldn't have out and out ignorance. That didn't mean he wouldn't challenge Zimmer.

"What the hell are you doing Zimbarco, opening up your own chain?"

"Just turn your head, Frank," Zimmer called back to the box. "Pretend we've all just put on a little weight," as he led the Lumpers across the driveway basin after clocking out, at the end of Thursday, Thurs-raid nights.

Frank, with his tortured conscience, his polarized loyalties, who had to give report at the end of their shift, needed reassurance that it was worth his while to remain silently privy to their actions.

"I should take it out of everyone's paychecks," he'd yell after them.

"Paychecks are already cut, Frank," Steph would remind him. "Everyone enjoys dinner at Fill, right? That's all we've got, Frank, enough for dinner."

Frank huffed and grumbled, but eventually turned his back every other Friday morning. More than provide for a hell of a meal come Saturday afternoon, it also meant he'd have workers when Sunday night rolled around. It was the only way they could all painlessly contribute to the dinners.

If Frank was ever genuinely pressured from his superiors about the discrepancies, he could tell them, in his defense, that Zimmer never exactly told him which night he was raiding the warehouse, although it was hard to miss. All night long he busied himself with course sequencing and quantities, asking Bruce, say, "Hey, big guy, how many rolls you think you can eat?"

Then, an hour or two before the end of the shift, a time when Zimmer wouldn't get much work done anyway, he stole around the platform, the various containers and alcoves, like any other shopper strolling the aisles of a brightly lit supermarket somewhere. He lifted a huge can of baked beans, shuffling it to Steph on his way by, astride Clementine. Then he tossed a couple of cabbages to Mickey, who worked produce. "Here, Mick, grow tits." He stuffed a thick turkey roll down the front of Bruce's Phillies jacket.

"Brrapp," he said. "Needs salt."

Then Zimmer filled his own pockets, every one of the countless pockets built into fatigue jackets, with a two pound bag of flour, some corn meal, a jar of peppers, a slab of bacon.

They met, minutes later, at the Bee-atile, to relinquish their bounty. Only when the collection was reassembled in the back seat of Abby—even though any one of them might be concealing the main course—would they start to wonder, maybe ask, "What's for dinner, Zimmer?" a question, like any other question, that he'd never fully answer, that he'd leave lingering on the cold parking lot of the Regency Warehouse, after a long, hungry night.

He might tease Bruce, who otherwise subsisted on drive-thru hamburgers and toaster waffles, who starved himself from midnight on those Thursdays until dinner on Saturday, who would stare at the food through Abby's rear window, "Come on, Zimmer, give me a hint."

"You want a hint?" Zimmer said, from halfway inside the driver's side door. "Get us rolling, I'll give you a hint."

"Piece of cake," he agreed, shoving the Bee-atile into motion.

"You're going to need plenty of napkins," Zimmer shouted, only after he'd reengaged the clutch, and Abby was winding up, and they were accelerating away from Bruce's curses and threats.

Bruce's frustration, and his fasting, were tests of the system, sacrifices of the truly devoted, as was Steph and Zimmer's bypassing the retail store, and Angela, on payday mornings. They still rode through Dagaton Woods, because some things are always essential—Inflexible, Zimmer would say, even before the question came up—and they still had maybe one beer back at Fill, standing in the kitchen gazing through the windows out over the park, Tripoli. They didn't eat breakfast those mornings, both in respect to Bruce's sense of ceremony, and to save time, to get to sleep quicker, not that Steph needed much help. Those Fridays, between Thurs-raid night and the feasts of St. Fill-up, were Halfzies, because they rushed home, hurried to bed, only to wake up earlier than any other day of the week, for they had early appointments.

"That's the problem."
"What's that?"
"Starting over."
"You're done, Steph."
"But..."

The transition, those payday Fridays, was a complete blur until late into the afternoon. And that meant, most of the time, that Steph'd just move from one kind of blur to another, from the insensitivity of fatigue to the confusion of intoxication, or both.

"Ah!" Steph said, with one final attempt at lucidity. *"That's when it started."*

"Yup. But that's not when it all began," Zimmer said wistfully, almost nostalgic, in his unguarded state.

"Oh?" he said, confused again, missing the tone from trying so hard to concentrate.

"Began with a bear."

"What? A beer?"

"Jesus, Steph. Go to sleep."

3. LEAVING VERMONT

A Vermont bear:

Victor danced on the cold flagstones that wound down from the front porch of the old farmhouse. He hopped from one bare foot to the other, rubbing the bottom of each elevated foot against the opposite shin for some warmth before shifting his bulky weight again. Only the first week of October, mornings were already cold in Vermont, overnight temperatures dipping into the thirties, threatening freezing. Zimmer watched Victor hop, rub, hop, knowing what was coming.

"You sure you got to go?"

Victor kept asking him the same question. That's what happened to him in the winter, as if the effort to stay warm became such a preoccupation that everything else was narrowed down to singular, obsessive lines of inquiry or expression or activity. This was just the first indication, but Zimmer knew what was coming. He'd already spent a couple of winters with Victor, and Jessie, their kids. The faint grey puffs of condensed air that Victor grunted out from all the exertion were a kind of sign that Zimmer could read well enough.

"You sure you got to go?"

"I can't stay, but thanks for asking."

Victor had to think about that, hopping, rubbing. He looked like a circus bear, performing. He was big enough, certainly, six-two, two-fifty, or about. And he was hairy enough, his full head of dark tangles sticking out in various directions. His beard was both untrimmed, and unruly, reaching from just under his eye sockets all the way down his neck so that it kind of blended into his chest hair. And Zimmer knew that he was just as hairy, and completely naked beneath the faded red terry-cloth bathrobe.

Victor knew no shame. It was a trait that both fascinated

and scared Zimmer. The fascination was starting to swallow him up. He couldn't imagine another idle winter in Vermont. Two had been too much, already.

"You sure you got to go?"

"Yeah, I got to."

"You don't even have any heat in that thing," Victor reminded him, motioning with his chin in the general direction of Zimmer's car, the light blue VW Beetle.

"That's one reason to go now," Zimmer said, surveying the morning sky. It looked like rain, or worse. "Before we have any of those nights where the battery freezes."

"And you need new tires. You need a new starter. Fuck, Z, you'll never make it."

"Shut up, Victor."

"All right, all right. Why Florida? Why-- What's that place called?"

"Panama City Beach."

"Sounds like it has an identity problem."

"I spent a weekend there, a few years ago. Seemed like a nice place."

"What, you gonna start surfing or something?"

"I don't know."

"All right," Victor said, bending and reaching behind the porch steps for a mayonnaise jar and holding it out to Zimmer. "If you say you got to, I guess you got to."

Zimmer took the jar, saw mostly hundred dollar bills stuffed into it. "What's this?"

"Christmas bonus."

"Victor, this is too much. You're crazy."

"Forget it," he said, grinning through his beard. "Take it, in case you break down. Or if you find any good dope down there, send it our way. And you know you can come back, if you get bored."

"Bored?"

After two and half years with Victor, being bored was probably what Zimmer needed most. At the very least, he yearned for the peacefulness and isolation that always came with driving. He needed the peacefulness of solitude, the isolation of the open road, so that he'd only have himself and his own voices to answer to.

He knew one thing, at least. He had to leave Vermont. He had to leave Athens, anyway, leave Victor, and Jessie, and the kids. He absolutely knew that. He could feel it. And he could hear it, driving. To the constant whine of the VW's tires he would answer, "Got to go. Got to."

By the time he was nearing the Vermont border, south of Brattleboro, cruising opposite all the chartered tourist buses on their annual leaf pilgrimages, he'd already told himself a couple of thousand times, "You've got to go, got to."

Zimmer talked to himself a lot. He's spent most of his near thirty years alone, or trying to become alone, and it's an easy habit he's developed, letting thoughts out loud. He talked to himself all through New England—Massachusetts, Connecticut. Talked a little louder, and not always to himself, as he made his way through White Plains, Mount Vernon, to the tip of Manhattan where he escaped across the George Washington bridge for New Jersey. Before he knew it, he was in Paterson, remembering a Dylan song, *Hurricane*, singing, "Why'd you bring him in here for, he ain't the guy..."

That's why he talked to himself. He had all these snatches, song lyrics, movie lines, unfinished conversations, potential conversations rambling around in his head. Always, unfinished conversations. He wondered if it could ever be otherwise, if you could ever really finish a conversation, if anyone ever asked all the right questions.

The desolation of Paterson struck him. All the vacant warehouses and ruined housing projects, the blank stares of the people, huddled in empty storefront foyers, sitting on bus stop benches with old newspaper pages billowing around their feet, made him feel privileged, somehow, almost lucky, which he welcomed, easily enough, but couldn't trust. The blight repeated itself through city after city, lending urgency to his escape, if nothing else.

But he didn't want urgency. Didn't really want escape. He only wanted to get some place where he could get it right, for once, could have that genuine conversation, finally. He didn't know. His attitude shifted some as he started entering towns where the schools looked like they contained some semblance of vibrancy, where there were green yards, and parks. He slowed and exited the interstate a few times, at Netcong, Allamucy, and Hope, New Jersey, encountering order, in the traffic control, in the school crosswalk guards who went about their jobs with a certain vigorousness—their eyes searching out danger and surprise from whatever direction it might approach, white-gloved hands following, orchestrating, protecting the innocent children, the future. He felt a loss, somehow, or a yearning, but a yearning that held promise, too, and he was glad he'd veered away from the big east coast cities rather than just skirt them.

He didn't want to feel any urgency, didn't want to hurry. He welcomed the idleness of driving, "The chance to become bored," cruising westward, slicing into Pennsylvania. He wasn't even working from a map, by design. Victor had pulled a Rand McNally Atlas out of a kitchen drawer and tried to draw a route for Zimmer to take, down the coast, zig-zagging the larger cities.

"You can fly on the Jersey Turnpike," he said. "Between toll booths. There's a beltway around Baltimore, and Washington. I'm not sure about Atlanta."

"Atlanta?"

"Got to go through Atlanta."

No, he didn't. He looked at the map long enough to find Panama City and trace the big green veins of interstate—he didn't want to have anything to do with toll booths, actually— back to Vermont, in straight lines and right angles, a simple, direct approach. He was headed for Ohio.

"That's crazy."

"He said."

"You'll add hours to your trip."

"Doesn't matter."

Truth was, he wanted to steer clear of New York, which was easy enough. There were too many memories there, unfinished memories, and he was afraid he'd be tempted to go back and try to work them out. He neither wanted to do that, nor did he want to drag any of them along, south. He wanted new. He wanted to start over completely. If he learned nothing else from the experience in Vermont, he learned you couldn't fix things. Once gone wrong, there was very little chance to recover. There might be answers, but probably never The answer; and sometimes, the only answer was nothing, forget it. Leave.

Take Maryland. He had to avoid Maryland. There was a bench warrant for his arrest there. He'd accumulated enough bad checks and DWI's, enough speeding and parking tickets, in the year and a half he'd been in College Park, they'd throw him in jail, impound the VW, strip him of his license, and who knew what else, if he ever got stopped on those roads. So he cruised westward, toward the heartland, hoping he could blend in.

Though he's never been able to do that. The opposite, in fact. He's always stood out, for some reason. That's what happened at College Park. He couldn't ever settle. He was a victim of too many possibilities at the university. Each class he took seemed like a field of study he might want to major in, until the next class. He went from English, to Anthropology, to Fine Arts, to History, then back to literature. All the liberal arts. But the G.I. Bill which funded his schooling wasn't quite enough to support his indecisiveness. While he strung out any move toward a commitment, waiting until he knew, absolutely knew what he wanted to do, life in general hunted him down, through bills, and collection agencies, and court summonses. His mistake was in waiting until it was almost too late, waiting for that decision that was supposed to bring the chaos to a halt, before fleeing, a mistake he should have known better than to make, by now. Once ensnared in that trap, he had no more choices but to run as fast as he could, as far as he could.

He was almost to Canada, sitting at a lunch counter in downtown Athens a couple of Aprils ago when Victor burst through the door hollering, "Anybody in here willing to bust their ass for twelve bucks an hour?"

Zimmer looked up at him, took the last bite of his burger, finished his Coke, and said, "Sure. Why not."

"Another mistake."

The trip through Pennsylvania, heading into the setting sun, was a game of peek-a-boo, as he crested hills and descended into valleys where small towns and villages huddled in the shadows. They were complete and contented in their isolation, with their own particular religious denominations, their own volunteer fire departments, generations of residents, cooperatives living their histories. He could feel himself being drawn to the towns, from the interstate, but he resisted, and kept driving, up the next incline, cross-sectioning the state, the series of mountain ranges which striated Pennsylvania, north to south, very much like the prow of a ship—or a surfboard— slices through ocean waves. He wouldn't allow himself to stop at any of the towns or turn toward the south just yet, not until he was far enough away from New York, and Maryland, and Vermont, until the momentum that had built up from his repeatedly telling himself, "You've got to go, got to," had worked its way past the point of resignation to a more relaxed posture, until he could indeed be bored, if he wanted to, something that couldn't possibly happen as long as he was within hearing, or striking distance of Victor.

Summers, working the construction jobs in and around Athens, had been fine, or at least mostly tolerable. They pulled concrete, Victor, Zimmer, and the three other workers who comprised the business. Victor would prowl through the pre-dawn farmhouse, snarling at Zimmer, "Get up, get up, goddammit!" only a few hours after drinking and laughing late into the night. Zimmer would lie there, pillow and blankets over his head, and in-between wondering if that son-of-a-bitch ever got tired, ever took a day off, would pray for rain, until Victor snatched his covers away. And so, all of them converging in three white Deconstructo Concrete trucks, they'd beat the sun to the site.

They laid foundations, climbing down into excavated holes, pounding spikes into the dirt and rocks that would brace the two-by-eights marking the perimeter. And after the cement truck came and vomited up its churning sludge, they'd smooth it out, with long squeegees, level it, and return the next day, after it dried, to frame the basement walls.

They carried the wooden wall forms, big as twin bed mattresses, but heavier, off one of the trucks, no more than two at a time—inside, outside—down into the hole, bent beneath the weight, the palettes angled across their shoulders, one hand steadying the load up high, the other scrabbling among the loose dirt and bared roots of the embankment for balance. Two by two, until they had enough of them leaning at all kinds of angles around the periphery of the dried slab. An ache settled across their shoulder blades, reached up the napes of their necks, like they'd been hung on a peg in a closet somewhere. It wouldn't go away no matter how much twitching and craning they did. They puzzled the forms into place, securing them together with latched bars of iron, top and bottom, and fitted the steel rebarb through the holes in the forms, every two feet, three, sometimes five tiers, all the way around. Then the hard part: the cement truck backed up to the ledge; the driver swung the chute out over the forms and they had to shovel the oozing concrete out of the snout down into the vacant walls, pushing it along, keeping it as uniform as they could, working fast as they could before it could have any chance to stiffen, yards and yards and yards of the stuff. The pain in their shoulders moved around to their pectorals, down their triceps, into their elbows, and wrists, pulling at the continuing flow. Ten, twelve hours a day. Sometimes they poured two jobs at a time, if they didn't run out of forms. Or they poured one in the morning, and dismantled the forms at another site, transferring them to the next site, the foundation they'd poured the day before. Every day, all day, from May, maybe April, until October, at least.

Every day, all day, Victor's voice, never very far away, anchoring them to the spot, the job, bellowing, "Isn't this fucking great!"

Victor was so convinced of that, so enthusiastic about the work, he'd start drinking at lunch-time, guzzling a couple of sixteen ounce beers along with the sandwiches and chips Jessie packed for him. Sitting on the back of one of the trucks, he'd tilt the cans upright, letting the beer drizzle down his beard if it wanted to, belch and laugh out loud, utterly uncaring of what anybody anywhere thought of him, which was considerable.

"Fuck 'em all!" he liked to say.

Victor had a monstrous reputation, among the other construction workers, in the minds of almost everyone in Athens, that he was constantly reinforcing. And Zimmer, through working with him, living with him, was too close not to be caught up in that reinforcement, too close not to become part of the reputation.

Some days Zimmer felt on the edge, that at any moment he would take his shovel, coated with splotches of dried cement three-quarters of the way up the handle, and swing it at Victor, aiming high, catching him right in the middle of, "Isn't this fucking gr--" the work was so grueling, so continuously and completely grueling.

But it was grueling in a focused way, an immediately recognizable way. There was a point to the effort, a product they could look at, where Zimmer could say to himself, That's good, this is worth it. As bad as the summers might seem— sometime in August, on any given Thursday afternoon, say, when it felt as though the day would never end, there would be no let up from the work—the winters were worse. As focused as the summer work was, the winter leisure was as chaotic. Victor had too much of that enthusiasm for living, experiencing, creating—whether cellar walls, or sensations—to ever be satisfied with any kind of peaceful hibernation. And he made too much money from the summer's work.

That's what Victor did during the winter, pissed away the money, or tried to, on cocaine, beer, and women. He stashed enough of it away in the walls of his old farm house to keep his wife, all their kids, living stylishly, but he could have retired long ago if he'd saved some of it, maybe reported some of the profits so he could invest them.

Instead, he luxuriated himself during the long, cold winters. He'd sleep into the afternoon, sit on the couch and smoke pot with Jessie, the whole family watching soap operas. Then he'd get coked up and want to go out drinking, driving Zimmer all over the back roads of Athens in the big white company pick-up, sloshing around corners, skidding through intersections, looking for ski tourists to run off the road.

Victor had tabs at all the bars in Athens; most of the hotels, too. As often as not, he'd drink himself into a stupor and spend the night in town, shacked up with some new female acquaintance.

"Strange pussy'll never hurt nothing," he'd tell Zimmer, who just as often would pass out on a couch down in the hotel lobby.

And true, Jessie didn't seem to care. She knew all about Victor's habits. Everyone knew everything in Athens. (The tabs consisted of a running total kept in the proprietor's head that Victor like to argue down and then tip the difference, plus.) He was good to her, the kids. It wasn't out of intimidation or insecurity that Jessie allowed him free rein. She had her own habits. She was fond of walking in on Zimmer's baths. "Seen my bra?" she'd ask, and then offer to climb into the big iron tub with Zimmer and give him a proper lathering, which was tempting enough. Or she'd invite Zimmer into the big bed that the whole family slept in—a huge waterbed Deconstructo had built himself: had to be king-and-a-half, easy. But the thought of sharing sleeping space with big, burly Victor and all those kids angled every which way was enough to make Zimmer decline, volunteer to sleep out on the kitchen floor and monitor the stove. Jessie'd even used that as a ruse, more than a few times, padding her way to the kitchen in the middle of the night to stoke up the fire and then slipping into Zimmer's sleeping bag, nestling up to him, shivering, pressing her bare nipples against him.

Zimmer had to get away from that. It was too disorienting. He had to leave. "I got to go," he'd told Victor, Jessie, the kids, as he stood backlighted in their bedroom doorway, shortly before dawn, dressed, in his fatigue jacket, duffle bag slung over his shoulder.

"Go where?" Victor asked.

"South," was all Zimmer said at first. Then, "The Gulf Coast, I think. Panama City Beach. In Florida." It had seemed like the right idea as soon as it occurred to him, which was more than enough substantiation. He had to leave.

When Jessie asked him, "Who's going to bake for us?" he had second thoughts. He thought it'd be funny to suggest, "Victor?" He thought he was being hasty, remembering some winter mornings at the kitchen counter, two or three of the kids standing on chairs beside him, helping, pouring flour, cracking eggs. He thought he'd miss that, and almost relented, almost shrugged the jacket off.

But then she got out of the bed, asking, "You sure you're warm enough?" trying to dress Zimmer up in Victor's scarf and hat, standing nude before him, at five-five, almost a foot shorter than Zimmer, looking up at him with a teasing glint in her eyes that provided necessary validation for his decision.

Except for Maryland, he's always known when he had to leave. Knowing exactly where to go sometimes presented a problem, but he's always known when to leave. He knew he had to leave upstate New York, both times, as a teenager, and then again when he'd returned after his discharge. He knew when to leave Colorado, and Mississippi. He has a long list of points of departure.

He had to leave. The disorientation, from the unrelenting fascination, was from Zimmer's feeling like he was becoming a replicate of Victor. It was a feeling he was familiar with, and did not like, but was less and less able to resist. He did not want to become someone else, especially someone like Deconstructo, who had graduated college, North Carolina, as a mechanical engineer, with honors, and has been gleefully dismantling his career ever since. "Had to leave."

The farther he got from Vermont, the better he felt about leaving.

"Which is good, isn't it?"

The success and validity of his decision became incumbent upon the completion of his plan, upon reaching Florida.

"The sooner I get there, the sooner I can start. Start starting over."

He veered into the emergency parking lane and ground the VW to a halt.

"No, no, NO!"

That was an old attitude. Eleven hours into the trip and he'd been thinking, Hell, this keeps up, I'll drive straight through!

"Then why did I take this out of the way route to begin with?"

For the trip.

"The transition."

To get it right.

"To get it all right."

The process.

"Fuck the destination!"

That didn't mean, however, that he wanted to spend the rest of his life on the Pennsylvania interstate system. No sooner had he eased back into traffic, he saw an orange construction sign: ROAD WORK AHEAD. And then another, LEFT LANE CLOSED, 1 MILE. 1500 FEET. MERGE RIGHT. His thoughts, the VW, the whole world slowed to a virtual crawl in a procession of cars idling along in the only opened lane behind a loaded down eighteen-wheeler dieseling its way asthmatically up the steep incline, from seventy, to twenty, fifteen, EIGHT miles an hour. A perfectly good passing lane lay cordoned off behind orange cones, though otherwise completely unattended. No graters, or cement trucks, no asphalt rollers, no road workers. And it wasn't for the usual stretch of highway, not the customary half-mile, mile of resurfacing or bridgework. It went on for miles, ten, twelve, fifteen unending miles.

"Unbelievable," Zimmer kept repeating, at the approach of each curve, the crest of each roll of the mountainous terrain. Around the bend, over the hump, were always more cones, and a ribbon of brake lights. He watched the cars file into line behind him, like lemmings.

"Unbelievable."

When the procession bunched up, and had to stop, like many other drivers, he'd stick his head out the window trying to make some sense of the scene. He wanted to lean on the horn.

"At what, though?"

He could see other drivers becoming agitated, silently waving their arms, or mouthing obscenities in his mirror.

"This is nuts!" he screamed, and swung his door open as he was passing one of the cones, clipping it.

"That felt good."

He repeated the gesture with the next one, and the next one, and felt better after each.

Then he started bumping the cones with the left front fender, before finally crushing one as he swerved into the empty lane altogether.

"Gotcha!"

He jumped out of the VW, ran and scooped up the flattened cone and hurled it into the median.

"Yaaa!" he growled and looked around for more victims, arms raised in defiance.

A Pennsylvania State Trooper came speeding at him from the opposite direction, a singular blue light twirling atop the car. Zimmer stalked toward the trooper so fast that he crouched down behind his opened door, resting one hand on his holster, calling, "Hold it right there!"

"It's about goddammed time!"

"Step back from the car."

"What?"

"I said step back."

"Jesus."

"License."

"What is this?"

"You been drinking son?"

"What?"

"I want you to count backward for me, from 42 to 29."

"You're kidding, right?"

"Not at all," he answered, walking around to the rear of the VW.

"42, 41, 40, 39—What is it with this construction?" Zimmer asked, following. "Look at the mess it's making of traffic."

"Got nothing to do with that."

"What? This doesn't make any fucking sense at all!"

"You can register a complaint with DOT if you like. But you can not endanger other motorists."

"Endanger? Are you serious?"

"Very much. Please keep counting."

"38, 37... What's that?"

"A traffic ticket."

"For what?"

"Reckless driving."

"Reckless driving?"

"You have your choice of paying the fine now, or waiting for court. The date is on the back there."

"A hundred and seventy-five bucks?"

"Cash."

"Jesus." Dumb-struck, Zimmer just stared at him for a few moments, before saying, "Guess I'll take my chances in court."

"Have a nice day then."

The trooper stalked away.

"What about the counting?"

He didn't hear, or didn't answer, which is good. Zimmer might have gotten the numbers wrong at that point.

"A hundred and seventy-five," was the number he kept saying to himself as he turned the VW around again and reentered the traffic.

"Hundred and seventy-five?"

By the time he saw a green exit sign in the distance he'd

become so flustered he went speeding down the emergency lane heedless of further entanglements with the law. He just wanted out.

Safely down the ramp, he pulled into a nearby Quick-Stop and bought two sixteen ounce cans of Iron City beer, walking out of the store with one cold can pressed to each temple. He sat on the curb outside the store, popped the top of one, drank down half of it, held it against the middle of his forehead, and said, "A hundred and seventy-fucking-five goddamn bucks!"

He continued like that, alternately drinking, and then using the cans as a kind of compress, until the alcohol effectively soothed him.

"Isn't this just fucking great?"

Nobody answered.

Zimmer sat, listening, thinking, before he finally had both cans empty, again, one pressed to each temple, and could only think to say, "More beer."

4. SOMEWHERE IN PENNSYLVANIA

ZIMMER woke up in the Viewway Motel, little by little, with less of a start than he might have imagined. He'd fallen asleep with the lights still on, so as soon as he opened his eyes he could see the room's paucity of furniture, its inert carpeting and wallpaper. In bed with him, he discovered when he tried to roll over, was food, the remains of his dinner: half a sack of sliced pumpernickel; a wedge of hoop cheese; a ruined tomato; part of a log of Braunschweiger; a jar of spicy brown mustard; and five, "Six. Seven. Eight," empty beer cans.

"No wonder."

Little by little: He remembered he'd had to hack at the cheese and the tomato with the Volkswagen ignition key. Spread the mustard with it too. Any other time he would have considered such logistical problems beforehand, but he'd been in a mood last night not to take responsibility for any necessary decisions, just to take whatever came along, and there it had all been: The deli was next to the Quick-Stop. The bakery was about a mile further south. And then the motel. He recalled just then that he'd even found a radio station he could live with.

"What's to argue about?"

The food was spread out on pages of newspaper, which he had to look at to bring to mind the town's name: Tripoli.

"Tripoli, Pennsylvania."

He'd only scanned the paper, between sandwiches. He reached for more of it, pushed down toward the foot of the double bed, and as he unfolded it the yellow traffic citation fluttered to the floor, and he remembered that encounter too.

"Hundred and seventy-five fucking bucks," he said, collapsing against the pillows and drawing the covers over him.

Then he looked to his left, to the nightstand, and wondered how warm those last two beers were.

"Fuck it," he said, reaching for one of them, popping the top. It was plenty warm. "Doesn't matter." He was going to get up and hit the road again soon enough. He figured to be in Florida long before they ever thought to look for him. And then he thought of not being able to return to Pennsylvania, or Maryland, and tried to bring to mind the atlas that Victor had held before him. "Was that only yesterday?"

He figured it'd be pretty tough to get to anywhere in New England, New York. "Pennsylvania's a big fucking state."

Oh well, like just about everything else since the trooper had bid him a Nice day, "Decision's been made."

Zimmer propped himself against the headboard, settled the beer can in a little hollow of covers, and returned to the newspaper. It suffered from terminal localness. Page 1 headline: "Shelter Denied Space Near Guthrie Spread: Moved to Newer Development." Beneath it was a grainy photograph of seven men standing around a shrouded street sign, identified by first names only. "Chummy." It made Zimmer feel excluded, almost unwelcome. He kept turning pages, thinking, "Fuck them. If they don't want me, or my money..." He barely read the other headlines, much less the attendant articles, about monster pumpkins, monster truck pulls, plowing strategies, and the like. And then, in the margins of the last page, number 19, he saw handwriting. Familiar handwriting. Familiar left-handed handwriting. He stood up on the bed, holding the page out at arm's length. He'd forgotten that. He'd made a phone call last night.

"Well, it was there," he said, walking the length of the bed, toppling the mustard, his beer. An ad for an apartment. When he'd finished with the paper the night before, it'd jumped off the page at him. "You don't fuck with providence," he tried, holding the page in one hand now, shaking it at the walls.

"Right?"

He looked around the room for a clock, his pants, and then stood in the opened front door, in his boxer shorts, to try and gauge the time of day. The marginal notes were directions to the apartment. He had an appointment to see it first thing in the morning.

"I'm a morning person," Zimmer remembered the man saying. "Best time to catch me is before the sun does."

In the bathroom, bathing more like a bird, than a human— in the sink, splashing water onto his face, under his arms—he looked at his reflection and repeated, "Right?"

He didn't know exactly what had prompted him to make the phone call; and he didn't know why he was going to keep the appointment, except, "There it is," he said, waving at the paper, that he'd carried into the bathroom, draped over the commode.

Suddenly—"Suddenly? What, ever, really happens suddenly?" he said, through a mouthful of toothpaste— suddenly, reaching Florida didn't seem like the only way to leave Vermont, to start over. Or at least Tripoli seemed like as good a chance as any other, a chance to start simple, and maybe get it right, for once.

"Who're you kidding?"

He could settle his business in Tripoli, something he never really did anywhere else.

"Right. That's the way *every* successful executive meeting begins. Old business? New."

Out in the Bee-atile, he told the rearview mirror, "The directions are easy," what was almost a question, as if seeking some kind of clemency.

He knew how imperfect his argument was, but then thought, "Maybe *that's* the problem?" His plans have always had to be perfect, to be successful. "No wonder. No fucking wonder." He checked the directions again.

"Take 13 south," the voice had said. "Past the park. Take a left at the second light, the Turnpike. Fillingim is about a mile up the hill, on the left. Got it? You shouldn't have any problem."

"I could stay long enough to get you fixed, finally," he said to the ignition key, which still had residue of cheese in its grooves.

"Right."

Fillingim was a short, truncated road with only twelve homes on it, all of them early Americana wood and stone, multi-storied, with high slanted roofs. Simple, and stately, from their position up on the hill, overlooking the rest of Tripoli. The houses had narrow, decorative yards in front, all of them nearly the same distance from the curb, and long sloping yards in back, on lots large enough to need access roads behind, even service driveways between some of the abutting yards. Number nine Fillingim had an arching half-moon driveway in front that curved around a rock garden, the center piece of which was a large bird bath--three seahorses with a huge ceramic basin balanced on the crowns of their heads.

Zimmer had been directed to the back, the carport—an arbor, really, with a loft—covering two deep, pebbled parking slots. He guided his noisy VW all the way in. It was tough to see, in that shadowed space, as he groped for the side door to the garage.

The owner, Donald Moseley—his name came to Zimmer just in time—came striding down the yard towards him, as he stood out on the grass, examining the large main house, squinting against the morning sunshine, just creeping over its roof. "Mr. Zimbarco?" he asked, from a few feet away.

Zimmer nodded.

"Donald, Donald Moseley. Nice to meet you," he said, extending a hand. "Come on up to the house. We'll get some coffee, and the keys. You can meet the wife." He pulled Zimmer up the slope of lawn.

In his split-level den, which looked down the yard through venetian blinds at the apartment, 9 1/2, Donald told Zimmer, "Built it myself," while he rummaged through a desk drawer. "For the kids, nineteen... What year was that honey?"

"Sixty-six," Rachel Moseley said, behind them, from the middle of a white davenport.

"Actually," he said, as they exited the sliding glass doors, "I had some help. Former clients, who needed to work off their bills. A plumber who needed to keep his driver's license; a carpenter who'd challenged his divorce decree, that kind of thing."

He led Zimmer up an outside staircase along the back of the loft, wearing deck shoes, khaki pants, an unzipped, lightweight London Fog. The apartment looked like a boathouse. Zimmer could imagine it perched above a grey wooden pier, creeping out from a lakeshore somewhere, except it didn't have enough windows, no screens. It didn't have any along the entrance side.

Donald kept talking about his "big picture" for the dwelling, key poised at the door while Zimmer took in the exterior, what had been his overall plan—having his children stay at the apartment during breaks from college, maybe starting their own families there.

"But you know how bogged down big projects can get," he said.

"Absolutely," Zimmer said, standing just inside the threshold.

Donald flipped on an overhead light. "So," he said, "you're not from Tripoli, are you?"

To the immediate left was the bathroom: tiny, built out from the wall, like a transplanted outhouse.

"No, no I'm not."

"Somewhere else in Pennsylvania? Philly?"

"No, actually. New York. Upstate."

"Ah."

Zimmer stood in the middle of the main room. It hadn't looked nearly so big from the outside. It reminded him of a gymnasium; half a basketball court, easy, just darker, with a lower ceiling.

"There would have been some partitioning walls for a bedroom here, a dining room up here," Donald said, fixing walls in the big empty space with his hands. He moved to a swinging door at the far end of the room. "Kitchen's through here," he said, holding it open. "What brings you to Tripoli?"

Good fucking question, Zimmer thought, and almost said. Mistake, he almost admitted. This whole crazy idea. He nearly fled then and there, faced with the question. He could imagine himself, twenty, thirty miles down the road, safely beyond whatever spell he seemed to be under, asking himself, What the hell was that all about? when Donald asked, "Do you cook?"

"Well, yeah," Zimmer said, stepping into the room. "Some."

The whole westward facing wall of the apartment was glass—must have been six feet of windows, top to bottom, a few inches of metal framework separating individual panes. The room was small, about three feet of walking space between the windows and a file of appliances and counters. The floor slanted ever so slightly down, but the windows were magnificent, overlooking the park spread out below, still showing plenty of its autumnal coloring.

Zimmer inspected the rest of the kitchen the way some people would a new car. He traced his hands along the countertop, testing the quality of the Formica. He turned on one of the eyes of the stove, to test the pilot light. He looked to be sure there was an exhaust hood and tried its fan. He bent to open the over door of the old Roper, bumping into a shelf buttressed along the wall of windows. There were two racks in the wide stove, and a real broiler compartment below: plenty of barbecuing space. Maneuvering in the narrow space would be tricky, he thought, as he danced from the sink, back to the stove, to steps only he knew, pirouetting back to the windows. "But doable."

"There's not a finer view to be had of the city," Donald said. "Sometimes Rach and I come out here and picnic." That road construction probably goes on for miles and miles and miles, Zimmer reminded himself. He was thinking contingencies. The refrigerator, in the far corner, opened the wrong way: into the room, rather than the corner. But these windows...

"I'll take it," he heard himself saying.

"Fine, fine. Let's go back up to the house, get another cup of coffee and take care of the paperwork."

He had about ten weeks before traffic court anyway. "Right?"

"Excuse me?"

"What about the couch?" Zimmer asked, pointing to a low, plaid sofa, more like he was still looking for an excuse than cementing a transaction.

"Comes with the place," Donald told him, pulling off the cushions. "It's a day bed, left by a former tenant. There's a chair that goes with it underneath."

"Perfect."

Then, climbing back up the yard, leaning into the slope, Donald asked, "Tell me more about yourself, Mr. Zimbarco. Do you work here in town? Got any references?"

"Listen, call me Zimmer." He stopped, reaching for his wallet. "And look, I just got to town yesterday. But I can give you two months rent and the security deposit right now," he said, unfolding four one hundred dollar bills, before adding, "Part of my separation pay from the military."

"Ah, a veteran," Donald said, reaching for the money, before draping an arm across Zimmer's shoulders, leading him back into the den. "Fine. Just fine."

Zimmer didn't know why he lied. "They might be the same bills?" he said, back up in the apartment, unpacking his duffel bag. But he doubted it. "It's been what, five years?"

Gradually, over the next couple of days, he absolved himself of the transgression, as he realized that absolute honesty hadn't been on either of their agendas.

"Partially furnished" fell pretty short of describing the apartment. He'd found out what a hazard the railing for the staircase was when he was hauling his bags up that first morning. Other flaws materialized. The place was more like a barn than a boathouse: drafty, incomplete, meant for cattle, at best.

And he found that he'd have to make do, like with a used car, with those ominous signs in their windows: As Is, No Warranty. It only took a few more encounters with Donald, Zimmer laying in wait for his landlord, outside, sitting at the top of the stairs, drinking a beer, sprinting up the yard when he spotted Donald's white Seville arching around the rock garden, asking about the gaps in the flooring, under the carpet, "Which floor? Where?" or if the baseboard heater was supposed to make that noise, "What humming?"

"Fuck it," he decided one evening, at the top of his staircase, glaring at the Moseleys, whom he was sure were watching him from one window or another. "I'll make my own goddammed adjustments." He'd pound an extra nail or two into the handrail. He'd duct tape everywhere. He'd wear his fatigue jacket when he sat on the commode, and use one of the two eyes that actually worked on the stove to warm his hands in the morning. "You think I'm going to worry about conservation when you're paying the utilities?" he called up to the house. "Who me?"

He never asked Donald about those other two gas lines for the Roper, or about the near complete absence of water pressure, leaving him pretty much alone, expecting the same. If Donald ever bugged him about being late with his rent or making too much noise, he'd answer, "Which month?" or, "What music?"

He found the chair—which didn't match the couch, not by a long shot—his first evening at 9 1/2, returning from the Goodwill store where he shopped to outfit the kitchen. It was stashed back in the farthest recesses of the garage, overstuffed, its upholstery split down the seat back, wood framing showing through one armrest, spotlighted in the headlights of the VW. Its faded orange maybe blended with the tan and yellow plaid of the couch, but just barely. What's more, there was a cat staking a menacing claim to it, staring fiercely into the light, then hissing when Zimmer tried to approach him, or shoo him away. Zimmer tried to pacify him, befriend him, reaching a hand out, palm upward, which the cat promptly swiped, drawing blood.

"This, I don't need."

The next morning Zimmer was sure to beat the sun to the Moseley's front door.

"Whose cat?" Donald sleepily asked.

So he tried table scraps, instead, leaving the leftovers of a scrambled egg, crusts of pumpernickel toast a nice safe distance from the chair on his way to another shopping spree.

That afternoon he caught the cat peeking around the side of the building at him. He poured some beer onto the last step, then climbed back up the stairs, mumbling, "You got twenty-four hours to change that attitude, pal."

He turned around at the top to see the cat squinting up at him. "Aw, Jesus. Listen to me. I'm sorry," he said, moving back down the stairs and sitting. "Look, I know you were here first. I just want to borrow the place, all right?" He poured some more beer out. "I'll be gone soon. Promise." He left a bowl of pork and beans out at the top of the staircase that evening and sat inside with the door open, watching.

It took two days of such negotiations, but at least they were pleasant encounters, no hissing, no growling, no sparring. At the end of the second, while the cat was enjoying another helping of bean juice, Zimmer snuck downstairs and hauled the chair up. The cat followed him into the apartment and reclaimed his seat, nonetheless.

"Oh, no, no, no," Zimmer said, but the cat didn't budge. They sat there, on their respective pieces of furniture, eyeing each other, the rest of the evening.

And they woke up at the same time the next morning. At least when Zimmer opened his eyes and looked over, the cat was already awake, sitting sphinx-like on the seat cushion. "You're not going to go away, are you?"

"Why should he?" he answered himself.

The next night, in the kitchen, Zimmer was sitting up on the counter, looking out over Tripoli, sharing a beer with the cat, who slurped it out of a gumbo bowl, down on the floor. He was still trying to figure out who ought to leave, who would leave, not to mention when. What he finally said to the cat was, "You need a name, is what you need."

First step in any diplomacy, he figured: Find out your adversary's name.

"Ali?"

"Bruce?"

But Zimmer named everything, tagged everything. He'd named his car shortly after he bought it, back in 1970: Abby, on the road. And just that day he'd named the apartment: Fill. "On the hill," he said, looking out at the sunset. He would have said that things named themselves, presented their tags, if you looked hard enough, paid attention. He even gave himself different monikers, according to the moods he found himself in. "Nice, Mr. Asshole," he'd say to himself if he pulled into traffic too quickly. Or, "You fucking numbskull," when he'd pounded a thumb instead of the nail head. He could do that because those moods, those actions were indicative of personalities he was trying to be, for whatever reason, rather than just being himself. "You deserve a name that fits, if nothing else in this world, right?" That was Zimmer trying to be Mario Andretti, or Bob Vila. That wasn't Zimmer being Zimmer.

"King?"

He tried to remember if there'd been anything in the lease about pets, but couldn't. "I'm not saying you can stay."

He didn't know if he could even find the lease, after only a few days. That's how much of a housekeeper he wasn't, wouldn't ever be: "No Hazel here."

"Doesn't matter." He'd play dumb. "Pet? Who me?"

That's what he'd named Donald, "Who me?" dismissing his part-time landlord, part-time lawyer.

"That's it!" he said, and jumped to the floor.

The cat skittered backward out of the room, like a startled crab, but then peeked through the doorway again, stealthily leaning across the threshold.

"Nice to meet you, Whomee," Zimmer said, stooping down and extending the hand with the scabbed over scratch marks. Whomee leaned forward some more and rubbed the side of his face against the palm, as Zimmer poured the rest of his beer into the bowl, asking, "How about some dinner?"

This was Zimmer. "Do I cook? Who me?" he said, looking down at the cat, who looked up. "Does a cat--" He tried to remember. "Shit in the woods? No, that's a bear." Zimmer loved to cook. He loved to cook more than he liked to eat, which presented a bit of a problem, at times. "Doesn't matter, though." He liked to cook for others, mostly. Loved to see their pleasure. It was better than sex!

"No. That's sneezing."

He'd only gradually begun the task of stocking his kitchen, going about it slowly, as he found out what might be available in Tripoli. He had just the beginnings of a spice rack. Today he found a grocery store where he could get the right kind of flour—highly glutinated—and bulk yeast. He was assembling pots and pans and other utensils piece by piece.

Zimmer pulled the rest of today's groceries from the sacks. He gathered up the yeast, beer, mustard, more of that hoop cheese, a couple of fresh tomatoes that he held, one in each hand, like rare gems, and moved for the refrigerator. When he stood, he reached up to the top of the box and turned on the radio. It was one of the few personal items that he'd brought with him from Vermont, along with his clothes, his car. It was something he'd never leave behind. He left a complete reel-to-reel stereo in Colorado, his last station in the military, but the radio—a GE clock radio, whose analog clock hands and tuning indicator had stopped moving a long, long time ago—was something he's been hauling around since high school. It was the first thing he set up, the thing that marked his space. "Like any other respectable cat."

The bike he did leave with Victor and the kids was something that they'd enjoy much more than he ever would, though it was difficult to decide just who derived more pleasure from riding it across the fields, crashing into the icy mountain creeks. It was just a passing fancy, like the rest of that experience, "Thank God," something that belonged to that time and place. He wouldn't have been able to fully extract it anyway. The radio was different.

It still played music just fine. Zimmer dialed through the airwaves, to the left, fishing for that radio station, WTPY, and found it paying tribute to John Lennon, on his birthday. "An hour and a half of his music," the DJ said, "from the Beatles days, and since."

"Perfect," Zimmer answered, though with just that little bit of providence, he was no longer contained enough to put together a real meal.

He settled for warmed up pork and beans again, knowing it was something Whomee liked, at least, warmed up and eaten from the can, after pouring off some for the cat, like C-rations. They shared the last two cans of a case of the stuff he'd gotten from the Quick Stop back near the interstate exit.

Zimmer used the last slice of bread to sop up the juice—he'd start baking his own in the morning—singing along with the radio, even dancing in the flickering candlelight as the chorus of the final song played over and over again, "Allll we are sayyyy-ing," standing at the windows, waving to the park like a giant stalk of meadow grass, "Is give peace a chance..." bending from side to side, careful not to spill his beer, but otherwise completely oblivious. "All we are sayyyy-ing..."

Perfect enough. He figured he had enough of Victor's money left to either last the two months he'd already paid for Fill, or to get south. "Or both." He'd decide later. Might even look for a job. "You never know." For the moment, he'd just enjoy the cold beer, the music, the shadows the candles created and the dark expanse of woods outside his glorious windows, exploring more and more of Tripoli each day, letting decisions present themselves, "Like names," if decisions had to be made.

5. DAGATON WOODS PARK

HE explored the interior of the park, Dagaton Woods, by mistake, on his way back from town the second day of his job search, or at least what had all the pretenses of a job search.

"I don't want to talk about it."

It's another one of those things he's not too good at, yet finds himself attempting again and again and again.

"What'd I say?"

He'd been headquartering the search from the Quick Stop, from the pay phone cubicle bolted to the side of the store. With the telephone draped over his shoulder, he held the classified section of the day's *Header* or the phone book he'd borrowed from inside against the lumpy masonry of the building, making marginal notes or circling numbers before dialing. He'd tried working from his strengths, at first, looking for jobs painting houses, something he'd done a lot of in Denver, calling paint wholesalers, building contractors. He even called the couple of telecommunications outfits in town, something closer to what he did for the Air Force.

"I certainly don't want to talk about *that*."

After an hour or so he found himself sitting inside Abby, parked out at the curb, drinking a beer, listening to the radio, trying to ward off the resultant frustration.

"I don't really need a job. Not yet. I'm probably leaving." He tested the starter. "Tomorrow." Tomorrow he'd call back the construction people he'd talked to and ask if any of them needed help pouring concrete, dreading their answers, already.

"It's a job," Victor always said, then laughed, "Haw, haw, haw!" Least and only qualification he ever needed.

"I know I don't need a job *that* bad."

What he needed was a good deep-fryer. "With a thermostat." And some dark rye flour, so he could bake his own pumpernickel, though he's been looking for that for years and years.

He was cruising south along 13, scanning both sides of the road for possibilities. He asked at the bakery, but of course they didn't know exactly where their supplies came from.

"Philly, probably."

"Would you sell me some?"

"I just work here."

Across from the main entrance to the park was a hardware store. He pulled to the side of 13, ever hopeful. He entered the double doors, looking more like a sheriff than a customer, and paced up and down the aisles. He found the small appliance shelves, what few there were. He found toasters, a waffle iron that he considered as a possible substitute, and then a couple of small french fryers.

"Hmm." They wouldn't really suit his purposes.

In the back of the bottom shelf, after he'd bent and pawed around, was a lone, scuffed up box: a Samson deep fryer.

"Samson? Wonder who it's made by."

He sat on the floor and opened it up. It was beautiful, deep, round, stainless. On the bottom was a little metal tag riveted to the frame: Made by Carrier Corp.

"Carrier? The AC people?"

He couldn't think of a reason why that would be bad news, so he scooped it up and walked toward the registers.

"Where's the box?"

"Back there."

"Back where?"

"In the aisle."

"Don't you want it?"

"Nope."

"What about directions?"

"Don't need those."

He walked out of the store hoisting his Samson like it was the Stanley Cup, then looked across the street to see a guy dribbling a basketball at the entrance to the park. It was a half-moon recess in the road, with low stone walls and lamp pillars bordering the entranceway, no more. "Strange."

By this time the guy across from him had stopped dribbling, at the sight of Zimmer carrying the deep fryer over his head, the electrical cord, dangling down.

"Real strange."

Then a white Plymouth Fury pulled into the entrance and the mysterious dribbler climbed into a back seat, to be whisked into the shadows of Dagaton Woods.

Zimmer put Samson into the back seat, got in Abby, got her started, and turned into the park, to follow.

He only caught a couple of faint glimpses of the car as it zig-zagged through the turns of the park road. And then he managed to get completely lost in the maze, tracing and retracing the unmarked, two-laned roads that would end abruptly in cul-de-sacs or in empty parking lots—the barrage of trees parting suddenly before a football field sized area of painted lines and blacktop and then rippling green lawns that rolled into the distance.

In the middle of one of those parking lots—or it might have been the same one he just kept coming back to, as far as he knew—he stopped, gave up the search.

"Need to find some peanut oil anyway."

Only when Abby stalled out did he hear the noise, the squeaking sneakers, the chink of metal-mesh nets, the louder echoes of the rattling goal when someone missed, then a human voice—the same someone, probably, cursing. Zimmer left Abby where she was and trotted off in the direction of that noise.

The basketball courts at Dagaton Woods were in the very center of the park, and were the focus of just about the only human activity within the park during the winter. The Olympic sized pool, located within the same cluster of recreational facilities, was empty, with nothing but a puddle of stagnant rainwater in the deep basin beneath the diving board, and a layer of dead leaves and branches, a couple of dead squirrels covering the rest of the aqua floor. The two fenced-in tennis courts didn't even have nets. The clubhouse, the centerpiece, might be used a couple of days during the off months, for Scouting retreats, a Christmas party, but was mostly locked, and dark. The basketball courts, side-by-side rectangles of asphalt, were popular year round, and Zimmer had no real trouble finding them, from all the noise of two or three games that were being played simultaneously that early in the afternoon.

He did have to do a little trailblazing, though, making his own path, to keep the search as direct as possible. He clawed his way through thick underbrush, climbed over boulders, and threaded his way through tight clusters of pine and birch and elm trees before he broke into the clearing where the sounds emanated from. As soon as he emerged from the woods, looking like a forest hermit returning to civilization—with leaves in his hair, small tears in the sleeves of his sweatshirt—he was picked by one of the teams to play.

"No, no," he tried to tell them. "I just want to watch."

"Come on, we need a center."

"No, really..." he said, turned, gesturing back toward the way he'd come. "I'm just out shopping."

When he looked back, the games had stopped, and everyone was staring at him. Shopping?

"I needed some flour, and oil."

"Right."

Rather than try to explain himself, he consented, bending to one knee, then the other, tightening the laces of his sneakers.

"All right, all right: we got the chef!"

"The gourmet!"

"The frontier gourmet."

Zimmer laughed, shook off the harassment, and took his place on the court. He hadn't played any basketball in years, not since high school, not counting a little in the service. Having been compelled to play let him off the hook, though. Never exceptional at the game, he was always first picked because of his size, on the assumption that anyone who stood six-three, with two-hundred pounds spread over a large frame, must play basketball. He grew tired of the very question, "You play basketball, don't you?" as well as the game. But here he was, in October, 1979, taking up a defensive position, the pivot man for his team, in a half-court basketball game, probably seven years since the last time he's touched a ball. It had to show.

Not so much on offense, where size really could make a difference. Zimmer knew at least that much about the game. He could camp out under the basket, using his bulk to get and keep position, calling for the ball, holding up a large left hand, able to jump high enough, once he worked the stiffness out of his legs, to take those high percentage shots, lay-ups, even dunking the ball a couple of times. And he was an able rebounder, kind of liked banging bodies again, liked the exertion. Because he'd been coerced—"I didn't ask to play, did I?"—he didn't feel the slightest need to offer excuses or modify his behavior in any way, which was good. Because on defense, he was vulnerable.

Never quick footed, he had to rely on positioning there, too, which meant he had to do a lot of anticipating, a lot of getting in the way. But when he guessed wrong, he looked, and felt, woefully inadequate. He ended up guarding, that first game, the mystery dribbler. Matched against each other because they were about the same height, Zimmer had a tough time keeping up with him when he had the ball. Dribbling around the perimeter, weaving in and out of the other players on the court, he would streak around Zimmer or shear himself from Zimmer's shadowing with the help of a well-placed pick that Zimmer had to fight through. The guy was a rabbit on the court, dancing, floppy, always on the move. He was skinny enough that Zimmer could push him around under the basket, could exert a certain measure of revenge, so that they looked like they were balancing each other out, but any time he got the ball and skipped back beyond the painted outline of the key, Zimmer would get this sick feeling in his stomach as he followed him, which he could only quell by getting progressively more aggressive.

The next time they faced each other, that aggression, and the mistaken sense that he'd seen enough of the guy's moves, made him vow, awaiting the initial inbound pass, "I'm going to get you this time."

It became a kind of obsession with Zimmer, chasing him around the court, lunging into his jump shots, leaping into his passing lanes, colliding with the players setting picks for him, grunting from the effort, groaning with contact, hollering with any success, "Yeah, now I got you!"

If was fun, for Zimmer, even if the result was the same—his team losing. He could act any way he wanted to: he could be animated, frustrated, and frustrating; dominating, given half a chance, from his mere presence. He could be foolish, just as easily, swatting at thin air. He didn't feel any restraints, even while he wasn't playing, but stalking the sidelines, yelling, "Watch him, watch out. Pick, pick! Cut him off, at the fucking kneecaps, if you have to!"

To the other players, he was distracting, at the very least. Some found it amusing. Others, like the mystery dribbler, found it almost frightening, enough that with Zimmer screaming threats from the side of the court, his game fell apart and their team got clobbered. He walked off the opposite side of the court, after giving Zimmer a Why me? look and headed up to the water fountain. Finally feeling more like himself, feeling some remorse, Zimmer followed.

Keeping one eye trained on his nemesis at all times, the dribbler bent to slurp at the running water.

"Hey, you know I didn't mean any of that shit down there," Zimmer said to him, waving his arms, wagging his head, like some giant St. Bernard puppy caught devouring a piece of furniture. "I was just fucking around."

"Swear?"

"Swear. I'm harmless."

Steph choked on the water.

"Really," Zimmer said, slapping him on the back, trying to help.

"Forget it," Steph coughed, standing, backing away. "Don't

worry about it. Part of the game."

"Yeah, well, if I was as good as you are, I could just shut up and play," Zimmer said, turning down the hill.

"What are you talking about," Steph said, walking along with him. "You're not so bad. Shit, I know I've got bruises."

"Right."

They stood on the side of the courts opposite from where the pool of players congregated between games, forging or dissolving teams, anteing up for the challenge.

"Listen, are you bound to those guys you're playing with?"

"Doubt it, after last game. Why?"

"What if we teamed up?"

Steph shrugged. It wasn't the worst option he could think of.

"Bruises, indeed."

Guarding Zimmer hadn't been any picnic.

"Like trying to move a piece of furniture down six flights of stairs."

Steph had never felt like more than a pest, as Zimmer kept him easily at bay with a well-planted elbow to the chest, nudging him into another orbit like he was completely weightless whenever they jumped after the same rebound. There were moments, actually, when he felt frustrated enough to want to leap onto Zimmer's back, lock him in a half-nelson and drag his ass to the ground, though he'd never do anything like that. He'd imagine himself doing it, from time to time, but would never follow through. In fact, he worried that Zimmer had somehow read his mind, as he watched him lumbering up the hill after him. The relief of those worries, perhaps, prompted Steph to say, "Why not?" in response to Zimmer's suggestion.

"Great," Zimmer answered, shaking on it. "I'm Tony Zimbarco, but call me Zimmer," he said, pounding Steph on the back again.

"S-Steph. Steph Abrams."

It turned out to be a natural collaboration, the two of

them—something Steph has always been keenly aware of: naturals. Though that's not how he would put it, later, on his way home, reminiscing their winning streak while he walked through the park.

"It was a damn dynasty!" he said, to the darkness, the chill closing quickly around him.

It could be a long walk out of Dagaton Woods, if you stuck to the roads, which Steph had to, if he hoped to get a ride. It was an even longer walk on fall evenings, October evenings, when the temperature seemed to drop just as quickly as the sun into the Pennsylvania hills. It wasn't frigid yet—Steph knew that true Arctic conditions were still a few weeks away—just cold enough that the sweat he'd generated through the afternoon's basketball, which had soaked through all three layers of shirts, cooled quickly. Steph had to put off any real possibility of a ride until he got out to 13. He walked along kind of huddled within himself, basketball tucked under his right arm, chin scrunched down into his shirt collar, hands shoved into the pockets of his jeans, folding himself as best he could to ward off the elements, cutting the tangents of the curving roadway, crossing from one curb to the other, kicking at stones to mark his progress. He had to wonder just what the hell he was going to do for another winter without a car.

He still lived at home. Being the eldest child of an otherwise typical family—three kids, two cars—and being their largest disappointment so far seemed to attract extra attention to his failure in life. Still at home when he ought to be graduated from college and off on his own, asking for rides or the use of an idle vehicle carried mostly unpleasant consequences, questions which usually led to lectures of one sort or another. The lectures—advice, supposedly—were all right, tolerable, on their own, except they never were, unaccompanied, independent lectures. They carried an increasing amount of baggage; comprehensive, all-encompassing, complete historical rendering kinds of baggage. Phrases like, Every time, and, Always, and Never ever, would slip into his father's diatribes as the volume rose. His mother made more subtle allusions to Patterns, Habits, which was maybe worse, maybe harder to deal with, or answer to. It was all an unanswerable puzzle, he could shrug and confess, a trap he'd created by himself, he knew, "But what can I do?"

"Do something!" his father would bellow, and stomp out of the room.

"Stephen, honey, you've got to at least try."

"Yeah, I know. But try what?"

His father answered, shouting from the other side of the house, "Anything!"

His younger brother, Jack, who couldn't be kept out of any family discussion, suggested, "Experiment. Take some classes at the JC. Find out what you like."

Steph never knew what he liked until he was already doing it, though he was willing to try, willing to take Jack's advice, even if he could already tell them that it wasn't the kind of advice suited to him. Steph couldn't make things happen, like his father, like Jack. He knew that much. He always had to let them happen, and then adjust.

"It's like basketball," he'd tell them, if he thought they'd listen.

If you looked hard enough, you could always find open court space, you could find the least challenging route, could slip between obstacles, to a rebound gone astray or an easy lay-up.

"Is that really wrong?"

To Steph, the whole secret of basketball—and life—was trying to perform with as little contact, or damage, as possible. His father, of course, thought he should give himself challenges, should erect his own obstacles, so that he could prove to himself something or other.

"Goals."

But there were always four Jacks for every Steph, or so it seemed. He had to be yielding. He wasn't left with any real choice, even if only because of his physical make-up. He was tall, and skinny, in a way that everyone always thought would change, even still made comments like, "Oh, you'll put some meat on those bones soon enough," like that was just another potential he wasn't realizing. He wasn't weak, or frail, so much as lean, wary. If anything, he looked like one of those underprivileged, third world poster children, who'd really managed to survive childhood because they'd learned to make do on their own. He was dark complected, even, with black, shaggy hair, unruly eyebrows over deep set, brown eyes. He knew how to get along with the tools he'd been given, surviving, absorbing impact on the basketball court and keeping on the move, adjusting, looking for least resistance, as elusive—and as dangerous, considering his shooting eye—as electricity.

He could take the lectures, act on the advice, and the harassment from the other players at Dagaton Woods—when he told them that he had to go, had to get home before dinner, or his mother, "Yes, my mother," would have a fit—for the same reason that everyone felt they had to lecture, advise, and harass.

"Does that make sense?"

He had to wonder, though, when Zimmer had broached the subject, hollering from the sidelines, "I know what it is!" after Steph had slipped free from a double team for an easier shot, "He's malleable, like fucking putty!"

"What the hell does that mean?"

He would find out, soon enough, that Zimmer had a completely different method of answering such questions, maybe all questions. For the rest of the afternoon, Zimmer would bellow only, "Like fucking putty," but then would grab Steph by both shoulder blades, kneading his huge thumbs into Steph's neck muscles to prove his point. Steph told himself that Zimmer, a disturber of space, surprised that someone who used so little force could accomplish so much on the same court, had to react more physically, couldn't possibly settle for just slapping palms.

"That's just him."

Steph was comfortable with that, though it took a while for him to figure out how to adjust. For the first three of their streak of victories, Steph scored the final basket on a play that they never really discussed, or practiced, a modified give-and-go play.

"We talked about this. I told you the secret to this kind of basketball, didn't I?"

Usually, Zimmer planted himself on the side of the key, high-post. Steph slipped past, plucking the ball from Zimmer's grasp, stepped back and took a jump shot if he was open; if not, he faked the shot and hurled a pass into the streaking Zimbarco, who would then maul somebody and muscle the ball up into the goal. It was a basic half-court play, where plays had to be kept basic to be successful.

They'd been playing three-on-three when Zimmer first got to the courts. Later, playing had dwindled down to two-on-two. Where three-on-three was maybe ideal park basketball, for its combination of variables and the lack of a crowd, two-on-two was a more elemental game. Options were limited. With only two players, one had the ball, the other didn't.

"*That's* the secret. Making the defense think you're going to do the other thing."

The secret was giving a believable head and shoulders fake, making it look like you were committing yourself to a jump shot while keeping your feet planted, keeping enough leverage to give some velocity to a pass underneath, something Steph was very, very good at.

But then he modified it. He couldn't say why, or how, even, at Zimmer's pestering, except, "It was game point. I don't know. Seemed like the thing to do."

He faked the shot, faked the pass, and just went back up in the air, shooting off the fake, instead of the dribble, which is maybe what surprised everyone, swish, or, "chink."

The first time he tried it, he was freelancing, acting on instinct.

"Which is best."

Zimmer had expected the ball and stopped underneath the basket with his hands up, his mouth ajar, just as dumbfounded as the two guys on the other team.

The second time, Zimmer was more prepared, even acted

his own part in the charade, following through, jumping toward the basket and then circling all the way around the court, arriving back at the spot where Steph had launched the shot not too long after he'd returned to the court, catching him in a sweaty Zimbarco bear hug.

The third time, Steph was ready for the end of the play—not tracing the ball's trajectory through the chains, but watching Zimmer, backing away from his suffocating hug. Zimmer was left to just grab at Steph's shoulders, digging those thumbs in, bellowing, "Beautiful!"

They continued like that, four, five, six more games, modifying the end of the play, while the central part, the shot, didn't change much. Steph figured right away that people were probably always modifying themselves around Zimmer. He was one of those people who were too big to be so exuberant. Or, because of his largeness, his exuberance was more pronounced, a non-linear, order of magnitude kind of thing. He wasn't big, fat, hulking, bulky large, really. He was built, big arms and shoulders. Huge hands. He conducted himself largely, more than anything else, with all that banging and grunting and yelling. And too, he was left-handed, so everything he did had that contrary look to it anyway.

Steph stopped in the middle of the road, no more than half the way to 13, remembering how Zimmer loosened up after that first game, how he started yelling out things, how funny that got to be: parking himself beneath the basket, spreading out, elbows high and wide, occupying the space of about three of anybody else, hollering, "Mine, it's mine! Get outa here!" Everything about Zimmer was pronounced.

They were standing on the sideline after a rare loss when Zimmer turned to Steph and asked, "How do you do that?" imitating the fakes, like a bad marionette.

"I don't know. I just do."

"I mean, it's like you got no bones or something," he said, continuing with his near-seizures, reaching for Steph's shoulders, "Like fucking putty."

Steph tried to remember other things Zimmer had said

throughout the afternoon, wanting to relish both the winning streak and the chance meeting, knowing that because it was chance, unforced, natural, in its development, it probably would not be repeated.

He heard Zimmer yell, "Now I got you!" and wondered if he really heard anything—he couldn't possibly hear what was going on at the courts from this distance—or if it was just more memory tricks. He did say that, early on, Steph was thinking, when he heard his voice again, "Yeah, you little motherfuckers, now I got your asses!"

Steph shook himself all the way out of his crouch, the reverie, trying to figure the direction Zimmer's voice had come from, when he heard it again, to his right, "Ouch, god-*dammit*!"

He stepped over the curb and fought through the bushes and whiplash tree limbs. On the other side, from the fringes of a parking lot, he saw Zimmer, spot-lighted in the circle of a high yellow lamp, wrestling with three or four little creatures.

"Kids."

Steph squinted, trotting over to the scene, then saw a fifth—Zimmer had one wrapped in each arm, one mounted and clinging to his back, and one tugging at each of his legs.

"No," Steph mumbled to himself, "six," as another one backed out of the pile and swung a little fist against Zimmer's chest. The one riding bareback grabbed a handful of hair and yanked. Zimmer roared and shuddered, all the while squeezing those he had a grip on till they cried, a grizzly fighting off so many jackals.

"Jesus," Steph said, before joining in. He dropped his basketball and sprinted the rest of the way, screaming a battle cry that cracked in his throat, and jumped onto the whole melee, toppling everyone.

The kids popped up and scattered. Zimmer lumbered to his feet, looked down on Steph with a snarl, spotted the six different directions they'd gone in, picked one and hauled after him, hollering, "Blooood!"

Steph got up and chased him down again. "Whoa, Zimmer,

wait. They're just kids." Then he hopped up on Zimmer's back, looping a skinny arm around his neck and hollering in his ear, "Stop!"

Zimmer stumbled on a few more steps, still screaming, "Blood! Blood!" before falling, taking Steph with him, who asked, "What blood? Where?"

"Not my blood, damnit," Zimmer answered, pushing himself up once more. "Theirs. I want their blood."

Steph grabbed a handful of sweatshirt. "Why?"

"Why?" Zimmer repeated, and only then stopped. "They broke into my goddamn car, that's why."

"Broke into your car?"

"Yeah, my car," he said, turning and pointing back toward the center of the parking lot. "Abby. They probably stole Samson, too," he said, trotting back to his car.

"What?"

Steph loped off to retrieve his basketball, then turned around to witness more of Zimmer's anguish. He paced around the VW, patting it, rubbing it. "Poor Abby." He picked at chunks of glass from the broken passenger side window, stared at each shard a moment before heaving it to a distant part of the asphalt lot. Steph watched him repeat the ceremony five more times. Once for each kid, he figured.

"You didn't say you had a car."

"What'd you think?"

Steph stared at him a moment, before saying, "I don't know." Then, "Why'd you park all the way down here."

Zimmer didn't answer, just said, "This is turning into another shitty day." He opened the passenger door all the way and brushed the rest of the glass to the floorboard. "Least they didn't fuck with Samson. I need a drink. How about it?"

"Sure."

Steph started to get in, careful about arranging his feet amongst the empty beer cans and the crumpled chip bags and the glass, as Zimmer turned the key and got no response.

"Of course," he said. "Of fucking course!" Then, "Wait Steph." He climbed back out, adding, "Need a push."

"Huh?"

"Push. I need a push, to start her," he told him, leaning back into the car.

"That's why you parked way the hell out here. The hills."

"Right," Zimmer said, wagging his head, as they nudged the small car into motion.

"Okay, that should do it," he said, hopping back into the rolling VW.

Steph copied the maneuver, skipping, hopping, then jumping through the opened door, just as Zimmer was threading the gear shift into second, before finally slamming the engine to life, and only then asking, "Where to?"

6. LEAR'S

"THEY violated her, Steph."

"Not permanently though."

"What do you mean not permanently? They forced their way in, what's not permanent about that?"

"You can fix the window."

"Just suppose it was your car. You've got a car?"

Steph shook his head.

"What?"

"No. No, I don't have a car."

"Hmm." Zimmer leaned forward, propping his elbows onto the bar, reaching for an ashtray and spinning it absently, otherwise remaining silent.

The silence continued; and continued. No arguments Steph thought to offer seemed worthy, or pertinent. He didn't have a car. He couldn't relate.

Steph hated such silences, though was usually powerless to do anything about them, as other sounds of Lear's sifted into the empty space: the muffled chatter of all the faceless drinkers sitting around the main room of Lear's; the tinkling of ice cubes in their glasses; and an occasional eruption of noise from the game room at the rear of the building, contentious voices or the crack of pool balls colliding. Otherwise, noisy silence: the buzz of indecision inside Steph's head, and the empty rattling of glass against the polished bar surface.

They sat bridging the corner of the bar closest to the front picture window, where Abby was parked, just the other side of the wall. When Steph had directed Zimmer to Lear's, telling him, "There's a parking lot in back," Zimmer had, instead, dissected the crosswalk, jumped the curb, and parked on the sidewalk, as close to the front door as possible.

"I need to keep an eye on her," he explained. "I'd hate for anyone else to fuck with her."

"Ah, okay," Steph agreed, then peeked over the vacant window frame at the six inches of space between the car and the brick and glass of the building before climbing over the hand brake to get out of the driver's side.

Zimmer was holding the door to Lear's open for him, saying, "That car is sacred to me, Steph. Your car has to be, or it isn't worth a damn thing."

"But Zimmer," Steph said after a while, as Zimmer sat there quietly staring past him at the shadow of the car through the dark glass. "All they did was break a wind--"

"They violated her!" Then he asked, "Are you married?"

"Me? No."

"Ever?"

"Ever what? Married? No, un-uh."

"Hmm."

Zimmer looked around, asking the only other patron on their side of the bar, an old man sitting propped up on a stool at the other end of the window, who'd been sitting there with his back to the wall, silently smoking, watching them. "You?"

"Certainly."

"Then you know what I mean."

"Indeed."

"I didn't take care of her."

Steph pivoted and stared through the window. A street lamp illuminated the front portion of Abby. He could see one drooping headlight.

"*Faites attention*," the old man said.

"What?"

"It's a French phrase. It literally means, pay attention, but idiomatically it's used to say be careful."

"That's right," Steph said.

"That's it. I didn't pay enough attention."

"And they violated her?"

"There's really no other term for it."

Finally, Zimmer stood, grabbed his glass, their pitcher, and said, "Let's play pool. Something I think I can do."

Welcoming any breach, Steph said, "Great," but did think to

offer, "I'm not very good at this, though."

"Don't worry about it," Zimmer told him. Then, spying Abby again, he waved toward the window, asking the old man, "Would you mind?"

"Not at all."

"Thanks," he said, striding for the partitioning which separated the game room from the rest of the bar.

"Maybe I'll just watch," Steph tried, following.

"Come on," Zimmer told him, finding them a table, anteing up for the next game. "I need a partner. It'll be just like basketball."

It will? Steph thought, remembering their streak at Dagaton Woods. How could he argue with that? But then he had a second thought, which almost always came too late, if at all. He remembered where he was supposed to be: home, eating dinner. He knew he was late, at best. He looked around for a clock anyway. While he didn't agree with his father or his mother about the severity of that infraction, he could guess the amount of grief it would cause. He should call.

"It's a perfect game, because it's so simple," Zimmer was telling him. "There're only three things you need to know to play pool," handing Steph a cue stick.

"First: pool is a gentlemen's game," he said, sliding two quarters into their slots and pushing the plunger. He watched to be sure all the balls tumbled out then let go and stood. "I don't know where all this bullshit about it being a brute's hobby got started, but I'll tell you a secret, brutes are the very people who should stay away from a pool table. They'll only wind up breaking something. You can't force anything in pool. Nothing. That makes pool shooters respectable, don't you think?" he said, thunking the eight ball into the middle of the rack, sliding the arrangement along the felt, lifting the plastic triangle and slipping it back into its slot, before offering the break, which wasn't theirs, as challengers, to offer: "Gentlemen."

They, their opponents, had been standing at the head of the table, waiting on Zimmer, listening to his speech. Steph wondered what they thought, more than about whether or not he agreed with Zimmer. Back at their seats, he tried to tell him again, "You may have to be a little more elementary, Zimmer."

"Elementary?"

"Specific."

"Re-lax," he said again. "You'll do fine. I've been watching your hands."

Steph squinted over the table at him, then down at his hands. "See, you're still over my head."

"Listen, you can tell a lot about pool players—anyone, really—by their hands. Watch these guys," he said, motioning to an adjacent table. "That one, gripping his cue so tightly, watch out for him. Too intense. And there, see how he bridges?" showing Steph a contortion of his own fingers, what looked mostly like a shadow puppet. "He knows how to play, but isn't executing: negi day."

Steph forgot about hands. "Negi day?"

"Happens to everyone," Zimmer said, holding up both hands. "You know, balance."

Steph closed his eyes, shook his head, feeling something more than disbelief or exasperation. Overload, maybe?

The other team sank a high ball on their break, but missed the follow-up shot. Zimmer jumped up and took two loping strides to the table before turning back. "We, ah, didn't discuss this. Mind if I shoot first?"

Steph turned his hands palm up, said, "Are you kidding?" He just wanted to watch, really. Or he wanted to hear those other two things first, though he didn't hold out much hope that he'd understand them any better. "Sure, shoot first. Shoot always."

Zimmer clumped around the table, grunting to himself, sucking in air between his teeth, visibly flinching from one idea, another strategy. He stood a little back from the table, still studying it, and reached, without looking, across his body for the powder block hung on a wooden peg in the corner. He rubbed the whole palm of his right hand white as well as the spaces between the first two fingers and his thumb. Steph watched, a little puzzled. There wasn't anything odd or uncustomary about what Zimmer was doing, just something confounding about watching him do it. It wasn't until Zimmer powdered the cue and slid it a few times through his bridged right hand that Steph remembered, "Southpaw." Then he watched the same wave of realization wash over the faces of their opposition.

"That's why he studies hands," Steph said to himself. Or, because he was left-handed, only he would *think* to study hands.

Zimmer crouched down low over the tabletop, nose to the rail, still not having taken a shot. It seemed an exceedingly laborious prelude. To Steph, pool was a matter of whacking away at one ball, maybe two, getting the embarrassment over with as quickly as possible. He hadn't ever seen anyone, at any level of accomplishment, conduct the kind of large and loud waltz about the table as Zimmer.

Steph had to wonder how much of it was just show, especially when Zimmer finally bent over a shot.

"Hell, I saw that one, from all the way back here."

But then, after the shot was made, and the cue ball bounded across the corner pocket and traced a parallel path back to very near its origin, the chalked end of Zimmer's cue, he forgot those thoughts. He tilted his head a couple of degree to the left—to get the same kind of picture Zimmer would—and watched him reel off another, then a third shot without having to move more than a step, which was amazing to Steph, though Zimmer seemed less than pleased. After that, after the seven rattled around at the side pocket before falling, Zimmer stood all the way out of his crouch, grumbled a little, reached for the chalk and started his pacing again.

The last three low balls sat huddled together, trapped by several opposing striped ones, against the cushion, never completely broken from the rack. Zimmer shrugged, slammed the cue ball into the crowd, sinking the six, but not before sending two of theirs home first.

"Now that looked like something I'd do," Steph told him as he came back to their table.

"Only way I could bust them out. It was either that or we'd be trying desperation shots while they cleaned up—bank shots, combos."

"They're bad?"

"On this table they are. Rails are shot. Banks closed. Usually," he said, holding up two dusty fingers, "all other things being equal, there're two kinds of players: shooters and slammers. Shooters shouldn't have to resort to slamming."

"Forcing."

"Right."

"Is that number two?"

"Number two?"

"You know, the three things..."

"Oh, no, no, no. But," he said, holding up just one finger, "if I'd kept my shape," leaving a white smudge on the Naval insignia of his sweatshirt, "I could have run the rack."

"Shape?"

"Yeah, you know. Where you leave the egg."

"Oh..."

"Got to take care of that darling," Zimmer said, sipping his beer. "Can't play the damn game one shot at a time..."

Steph just blinked.

"Only in pool, you have those absolute relations between cause and effect..." Zimmer stopped. "You really meant what you said, didn't you?"

Steph could only shrug.

"Oh, well. Too late now."

"Huh?"

"You're up," he said, waving at the pool table with his cue.

Steph had almost forgotten why they were there. He gulped down the rest of his beer, swallowing wrong, which he took for the worst of omens. He stepped up to the table and plucked the chalk off the rail before turning back to tell Zimmer, "This could get ugly."

Zimmer held his hands up, and Steph knew exactly what he was thinking: Re-lax.

"Right."

The game had wound down to a critical juncture. Each team had two object balls left, plus the eight. "What's the worst that can happen?"

Depends. He tried to think in terms of what Zimmer had said. "Disrespect?"

Didn't ring, just as imitating the stalking, the noises, or powdering both hands didn't settle his anxiety any.

There was a shot, though. A long, but unobstructed one: the three ball still down by the far corner. He gave only passing consideration to his shape, "Sinking that one ball would be accomplishment enough, thank you very much," and perched over the table.

He knew alignment, at least, sighting over the cue ball. He tried a few practice strokes before shooting. The cue ball banged the three with a pop, knocking it into the pocket, but then followed right along, "Like it was on a leash." Scratch.

"Only in pool," he remembered, as he caught sight of Zimmer, over at their table, leaning forward, elbows on his knees, hanging his head, shaking it, can success be so immediately and totally replaced by failure.

"Is it, ah, past the trading deadline?" he asked, standing between Zimmer and the game table.

"No, no, don't do that to yourself. You're thinking too much. I could hear you."

Hear me? Steph thought.

"You should just shoot. Here, look at this," he said, slouching over their tabletop, tracing an outline of a pool table in the moisture, positioning empty shot glasses as pool balls. "Your form's not bad," he said while he arranged other props. "Just don't torque your elbow. Watch." He pointed to another player. "Pendulum, see? But your form's not bad, it's just that... You don't mind this, do you?"

"Mind?"

"Good. Listen, the ball's going to scoot in a straight line, a line drawn from the point where the cue ball hits it right through the center of the ball, boom, like that," he said, smashing one faceted shot glass against another.

They looked up from the mock game, from more noise than Zimmer'd expected, to find most everyone else in the room watching them. Zimmer guessed, "I'm up?"

He got up and moved toward the table, reaching for chalk, more powder, circling, making his noises, rubbing his head, frosting it blue and white. Steph tried to concentrate on the game, but it was so damn hard to ignore Zimmer and his movements, his expressions: His eyebrows shot up his forehead as a plan worked itself out inside. Steph remembered a high school French teacher who used his eyebrows like a third hand, to emphasize pronunciation, accent. "*Faites at-ten-zion.*"

"That's it!" he said, slapping his own forehead, interrupting Zimmer's ritual. "He's got *two* left hands!"

Zimmer shook his head at him, then elaborately swung his primary left arm freely, sliding the cue smoothly through his bridge until he was certain Steph was paying attention. Pen-du-lum, he mouthed, and waited for Steph to answer, "All right, all right, I got it," before he would continue.

And then, in a lightning succession of shot, chalk, shot, he dispensed with the yellow one ball, and the eight. "Game."

"Yeah," Zimmer burst out, before being pulled aside.

Steph watched, and assumed the worst.

"Who wouldn't?"

He figured Zimmer was having the same kind of conversation that they'd had by the water fountain back at Dagaton Woods.

"And who could blame him?"

The beer was empty, the game over, and Steph had so much as told him he would need to find another, better partner.

"And then went up there and proved my point. Jesus."

He saw Zimmer circling around the partition and supposed he might as well move on too, home to dinner, that was over by now, clearly, though maybe not so cold that the interrogation wouldn't last all night.

"Commiserating with a friend?"

"What friend?"

"Over what?"

"His car got banged up." Or should he say violated? Would that be more believable? Less of a stretch?

"Got to go?" Zimmer asked, clunking a fresh pitcher of beer onto their table.

"No, no, not really. I just thought..."

"Good. We got a rematch with the guppies."

"Guppies?"

Zimmer chugged down most of a glass of beer before saying, "Fuckers say I didn't call my shot on the eight—like there was any question." He put the glass down, refilled it, Steph's. "Story of my life."

Steph thought, At least you've got a story.

"Fucking guppies," Zimmer said, a little louder.

"You think it's a good idea you call them that?"

"Why, you know these guys?"

Steph looked around the room. "A little."

"Hell, Steph, if that's the way they're going to act, always nibbling..."

Steph shook his head.

"Right, right, you're right. Pool, we'll keep it at pool," he said, waving the mood away. "English, that's what separates us from the guppies. That's the trick," spinning one of the shotglasses.

"*That's* number two."

"Right. The spin determines where the cue ball will end up. Topspin," he said, twirling the index finger of his right hand, "will make it run. Bottom, and it'll stop, dead; reverse even. It gets a little more complicated after that, when you start using side spins, start combining, bottom-right, top-left. The cue ball transfers energy, reverses its spin whenever it collides with something else, shit like that. Ever had any physics?"

"Hell, yes. Too much."

"See, I could tell. It's like that, predictable. Only in pool. You'll get the hang of it. Just fool around with it some. But try not to think too much about all that other shit."

"What other shit?"

"You know," he said, standing, looking over either shoulder at nothing. "*That* shit."

Steph just stared at him.

"Forget these guys," he said, waving at the other team, who'd been waiting on them again, to break this time. Zimmer leaned over, whispering, "They're guppies. Just shoot."

He straightened back up, moved toward the head of the table before stopping, turning, and asking a little too elaborately, "May I?"

Steph had settled back into his seat with his beer. Caught in the glare of Zimmer's showiness and the attention of everyone else in the room, he choked, and couldn't answer. He wondered, though, if it really was just a show. "Maybe he's just constantly contrary." As his teammate, of course, Steph would like to think so. Wasn't this the same Zimmer he'd played basketball with? "Only more in his element?"

Zimmer sent the cue ball crashing into the rack. One, then another, and a third ball fell into pockets off the break.

"He's just left handed. It just looks like a big production."

He didn't make any kind of show about calling his shots, as he proceeded. He just nodded, twitched his head, twelve in the side.

The guppies weren't taking it all well. They watched, following Zimmer's every move, studying the spectacle, leaning against the wall or sitting nervously in chairs, mouths either slackened in amazement or pulled back into tight grimaces. Forgotten cigarettes burned away in ashtrays, single undisturbed columns of smoke rising from the ash. Zimmer just kept shooting. As his targets grew scarcer—nine ball, tracking the rail, into the corner—and scarcer, Steph felt a little puny about questioning any part of Zimmer's behavior, and terribly odd that he should be holding a cue stick in the same general vicinity as Zimmer. He wondered if it was that same sense that caused the two who had challenged Zimmer's protocol to jam their cues back into the wire rack, like the sticks had failed them.

"Well, we certainly showed them," Steph said, welcoming

Zimmer back to the table with a beer, and a salute. "I do appreciate you sparing me the nuisance of having to shoot."

"Think nothing of it."

One of the guppies came back from the bar, by their table, with two shots of Jack Daniels, their bounty, and slapped them on the tabletop as disgustedly as he could.

"See what I mean?" Zimmer said."Nibbling. Wouldn't that piss you off?"

"Nope," Steph said, raising a toast. "You keep this up, and I may have to get drunk."

"That's why," Zimmer answered, clanking glasses with Steph, letting him get a mouthful, "it's your turn.

He watched Steph struggle to keep from spitting back over the table. "I'm tired."

Steph just stared at him.

"Go on, let me see if you've been paying attention," Zimmer said, thumbing toward the awaiting game. "You break."

It's just a break. "Got to be haphazard enough to conceal lack of talent, lack of experience, right?" But he knew better. He'd seen games where there'd been lousy breaks, where the players either racked the whole thing over again, or spent the rest of the game grumbling about what a shitty break it'd been.

Steph remembered picking up the chalk, but can't say what he did with it after that. He remembered thinking, Just act, shoot. "Instincts. Like any other animal." And then he almost turned to the guppies and said, That's where the grunting comes from! But as he looked up, and around, he could see Zimmer watching him, frowning. That look: You're thinking too much.

That's probably the moment he started holding his breath, sucking up a chest full of air, trying to expand his ribcage, diaphragm, trying to lose that suffocating, panicked feeling.

He stooped over the table and tried to pump some life into what felt like a faltering, twitching heart, sliding the stick back and forth over the rail. Failing that, but with nothing else to do, not daring to look up again, he jabbed at the cue ball finally with whatever might he had left. The tip of the cue glanced off the ball and it hopped against the rail and then just bumped into the awaiting squadron of balls, dislodging only a couple of them.

"Oh, Jesus," he cried, letting out that air finally, seeing black spots spinning crazily before his eyes, falling to the ground.

He remembered thinking, Great, a trap door! And he thought he heard Zimmer hollering, "Epileptic! Epileptic!" but doesn't have any recollection of how he ended up on the floor of the bathroom clear on the other side of Lear's, Zimmer standing over him.

"Was that your very first break?"

"Showed, huh?"

As Steph blinked back to life, Zimmer held a paper towel compress to his head.

"Shit..."

"Zimmer, look, I can explain."

"Explain? Did you use the chalk?"

"Well..."

"Steph, how many times have I got to tell you, relax! Get floppy, like you're going baseline."

"I wish," Steph said, checking himself in the mirror, looking for bruises, or blood along his scalp line.

"Get Steph-like, goddammit," Zimmer said, kneading his shoulders. "What are you worried about?" he asked, stepping back, frowning at him through the mirrors. "Listen, you don't care, right? Forget them."

Zimmer started out of the bathroom, but stopped to say, "Oh, and listen, you don't have to hammer the damn cue ball on the break. Just stroke it, like any other shot. Force comes from body weight. Rock back on your rear foot, like this, and bring everything forward, through the hips," demonstrating with a little hula dance. "See?"

He did it a couple of more times, "Rear foot, hips, through the stick to the ball," like a waltz routine.

When Steph tried it, the question was, What body weight?

Zimmer gave up, said, "Let's go take a look at the damage," leading Steph out of the bathroom with a steadying arm draped across his shoulders.

In the glare of everyone's awaiting their return, Steph panicked again, slipping out from under Zimmer's arm, veering across the room on the wrong side of the partition, to the bar. He ordered one shot of tequila to either steady himself, get floppy, or both, then ordered two more. Just as he picked them off the bar, he thought, "Is that number three?" and tried to remember to ask Zimmer.

Back at their table, waiting, Zimmer told him, "It's not that bad."

Steph looked. He saw a mess of balls huddled very close together on about a third of the table. "Not bad?"

"Trust me," Zimmer said, downing the shot, going to work.

In fact, he quickly recovered any advantage Steph had squandered, but it was at least three games later before he would trust Steph to go up to the table by himself. He stomped around behind Steph, hovering largely, like a left-handed Goodyear blimp, staying just within Steph's periphery, making comments, clearing his throat if he thought Steph was positioned wrong, getting too floppy, or not floppy enough, heedless of the increasingly hostile guppies.

Steph worried about why they seemed to be so irritated whenever he was caught in the glare of their seething animosity, bending over a shot, discussing strategy. He knew he shouldn't pay any attention to them, should just shoot, but these were guys he's seen countless times, in high school hallways, gas station doorways, guys he's traded familiar nods and relaxed greetings with all his life, guys he could easily empathize with, could commiserate each other's parallel, dead-ended existences, even if they didn't ever get down to specifics. He couldn't rationalize how a game of pool could bring the tight-lipped snarls and narrowed eyes, and his attention would wander off trying to see what was so important about the game until he'd hear Zimmer's voice cutting through all the others, both inside and outside his head, "Baby that thing, Steph. Don't be a slammer. Pretend those are balls you'd like to take home with you."

Zimmer was a traffic cop, giving directions, pointing to the impact spot on the object ball where Steph should aim. And, as Zimmer knew, once he relaxed enough, Steph proved to be a pretty dependable student, so that it wasn't too long before they really were a team again, on more or less equal ground, acknowledging good shots or good attempts; and it wasn't too long before Zimmer was once again trying to fold Steph in half by way of congratulations.

Safely back at the table, out of the glare of the guppies, they just toasted themselves as the number of victims exceeded the extent to which they could harmlessly stack the shot-glasses.

It was later, what seemed like hours and hours later, when Steph, leaning over the pool table, squinting at the blurry colored balls so far away, readying to break again, had a sense of premonition, or *deja vu*, course through him, what honestly felt like a real seizure. He remembered every little bit that Zimmer had told him, rocking back on his heels, but couldn't help giggling at the memory of his sashaying in the bathroom, bringing his weight through his bony hips, "Hips, sticks, baby balls," swinging his cue stick forward, this time missing the cue ball completely. He still managed to dislodge the same number of balls as before, though only because he couldn't stop and crashed into the table. "Does that count?"

He squinted in the general vicinity of where Zimmer was supposed to be sitting. "Where the fuck did all those other white balls come from?"

Zimmer stepped into the light around the table, tossing a paper napkin into the air like a referee. "Game," he said. "Partner's turned into a pumpkin." He reached and slid two quarters onto the edge of the table to pay for the next one, gripping Steph by the shoulders and steering him for the front door.

"What about our drinks?" one of the guppies called when they were halfway past the bar, already past the bartender.

"Drinks?" Zimmer said, still facing the bar, the old man. Then he turned around. "Drinks? He could probably still beat you!" he told them, and left Steph clinging to the bar rail.

"They're nibbling again," Steph said carefully, crumbling to his knees, still holding the padded rail above his head. The voices were coming to him in bits and pieces, though he could well enough sense that it was time to either go back and shoot more pool—which wouldn't have been impossible, he figured, if he could maybe get someone to hold him up—or it was time to go jump on Zimmer's back again, like he had a long, long time ago back in the parking lot of Dagaton Woods, "If I could just find my goddammed feet..."

A hand pulled him upright. He could see, squinting through one bleary eye, the old man leaning over the edge of the bar.

"Thanks, ah..."

"Boyles. Mr. Boyles."

"Right. Debreciate it," he mumbled, and then turned back toward the game room, pleased and surprised, really, to be still mobile, and at least a little lucid, crawling along the bar, using it for support as long as it lasted, ready to stand with his partner, arms locked in mortal combat, ready to beat hell on some guppies!

"I should think," Mr. Boyles said before Steph got more than two or three steps away, "that the most diplomatic thing to do at the moment would be to avoid any further confrontation. Give them their drinks, and save if for another day, eh? Randall?"

Steph turned and immediately agreed with him—something about his voice, so measured and unstressed, as if there couldn't possibly be anything else to do, or say. One part of him wanted to agree to the point of pleading, "This isn't really like us, you know. It's all that awful alcohol," while another was asking, "Who you calling Randall?" afraid that a case of mistaken identity would nullify everything somehow.

With one hand raised "diplomatically," though unsteadily off the bar to repeat the advice, "Give them their drinks, Zimber," he saw Randall, the bartender, a blur, really, heading for the game room with the drinks in hand, another pitcher, and a short stubby piece of lumber under his arm. He came back with Zimmer in tow, who said, "Thanks," to Mr. Boyles.

He bowed his head slightly in response.

Zimmer pried Steph the rest of the way off the bar and started for the door again when someone else yelled from the game room, "Thanks a lot, Abrams!"

Steph looked up, first, to the ceiling, and then traced the sound back to the guppies, trying to paste a snarl on his face, but then saw the biggest, fishiest guppy flipping him off—what looked like four or five fat middle fingers.

"They *really* need a lesson," Zimmer grumbled, to anyone listening, pausing, then sighed and reached for the door.

Mr. Boyles answered, "Admittedly," just as Zimmer was maneuvering Steph through the doorway. He raised his tumbler saluting them, Zimmer's restraint, adding, "Always will, no doubt."

Steph caught up with the conversation once outside, crawling over the driver's seat. "We ought to ask them," he said, peering through the gaping hole where Abby's window had been, through the darkened window of Lear's, "if they understand the implications of flipping someone off," sounding to himself a lot like Mr. Boyles suddenly, which worried him.

He closed his eyes against the motion of the car as Zimmer nudged her for the curb, then opened them again to stop the spinning inside his head, asking Zimmer, as he jumped into his seat, "Does this thing have any heat?" not sure he was cold, as much as fascinated by the clouds of his breathing.

"Sure," Zimmer said, once the engine was winding up, reaching into the back seat for a pair of gloves, "Round about May, or June, I figure."

Steph looked over at him, trying to process information that flat refused to fit, "June? Who's June?" until he remembered it was Zimmer who'd said it, "Left-fucking-handed Zimbarco," who glanced over at him, grinning, bouncing his eyebrows up and down, *a la* Groucho Marx.

"Oh, Jesus," Steph cried. "Now he's got six of those blasted eyebrows," covering his face. "Too much, too much. Goodnight Lear's. Goodnight world."

7. THE PINK HOUSE AT 11803 MOUNTAINSIDE VIEWWAY

THE first thing Zimmer had to know when Steph finally told him where he lived—when they toasted the place to an otherwise empty Lear's—was, "Is it really pink?"

Thirty-plus hours later, Steph was readying for war.

"Not war, really. Let's just say confrontation."

"But is it *really* pink?"

"Oh, yeah. Pink aluminum, too. So it'll never fade. It'll always be pink, always be visible, for miles and miles and miles. Forever. I'll never get away from it."

"If I'd known *that*," Zimmer started, but then stopped, short of guilt, short of saying that with that little bit of information he could've gotten Steph home two nights ago, and maybe they wouldn't be plying him with liquor this early in the morning, maybe he wouldn' have...

Instead, he asked, "Mountainside Viewway? I thought you lived on 13?"

Mr. Boyles laughed, "Heh," something like a squeak, something like a hic-cough, something they hadn't heard from him before.

"It's a long story, Zimmer. I'll tell you about it when I get back. If I get back." Steph stood, adding, "Wish me luck."

Zimmer held his shotglass up to him so that the morning light shining through the front window of Lear's, over the horizon of Abby's roof, made the amber whiskey glow. "You've got to be good to be lucky."

"It wouldn't have mattered," Mr. Boyles said. They both had their glasses raised, watching as Steph climbed into the Bee-atile.

"What?"

"Steph's house."

"Oh. I know."

Zimmer hadn't been in much better shape than Steph the other night. They were both functioning in a basal kind of way when they left Lear's. They were on automatic pilot.

"We wouldn't have peed on ourselves, say."

Otherwise they were pretty useless. Steph had huddled himself down in the seat of Abby, burrowing into his peculiar, soft-shelled cocoon, and wouldn't move past a particular point in the evening's conversation, like an album skipping on the turntable.

"Why do you suppose they got so pissed off?" he kept asking, slurring, "dooyoo-spose," about the guppies, sounding like he really never had been the target of anyone's wrath or anger or belligerence before in his life.

And Zimmer kept answering, "That's what makes them guppies," thinking he was moving the conversation along when he was really just completing the loop.

Neither of them were losing their patience, though. Zimmer, for one, was used to drunks, just as he was used to guppies. Victor, whenever they'd return to the farm house, to Jessie, instead of shacking up for the night, would get morose and apologetic, confessing his sins to Zimmer, crying, threatening to drive the truck right off the mountain ledge, and then promising to change his life as if the mere mention of dying were epiphany enough.

Steph, slumped all the way down in his seat, had started snoring, when he inhaled. When he exhaled, he was still mumbling about the evening. "Fucking guppies," Zimmer heard him say a few times.

Zimmer cruised the length of 13, south, and then turned back towards Dagaton Woods, hoping to spark some kind of homing device in Steph. At the main entrance to the park he pulled into the half moon cut out around the pillars and stopped, idling very near the spot where he'd first seen Steph. He tried to count how many hours ago that had been, thinking maybe if he went back to the source it might help.

"Starting over isn't always bad," he told Steph, but received no coherent response.

He couldn't leave him there. It was too cold to let him sleep in the car. Zimmer swung back out onto 13, headed for the Turnpike, and Fill.

Automatic pilot for Zimmer was altogether different than it was for Steph. Zimmer was still thinking, still assessing, still anticipating. He was figuring contingencies, logistics. But he was mistaken in expecting the same from Steph.

"I could have told you that."

"You were incoherent."

"You could have tried."

"I did. I tried to warn you about sleeping there."

"I'm sure you did."

"Just like I tried to warn you about the stairs, and the railing. You weren't listening to anything!"

"I was drunk!" Steph said, then winced, still feeling the effects. He stood in the corner of Zimmer's kitchen pressing a cold bottle of Iron City to his forehead. With his other hand, he was picking at little scabs in his scalp. They were the least of his injuries.

"So was I."

"But you live here," Steph said, waving one hand into the kitchen, the other at the doorway which led to the rest of the apartment.

"And I tried to tell you."

He tried to tell Steph about the rotten steps and the handrail, "Won't hold you," as he guided him up the stairs. Steph could manage only one or two steps forward before he would veer in one direction or another, right, into the wall with a thud, or left, teetering over the shaky railing.

Once navigating the stairs, Steph had shut the rest of the way down, collapsing into the first available space, Whomee's chair. Zimmer tried to tell him what might happen if he slept there, and even tried to move him to another spot, but Steph was beyond gone. He was unapproachable.

Zimmer wasn't at all surprised by what happened. When

Steph finally woke up—where Zimmer'd been up for more than an hour, was already baking, had been wondering, in fact, if he shouldn't go and check for a pulse or something—it was to Whomee, draped over the top of the chair, kneading his claws into Steph's head.

"Shit!"

"I knew it."

"Oh, God. What time is it?"

That took Zimmer back. "He's worried about time?" Zimmer peeked around the corner of the kitchen to witness Steph looking around wildly for a clock, while feeling along the carpet, under the chair, for his shoes. "About eight-thirty," Zimmer guessed.

"What?"

"Eight-thirty, give or take..."

"Oh, God."

"What's the matter?"

Steph stopped, stood up and pointed at him. "Zimmer."

"Right."

"Where am I?"

"Fillingim. Up in the hills."

"Near the interstate?" Steph guessed, looking around for windows this time. "Jesus. I got to go. I got to fly," he said, knotting his shoelaces.

"I can give you a ride, if you can wait about ten minutes," Zimmer said, showing his floured hands as evidence.

"Can't. I got to be home, like an hour ago."

"Take Abby, then."

"What?"

"Abby. The Bee-atile. Take her," Zimmer said, tossing his keys across the room.

"You sure?"

Zimmer frowned. "You can drive, can't you?"

"Drive! Shit," he said, struggling with his jacket, backing through the door, mumbling, "Thanks."

Still trying to get the right arm into the right sleeve turned the right way out, he crashed through a soft board three steps from the bottom, gouging a knee, screaming, "Fuck!"

"I told him about that, too," Zimmer said to Whomee, before returning to the kitchen.

Steph actually got the Bee-atile started, nudging her down the negative grade of the access drive from where Zimmer'd backed into the parking space last night. It's not so much that Steph could manage the maneuver, as it was that he remembered, period. Steph'd only seen Zimmer do it once, sober, and Zimmer didn't think he'd paid that much attention.

"Maybe he just pays a different kind of attention."

Zimmer reached to turn on the radio, now that there was no one to disturb.

"I got no car and it's breaking my heart..."

"Perfect."

Steph heard the same song in the Bee-atile, speeding down the Turnpike, "...but I got a driver and that's a start," though he wasn't really listening. He was thinking contingency. Driving was exactly what he was supposed to be doing that morning, though not some dilapidated, airy Volkswagen. He was supposed to be driving the family wagon to the service station for its winter visit: antifreeze, oil, tune-up, snow tires. He was supposed to have dropped his mother off at work at the mall and deposited the car at the Sunoco station downtown near the Tripoli Community College campus. He'd missed his mother, that much he was certain of. He'd missed his first class, too, though he wouldn't get upset over that.

"Calculus."

What other alterations there had been, he couldn't know. So he was thinking contingency.

"Stevie's home!" his little sister shouted almost as soon as his hand reached the doorknob to the side cellar door.

"Kathy, please," Steph pleaded, climbing the three steps up to the kitchen. He almost had time to ask why she was home, why the house wasn't empty.

"STEPHEN!" his father yelled from upstairs. He'd waited for the last plant bus.

The clock on the staircase landing said Steph'd gotten home

ten minutes before that ride would come.

"Where the hell have you been all night?"

"I, ah..."

"No. Wait. Don't tell me, let me guess," he said, standing over his son at the top of the stairs. "Hell, I don't' even have to do that. You stink. All I have to do is smell you to know what you've been doing all night."

"I was helping a friend move."

"Helping a friend move? What friend? Where?"

"Somebody you don't know. I just met him yesterday."

"What's his name?"

Later, standing in the corner of Zimmer's kitchen, he finally remembered the correct answer. "Zimbarco. Tony Zimbarco."

"I knew it," Zimmer said. "What'd you tell him?"

"Zimmer, of course. Bob Zimmer, I think."

"Perfect." As Zimmer was dishing himself up some breakfast, sausage patties and green pepper slices, a couple of fried eggs, a hunk of fresh French bread, he fixed a plate for Steph too, asking, "Eaten yet?"

Steph said, "Think I should?" supposing he ought to punish himself or something. The conversation with his father had ended with Steph being kicked out of the house.

"If you don't, Whomee will."

The cat stood poised on his rear legs beneath them, pawing at the air.

Steph took the plate, moved alongside Zimmer at the counter, facing Dagaton Woods, but he didn't start eating. He stood there waving the plate around in one hand, his half finished beer in the other, driving Whomee crazy. He was trying to detail for Zimmer what had happened, and why. But just like the night before, he was stuck at one point of the conversation, repeating his father's final words. "Out!" he'd said from the top of the staircase, "Out!" from the landing. And then finally from the bottom of the stairs, he'd turned and shouted, "I want you OUT of this house!"

Steph stopped, took a drink of what had become warm beer.

Zimmer drank too, wondering if Steph was ever going to eat.

Steph put down the bottle, reached for a fork, but then said, "And you know what? You know what I was thinking at the time?"

Zimmer just stared at him, wincing, anticipating Steph's pain.

"I was trying to make some goddammed joke about three outs and your struck, but couldn't make it work," he said, as Zimmer spat his beer at the windows. "Is that fucking sick, or not?"

Finally, Steph took a bite. "Hey, this is good. D'you cook this?"

Zimmer only nodded.

The only interaction between them for the rest of the meal was the bread, as first Zimmer, and then Steph would hold the loaf for the other to rip off a warm chunk for each of them, replacing it onto the wire cooling rack behind them on the counter. Every once in a while, Steph would grumble, "Out!" and Zimmer would laugh, almost choke.

Only after he finished, and slipped his plate into the sink, did Zimmer ask, "Now what?"

Steph took his last bit of moist bread and squashed it into the yoke of an egg—the only other survivor on his plate—once, twice, until all the goo was soaked into the bread and the cooked underside lifted off the plate, leaving only the rim of white, like an empty eye socket in a skull. He finished the soggy piece of bread, remembering that his father would cook breakfasts like that, but only on Sundays.

He set the plate on the floor for Whomee to finish the ghostly egg and lap up the grease, answering, "I don't know, Zimmer. I really don't know."

"You got a job?"

"Nope."

"Want to go make some phone calls?"

"Would you hire me?" he said, picking at yesterday's sweats, crusted with salt lines, dirt, bloodied at the knee. Had it really been less than twenty-four hours ago that he was setting out for Dagaton Woods, not a care in the world except for hitching a ride home afterwards?

"Good point."

"Shit, Zimmer," Steph said, bending and picking up his plate, sliding it into the sink. "I feel like getting drunk."

"That was my very next suggestion," Zimmer said, leaving the kitchen and heading for the door without any further hesitation.

He stood holding the front door open for Steph. "Lear's?"

"Why not."

Why not retreat to the dark, the relative warmth and the isolated acceptance of Lear's? He could find a seat in Lear's, he knew, some place to call his own, for a while, at least. That's what he needed most right then. Once there, settled, comforted by the swivel chair, the alcohol, then he could deal with plans, could approach decisions, could scheme: he'd get his clothes, whatever, tomorrow morning; he'd find a job, first of the week. He'd get by.

Steph, of course, hardly gave any of those things a second thought all during the long day of pool, and beer, and whiskey. The courage and conviction he found in Lear's that morning flagged a little as the day wore on, but not much. It didn't dwindle nearly as quickly as his sobriety, say, and then his consciousness.

If he woke up the next morning, in Whomee's chair again, with a start, with that same panicked feeling charging through him, the same dread and remorse and fear, it only took a return trip to the bar, a couple of shots on an otherwise empty stomach to screw him back into action, ready him for facing his family. It only took a little bit of liquor, and Zimmer's ready encouragement, "You've got to be good to be lucky..."

He meant it as encouraging, anyway. Steph did wonder, pausing as he pushed Abby off the curb, How is that supposed to help? "And does he think I'm either?" which was the worst thing he could wonder at that moment. Then, trying to think in a Zimbarco kind of way, Steph figured it had to have something to do with balance, which was a little more comforting.

"It's just one of those lines," Zimmer would have told him. Just a pool player's, "A respectable pool player," quote, a response to the meddlesome queries of the uninitiated.

"Masconi," Mr. Boyles said, many minutes after the sound of Abby's engine faded into another silence, "I believe."

Zimmer moved to a seat next to the old man. "You know that line?"

"Certainly," he said, facing forward. "It surprises me some that you do. Seems you're a student of the game, as well as an accomplished player."

"He's the greatest," Zimmer said, raising his glass. "To Willie."

"Randall," Mr. Boyles called, "Have you officially met, ah, Zimmer?"

"Zimbarco, actually. Tony Zimbarco. But, yeah, call me Zimmer."

"Meet Anthony," Mr. Boyles said, slowly, almost correcting him.

"How ya doing, Randy," Zimmer said, reaching over the bar to shake hands with the bartender.

"Greetings," Randy responded, in fair imitation of Mr. Boyles, maybe even chiding *him* a little.

Mr. Boyles relaxed then, allowing himself a half grin, chuckling, "Excellent, Randall, excellent. Now then, pour a round please, yourself as well. We're going to toast a great man. A gentleman. True, Anthony?"

Zimmer looked over at him, quickly, like he'd been caught stealing or something. Mr. Boyles sat implacably forward, watching Randy measure their shots.

They drank, savored the liquor, the memory, the silence. Something about Mr. Boyles' demeanor made Zimmer feel like a kid again, as he started quizzing the older man about *his* pool knowledge. And as a father might, he only answered the specific questions—not intending to discourage curiosity so much as trying to avoid questions into realms where he might not be able to answer everything perhaps—allowing only, "Yes, some," to questions about whether he played the game. Only, "On occasion," as answer to if he'd ever seen Willie play.

Randy, polishing glassware, leaning against the shelf of bottles at the rear of the bar, helped, some, prodding Mr. Boyles' silences with intimations of tournaments, and touring, of rolling the nine in Atlantic City, in New York, Jersey, gesturing towards an array of dusty trophies occupying the highest most secluded shelf above him, pushing his old friend.

"My dear Randall," Mr. Boyles said at one point, "professionals do not *roll* the nine."

"Professionals," registered with Zimmer, and he took another look at the trophies. Mr. Boyles sat facing forward, as always. Zimmer watched him drink, and smoke.

"You a lefty too?"

"Excuse me?"

"Left-handed," Zimmer said, motioning his. "I just noticed—
"

Mr. Boyles was holding both his cigarette and his glass in his left hand.

"Oh, that. No. Just I habit I got into."

Zimmer waited.

"After I quit playing," he said, waving his right hand, "I took up writing for a time."

"Writing?"

"Stories," he said, smiling. "Lies, mostly. So you see, while my right hand was occupied..."

"Oh, sure, sure," Zimmer said, nodding. "Maybe we could play sometime?"

"You think so?"

"Well, you know, no big deal. Maybe you could show me a couple of things."

"Oh, I doubt that."

"You could try!"

"I should think you've already helped enough, Randall," Mr. Boyles answered him, peering over the top of his glasses. "I can tell you this, though, Anthony: On a good table, I mean a really good table," he said, sneaking a glance at Randy, "You can cut anything."

One of the first things Steph's mother had to know was, "Just who is this Bob Zimmer, Stephen? Where do you know him from.

Steph stood in the kitchen of the pink house, a kitchen that couldn't be any more different than Zimmer's, with its matching appliances, the color coordinated tiles and countertops and linens, even the cookware, "The telephone!" And space. There was so much space, Steph was kind of floundering in it, yet feeling cornered, too, like some crook cowering before the family Doberman. But it'd been Kathy who'd caught him, with her irritating, "Stevie's home!"

Actually, it caught everyone by surprise. His mother, sitting at the dining table with his brother Jack leaning over her shoulder, had been working the *Header*'s Saturday morning crossword. She looked up with mouth ajar.

His father came in the sliding back door, from his redwood patio progress, took a pencil out of his mouth, and said, "Son?"

Steph answered, "Hi," unsnapping his jacket.

"Stephen, your... Those..."

Jack finished for her, like with the puzzle, where he had right answers only because she had wrong ones. "Where'd you get those clothes?"

That wasn't the exchange Steph'd been rehearsing. He tugged at Zimmer's sweatshirt, which hung on him, hung over his belt, which was cinched all the way up, the only thing that kept Zimmer's painter's pants on his bony hips.

His father asked, "Whose car you been using?"

"Well, that's all part of what I wanted to tell you."

"Stephen, is everything all right? You're not in any kind of trouble, are you?"

"No, Mom, nothing like that."

"Are the police coming?" Kathy said, pulling the cellar door open and looking out the window, looking for flashing lights, listening for sirens.

"Kathy, why don't you go watch some television, okay baby?"

Steph stepped back and leaned against the counter in the corner of the kitchen nearest the back yard. Little starlings hopped around out there on the lifeless lawn, the last few hanging around town, he guessed. He found himself wishing he was at Lear's, with the one-way anonymity of that window, or at Fill, looking out over Dagaton Woods. He heard a pigeon scratching the pebbly roofing of the back porch overhang, just above his head. They didn't go anywhere for the winter, just got a little slower, a little dumber. "Or maybe it was a squirrel."

His father stepped after Kathy, watching as she tuned the television to American Bandstand and settled herself on the couch. Stephanie Mills syncopated down the hallway. Mr. Abrams turned from the sound, back into the kitchen. "So?"

So. Steph couldn't help but squirm and wish again that he was back at Lear's. Maybe there, just the two of them, leaning over one of those small, round tables, maybe then they could drop the antagonism. "Not here in this kitchen," where it was put upon one or the other of them to do something.

"I'm moving out, moving in with Zimmer."

"Zimmer?" his mother asked, still seated over her puzzle, marker at the ready, poised to jot the name in the margin. "This the one you helped move?"

Jack didn't help, asking, "You sure there's no woman involved?"

"Jesus," his father said, turning to check on Kathy.

"Yes," he said to his mother. "You don't know him."

"Didn't sound like you knew him much the other day."

"Jesus," Steph mumbled. "Dad, listen, isn't this what you said would be the best thing for me to do?"

"I said, it would be best if you started taking some more responsibility for your life and those around you. *That's* what I said."

His mother, bless her, reversed the conversation a little. "Is this someone *you've* known long? Someone from school?"

He almost grinned, that humor which can only come from

exhaustion, the mingling of a three-day drunk and requisite hangover, or from bourbon on an empty stomach. He didn't know, didn't know much but that it was so typical of her to have to have things settled, understood, in an orderly, chronological way. It really seemed funny, until Jack pressed, "From State?"

"No, no," Steph said, sounding tired, especially to himself. "I met him a couple of days ago in the park. He's from New York, just moved here."

"The park?" Steph could hear his father's patience unraveling. "The *park*? You play basketball with someone and all of a sudden you're driving his car, wearing his clothes, and he's got room for you in his house?"

"Apart--"

"Jesus! What a prince."

"Dad, he's just trying to help..."

"Who can blame you?" his father said, pacing again. He wore a path across the kitchen linoleum, across the hallway that led to the front of the house, into the adjoining dining room where he'd spy out the bay window at the neighbor's son waxing his car. "A real home away from home. Why, Stephen?"

"Why?" Just then Steph got the feeling they were reading more into it than there was. "Jesus. Why not?" he asked, in earnest, which had an immediate negative effect. He pulled at his hair and glanced to check on the birds. They were gone.

"Just who is this Bob Zimmer, Stephen?"

Steph wanted to sit at the table, across from her, because she had the power to call all this shit off. She was in complete control, always, whether or not any of them ever admitted as much. She was emotionally detached enough not to be caught up in the anguish and anger and dread. He could explain it to her. "It's simple," he'd tell her. He'd get a job, work for a while, then try to decide what he was going to do, and where. "You're *right* Dad!" On his own he would make more responsible decisions. But they wanted details.

"He's just a guy, Mom."

"Oh, *GREAT*. That tells us a lot."

"What does he do, honey?"

"Work for parks?"

Shit. Steph took a breath. "Right. That's right, Jack. That's how I met him," he said, tossing one of his own indignant glares back at his father. "I was asking him about a job."

"I thought he just moved here? You were helping him move in?"

"That's right. He was transferred. Anyway, he paints houses on the side, said I could help him out with that, as soon as he gets going."

His father started to challenge, "What?" but was distracted by some Lionel Ritchie vocals wafting up the hallway from the television room where Kathy had been steadily increasing the volume and was now singing along.

"How can you watch that crap?" he yelled at her, stomping into the den.

Steph heard him chop the dial through a talk show, the gunfire of a matinee western, a couple of news broadcasts reviewing the first full week of the hostage situation in the Middle East, finally to a college football game, "The twenty-second consecutive meeting between the University of Pittsburgh," never attenuating the volume.

Steph reached under the sink and slipped a big green trash bag off its roll, stepped past Kathy at the foot of the stairs and retreated to his room.

He sat on the bed and noticed immediately that his mother was already accepting of the situation, was already making the necessary changes. She'd made up his bed, closed the window that he almost always kept open, and she'd begun shifting his things on the desk, the bureau, into neat piles off to one side or another. He could see the room evolving into the guest room she'd always wanted, right before his eyes.

It annoyed him that they were torturing him so much about the transition when she seemed so relegated to it. "Anxious, even." And it kind of hurt. But that was her way: Calculated, orderly, controlled. "Cold."

He heard voices from below his room, filtering up through

the duct-work and the floor vents. Jack's deep grumbling, Kathy's high-pitched, insistent whine, and his mother's reassuring murmur, answering both of them, "That's between Stephen and your father."

As younger children, Jack and Steph used to lie on the floor on summer nights when their parents had parties, listening to the laughter, the joking, the tinkle of ice-cubes and the clanging of bottles, echoing up from below. It always seemed like it was a lot farther away, not just a matter of twenty stairs, like they were listening in on a party in Hollywood, or Monaco. The parents they lived with day to day were not the socialites they could hear. Jack always talked about what it would be like to attend such gatherings, how he would be. Steph always wondered about that discrepancy.

He heard from the front of the house, "Intercepted at the TWO YARD LINE, Oh, myyyy..."

"Jesus."

He stood, pulled sweatshirts, tee-shirts, socks, everything from the bureau, stuffing it all into the bag. "Ho, ho, ho," he said, hoisting the bag over his shoulder and climbing back down the stairs.

He set the bag down in the middle of the kitchen, snapping his jacket back up, to the silent, expectant vigil of Kathy and Jack and his mother still at the table. He tried to think of something to say to them, something light, but because his leaving was so totally out of context, not at all like those Coke commercials or war movies, he didn't have any idea what would be appropriate. And they were no help, leaving the burden entirely his. He shrugged, picked up his sack again, and told them, "See you."

"Stephen, how will you..." his mother blurted out as he started to turn away for the cellar door. Again, he heard in her voice that she preferred him gone. Why couldn't she just say goodbye.

Jack came around to the front of the table, finishing her question, louder, "You got any money?"

Steph gave him a "Fuck you" look he was sure to

understand, maybe even translate for everyone else, should they ask.

But Jack's question had been loud enough to bring their father back into the kitchen, cigar smoke billowing around him. He only smoked these days when he was either overly content, or agitated.

"You just gonna sneak out?"

"Come on, Dad."

"When we gonna see you again? Passed out on some bus stop bench?"

"Is Stevie gonna be a bum?"

Steph knew she must have heard the association from somewhere else. "I've got a place to stay."

"Where?"

Details. Now his father wanted details too. "Up off of Fillingim."

Jack said, "Those places?"

"Stephen?"

"It's a garage apartment. A guy named Moseley owns the place."

"Donald Moseley?" Jack tilted his head a little. "On the Chamber?"

"I guess."

"How much rent you paying?"

"None, yet."

"This Zimmer paying it all?"

"Yeah, for now. But I'm going to get a job. I may not even stay there."

"So you *don't* have a place to stay."

"Look, don't worry, all right," Steph finally shouted. An empty gnawing anger swept in after the exhaustion, after the hapless humor. It crawled into the pit of his stomach and just wrestled with itself there, like Whomee trying to get comfortable. "I'll take care of myself, all right."

"Oh, you will, huh?" his father shouted back, his face glowing crimson. "You think it's that simple?"

"Yeah. I do."

Mr. Abrams took an angry step toward Steph.

"John," his mother said, composed, composing, still gathering data. "Stephen, will we hear from you?"

"You better believe we will," his father answered, turning for the television room again, trailing smoke, disgust.

"Shit. Look, I'm leaving," Steph said, holding his hands up against any more interrogation. "I don't know anything else right now, just," he pivoted for the three short steps that led outside, "just goodbye, all right. Goodbye, I'll see you."

He resisted the urge to slam the door, felt better, stronger for that, walking up the side of the house for the curb, and Abby.

The bag tore when he pushed it through Abby's broken window, and the battery didn't cooperate when he tried the key.

"Shit."

He's watching, Steph told himself. "I know he's watching." He rolled down the driver's window, slipped Abby into neutral, and let off the brake. Sure enough, Steph could see a part in the living room curtains as he bent over the driver's side door post.

"Go ahead and gloat, you mother," he grumbled, nudging Abby into motion, "fucker."

Zimmer's pants billowed around his legs like collapsed main sails as he pumped harder and harder, pushing the Bee-atile down the middle of 13.

This was not how it was supposed to be, he thought, running alongside Abby. He pulled open the door, hopped in, worked the stick into second, let the clutch out with a jolt and Abby coughed to life.

He pushed on the accelerator until the engine was screaming before shifting up, third, fourth, going fifty, sixty, and then he screamed, "Gloat NOW!" out of joy, or release, or just to scream, and then rolled the window back up.

The echoes died down pretty quickly, just sort of fell to the floor among the glass and the food wrappers, the empty beer cans, and it felt kind of hollow in the Bee-atile.

"What the hell am I doing?"

Just as full-fledged panic started to set in, he poked at the ON/OFF knob for the radio: "Well Ah'm sooouthboooound..."

"Perfect. It's only about a thousand miles to Georgia," he guessed, and smiled. And then a couple of hundred miles further down the coast to Florida, Fort Lauderdale, swimming in the Atlantic surf, parties on the beach, bikinis, sunshine, a ton of beer.

He'd never been, of course. Those thoughts were accumulations of postcards he's seen and stories from friends who'd gone down on spring break; pictures only: stooped palm trees leaning over sugary dunes and crystalline cobalt water frozen in hypnotic undulation.

Why hadn't he gone? What was keeping him from going now, now, even, in November? Hell, he could go wherever he wanted to, "Right?" Fort Lauderdale, Miami. "Honolulu!"

"Except," he said, and almost didn't recognize his own cautionary voice, belying his rock and roll heritage.

Except, if he were to pull up what stakes he had and leave, what would he have, besides a more or less two dimensional postcard representation of himself, of some self. He wasn't sure of anything suddenly.

Outside the Bee-atile, the day had clouded over and gone grey, sullen, anticipative of another miserable Tripoli winter. "Rain, probably." He passed the Mercado plant where his father worked and couldn't remember what the hell it was they made there. That thought spooked him.

Then Warehouse Road, without the usual tangle of eighteen-wheelers coming and going. After that, for a mile, then two, there wasn't much scenery, just a rare house, then another: large ranch style sprawls set off the highway. He never knew who lived in them, but heard they used to be owned by the mining barons before they packed up and moved away. How the hell could he live in this town twenty-three years and not know everyone and everything? And if he never cared to find out—which he didn't—what held him to Tripoli?

Even as he asked that question he felt an increasingly

discernible tether on his life, or what he supposed was his life, pulling, yanking him back. But he had to wonder if it was becoming taut because of its hold on him, or his dependence on it? What would he be without that tether, that umbilical connection?

His life, as he supposed it, was defined, in decreasing spheres, by Tripoli, Rt. 13, the pink house, and the square shadow of his father. Spheres, layers, that just kept peeling away, like an onion, with no core, no sovereign definition of Steph Abrams to be found.

He passed the Tripoli Auto Salvage yard—bleak, abandoned cars, standing sentinels inside a twelve foot chain-link fence, propped up on cinder blocks or rusted tire rims. He looked over at the carnage and actually felt jealous. He pulled to the side of the road in front of a green mileage marker just past the corner of the fencing to try and figure out why. Worthington: 22 miles, the sign said. He turned and looked over his shoulder at the cars. There they stood, proud and eager to tell the stories embedded in each dent or scratch, ground into the ring on the dashboard where the St. Christopher's medal had been mounted, layered upon the mildewy odors of the old upholstery. It hit him: What stories did he have? What scars could he show for his years? None, all by himself, because he's always been part of another, larger package.

He'd never considered himself outside of that package, never just Steph Abrams who *could* have his own story. It was always Steph Abrams, from Tripoli, from the pink house at 11803 Mountainside Viewway. Even when he was away from home, at college, a year in Baltimore, another at State, definition was always linked, traceable to that concise historical origin: the pink house, in Tripoli. *That* Steph Abrams. He's always been the son, or the brother, the little boy. He was the first Abrams grandson, the eldest cousin. "Layers." No core.

"Jesus." He pushed the gear shift into first and swung across the traffic lanes, skidding in the gravel of the opposite shoulder, heading back to town, yet again.

"Welcome to Tripoli," the sign said, "Part of Pennsylvania's cast iron core."

Right. "Was I gone long?" No, not really, despite getting kicked out, he still wasn't really gone. It was another layer. Steph Abrams, who *used* to live at 11803 Mountainside Viewway. "That's worse!"

Then he wondered if that was what Zimmer really meant by that evasive answer of his, "Somewhere in New York."

"No." He's got stories. He just wasn't telling them. "What have I got?" Layers. "More like deposits," like the interstate, where they never really fix the damaged roads, just slather another covering of tarvia over them.

He took his foot off the gas, just to test the sound of "Somewhere in Pennsylvania..."

Nah.

But Abby responded, a hitch, cough, and a backfire, what he took for approval, "She likes it," pushing on the accelerator again.

He was still building speed, holding Abby's pedal to the floor, accelerating like a cyclotron, trying to throw himself out of the orbit of the pink house, as he passed it again. He remembered his father, "You better believe he'll be back," and answered the memory, as well as the blur of pink aluminum, "I don't thiiink sooo..." trying not to focus on the receding image of the house or his family or any of their nagging questions of How? or Why? He tried not to think about anything but, "Goodbye, I'm gone."

Lear's was filling up. All the parking spaces at the curb were taken, but they were still parking Abby within eyesight, as they had that first night. Out of easy habit now, what Steph called easy habit, Zimmer called inflexible absolute, he checked the rearview for traffic, then forward for oncoming, and swung Abby around 180 degrees, climbing the pedestrian curb and onto the sidewalk in front of the bar. The maneuver was extra pleasing because he could accomplish it—thanks to the tight turning radius of the Bee-atile—in one clean swing, without any hitching back and forth, without a three point turn. He remembered when his father had taught him how to drive, in the clumsy family station wagon.

"Three points, Stephen, sixty degrees at each point," showing Steph the measure of the angle with the thumb and forefinger of his right hand, as he sat sprawled across the passenger seat of the Chevrolet, left arm along the bench back, his sixteen year old son cowering behind the wheel, hands locked onto ten and two o'clock. "Sixty degrees at each point. Don't even try to get it all on one swing."

He shook the memory from his head and unfolded himself from the Bee-atile. He stood on the sidewalk glancing in either direction, ready with the story about Abby's window in case he had to defend her presence there on the concrete.

Inside, Zimmer and Mr. Boyles sat poised on their stools, still side-by-side, backs to the bar, glasses raised, awaiting Steph's entrance.

"Greetings," they offered, and Zimmer couldn't help but start snickering. He'd been practicing the salute all morning, as more and more of the regulars showed up, and introductions were made.

Steph stood in the diminished light of the doorway, his face creased with pain. "What's so fucking funny?"

"Everything is, Steph. It's got to be. Got to find a way to turn tragedies into comedies, or else we're all in a lot of trouble."

Steph shook his head, managed a grin at least, and moved toward the stool to Zimmer's left.

Mr. Boyles guessed, "Shakespeare?"

"No. Jimmy Buffet," Zimmer said, turning from Mr. Boyles to Steph, eyebrows alive, active, mocking.

But Steph was still drifting in and out of that unconnected feeling. "It's neither. It's a mess, a big fucking complicated mess."

"What's complicated?" Zimmer answered him, pushing a shot glass in front of him. "This is Lear's. That's Randy," pointing, then leaning back, "You remember Mr. Boyles..."

He raised his glass.

"And that's Jack Daniels." Zimmer picked up Steph's glass so that he'd take it, hefted his own and the three of them drank. "That's all the recipe you'll need for hours."

"What's it all add up to?" Steph asked him, holding the empty sculptured glass in front of his face, studying the facets, feeling its bulk.

"Nothing." Zimmer pushed another round on him. "Drink."

Still, Steph wouldn't let go. "You should have heard them, my mother, all of them. What are you going to do? Where will you stay? Jack, fucking Jack, quizzing me, Donald Moseley, on the Chamber?"

"Drink," Zimmer said again. "What'd you say?"

"Shit. I got just as disgusted and irritated, shouting along with my father, Jesus! One big happy family..."

"Chase," Zimmer said, pouring a beer for him.

"I'm so beat. Like twelve, fifteen rounds beat."

"It'll be clearer later, trust me."

"Yeah? When?"

"When you're bulletproof. Drink."

Steph accepted the shot, mumbling, "How in the hell can that be?"

Mr. Boyles offered his own toast, not really circumventing nor negating Zimmer's attempts but offering an alternate track. "One thing is certain, at least," he said, hoisting his tumbler of rye whiskey, "nothing is ever clear at Lear's."

That gave Steph pause enough to remember where he was, who he was with. He sat back in his stool and peered past Zimmer's back at the old man. While Randy refilled Mr. Boyles' glass, he took his cigarette case, which served as a coaster during rounds—a worn, Naugahyde coaster—and pulled an unfiltered cigarette from beneath the elastic band inside. He tapped each end against the closed case three times, quick little tap-tap-taps, pivoted, banged the first end two more times, then slipped it between his lips, sucking flame through the tobacco from the match that Randy held for him. He exhaled, pulled a piece of tobacco from his tongue before meeting Steph's eye and repeating, "Nothing."

It didn't sound at first like much in the way of paternal advice, though it wasn't merely an indictment either. And as Steph and Zimmer sat quietly looking around the bar, with its constant smokey haze, with what daylight that could sneak through the window and the door glass diffused by cigarette smoke, arrested by the dark furniture, witnessing the fact that whenever someone stepped into the bar, they hesitated on the threshold a moment or two, while their eyes adjusted to the shadows, they realized it was just a simple truth.

Steph figured, without saying anything, that maybe he'd do well to stick to simple truths for the moment. He stayed leaning back, arms folded, half a shot untouched on the bar, that Zimmer kept nudging toward him. But he wasn't ready for it just then, or maybe didn't need that therapy at all any more. Maybe the point wasn't obliteration so much as the soft blurring of those harsh lines of reality. "It's good enough for now, though," was all he'd say.

Zimmer sat there tensed, elbows on the bar, turning from Steph to Mr. Boyles, not too fond of those cryptic remarks arching over him. In his pronounced way, he grumbled, "Of course it's good enough. We're here, aren't we?"

"Hell yeah, good enough," Steph repeated, then sat up. "Anybody got a quarter?"

Zimmer pushed around the pile of crumpled bills before him on the bar. "You're not going to call home are you?"

"No. I'm going to play," he said, arching his back, searching his pockets, "the jukebox."

"Think they've got anything besides Frank Sinatra on that thing?"

"Certainly," Mr. Boyles answered, one, or both of them, pushing a coin along the bar, like he was serving up a stein of beer.

Zimmer found two of his own, adding it to Mr. Boyles', saying, "Let me," holding Steph to his stool.

"Certainly," Steph said, relaxing again, trading nods with Mr. Boyles.

The older man turned a little into the space which Zimmer

had vacated, crossing his bony legs. He brought the cigarette to his lips once more, tilting his face up and squinting his eyes as the little nub glowed, only half an inch from his nostrils. His fingernails, of that smoking hand, at least, were coarse and yellow, an orange, nicotine yellow, as were the insides of the first two fingers, where a burning cigarette almost always sat, as he ground out this latest. Otherwise, his coloring made him look like a specter to Steph, like one of those figures in a wax museum. His skin was thin, almost translucent, with a pink pall to it, as though you could look through it and see veins and tissue, organs, only barely keeping the inside separate from the outside. He had brown spots on the backs of his hands and on his forehead above his black framed glasses. His sparse hair, pasted down and combed straight back from his high crown, had yellowed too, from age, or infrequent cleaning; it looked like cords of fine porcelain or the bone China wedding service that's been sitting in some widow's curio for years and years and years. "It's never as bad as you think," he said to Steph, once he'd completed his survey.

Steph thought, then, the welcomest, best thought he could have anticipated, wished for, Perfect.

The opening groans of Elton John's "Funeral for a Friend" reverberated through the bar. Steph acknowledged, and appreciated the effort, Zimmer's left-handed forcing of rock and roll's providence for him.

Zimmer came back to his stool, saying, "That should just about do it."

"Just about," Steph answered, raising his shot glass finally.

8. INCOMING FLIGHTS

THEY stayed in Lear's the rest of the day, through Saturday night, and into Sunday morning, anchored, pretty much, to those stools, except for trips to the rest room, the jukebox, and a late evening's adventure across 13 to the small grocery for a bag of Chips Ahoy cookies. This was after they'd exhausted Randy's supply of pickled eggs and the tiny rack of chips and nuts propped up next to the cash register. They stayed until again they were the only customers in the bar, though Steph had passed out a few hours earlier. Mr. Boyles sat elegantly erect in his corner stool, with Zimmer between them, slouching, fading.

When Zimmer tried to gather Steph and hustle him outside to the awaiting Bee-atile, all he managed to do was knock him off his stool, and then stood leaning over him, swaying, urging, "Come on Steph, old boy. You can do it," to Steph's inert body.

Randy came around the bar and picked up Steph with Zimmer's dubious assistance, and drug him to the back of the building, where he'd set up a couple of cots in the storeroom, at Mr. Boyles' urging. "Why don't you sleep it off too, Zimmer," Randy said, as Zimmer turned from the dark room.

"No, no, no," Zimmer said, weaving his way back through the poolroom and the tables. "I've got a starving cat at home. Gotta go."

Zimmer was greeted, on the sidewalk outside Lear's, with a yellow parking ticket flapping underneath Abby's driver's side windshield wiper. He didn't really see it until he had the car started and was turning around on the empty lanes of 13, headed back toward Dagaton Woods. He slowed at the entrance to the park and turned on the wipers in an attempt to retrieve the piece of paper, what he thought at the time was some kind of advertisement, "Some goddammed new pizza place, I bet." But he missed, and it fluttered to the ground in the darkness.

At Fill he was greeted by a truly angry animal. He could hear Whomee inside as he fumbled for the key—snarling and hissing—and opened the door slowly, calling, "Honey... I'm ho-ome." The only time he cursed his drunkenness was when he couldn't find the light switch, panic setting in while Whomee growled at him in the darkness of the apartment.

Whomee settled down some after Zimmer dished him up a bowl of tuna, but it was a while before he would let Zimmer sleep. He paced around on the fold-out, complaining. Zimmer tossed and turned, pillow clamped to his face, mumbling, "Come on, Whomee. I said I was sorry."

Not more than four hours later, he was awakened by Donald Moseley's determined knocking. Zimmer answered the door still holding the pillow to one side of his head.

"Oh, sorry," Donald said. "Thought you'd be up by now."

"Nope."

"Listen, Anthony," Donald said, peering around Zimmer into the apartment, "do you know a Steve Adams?"

"Hmm?" Zimmer's head was tilting, sinking farther and farther into the pillow.

"We just got a call from a Mrs. Adams. She seems to think her son is staying with you."

"Adams. Abrams? Steph Abrams?"

"So he is here? You have a roommate?"

"What? Steph? No, he's not here."

"Mr. Zimbarco, my point is--"

"He's not," Zimmer said, showing Moseley the empty room, except for Whomee, entangling himself around Zimmer's feet, one of which still had a sock on.

"I'm not at all concerned with your personal life."

"What?"

"But if you're going to have a roommate we'll have to discuss the terms of your lease. I thought we understood each other?"

"Mr. Moseley, Steph stayed here a couple of nights. That's all."

"Mm-hmm."

"Sorry about the phone call," Zimmer said, gently closing the door. "Wonder what she wanted?"

That's the thought that kept any further sleep at bay, or its companion: "Should I tell him Steph's at Lear's?" Or it was just Mr. Moseley's voice that wouldn't go away, "I'm not at all concerned with your personal life..."

"Jesus," Zimmer said, sitting up. They'd recently changed the time back, so he had a harder time than usual gauging the hour. "Seven?" He had to work from a formula, "They turned the clocks back an hour, so it's lighter, earlier," which was annoying. Like cooking from a recipe, it was better if it was spontaneous, "If it has its own kind of internal sense."

"Seven-thirty, tops," he said, but without much of that true Zimbarco conviction. He wasn't sure. He wasn't sure of anything, padding around the apartment. He knew two things: he couldn't sleep, and he was desperately tired.

"Two things? That's it?"

He'd never be able to do any cooking, which is what he usually did when he woke up early. The coffee pot, perhaps the simplest of kitchen preparations he might be expected to undertake on any given day, was a complete mystery. He spooned grounds into his coffee cup instead of the filter basket. When he realized that, he poured the grounds into the sink, rinsing the cup, soaking the grounds. When he spooned more grounds into the basket this time, he'd forgotten the filter paper, "Jesus fucking Christ, Zimmer." After he poured those couple of spoonfuls into the wet cup--meaning to save them, while he put the filter in place—he gave up. He went back into the other room, rummaged through the tortured sheets on the foldout, fishing for his other sock. He laced up his sneakers, pulled on his fatigue jacket, and moved toward the door, thinking he was headed for coffee, but ending up at Lear's.

"Muscle memory," he said, seated in the Bee-atile, on the sidewalk, his head starting to pound. "Or I'm just starting to notice things."

The bar was closed, that early on a Sunday morning. He sat there staring through the hole where Abby's window had been, at the darkness, either willing it would open, or hoping an alternative would occur to him, when he realized there was someone moving around inside. He couldn't make out who it was until he got out of the car and pressed his shaded eyes against the glass, giving only the briefest of thoughts that it might be someone who wasn't supposed to be in there. It was Steph, mopping the floor. Zimmer rapped on the window with his left index finger. Steph looked up, came over to the window, mouthed, Coffee? then went and opened the door.

"Greetings."

"Where is everyone?"

"Up in bed, I guess," Steph said, motioning upstairs with the mop handle.

"And what are you doing?"

"Earning my keep," he said, showing Zimmer the coffee maker plugged in at the end of the bar, dragging the damp mop across the room.

Zimmer sat there holding his coffee cup with both hands, sipping it slowly, savoring those first effects of caffeine—like it was cognac—while Steph explained his arrangement. "I can sleep in the back, and work off the rent," he said, "cleaning up. It's perfect."

"Hmm, perfect," Zimmer echoed, holding the coffee cup against his head between sips, moving the compress from place to place as the pain shifted.

Steph finished with the mopping. They heard Randy moving around overhead, then coming down the stairwell over the stockroom. Mr. Boyles followed him shortly afterward into the bar.

"You live here too?"

"You sound surprised, Anthony. Good morning," he said, taking his stool.

"Well, I didn't know."

"I was Randall's first *de facto* adoption, I believe."

"Many, many years ago," Randy said, behind the bar,

flipping on lights, plugging in appliances, bringing Lear's to life the way an airline pilot revs up a jumbo 747.

"All we need now is breakfast," Steph said, gathering up his accessories, the mop, a bucket, some rags, a can of Pledge.

It was the first time Zimmer had actually thought of food that morning, which surprised him some.

"Liquid?"

"Why not," Steph said, finding himself a seat at the bar.

"I suppose. Randall?"

"Got just the thing."

"Steph," Zimmer started, wanting to tell him about his mother calling while he was still mostly sober—bloody Marys always taking him through the entire spectrum, from hungover, to something like refreshed, or at least steady, back to tipsy—but stopped. He sat there, index finger poised, but his head twitched a few times in slightly different directions, nostrils flared. He smelled something. He sampled the stagnant air of Lear's noisily, like some kind of hound.

"I know that smell," he pronounced.

The rest of them sat unmoved, waiting.

Memories of Vermont flooded in nearly drowning him. "Somebody smoking weed?" he asked.

"Nearly every morning," Mr. Boyles told him, raising his glass. "Part of the ablutions of the elderly."

Steph nearly spit back his beer. "Really?"

"Certainly. I find its medicinal effects incomparable."

"Medicinal effects?"

"I'm rather surprised that's news to you, Anthony."

"Guilty, and on this morning," Zimmer said, holding his head lest it wobble off and roll out amongst the tables, "especially interested."

"Since antiquity, the Greeks and Egyptians. Did you know cannabis is one of the fifty fundamental herbs in traditional Chinese medicine."

"I did," Steph said.

"I'm sold."

"But where do you get it?"

"Randy?"

"I know a guy, or two."

"No kidding," Steph said, as both he and Zimmer looked upon the bartender with renewed admiration, and eagerness.

Zimmer never did tell Steph about the phone call Mr. Moseley had gotten. He meant to, certainly. It had been the reason he'd ended up at Lear's, "Right?" And he meant to every ten minutes or so, those first couple of hours. Still fogged in as he was, he suffered from a kind of a delayed recognition syndrome, where, during pauses, he'd think there was a comment, a bit of news he needed to give Steph. He'd only remember exactly *what* the comment or news was a little later, after conversation had resumed around the bar, or Steph had jumped up to feed the jukebox, or other customers started arriving, shortly after noon, and they'd have to adhere to *that* ritual, and whatever urgency Zimmer may have felt would once more be blunted, obscured, lost in the accumulating fog, and he'd forget, again.

After a while, into the afternoon, once they started playing pool, it all turned into the vaguest of notions that there was some bit of business he needed to tend to, before he got into this game, before he refilled that pitcher, before he got too drunk. He even said to Steph a couple of times, "There's something I'm supposed to tell you, I think..."

Steph answered, "What?" the first couple of times, but then quit probing, and never did guess what it might be.

Zimmer didn't think of it again until he was leaving, after dark, pushing Abby onto 13, arching back northward, spying another parking ticket flapping on the windshield, wondering what that was, then remembering the advertisement from yesterday, remembering yesterday, leaving Lear's alone because Steph was passed out in the stockroom because they'd been drinking since about eight in the morning because Steph had gotten kicked out of his house because he hadn't gone home a couple of nights ago because he was passed out again and Zimmer didn't know where he lived and just stayed at Fill, "That's it!" Zimmer hollered, easing into the entrance to Dagaton Woods. "Your mother called," he said to the vacant seat, the airy window, the shadows of the park.

"Ah, I'll tell him tomorrow."

Zimmer started into the interior, saw the ticket again, turned on the wipers, but missed again.

Tomorrow, Monday morning, by the time Zimmer got up, got some coffee, started some bread, turned out to be almost exactly twenty-four hours, he figured, standing in the kitchen, watching the morning advance down the hill, since Mr. Moseley had awakened Zimmer, banging on Fill's door.

"That's not bad," he said, "as notification standards go."

The military gave themselves three days to notify next of kin in a death. Even the Red Cross gave themselves twenty-four hours.

"Hell, you're not even considered AWOL until after you've been missing *over* twenty-four hours."

So he didn't feel too bad, until he wished he had a phone at the apartment so that he could go ahead and call Steph at Lear's. He relegated that wish to a growing list of things he might want to think about spending money on, once he managed to concoct some more dependable way of bringing in an income. Shooting pool could be counted on to keep him drinking, "But that's about it." He decided he'd stop by the bar as soon as the bread was ready, and stepped away from the counter to check the temperature of the oven.

When he got there, Steph and Mr. Boyles were seated at the bar in their usual places, more or less, with their backs to the window, intent on something, so it seemed. Steph was slumped over the bar, and Mr. Boyles was huddled close by, with an arm draped over Steph's shoulders. When Zimmer slipped into the stool on the other side, he heard Mr. Boyles telling him, "That is precisely the point, is it not, that no, there probably is not a thing you could do at this particular juncture, to satisfy them."

"Yeah, but..."

"What's up?"

"Don't ask."

"Oh, Steph, before I forget, your mother--"

"I know, I know..."

Steph had called home earlier in the morning, to tell them where he could be reached, had only gotten as far as, "Hi, Mom, it's--" before listening to a twenty minute tag-team lecture, as first his mother, and then his father bitched and moaned about how worried they were, how callous he was, how disappointing he'd become, "*Etcetera, etcetera...*"

The conversation dwindled into a communal funk, so Randy moved to turn on the television that hung over the corner, but noticed strobe lights reflected in the dark screen. "What the," he turned to look outside, then said, "Uh-oh, Zimmer, you, you better take a look," sounding about as flustered as anyone had ever heard.

Outside, on the sidewalk, a tow truck had maneuvered into position and was hoisting the Bee-atile in its sling.

"What the fuck?" Zimmer said, choking on his drink, then rushed outside, followed by Steph, then Mr. Boyles.

"What the hell are you doing?"

"Impounding."

"What?"

Steph stepped between the two. "What's the matter?"

"This your car?"

"Can I help?" Mr. Boyles asked.

"Shoulda read those tickets before tossing em," the driver said to Steph.

"What tickets?" Zimmer said.

Steph reached and slipped the third one from underneath the wiper. "Zimmer?"

"What tickets?" he repeated. "I haven't gotten any--" Then he remembered. "Fuck."

"Yup, thought so. Every time. They come out bitching and frothing and crying What are you doing? Why me? Why're you picking on me? all the time knowing they're guilty, guilty, guilty." The driver had been rotely going about his business, attaching hooks to Abby's axle, taking the slack out of the lines by pulling on a lever. He gave Zimmer a card that had the address of the pound on it, ducked under the hook up, and climbed into the cab of his truck.

Mr. Boyles opened the passenger side door. "Isn't there anything we can do?"

"At this point? Only cash. Once I pick up, I gotta charge."

"How much?"

"Seventy-five."

"Seventy-five *dollars*?" Zimmer said.

"Cash."

"Jesus," Steph said, looking at the Bee-atile, as if to gauge relative worth.

It was later that night, or the next, when Zimmer realized the solution. "I've decided." After he'd tallied up how much it cost him to bail out Abby: the tow charge, the three tickets, not to mention that other pending legal business he'd all but forgotten in the midst of everything else. After he figured how much it would cost him to get Abby efficient, secure again. After Steph told him he wasn't clearing even enough wages to cover his bar tab. And after Zimmer realized how quickly he'd emptied the mayonnaise jar Victor had given him. "I got it all figured out," he said. "You can move the cot up to Fill," not yet tallying in what that would do to his rent, "and we'll get jobs."

He'd decided. Then, having decided to earnestly look for a job in Tripoli—even after three more days of frustration and rejection: it would be weeks before the next civil service test, before they could apply at the post office; they didn't have the experience to land anything at the tri-county airport; and they didn't have the training to do anything but custodial work at the hospital, which was contracted—he became the deciding factor in their getting jobs at Regency.

Steph certainly didn't know what was going on. They were sitting in the administration building's lobby, filling out the forms, information they'd given out probably two dozen times already, when Zimmer just up and stomped down the hallway. Steph chased him into the corridor, mumbling, "Oh, Jesus, here we go again..."

Zimmer barged into Frank Curry's office, then a personnel assistant. Frank, like Steph, didn't know what to do but sit there and listen. He'd been given no warning, certainly, and hadn't ever seen anything like it at Regency before, not in the nine miserable months he'd been behind the desk. He wasn't nearly able to push himself out of the chair and pull his cigar out of his mouth in order to tell Zimmer, and Steph, to "Get the hell out of my frigging office!" He just sat there and glared at them.

"We need jobs," Zimmer started. "We don't need to spend three hours outside your door there waiting for you to tell us we're on a waiting list. That's kind of redundant, don't you think?"

"What?"

"We don't want to be put on file for a hundred and twenty days. In our case, it would be a waste of file space. We need jobs now, and we'll find them somewhere, if not here. I know, I know, we'd stand a better chance if we went about it separately, but he doesn't have a car, and I'm new to town... Circumstances dictate, don't you see? This is just the way it is. So, if you have work, great. Thank you. If not, we'll leave and won't bother you with a pointless interview."

Frank looked at the frothing figure of Zimmer leaning over his desk. He pulled out the cigar, finally, and pushed his glasses back up his nose—which he only wore for paperwork, consequently, they didn't fit so well—and squinted at them, measuring them, a Clint Eastwood impression, trying to convince himself that he either had to drag them out of there himself or call security to come and do the yanking, except, "Son of a bitch's right."

He laughed at them. "You want jobs, huh?" He asked for their names, address, a phone number, jotting the information down on his desk blotter, then stood up and crossed his arms. "Sure, I got work, if you can handle it. What day is this, Thursday?"

"Right," Steph said. He was standing beside Zimmer by now.

"Come back at midnight. But for now," he said, jamming the stub of his cold cigar back into his mouth, "get the hell out of my frigging office," what came out, through clenched teeth and another exaggerated snarl, as, "gedde'ell outamy frigginoffice."

The imitations didn't fit Frank any better than the eyeglasses. In fact, not much of anything about Frank and the office coincided, not the starched white shirt—even with the ash smudges or the back untucked—not the necktie—even with the loose knot—and definitely not Frank's temperament. He was completely unfit for the interviewing process, finding himself either impatient with its tedium and benevolence, or overly accepting and kind-hearted when he needed to be brutally corporate minded.

He stood out in the hallway watching Zimmer and Steph leave, thinking he liked their approach so much he ought to try it on his own boss, because, secretly, he *hated* that office. He wanted to get back to real work, the work he'd done at Regency almost non-stop for the past twenty-three years, on the platform, at night. "I don't want to push pencils," he confessed to the water cooler, as he slugged down two, three conefulls. Sure, he knew it had been a promotion, with a tidy raise. "Why would I want to go back working nights? That doesn't really matter, does it? I just do. And," Frank further reasoned, "I can do it," intimating that it wasn't getting done at present.

"Just stating the obvious," which was what really made him a good night shift supervisor in the first place.

"He's right," meaning Zimmer, the fleshy knuckles of his balled right fist poised at a VP's door. "You don't need a detailed history to work that shift, just hard, determined workers. If you get lemons, you deal with that later."

Inside, he said, "By and large, sir, if folks sign up to work shift, are prepared to show up, night after night, they're worth keeping, at almost any cost—though they don't usually ask a whole lot. It's a pretty simple system that not everyone understands."

Frank didn't get nearly the resistance he expected, not from his boss, nor his family. His rationale was almost too simple to argue with, like Zimmer's presentation, as was managing the night-time workings of the Regency docks, the grocery chain's principle warehouse and trucking hub. It was far simpler than the politics of day shift administrative work, which most days drove him home in as foul a mood as his family has ever seen. That's why he wanted to go back on shift, despite appearances, his age, or the fact that the step was a sidestep, maybe even a backwards leap in his career. And why wouldn't the Curry household prefer a peacefully sleeping Frank on their hands as opposed to the nine-to-five time-bomb? Eventually, everyone concerned would come to accept the logic, the move, though some would wonder from time to time—Patty, his wife, for one, "Is he losing his mind?"

Frank, of course, would say just the opposite. "Musta been ouda my frigging mind to take that weeny job."

Working the warehouse dock, at night, when the world was left alone to recoup after a busy day's worth of dayshifting, when all those things consumed during the course of the day had to be replaced, or replenished, when all the workers everywhere had that one express purpose to their jobs—or only slight variations: babysitters, watching their part of the world, the big office buildings, the hotel lobbies, the side streets and bank foyers—getting everything back to a neutral position or watching that it didn't keel over altogether, "That's the only sane work." It was just too simple not to enjoy.

"It's simple," Frank told Steph and Zimmer by way of orientation that first night. "If the drivers make it, we all work our buns off."

"Right," Steph said.

"Doing what?" Zimmer had to know.

"Lumping," they were to find out.

"Fucking lumping."

"Numb fucking lumping."

"11 to seven, half-hour for lunch, if there's time, five days a week, Sunday through Thursday. You got that, Sunday through Thursday?" Frank had learned to emphasize the days. It was from more than personally knowing how twisted around you could get from the hours. There was no telling how many times he'd hired somebody new for the shift, and they didn't show up that first Sunday night. "Sunday through Thursday."

Fridays were different. Even for Lumpers. "Especially," for the Lumpers, Steph might say.

"Absolutely."

"Not always."

"Yes. Always."

"Even in the beginning?"

"Always."

"Not this different."

"What? Different is different, right?"

"This is more different. Twice as different?"

"More different?"

"No. Half. At best."

"Shut up, Steph."

They were all inside Lear's. Normally, at eleven-thirty in the morning, Randy wouldn't even have the bar open on a week day, much less full of resurrecting Lumpers.

"That's twice different, right?" Steph asked, holding up two fingers.

"No," Zimmer answered again, shaking his head slowly. "We're always in Lear's."

"If it's open, we're here."

"Right. But we're not here because it's open, it's open because we're here. So that doesn't count."

"What?" Steph demanded, utterly confounded by the logic, normally a confortable enough domain for him, but Zimmer's grin and the chorus of snickering stopped him. "Jesus."

Although all of them—everyone but Bruce, that is—was suffering some, varying effects of the time change, the flopping back to a more normal schedule for about sixty short hours, "Like jet lag, you know?"

"You've never been on a jet."

Only Bruce sat there semi-lucid, mostly eager, and not

struggling to resurrect some semblance of wit or wisdom. He credited his caffeine laden Mountain Dew for his recovery from the week's worth of night shifts. More probably, hunger pangs were juicing his cerebral cortex. But Bruce didn't know nothing for endocrinology, or anatomy, for that matter. He did know caffeine: "And we're talking mega-dose here, folks," he said, holding up the green bottle and pointing to it, like any good commercial spokesman.

Steph, who supposedly knew numbers, facts, was having the hardest time, was finding it difficult to figure anything out: He'd stare at Randy for long, empty moments before he recognized him enough to order. If he concentrated enough so that the print of the morning's *Header* didn't slide around too much, he could maybe trust it to tell him what day it was. But if he tried to read the line scores from last night's NBA games, to see how many points Doctor J. scored, say, he just couldn't focus. He sat next to Bruce and would, from time to time, agree with Bruce that he needed some Dew and allow him to pour some into his coffee cup. All that did was jar his taste buds and flutter around nauseously in his empty stomach.

"Serves you right," Zimmer told him, who winced at everything Steph stirred into his coffee—all three scoops of sugar, each glug-glug of milk and whatever else he'd try so that it wouldn't taste like coffee.

For someone who found the job and the hours least agreeable, Zimmer had an easier time of coping with the trip back to normalcy than he might have expected. But he'd always been able to function on a minimum of sleep. He could sit there and will the negative effects into submission after one, two, as many as three cups of black coffee. He would at once consider the trait facilitative for their chosen lifestyle, and then decide it was damning, trapped by its merits. He thought of Mr. Boyles, who Zimmer always sat next to now, who'd already spiked his coffee. His constitution seemed conditioned to coping with however much alcohol and marijuana and nicotine he gave it. Did that mean he was perfectly suited to his life as a boozer? Did Zimmer's recoverability mean he should always work shift? Was that the best he could hope for? "The least I can do?" Did Mr. Boyles ever wonder if it was a waste of time for him to drink? "Or is he the only person who *should* drink?"

Zimmer could imagine Mr. Boyles deflecting the questions, much like himself, answering, "Apparently so, Anthony, apparently so."

Zimmer, Steph, all of them appreciated Randy silencing the insipid Billy Joel song that was seeping out of the easy listening radio station and turning up the television. Any other day it would remain flickering mute grey images over the bar. But Fridays were different. Fridays they were there *for* the television.

For Steph it was therapeutic. The successful grafting of sight and sound provided an easy example of merging disparate sensations into a single, soothing whole. "I need directions, sometimes."

The sound was of a whining turbine engine, and an announcer droning, "It's time for another soaring episode of *Incoming Flights*," as necessary a tonic for the halfzied Lumpers as the beer Randy drew from the tap and doled out, replacing their coffee and soda.

Mickey pushed his Coke away, unfinished, though grumbling, "Do we have to?" meaning the "soaring episode."

"Mick?"

"That's why we're here."

Steph, on the other side of Mickey, nodded his head in agreement with Zimmer, piecing together information finally, "Yeah, yeah, that's right," remembering at last that if it wasn't noon, or Friday, if they weren't Lumpers, they wouldn't be there. They'd be working somewhere else. Or sleeping, "Anywhere."

Still, he wondered, "How does half the sleep factor out to five times as tired?"

"It's that new math stuff."

"Here we go," Bruce said, as the show started.

The airliner was peeking down out of billowing clouds.

"Brighton tower, Brighton tower, this is Hemispheric flight four-o-four requesting final landing instructions, over."

A thin voice shot back, "Negative, Hastings."

After a few silent moments of just the engines humming, the camera shifted from the looming aircraft to the flight tower, to the haggard traffic controller, smoking a cigarette in a room filled to capacity with tense people and cigarette smoke.

"Brighton tower, Brighton tower, this is four-o-four again: please repeat."

The controller pulled a couple of times on his cigarette, saying in-between hits, "I said negative four-o-four. Continue at present altitude. Use alternate ground pattern Captain Hastings. Over."

"Ah, roger, Brighton."

"Like he's got a choice." The controller snapped off his microphone, ending the crackle of ground-to-air communications.

"That's Roy, isn't it?" Steph asked around the bar. "What's he up to now?"

Bruce leaned over and said, "He's going to kill them."

"All of them?"

"Stephen?" Mr. Boyles pleaded, gesturing toward the screen.

"Oh, Justin, please. I've got to keep this store open. It's all we've got, until Mark gets his wings back. You can't close us down."

Justin looked down on the woman. "Oh? I can't?" He folded his arms across his chest, his dark suit, standing in the doorway of the terminal novelties shop, looking off into one corner of the store, as a passenger flipped through magazines, and then another, where a mother pointed out ceramic souvenirs to her child. "You know better than that, Nancy. You know I have no other choice."

"But why, Justin?"

"I think you know the answer to that, too."

"He wants her," Bruce whispered. "That's why he's stalling."

"Who wouldn't?" Randy said, next to Bruce. "Such a good woman. Faithful. Pure hearted."

"I'm not real sure that's what he wants, Randy," Bruce corrected.

"Sex," Mickey said flatly, not so much guessing, as maybe knowing well enough how Bruce's mind worked.

"Ding, ding, ding, ding..." Zimmer sang, rubbing Mickey's head.

"Shh!" Mr. Boyles said, once the scene changed.

"Your connecting flight should be landing in a few minutes, sir, ah, Mr. Grayson. They'll be loading that flight right away, at gate twelve. That's flight twenty-six," the consultant sighed. "But it's a pity you have to rush away," with a lilting ascent to the end of her sentence.

The man, Mr. Grayson, hesitated, half standing, half crouching from where he'd bent to pick up his briefcase.

Before he figured everything out, before he could manage a snappy come-back, she repeated, "Flight twenty-six, gate twelve," laughing, and then bending into the cut-out of the counter to move his luggage onto the conveyor belt. "You'd better hurry."

"God, what a tease."

"Anth--"

Zimmer held his hands up preemptively.

"...scheduled to meet with a Senator Carrelli this afternoon to discuss my options. Some very important people, his sources tell him, seem to think I'd make a good run at Mayor of Brighton. Can you imagine that, Sam?"

"Excuse me, Captain Hastings?"

"Yes, Leslie?" the captain said, swiveling around in his cockpit seat. "Er, Ms. Walton—yes?"

"Sir, is there an update on our landing?"

"Sam?"

"I was just about to check on that, sir," Sam said. "Brighton tower, Brighton tower--"

"Hey, hey, Brighton," another pilot hollered over the same frequency. "Did you miss me? Open up them gates buddies, I'm a-comin in for a landing."

"Please identify."

"Shh... This is niner-niner-two, requesting permission to sit this here shiny bird on your pretty little driveway. Please? Pretty please?"

The camera cut to Roy leaning into his microphone. "Captain Jemison, you know the protocol. Please observe, over."

"Is that you, Roy?" Jemison said, pushing his flight cap back on his head. "Man, don't you ever get tired of all that protocol hocus?"

"Roger, niner-niner-two. Standby, please," Roy said, again slapping off his microphone. "Another one. Like this is some kind of damn game. We'll see about that. They'll all see..."

"Oooh," Steph said, as the scene, Roy's radar screen, clouded over, and the music swelled. "He's pissed."

"Such language," Bruce said.

"Oh, Christ," Mickey said.

The music grew ever louder—grand sweeping strings and horns—as the camera panned across the distance, over mountains, and fields, reaching a crescendo as a giant jetliner filled the screen, almost sitting on the camera with its landing gear poking toward the audience. The great silver airliner was superimposed with the title script, *Incoming Flights*.

The Lumpers adjusted themselves in their seats at the bar, sitting back, relaxing, after the frantic opening scenes. They waited out the three minutes of commercials.

"Wasn't it just a few weeks ago that Hastings was dropping his ministry so he could fly again?"

"Yeah, except they didn't say anything about his being a pilot in Nam for a long, long time, remember?"

"Right. He just kept saying he was going to heaven."

"And everyone was speculating about illness, suicide, shit like that."

"All he told them was, Before Christmas..."

"And those idiots started talking about a second coming."

"That's when this show really started to piss me off."

"Aw, Mick."

"Poof, he's a pilot. And *now* he's going to run for mayor?"

Randy got up and circled back around the bar, fixing another scotch for Mr. Boyles, a screwdriver for himself. Bruce worked the beer tap from the customer's side of the bar, as Steph and Zimmer slid empty mugs his way, receiving fresh beers in return. Mickey kept his back turned to the television and the workings of the bar. Mr. Boyles lit up another cigarette.

"This is the final call for Hemispheric Airlines flight seventeen, boarding at gate number nine for Las Vegas, Nevada. Passengers..." a quiet voice called through the terminal, as the camera stayed removed, distant.

"Who's that?" Randy asked, craning his neck up as he returned to his seat next to Bruce.

"... seating arrangements..."

"Sounds like Carolyn, doesn't it?" Steph answered. "Hastings' wife?"

"You mean Jesus' wife," Mickey said, still turned away from the action, watching the pedestrian traffic outside instead. "Weren't they announcing that flight last week?"

"Really?" Steph said.

"No, no," Zimmer answered, waving him back to the television.

The camera panned down the wide open aisles of the terminal, past a phone booth with a young sailor in it; past family clutches, grandparents or teenagers taking their leave; past businessmen checking the departure/arrival monitors. It picked up Mr. Grayson hustling for his flight, and then past the gate podium where he checked in, through the picture windows, to the runway, spying the flight tower, and beyond it, a plane glistening in the sunshine.

"Listen Leslie, we're going to be stuck over Brighton for a little while, it looks. I'll reassure the passengers. Let them smoke, even have another drink, I guess."

"I want to be *his* disciple!"

"Shh!"

"--wrong, Richard?"

"I don't know, some ground problem." They were standing behind Sam, whispering.

"But what about," she started, glancing over his shoulder. "Your *meeting*?"

"Meeting?"

"With the senator, stupid!"

"Or God."

"Oh, yes, let me check on that."

"Why is she worried about that?" Steph wondered.

"Come on, Steph..." Mickey said.

"Hurry up, would you, grope, kiss," Bruce said, rocking in his chair, crossing his legs and then uncrossing them. It was one of the unfavorable side effects of Mountain Dew. "I *need* a commercial!"

"Go on, will you," Zimmer told him. "Before you hurt yourself. We'll take notes."

"Notes!" Mickey said, sipping his beer. "Who needs notes with this shit?"

"... 0-four, requesting--"

"Continue to circle, four-0-four."

"Roy, I'm just trying to get some kind of estimate..."

"Captain Hastings--"

"Lord Hastings?"

"Hizzoner Hastings?"

"--something to tell you, you'll know, don't worry. I'll take care of you."

"Suuure you will."

Roy stared intently at the pale green scope with its orbiting tracers. "First they said I couldn't fly," he mumbled. "They put me in here, cramped, pressured," lighting another cigarette, "No respect, no appreciation, and now, now," as an image swam in the screen before him, not an airplane, "no love," but an apartment living room.

"Why Leslie, why?" Roy's voice echoed out of the monitor.

"That's why--"

"Shh!"

"Just tell me that."

"I'm leaving because I don't want to be stuck in this miserable airport the rest of my life, wearing silly costumes, always smiling. I want more, Roy," she said, standing there in his memory, on the screen, in heels, a beige cotton dress, holding her overnight bag, throwing dark unpinned hair back over one shoulder, then the other.

"I can give you more," Roy said, as she turned. "I can take you away from here."

"Ha. I don't think so. At least not as quickly as I want."

"How are you going to get out faster without me?"

"I've got plans," she said, gathering her coat from an armchair.

"Plans? With who?"

"With *whom*," Mr. Boyles corrected.

"Ha, ha, ha," she raked him. "You're pathetic, Roy. Is that why they wouldn't let you fly? No backbone?"

Her mouth filled the scope. "Ha, ha, ha, ha..."

"Helloooo... Roy, partner, you there?"

"Roger, Captain Jemison. Standby, please."

"Standby? Roy, buddy, listen, it's real import--"

"Roy, how about a break?"

Roy turned down his headphones to answer his supervisor. "I've still got two up, Conrad."

"Who?"

"Whom," Zimmer tried.

"Four-0-four and niner-niner-two."

"Hastings and Jemison."

"Roger."

"Well, bring them in, especially Jemison, and then take a break, all right."

"Yes, sir," Roy said, pushing buttons on his console calculator, lifting his eyes a few times to check the screen, telling it, "I told you I could..." Then, "Niner-niner-two, this is Brighton tower..."

"Well, it's about damn time..."

The shot flipped back to the terminal, the same elevator voice calling, "Hemispheric Airlines flight nine-ninety-two, from

Puerto Rico, is now arriving at gate six."

"How come all we ever get is Carolyn's voice now?" Zimmer asked. "We never see her."

"She's pregnant," Steph said, standing from his stool, heading for the bathroom, able to pace his first few beers with the eight or so minutes between commercials.

"In real life?"

Steph stopped, and stared at Zimmer blankly.

"Did I miss anything?" Bruce asked, wedging himself past Steph.

"Leslie's moving in on Hastings," Randy said, standing himself, for another round of drinks.

"What? They did it? Already?" Bruce said, pounding the bar. "I missed *that*?"

"Actually, they didn't do anything, yet. In fact, it's mostly a theory, at this point," Mr. Boyles told him.

"And Roy is after both of them," Zimmer added.

"I knew it!" Bruce groaned, standing on the foot rail and leaning over the bar. "I knew it was too quiet out here. Why didn't you call me?" he charged Mickey.

"Whoa, easy fella," Zimmer said, reaching across Mickey to ward Bruce off.

Randy held a fresh beer in front of his face to calm him down.

"Bruce, again: Anthony's merely speculating."

Bruce sat glaring at Zimmer.

"--speric Airlines, flight nine-ninety-two, from Puerto Rico, will be landing..."

"Whatever is the matter, Nancy?" Justin asked, polished, smirking, after Nancy had bobbled a customer's change at the announcement. "Why so suddenly nervous?"

"Oh, I'm not nervous, Justin. More weary, I suppose," she tried, her voice cracking a little. "I just remembered I need to make a phone call. Do you mind?"

"Be my guest," he said, waving to the other end of the counter.

"Sounds nervous to me," Steph said, settling into his seat, as the camera rotated across the wide aisle of the passenger terminal, to the airport lounge opposite Nancy's novelty shop.

"Noooo shit," Mickey said, resting his chin on his hands.

"Mark, telephone for you."

"Thanks, Shirl," Mark said, throwing down his drink before slipping off his stool. He walked the length of the bar, past only a few drinking travelers, with their carry-on wardrobes slung over adjacent stools, gulping their drinks in turn, checking their watches. Mark picked up the phone lying on the bar surface nearest the entrance and stood leaning back against the bar, with just the toes of his shoes poking into the light cast into the bar from the brighter corridor lighting outside. "Hello?"

"Mark, Mark, it's Nancy."

"Mark-Mark, mark," Zimmer barked.

Finally, Mr. Boyles lost enough patience to raise his hand, as if to cuff him. But then Bruce picked up on the idea. "Awwoo, wooo..." he howled.

Randy nudged him, almost off of his stool, and then traded satisfied nods with Mr. Boyles across the tangent of the bar.

"Nan..." Mark said, then stepped fully into the light to see the gift shop across the foyer. He squinted, held his free hand up to shade his eyes.

"No, don't," Nancy told him, clutching the mouthpiece close to her face. "Don't look over here. I've got company."

"Nancy, how did you know where I was?"

"Oh, Mark, where else have you been since they grounded you?"

"Listen, Nan, if you can't handle--"

"No, baby, it's not that. Peter Jemison's plane is landing, didn't you hear the announcement?"

"Yeah, so? You think I should go out there and give him a nice big welcome home hug or something?"

"Someone's got to meet him, Mark. Someone's got to tell him not to bring anything up right now."

"Ah-HAH!" Zimmer yelled, jumping out of his seat.

"I can't go," she said. "I'm being watched, constantly."

"Yeah, I've noticed. Has he come on to you yet, Mr. Spit-shined cop?"

"What a shit," Randy said.

"Randall?"

"Mark, please."

Bruce draped an arm across Randy's shoulder, but faced the other Lumpers, saying, "I think our confirmed bachelor here's got a crush on that little lady."

"And if I get caught? What then? You think they'll ever let me fly again?"

"Just get a message to him, then. Tell him to stash everything for now."

"You'd like to do some stashing, wouldn't you?"

Randy fought his way out of Bruce's embrace.

"Mark, honey, did you hear me? We don't have any choice."

"Okay, okay, I'll think of something," Mark said, hung up, and turned back into the darkness of the bar. "Shirley, give me another, will you?" he said, and the screen faded into the cool shadows of the lounge.

"Sounds good to me," Bruce said, reaching for the tap again. "Give everybody another!"

"Whoa," Zimmer said, dancing around on his stool. "I need relief first. My eyeballs are floating."

"Jesus," Steph said, staring at the remainder of his warm beer.

"Must you be so crude?"

"I'm not," Zimmer protested. "I speak the truth. See for yourself," he said, pausing, tugging at his eyelids for Steph to act as witness.

"Get out of here."

"Vulgar."

"Truth!"

"Welcome to Hemispheric Airlines, sir," the show returned, to the ticket counter. "May I help you?"

"Yes, ma'm. Ah'm going to New Orleans, Lewees-seeana."

"Oh, I just love New Orleans," the same ticket agent said, with the faintest of quivers in her voice, and her body—her nametag, which said Audrey, jiggled on her breast.

"Now *that's* vulgar," Mickey said.

Audrey took the man's ticket envelope and punched up his flight information on her computer terminal. "You're so early, Mr. Demmons."

"Thar's no problem with that, is there?"

"Oh, no, certainly not. We prefer it, actually," she said, breathlessly. "Realllly," she added, with a funny twisting of her mouth.

"Oh, boy," Bruce said, squirming in his seat again.

"And just one bag, Mr. Demmons?" she asked, leaning over the counter.

"Yep, just me. Maybe that's why Ah'm so early. Nothing much to do. Eager to get down there to sin city and have me some real fun, know what Ah mean."

"Yes, I think I do," she said, bending to tag his suitcase. "Maybe we can find a little bit of fun for you while you wait."

"What's that? What's that?" Zimmer said, rushing back to his seat.

"Well," Demmons said, watching her every movement. "May, be."

She stood, smiling. "Will that be smoking, or non-smoking?"

"God, would you look at that cleavage," Bruce said, hiding his face, then looking through his fingers. "Smoking. SMOKING!"

"Se-smoking, please, ma'm."

"Hah. Listen to him," Mickey said.

"Good," Audrey crooned. "That's just faahne," she said, winking.

"Just tell me this," Bruce turned, grabbing Steph by the tee-shirt. "Where's Brighton?"

"Well, you're all set here, Mr. Demmons. Now then, what shall we do with you? There's a lounge. An arcade? But you don't really seem like that type." She leaned over again and whispered, "If you know what Ah mean. Maybe you'd like to wait in our private lounge?"

"The hook," Zimmer said.

"All raaht."

"Gotcha!"

"All raaht," Audrey said, with that giggle again. "I'll just show you where it is. Hank, could you cover for me?"

"Sure, baby."

"My kingdom..."

"Bruce, honestly..."

Mickey leaned forward, past Steph. "How can you get so hot and bothered by that horrible acting?"

"It's always been a weakness of mine, I guess."

They all watched, just as mesmerized as Bruce, as the two of them strolled down the hallway of the terminal, very close, giggling, touching each other, on the elbow, the back. The Lumpers all leaned precipitously on their stools, following the dwindling rhythm of Audrey's tight skirt, down the corridor, along just one of the myriad of painted lines that covered the floor. Only when the scene faded, focusing on those lines before dissolving, and then lighting again on a North Atlantic shoreline did the sound of its punishing surf register.

"I know that beach," Bruce claimed, pointing. "I do, I know that place."

"Captain Hastings?" Leslie said, in the cockpit doorway, wringing her hands. "Any word on how much longer we'll be circling?"

"Easy, Leslie, easy," Hastings jumped up and said. "Why so upset?" he asked, sliding an arm around her shoulders.

"Yeah, why so upset, Leslie?" Steph asked the television.

Mickey leaned forward to look into his eyes.

"I was just about to check on ground status," the captain said, returning to his seat. "Brighton tower, Brighton tower, this is four-0-four, come in please."

"Like *we're* the one's going anywhere," Roy said. "Roger, four-0-four."

"Roy," Captain Hastings said, as Leslie shivered at the sound of Roy's voice. "What's the matter down there?"

"No runway yet, Hastings. Continue circling."

"But, Roy, I've got to start thinking about--"

"Over," Roy cut him off. "Jemison's right. Can't worry about protocol now," he said, as the scope modulated again, to the front door of the same apartment, it slamming, him yelling, "You won't get ANYWHERE! I can promise you that! You'll see backbone."

"Ready for that break?"

"Sure, sure, Conrad." Roy got up, erasing his module. "All clear."

"But?" Steph said, pointing at the set, looking around the bar.

"I told you," Bruce said. "That man's evil."

Zimmer started, "I can see it all clearly," holding his fingers to his temples, in a trance. "The tragedy, the human suffering and devastation..."

"He must be STOPPED!" Bruce yelled, pounding the bar, as Steph swiveled back and forth between them.

"You fellows straighten it all out, hmm. I'll be in the restroom," Mr. Boyles told them.

"You laugh," Mickey said. "They'll be making emergency phone calls any minute now."

"Yes. Randy, quick: 9-1-1!"

"Roger," Randy snapped back, scurrying around the bar.

Mickey stopped, from following Mr. Boyles. "You're kidding, right?"

Randy reached for Mr. Boyles' glass, not the telephone.

"But how?" Steph said, as Bruce handed him another beer.

"Let's just hope we can alert them in time."

"Maybe we should call the FAA?" Steph said, sipping his beer. Zimmer couldn't catch the expression on his face, from the beer mug, couldn't be certain Steph was actually playing along with them.

"Nancy, why do you do it?" Justin asked, as he scribbled comments he overheard from her telephone conversation.

She was breaking down in front of him. "Oh, Justin, I've told you that. For Mark. I love him."

"You could leave all this. You should've left Mark when they suspended him. Come with me, Nancy, I can see to it that you get cleared."

"Justin, please, don't," she tried, as he approached her, after bolting the shop closed.

"Justin, pleeease," Bruce and Zimmer mimicked.

"Yes, Nancy, I love you. Don't you see?" he told her, cornering her. "Say you'll come with me. Say you love me."

"Mick, Mr. Boyles, don't watch!" Zimmer warned them as they returned.

"Justin, dmmphh--"

"I'll be damned," Randy said, still standing within the bar's circumference, waiting on the show to finish up, before opening Lear's for general business. "Mark was right."

"So was I!" Bruce said. "And where the hell is he now? His woman *needs* him."

"Oh, Mark, why don't you go on home. You've had enough."

"You don't understand, Shirley," he said. "I've got to meet that fool brother of yours. I've got to get him a message, risk everything."

"Peter? What have you got to do with him?"

"His cargo."

"What?"

"De-dum," Zimmer chimed.

"Don't ask, Shirley. I can't tell you. I've gotten enough people involved already."

"But I know how to get a message to him, if that's all."

"You do?"

"Sure. Come on. He's landing now, isn't he?"

"Yeah, yeah. Great. Let me make a quick call first."

"Da-da-da-dum..."

"Oh-oh," Steph said.

The camera backed out of the dark recess of the bar, but didn't light on a scene any brighter.

"No, no, don't..."

"That's not *my* Nancy?" Randy said, squinting up at the tube from directly beneath it.

"Spoken like a true proprietor, Randall."

"No, please... Please, don't."

"Or is it?"

"No, don't. HELP!"

"Could be," Steph said.

"Helllp... Stop it, you bastard. HELP!"

"Naw," Randy decided, turning away from the screen. "She'd never talk like that."

"Or would she?" Zimmer said. "And are they going to go on like that for the whole weekend?"

The muffled screams of the incessant struggle and the soft anonymous rustling of clothing were lost in the fade of the camera. They were layered over by the equally relentless, impersonal pounding of the ever present shoreline, with the tide rising. Then all went black, but the credits, the same crescendo, and the surreal sound of a distant airliner.

"Yup," Steph answered Zimmer. "You think Hastings is going to circle all weekend?"

"He is as long as Roy stays on his break," Mickey said, finishing his beer, pushing the mug forward on the bar for a refill.

"Or is he going to crash?" Zimmer asked.

"And drown all those people?"

"They never get rid of any of these characters."

"But Hastings? The election?"

"*That's* a consideration."

"Oh, hell, they'll resurrect him in time to run. Probably show up on some goddammed island."

"Can't run for mayor from an island."

"Never heard of absentee campaigning?"

"We could run Zimmer for mayor."

"Let's not jump to too many conclusions, shall we gentlemen."

"What'd you say?"

"Yes, let us all, stay tuned, for the next, exciting episode," Bruce started, adopting the promo-man's voice and pacing, "of *Innn-coming Flightsss*... Yeee-owww..."

"You could be mayor."

"Think so?"

"Don't you?"

"ANY-thing can happen in these stupid shows," Mickey said.
"Hmm."
"Can I be your campaign manager?" Bruce asked.
"He's got one."
"You know who we should get? Audrey!"
"I don't think so."
"Why not?"
"She's busy."
"That crummy job?"
"No. Not that," Zimmer said. "You don't know?"
"What?"
"No, no, stop it you bastard!"
"Audrey?"
"Who else? Not Nancy."
"Not my Nancy."
Mickey lifted his head. "What?"
"Sure, sure," Steph said. "Had to be her."
"Had to be who?"
"Whom."
"Anthony..."
"What?"
Steph patted Mickey on the back. "Should've paid more attention, Mick." Then, turning to Zimmer, he asked, "You ready?"
"For what?"
"To meet with Senator Carelli."
"What?"
"The nomination."
"Oh."
They both tried to squeeze through the door at the same time. Zimmer asked, "You really think so?"
"Absolutely."
"Where the fuck are they going?" Mickey asked, as the door closed.
Outside, they had to hesitate on the sidewalk, had to allow for a moment or two to adjust to the bright afternoon light. It was impossible for them to navigate the few yards toward the

Bee-atile, blinded, without groping along the building's edge, squinting, bumping into each other.

"My mother always said God would punish me."

"Fucking dayshifter."

"My mother?"

"No, God."

Steph snorted.

"Did the guy create light first, or what?"

Steph slid down the wall, to his knees.

Zimmer helped him back to his feet. "If I *were* mayor, everyone would take a few hours out of each day and do what best relaxed them: a nap, a drink, a partner, whatever. If everyone stopped, like right now," he said, cutting the air with his hand, like he was a film director, "Who'd notice?"

They stood over Abby, hemmed in at the curb, gauging distances. They both had a "I knew we should have parked on the sidewalk" look on their faces.

"After two hundred years of democratic seriousness, I think it's time we brought back good old imperial tea-time," Zimmer said, rolling the driver's side window down.

He reached in and turned the wheel away from the curb, and started what would be multiple cycles of rocking the Bee-atile back and forth, trying to get her clear enough to push away from the curb.

"You know, you're right," Steph said. "You're abso-fucking-lutely right!" and quit being much of a help. "What're we doing that's so very important that it can't be interrupted for a few hours each day?"

"Remember kindergarten?"

Once Abby's right front wheel was clear and they could've pushed her out into traffic to jump start her, Steph veered away from the Bee-atile, instead of helping, veered onto the sidewalk. "Sir, sir?" he said, stopping a man hustling by. "Would you vote to bring back the British tea time rule?"

"What?"

"You ma'm," he turned to another person. There had already been a small crowd of people, who'd slowed to watch them jockey the Bee-atile. Steph just waded into the thick of them, thrusting an imaginary microphone into their faces, cupping his ear with his other hand as if he was getting instructions from network central. "Don't you miss kindergarten? Milk and cookies? Nappy time?"

Steph tried to explain, to the gawking bystanders, twirling around in counter clockwise circles, "Twenty-four hours is a long, long time. Try doing anything for twenty-four long hours. How much time do we devote to rest? Eight? Maybe nine? Surely we need some time, just a little, in the middle of that remaining fifteen, sixteen hours to relax, to let loose, at regular intervals.

"You don't have to nap. Our future mayor isn't dictatorial," he said, waving in Zimmer's direction, who ducked behind the bubble of Abby's roof. "Do whatever suits you, just for an hour or two. In the words of his honor," Steph stopped, tried to stand straight and tall, Zimmer-like, but wobbled, a little: "A nap, a drink, a partner, hell, take several hours, the rest of the day, if that's what it takes..." He broke the pose and lunged back clockwise. "I think the gentlemen in the audience can appreciate that!"

Zimmer had started for the sidewalk already, sensing which direction Steph's presentation was headed. "Come on, Steph," he said, pushing through the crowd to catch him before he tripped over any of the little kids and wound up flat on his face. "Got to go, folks."

"Ladies and Gentlemen I give you the next mayor," Steph said, as Zimmer was dragging him away, "Tony, Zimmer, Zimbarco!"

"Here, push," Zimmer reminded him. "And shut up before somebody calls the cops."

"Zim-mer, Zim-mer, Zim-mer," Steph chanted, mostly quietly, and pushed.

"Zim-mer, Zim-mer, Zim-mer," he said, as he trotted alongside the car.

"Get in, Steph," Zimmer hollered at him. "Get in and shut up!"

9. INVITATIONS

STEPH complied, partially. He got in, but he didn't quiet down, not while there were still sidewalks and porches, front yards with people milling about, or just the potential for witnesses, of voting age, or not. He kept up the chant, "Zim-mer, Zim-mer, Zim-mer!" He took to banging on the roof of Abby in cadence. And he even startled Zimmer more than once by imitating a siren, "Woo-ooo-woo..."

The last thing Zimmer wanted was another confrontation with Pennsylvanian law. "Steph would you *please* knock that off!"

"Zim-mer, Zim-mer..."

Steph was inaccessible though, still caught up in the diffusion of self, the mingling of reality, make-believe and down right fantasy brought on by *Incoming Flights*. He watched the show for just that reason, perhaps. It afforded him an opportunity to skirt authenticity, to make the rational world around him as malleable as he was, so that he could mold it, shape it, create a world where Zimmer really could be mayor, so that maybe he really did think they were headed for some high-rolling strategy session, instead of to Regency, to pick up their pay checks.

"Zim-mer, Zim-mer..."

At Zimmer's repeated requests, though—requests layered on both sides with increasingly hostile threats—Steph stopped the chanting, the banging on Abby's roof. He wouldn't exactly let go of the idea the rest of the way, and even sparked some renewed interest in Zimmer with talk of riding limos anywhere they needed to go, talk about real parties with unlimited guest lists.

"Yeah?"

"Oh, sure. Part of the job."

"What the hell does a mayor do, anyway?"

"Gets his picture taken a lot. Otherwise, shuffles paperwork most of the time, I think."

"That's Lumping, right?"

"Right, right. Just ask Frank."

At the employee parking yard, they cruised four aisles looking for a slot. And they had to walk single file along the fence up to the platform, giving way to trucks coming and going, swooping through the asphalt receiving basin around the loading docks, backing into narrow spaces alongside each other, to be emptied, refilled, and hustled away. The whole yard was teeming with heavy engine noise, diesel fumes, the whine and thump and clatter of forklifts, the voices of all the workers.

"Isn't this enough to make you want to be a Lumper forever?" Zimmer said, over his shoulder, meaning a nightshifter, disdainful of the commotion, the noise that they witnessed every other Friday afternoon. He could easily enough forget about the numbing fatigue that came over him about five in the morning those nights on the cold, dark and empty platform.

Steph leaned forward. "Doesn't it make you want to turn everyone on to the Lumper doctrine?"

"Lumper doctrine?"

"You know, halfzies, toddy-time. Think of it," Steph said, dancing around in front of Zimmer, "Hizzonor," as they continued the climb toward the platform, skipping backwards and crouching down a little, trying to engage Zimmer's forward lean. "Think of the crowds, the adulation. The babies!"

"Babies?"

"Think of speaking before thousands of anxious citizens. Think of holding those multitudes in the palm of your hand," he said, reaching for Zimmer's ample left hand, holding it up between them like a chalice.

"Actually..." They were standing at the base of the short staircase that led up to the stage where daytime Regency folks were busy wrapping up their day, their week, whisking boxes and bundles back and forth on forklifts, hand trucks. Zimmer waited there until Steph let go of his hand. "I was thinking about holding that scrawny neck of yours," he said, reaching for Steph's collar.

Through the crowd of busy workers, parked along the back wall, near the doorway leading to the administration cubicles, Frank was waiting for them. More than part of his duties as Chief Lumper, he used the bi-weekly afternoons as a reminder, much like Zimmer, that he too didn't want anything to do with the frenetic daytime operations of the warehouse. Frank was a company man, to be sure, holding hard and fast to the company line, but that didn't obscure all his personal limits.

Over the thirteen day interim between paydays, he sometimes faltered, confessing to Patty, his kids, that maybe it was time he took an office job again, that maybe shift work was for younger, freer folks, folks without the responsibilities he had. But then, for those couple of hours when he'd sit perched on his forklift, watching executive types come and go from their offices, he knew what he really preferred. If he needed to, he could bolster himself further by reminding himself that he could do the daytime shuffle if he had to, "Absolutely had to." And maybe none of those folks he spied on those Friday afternoons were capable of doing what he did for the company. Like Zimmer's physical compatibility or incompatibility with the workload, the hours, it went beyond career or professional considerations. There was something deeper, almost emotional at play.

On his paycheck, as a salaried manager, his title was Night Supervisor. The company, perhaps, had never heard of the term Lumpers, so Frank's more common designation, Chief Lumper—which was inscribed in gold lamé across the bill of a golf cap the other Lumpers had presented him—was honorary. He wasn't particularly comfortable with it, but if it was good for the shift, it was justified.

The genesis of Frank's association with Regency, how their two histories intertwined, a story which he's told probably once a week since Zimmer and Steph started working for him— filling otherwise slow hours in the middle of the night, crowded into his make-shift office, taking turns squatting over the heater—was a simple one. He'd signed on with Regency when he was seventeen. Except for that painful stint in the personnel office, all twenty six years—"Dwenty-six years," he always repeated, reclining back in his swivel chair, feet up, cigar plugged into his mouth, hands behind his head—of his employment has been as a Lumper. He attributed such dedication and fervor to the emotions of the times, "When people gave damb-boud wad-dey did."

Frank had missed his chance, cheated by birth date, to fight for the country in Korea. Thirteen years later, when the Army was again choosing volunteers and sending them overseas, he'd already had most of his family, so he stayed home, in Tripoli. That didn't mean Frank wasn't imbued with the war effort, recalling other war efforts, "De big one," when he was a child. He saw himself as some kind of moral equivalent, manning the home front, staying up all night, so the tuna fish and oatmeal and graham crackers would get through.

The result was that Frank knew better than anyone at the warehouse its intricacies, peculiarities; and everyone else knew Frank, knew to ask Frank those otherwise unanswerable questions. He seemed the obvious choice when the personnel position opened up. Not even Frank would've guessed, before they put him behind the desk, that what he really preferred was not upward mobility but the stability of always knowing what his job was, the surety of the cast iron cage of his forklift and the no-nonsense concrete platform under his steel-toed shoes.

"Steel-doed jews," the other Lumpers would mimic, when Frank wasn't out there with them, answering a call, maybe, banging their sneakers to the cadence of the exclamation, just like their boss. But they never tired of the story, especially Zimmer, who would prod Frank into it sometimes, asking, "Frank, don't you get tired of those young college guys badgering you with their memos, those management seminars?"

"Naw. They do what they gotta do. Just like the rest of us.

Keeps the food moving."

Frank'd tried. He'd tried wearing the neckties. He'd tried to learn how to be an effective manager, how to mingle along the carpeted hallways, how to joke and jostle at the departmental functions. But Frank just didn't have it in him, to play the politics, to push the paperwork.

It was just after Thanksgiving, about three in the morning, when he'd been back on the shift about a month, when he'd confessed that he just didn't have the vision or ambition to deal in that two-dimensional world. He found himself treating his office much like the platform, moving one pile of reports over to the windowsill, a stack of applications to the file cabinet, then moving them back and forth, telling himself he needed to at least look at them, but more often just leaving them there until it was time to move them again.

"Lumping," Zimmer said at the time, before Frank knew much about the term.

He wasn't sloughing his assigned work, he'd just been misplaced in the office.

"Is that a sin?" he asked them, bringing the chair upright in the dispatcher's office.

"You're a Lumper, Frank. You should've known. *They* should've known," Zimmer told him. "Once a Lumper, always a Lumper."

"It's a natural kind of thing," Steph told him, standing with the rest, break over, patting Frank on the back.

He wanted to believe them, because no, Frank wouldn't slough. He was of a generation which had things like duty and service and loyalty and responsibility ingrained in its psyche. He never would have made the choice just for himself.

The Regency chain of stores had originated in Pennsylvania. For a while, it seemed that the company would compete well enough with the Acmes, the A&Ps. When it was finally admitted that the boon had somehow skipped over central Pennsylvania and failing mines sent workers looking for blue collar jobs that weren't there—searching out industries which had been less determined employers of the citizens of Tripoli, that had packed it in and moved in search of a more prosperous America, like Atlanta, or Houston, or Denver— Regency was still there.

While Tripoli was anything but a ghost town, for Frank, for many other harried locals, the fact that Regency remained, planned to remain, was reassuring enough to foster his kind of loyalty. That's why he'd try the neckties, the paperwork, the office routine at a time and an age when not many employees would make those kinds of sacrifices.

"Sacrifices?"

"It *was!*"

That's what Frank had found out, what he explained to everyone back in October. He was genuinely better suited, more useful and competent in his old job, Night Supervisor, "Working all night wid-dyous guys."

A happy coincidence of the experiment was greater understanding of Lumpers in general which Frank brought back to the platform with him, how they denied normalcy, forgot all about humanness, almost, if that's what it took to get the job done.

"Just doing the job, Frank," Zimmer would remind him.

So, in part, it was Frank's appreciation of them that brought him in every other Friday, his day off, holding office on his forklift, parked back out of the way, handing out the yellow wage envelopes to his Lumpers personally. And though he'd sometimes squirm in the presence of their methods, in Frank's simple managerial system, the Lumpers showed up each night, and they did what was asked of them, "What's to really complain about?"

Steph strode across the platform, toward Frank, and Clementine, patting the tongs, "Looking good, girl," propping a foot on one while Frank sifted through the small stack.

"Frank, let me ask you. Don't you think Zimmer would make a fine mayor?"

Another reason Frank came in to hand out the checks had something to do with trying to isolate the Lumpers as much as he could from the rest of Regency's management and administration. "What if he'd asked Mrs. Harrington that?" He gave Steph his pay, asking, "Whaderr-you-dalkingbout?"

"Wouldn't you vote for Zimmer?"

"For mayor?"

"Yes, Frank. Yes. The next mayor," Steph grabbed his check and tried to get out of Zimmer's way, "of Tripoli, Pennsyl--"

Zimmer elbowed him quiet. "Humor him, Frank. He's drunk."

"What?"

"I am not," Steph said. "Think about it, Frank."

"He's delirious."

"I'm not delirious. Zimmer, would you shut--"

"No, you shut up. I'm not running for nothing!"

"Let's just get a second opinion, all right?" Steph said, backing up, keeping Clementine between them.

Zimmer turned back to Frank. "He's tired. Very tired. We're both tired. We were up all night..."

"Oh, well..." Frank said, handing Zimmer his check. Then, thinking about it, recalling where *he'd* spent the night. "Waydefugginminite."

"Jesus," Steph said, walking away.

Again, Zimmer thought he'd successfully censored Steph and didn't pay much attention to where he was sulking off to. He peeked inside his envelope. "No raise again, huh Frank. I guess you can come to dinner anyway."

Frank leaned over and out of the cab of Clementine nervously. "Gee, I dunno, Zimbarco. It is time for that again already?"

"Every pay-week Saturday, Frank."

Steph hadn't opened his check yet. He just stuffed it into his back pocket, still looking for that second opinion, one that would endorse his political intuition, still intent on campaigning.

"My fellow Tripolites!" he commanded the other workers at the platform, both the day shift and their relief. The other Lumpers arrived as well. There were always drivers idling about, and some of them were locals. "I ask you, are you satisfied with the current state of politics in our beloved city?"

Only the Lumpers would answer. "No!" Bruce yelled.

Mickey shrugged.

"Tell me, Zimbarco. Wad're we having for dis dinner?"

From where they were situated, they could see Steph, though with his back to them, and the truck traffic, they couldn't hear him clearly. He could have been just another worker, climbing up on the rungs of a hand truck weighed down with three cases of bananas.

"We want shorter work days," Steph hollered, shaking his fist.

"Yeah!"

Sounded to Zimmer like a sports headline: "Oerter Irks Mays," as he whispered to Frank, "Turkey."

Frank watched Steph, worriedly, but convinced himself that Steph had called out, "Order more mayonnaise." He turned to Zimmer, "Again? We had turkey for Thanksgiving. Christmas. New Year's turkey. You got another one for tomorrow. Where'd you get all these birds from, huh?"

"Let me explain, Frank."

Once someone took Steph's prop from him—to load the bananas into a cavernous eighteen-wheeler—he paced back and forth across the platform, climbing up on other machinery, jumping back down.

"We want a twenty-four hour post office and new nets at Dagaton Woods!"

"A turkey roll, Frank, not a whole bird."

Frank reinserted his cigar. "Wha-de'll'se-diffrence?"

"Just listen, okay?"

"No! More! Beer! Tax!" Steph chanted, hurling himself across the stage. He ticked off campaign promises just as fast as they occurred to him. "There'll be a round the clock hotline, so that you could always reach hizzoner."

"I'm going to stuff the roll with coleslaw and cornbread after it's almost finished roasting. And then, under a cool broiler, I'll barbecue the whole thing with my special thick sauce."

"Dat'll work?"

"Wait, wait. There's more."

"He's one of us, after all. Mayor Zimmer knows the things little people like us need. He needs them too. A vote for Zimmer is a vote for yourself, essentially. Mick, you'd vote for yourself, wouldn't you?"

Mickey turned to Bruce. "Can I do that?"

"I'll vote for you," he answered. "If you'll vote for me."

"Listen to this, Frank: on the side, bacon baked beans, hmm, with cheese?"

"We'll all be vice-mayors!" Steph promised, as the sun dipped in a hurry, as it does early on winter afternoons, behind the rolling hills and quiet smoke stacks west of Tripoli.

"And, as always, some onion rings."

"Nough. Enough," Frank said, getting up. "I'll be there."

"Oh, but lastly, Frank," Zimmer said, following him up to the front of the platform, empty now except for the sparse evening shift, who represented absolutely no threat to Frank, or his Lumpers. "A special creation, just for you."

Steph was skipping across the stage, waving his arms. "Zim! Mer! Zim! Mer! Zim! Mer!"

"Jalapeño pepper-chili dinner rolls..."

Frank handed Bruce and Mickey's paychecks down to them, and turned to Zimmer. "I'll be early," he promised, pointing his stub of a cigar at him as confirmation.

Steph stopped in front of them, panting, glistening with sweat.

"Tired, huh," Frank said, stuffing the cigar back into his mouth and walking away, muttering, "Fuggin lunitig."

Zimmer turned for the staircase. "Come on, Steph, we got work to do."

"You mean it?" Steph said, following. "You'll run? This'll be great."

"What?" Zimmer said, waiting for Steph at ground level alongside Mickey and Bruce. "What's he talking about?" he asked them.

"What am I talking about?"

Zimmer draped an arm across his shoulder. "Steph, this is Friday, right? We just got paid," waving his envelope in front of Steph's face. "Tomorrow is dinner day. Now, what does that mean?"

Steph actually pondered an answer.

"Two-far!" Mickey shouted for him.

"That's right," Zimmer said, guiding Steph down the lot toward Abby.

"Wasn't anybody listening to me?" Steph tried to protest, tried to turn and point back to the dock, but was kept moving forward, for the Bee-atile, a trip to the bank before it closed and on to Lear's.

"Yeah, Zimmer, is that true? You running for mayor?"

Zimmer just laughed.

Steph wasn't so much angry as he was feeling a need to at least act it. It was an urge to act born out of the rawness of being so tired, strung out on the efforts of the day, rather than further association with *Incoming Flights*, though. He'd all but forgotten the show, such was the immediacy of his concerns, his attention. He couldn't think of anything past the two or three feet in front of him, at the moment, or the crumbs of grit down at the very bottom of his pockets where he had both hands balled up and shoved. He helped get Abby started by just nudging her into motion with his foot. Then he stood there, rather than trotting after the lurching vehicle, daring Zimmer to take off and leave him.

Zimmer wouldn't, of course. At least not today. He knew Steph was suffering, was trying to find a personality which matched his physical state. Steph always suffered through the flip-flop, the metamorphosis. Zimmer circled back and picked him up. He drove along in silence for many minutes, before asking, "What's the matter?"

"Why do you do that?"

"Do?"

"Jesus." Steph knew the discussion was probably pointless. "Always cutting me off, yanking me around. Maybe I was serious back there. Did you think about that?"

"Come on, Steph. Serious? About me running for mayor?"

"Maybe."

"Well, I'll tell you. It's a ridiculous notion, and you know it. Just as it's ridiculous that you get your feelings bent out of shape. I mean come on. You? Serious?"

"Exactly," Steph said, throwing his arms up. "Maybe I don't want to be that person any more. Did you think about that?"

"Yes you do."

"I do?"

Zimmer stopped the car.

"Jesus."

"You want to be Steph. You *love* being a Lumper, remember?"

Steph sat, frowning.

"Steph, you don't have to be serious to be assertive, you know. You just have to know what you want."

"How did we get into this?"

"I see you struggling."

"I think I've already had this discussion somewhere," Steph said, collapsing into a ball on his seat.

They were chugging past the pink house, but that's not why Steph disappeared from view. He could look on the house with more and more detachment. He no longer wished they could take a back route to and from the warehouse, or that his seat in Abby was a reclining one. Though he still had a tough time visiting the family—for those obligatory functions: holidays, out-of-town visitors—and trying to maintain whatever definition he'd carved. For those occasions, yeah, he still assumed the persona they'd prescribed for him years and years ago. Otherwise, he didn't think he always "caved in," as Zimmer went on to characterize it. It irritated him that Zimmer thought so, though not nearly as much as if Zimmer'd been right. Sometimes Steph just hated the fact that the son-of-a-bitch was so fucking right.

As he was crawling across the seat of Abby, grumbling, "Assertive, huh," Steph decided he'd match Zimmer belligerence for belligerence. "What if I was serious?" he said to Zimmer, who was holding the door to Lear's for him, rolling back their conversation however many hours it'd been since they last stepped out of the bar.

"For Christ's sake, Steph..."

"This could have all been yours," Steph said, standing at the bar, waving his arms, pirouetting.

Randy asked, "What's that mean?"

"Pay no attention to him," Zimmer said. "He's tired."

"Jesus," Steph said, retreating to the bathroom.

Quiet confusion accompanied Zimmer's settling into his customary stool next to Mr. Boyles. Mickey and Bruce knew some of what had been going on, but couldn't begin to translate what they witnessed at the warehouse into any kind of sense. Randy looked more than a little concerned. Mr. Boyles said simply, "Private quarrel?"

"Yeah, yeah. Give him a beer. He'll be good as new," Zimmer said, reaching into one of the utility pockets of his painter's pants for a pencil, and then across the bar for a napkin. He had to try to recreate the menu he'd recited to Frank. He'd known before then, of course, what the general fare for tomorrow's dinner would be, had known since Raid Night. But some of the particulars he'd only figured on the spot, like stuffing the turkey. The idea for the rolls had come out of nowhere.

"Sending notes?" Mickey asked.

Even sitting next to him, Mickey was unable to see what Zimmer was scrawling, contorted and hunched over the bar in his wrap-around left hand writing pose.

Zimmer was working on the roll recipe. Chopped peppers? Or pepper cheese? He looked up at Mickey. "This is business."

"Business?" Bruce said. "What business?"

"For tomorrow."

Mickey repeated, "What business?"

"The dinner."

"What do you need to know, Anthony?"

"Well, who's coming, what time they'll make it, stuff like that."

"What, who's coming," Mickey exploded. "Who always

326

comes?"

"I just want to make sure, all right."

"Well, Randall willing, you can be sure I'll be there," Mr. Boyles told him. "Could you use an extra appetizer."

"Always."

"I'm in, you know that," Randy said, tapping an index finger on the bar, like he was calling for a card at blackjack.

"Holding?" Mickey asked, with more than a little eagerness.

"Maybe."

"Mick?"

"Maybe."

"Maybe?"

"I'll be there, I'll be there."

"Bruce?"

He nodded.

"Steph?"

Bruce pivoted around on his stool to see if Steph was coming back into the room.

"I think he's talking on the phone."

"Talking on the phone?"

"I think—Oh, no, here he comes."

They all watched his return.

"What?"

"Who're you talking to?" Mickey asked.

"Never mind," he said, taking the beer Randy had poured for him to the opposite side of the bar.

"Jesus," Zimmer mumbled, huddling over his notes again. Temperature for the rolls? 375? 350? Could he get away with the same temp for the broiler?

"What's he up to?" Steph asked after a few moments.

"Business," Bruce told him.

"Dinner business?"

"Yes, dinner business," Zimmer snapped. "You think these things happen all by themselves?"

"So, what's the question?"

"You coming?" Mickey asked.

"Good question. You know, I've been thinking."

"Bad sign, Steph."

"What if we brought guests?"

Zimmer's head popped up.

"A guest of honor, each time, say. We could fill that eighth chair, at least."

"Whomee sits there," Bruce reminded him.

Usually the chair in question, at the dinners, was the one between Bruce and Steph at the table. Bruce had been picked, on one side, because he'd found a way to get along with the cat that the others hadn't—claimed they spoke the same language. Steph kind of ended up on the other side.

"I'm talking about a real live person," Steph said. "An eighth hand. Someone who won't scratch your wrists when you reach past them."

"Who'd you call?"

Steph looked across the bar at Zimmer. "I mean," he said, like it was just the two of them suddenly. "What if we invited somebody like, Jack?"

"Jack?" Zimmer said, surprised. "Why?"

"Jack?" Bruce asked.

"Remember the day we got the table? That Jack."

"His brother," Zimmer clarified, though still staring a hole through Steph.

"Right, my brother. Why not? This is all about family, right? What if Frank wanted to bring his kids sometime?"

Mickey turned to Bruce. "Frank's got kids?"

"Scary isn't it."

Zimmer wouldn't be distracted. "You called Jack? Why? What's he ever done for you?"

"Al fresco Jack, right?" Bruce said. "He's already been to dinner, hasn't he?"

"Shut up, Bruce."

"Thank you Michael."

"He doesn't have to do anything. He's my brother."

Zimmer bent down over his calculations, figuring in an extra portion. "In his case he does."

After a noticeable silence, he added, "It's up to you."

"Whatever," Steph waved, finishing his beer, wanting to insist, "Damn right it is." He got up and moved toward the hallway, and the telephone.

Zimmer tried to ignore the expectation hovering over him. He turned to Mr. Boyles, the only person he'd allow judgement to. "He's not really like family, you know."

"Does not sound like it, no."

"We treat Steph a lot better than they do. I've seen it. I've been there."

"Yeah?"

"You should see them. It's like he's a stranger in the place, like he's come on some kind of appointment, or he's a neighborhood beggar that happens by once in a while."

"Even mom?" Bruce asked.

"She's the coldest one, the one Jack learned to be such an asshole from."

"Anthony?"

"I'm telling you, it's true." Zimmer got up, and paced around the bar. "I'll show you," he said, dragging three empty tables together near the bar. "We're over there for Christmas dinner, right."

"You spent Christmas at Steph's?" Mickey asked.

"Yeah, well, it was a lot like today. Day before, he kind of suggests I come along. We'd been talking about his going, how he doesn't really mind popping over there every week or so, doesn't mind the role-playing. 'It's what they expect,' he says. 'I'm used to it.' And they won't change. And he thinks I want to go with him? Come to find out, though, that morning, his mother's expecting me, has a place set for me."

"Did you go?" Mickey asked.

"Did I go?" Zimmer said, sitting at one of the small tables. "Did I have a choice?"

"Go where?" Steph asked, sitting at another of the tables.

"Christmas dinner," Bruce reminded him.

"Oh, Jesus, not this story."

"There we were, sitting at the elegant Abrams table, dutifully eating in this enforced silence—I know why you hate silences so much now," he said to Steph. "No one gets to say anything, unless Senior initiates a conversation. And then, everything he says is either directed toward the Mrs., or Junior. The *whole* fucking meal! Wonderful ham, honey, which it wasn't. It was dry as toast. How are the bowls shaping up, John? Or he carries on all by himself, not addressing anyone, like he was making a speech or something, rambling from the hostages to the weather to the fucking Olympics! So I'm thinking, I'm a New Yorker, I'll tell them something about Lake Placid, but *whoosh*, he's off, complimenting the lumpy mashed potatoes then making a bet with Jack on the NFL playoff games that weekend."

Steph was chuckling. "Tell them about the phone call."

Zimmer grinned.

"Phone call?" Bruce asked.

"He got this phone call, right in the middle of dinner," Steph started. "How did you do that? You never told me, did you?"

Zimmer only glanced toward Mr. Boyles.

"What happened?" Mickey screamed.

"My mother comes into the dining room, 'Bob?'"

"Who's Bob?"

"Another story."

"'Bob, there's someone on the phone for you, I think.' Zimmer says, 'Uh-oh,' then jumps up, talks into the phone, comes back to the table frothing about an emergency at the warehouse: refrigeration lost, starvation in three counties, grabbing his coat, me, and we're out of there before any of them can blink."

"You took a lot of shit for that, didn't you," Zimmer said.

"Jack's the one that figured it was a scam."

"See what I mean?"

"I hope he brings a lot of money tomorrow," Bruce said.

"Did you mention that?" Zimmer asked.

"No."

"What time'd you say?"

"About noon."

"Great. He's a teacher, you know," Zimmer said to Bruce.

"Probably pulls in about eighteen, twenty grand."

"Perfect."

"Yup," Steph said, starting to squirm in his seat. "But listen--"

"Yes?" Zimmer said. Everyone was listening, not just the Lumpers. Other patrons, both at the bar and out amongst the other tables were listening, keeping up with the conversation as it spread from the bar into the dining area. "You're not going to plead for clemency, are you? Jack's a big boy, don't forget."

"No, no, not that. In fact, he's not even coming."

"Oh?" Zimmer said, not relieved, seeing as how Steph was still anxious about something.

"Damn," Bruce said.

"You're kidding," Zimmer said, guessing. "The redhead?"

"I can call her back," Steph tried, getting pale, even in the dusk of Lear's.

"Her?" Mickey said.

"Angela."

"*Ange-la*?" Bruce sang.

"Nice girl, works the check-out at Regency, mornings," Zimmer went on. "Good looking too, you know"

"Jesus," Steph said, moving back to the bar, signalling for another drink, then burying his face in his arms, on the bar.

"We're having a co-ed dinner?" Randy asked, moving to serve him.

Bruce stood and moved next to Steph. "Does this mean there'll be a dress code?"

"That's right," Zimmer said. "We'll have to shave, too."

"Look, Angie doesn't even know if she can--"

"*Angie*..." Bruce sang again.

Steph elbowed him. "She's almost a Lumper. You said so yourself."

"Perhaps a nice dry Chablis would be in order, Randall."

"Sure," Randy said, pouring Mr. Boyles another scotch. "Or champagne."

"Champagne?"

"Stephen, if you intend to woo this girl, certain amenities

174

are required."

"Woo? What is that? Who said anything about woo?"

"Is it too late for invitations?" Mickey asked, sitting on Steph's other side.

Steph was left to only pivot and look on helplessly at each successive comment.

"We could use the bar's stationary."

"You've got stationary?"

"How about place settings?"

"I'll wear a chef's hat. A big white sucker."

"I'll be the doorman!"

"Or the door."

"*Ma-damn. Me-sure.*"

Everyone cringed at Bruce's accent.

"I'll be the maitre'd," Mickey said, draping a paper napkin over his forearm.

Mr. Boyles, who should have been able to resist, said, "We can have a receiving line for her."

"No, no, no, no," Steph cried, rising from his stool again. "No. I'm going to tell her it's off."

But he walked past the telephone, walked all the way down the hall, as they all watched.

"And you'll have to do that sitting down tomorrow!" Zimmer called. "Can't have all that splashing with a lady about."

"We'll make a refined man of him yet."

Usually, Steph would figure he deserved the agitation. He's always supposed, a function or a result of his passive demeanor, that he got what he deserved. He could tolerate it, if nothing else, and wouldn't erupt into reactive indignation. He might consider it, returning from the bathroom, might tire of being the target, but that would be an act.

It was kind of nice, as a way of balancing things, if Zimmer's calculations ever bogged down or got tangled up--over the real life complications of chairs or the amount of beer or the order of courses—up popped Angela, at least the subject of Angela, before anyone could get testy, indignant, serious. "Guardian Lumper benefactress," Bruce was calling her by the end of the evening.

The only escaping Steph attempted—which, without leaving the bar itself, wasn't an escape at all, especially with the other Lumpers following him—was moving from seat to seat along the bar, ordering different drinks each time, as if he could become someone else that easily.

"I should think," Mr. Boyles said at one point, "that turkey has to be very delicately barbecued, Anthony, if at all."

"Miss-ster Boyles," Zimmer answered him, from Steph's first former stool, next to Bruce, "it is absolutely no use barbecuing anything if it isn't good and spicy and half an inch thick."

Bruce had slipped off his seat, into the gap between them, was gnawing on Zimmer's shoulder, "Rrhhumm..." having missed three meals by that time.

"Or," Zimmer said, raising his left hand, pointing that index finger, dislodging Bruce, "Maybe Angela doesn't even *eat* barbecue? I mean," turning from one side of the bar to the other, getting dizzy with trying to keep up with Steph's migrations. "It's so messy."

Mickey was next to Steph, chin resting on his little stacked fists on the bar's surface. "Maybe she wears gloves."

Steph sat up and glared down at him, thinking, Who the hell wears gloves when they eat? But he didn't really want to prompt any more comments. He figured if he avoided challenging them, just got up and moved, they might forget about Angela for another few minutes, especially since they were all starting to show the effects of the alcohol.

Alcohol, and Lear's were usually antidote enough for the Lumpers, for their sometimes miserable lives. "Imperfect lives," Zimmer was always quick to correct Mickey. They had others. Sometimes, in fact, the number of prescriptive measures they resorted to teetered higher than the rituals, their distractive, cloaking devices.

One of the more passive of their measures was Dagaton Woods Park. It was Steph's idea, naturally enough, that wherever they were, or wherever they were going, their trip had to be through Dagaton Woods. "Especially, if it's out of the way," he'd said. "Dagaton Woods is like a really good book. You can open it to any page, any time."

On the other, less-than-passive, contrary, Zimbarco side, Steph's basketball was always rolling around in the back seat of the Bee-atile, accompanying them on any journey. "Something I should have thought of when I was married," Zimmer'd said, after their third or fourth installment of a running, day's end, one-on-one basketball game.

Steph had asked at the time, "You were married?" knowing the response would only be a left-handed, somewhere in New York, that was then, wave.

"So," Steph said, dribbling. The shadows cast by the movement of the ball and his arm, angling across the court's surface from remote lights, lights meant for parking lots and building security, looked disconnected from any source, or at least out of phase. "What's the big fucking deal?"

"Deal?" Zimmer said, guarding the shadows more than the shadower. "You mean the score?"

"What's the deal, the big fucking deal?"

Steph got more mobile with drink. He got completely floppy. As he hesitated at the top of the key, waiting for an answer, dribbling, slapping the ball to the asphalt, cradling its return, he kind of hopped from one foot to the other, swaying, rocking.

"Big deal?" Zimmer said, calmer, poised, crouched over a little, waiting. "You mean about Angela?"

"Yeah. Angela. *All* your bullshit today."

"My bullshit? Listen to you. You had me kissing babies, remember?"

"So?"

"So, sounds like you can't take your own medicine."

"Cli-che."

"Fuck you."

"They were just *hypothetical* babies, not real babies."

"Not yet."

Zimmer stood up straighter, smirking.

"Yeah, *that* bullshit," Steph said, pointing with his free hand, then faking a drive to the basket, jumping into Zimmer's sanctuary, skipping back. "That's what I'm talking about."

Zimmer crossed his feet, almost stumbled at the fake. "It was your idea to bring her up, to bring her tomorrow."

"Today," Steph corrected him, waving at the sky.

"Fuck you."

"Fuck you!"

Steph faked again, at Zimmer's right side, then streaked for the basket around his left.

Zimmer was expecting the move though, and recovered quickly enough to shoulder Steph as he lunged for the goal, altering his flight, that of the ball.

"Like a fucking kidney punch," Steph groaned, flinging the ball at the basket anyway, easily outrunning Zimmer for the rebound, starting the whole process over again. "Goddamn bonehead."

"Easy," Zimmer cautioned.

"Let's see if you can take *your* own medicine."

Steph charged the basket again, without any fake, driving right through Zimmer, slamming the ball through and toppling them both onto the dirt and dead grass off the edge of the court.

"See?" he said, sprawled out on the ground.

"See what?"

"See what being so obstinate gets you?"

"Yeah, I see," Zimmer said, getting up, retrieving the ball, grinning a menacing grin, waiting at the top of the key for Steph. "It gets you fouled," banging the ball against the court in cadence. "No basket."

"What I'm trying to tell you," Steph said, ambling into position, "is that it wasn't my idea." Then, presumably possum like, he flicked an arm out for the ball, where Zimmer was standing straight up, dribbling from about his shoulder. But Steph had drunk away most of his relative agility several beers ago.

"Right," Zimmer said, skipping by him, stuffing the ball through the basket with a vengeance.

"It's true."

"It just happened that way." He gave the ball to Steph to check. "Two zip."

"I was just calling Jack to piss you off. He wasn't going to come."

"Then how'd Angela get into it?"

"You mentioned her first."

"What?"

"Yeah. And then everyone got so worked up about it, it started to sound like a good idea."

"What? You hadn't talked to her before…"

Steph watched Zimmer recreate the timeline, then shrugged.

"Jesus," Zimmer said, through clenched teeth. Now he *was* pissed, mostly because he should have expected something so typical. He charged for the basket, taking a course that would run right over Steph if he hadn't moved.

Steph knew better than to try and draw this foul. He side-stepped Zimmer and snatched the exposed ball away as Zimmer lifted it toward the basket. Then he retreated to the wing and let fly an uncontested jump shot, "Chink."

"Two, up," Zimmer snarled, flinging the ball back at him. "Chickenshit."

"What?"

Zimmer stood back under the basket, arms folded in defiance, repeating only, "Go ahead and shoot, chickenshit."

"See?" Steph said to phantom spectators. "See what I mean? *That's* what started all this!" he hollered. Then, falling completely out of character finally, after the long, taunting night, resorting to Zimbarco jungle basketball, he grumbled, "Goddammit," dipping a shoulder, bulldozing for the basket, leaping up and crashing into Zimmer, jamming the ball through, rattling the whole goal. He tried to grab onto the rim to correct his flight as he came hurtling over Zimmer's back.

Zimmer caught him, breaking his fall, and set him back onto the ground. "Sounded like a good idea?" he said, before picking up the ball and heading for the Bee-atile.

10. Feast of St. Fill-Up

STEPH spent a considerable amount of time wondering if the shot counted. Zimmer hadn't said anything, hadn't claimed foul, though Steph knew he'd probably travelled, at least. That meant they were still tied. They could be tied, "Right?"

At Fill, while Steph didn't need to sleep in Whomee's chair any longer, not with the cot still on loan from Lear's, it had become his habit on Friday nights, after the long and painful transition back to the more normal method of sleeping at night, to collapse into the chair as soon as he made it inside the door, much like the first night he'd spent there. He could defend the choice in Zimbarco terms, "Starting their weekend by starting over, with the identical ceremony with which they'd started the tradition of the Lumpers way back..." if Zimmer ever took up the argument.

Zimmer didn't. He knew it was just more of Steph's least resistance crap, that yielding to whatever environment he found himself in. While Zimmer might have appreciated Steph's argument about starting over, collapsing in Whomee's chair was something Steph did just because he was Steph, no Zimbarco rational to be found, "Which is good." Zimmer didn't want Steph thinking like him, imitating him in any way, which is why he ended the basketball game, regardless of the score. If the last shot counted, could either of them be sure, in the darkness of Dagaton Woods, that it had been Steph who had scored it, and not some Zimbarco clone? Better to stop the game before they had to figure that one out. And if they remained tied, what's the worst that could happen? "Get to start the game over, right?" And surely Steph, Mr. Math, realized that tied did not nearly mean equivalent?

"Jesus," Zimmer said, holding his head with floured hands. "It's dangerous trying to out think him." And that's the problem, Zimmer knew, either of them trying to out-other each other.

"What?"

Steph's brand of dialectics infuriated Zimmer, stringing out the argument with no real choices in sight. He viewed it much like Steph's basketball playing, slipping between one opportunity and the next, instead of just meeting obstacles head-on, creating a kind of resolution.

"It's like cooking," he said. At that precise moment he could've instructed Steph on the secrets of cooking, life, with just that day's meal, with just those portions of it he was working on at the time—the roll dough, the beans, his sauce. "You have to have a desired endpoint, don't you?" he said. "That's what makes everything else about it so simple," turning and raising his hands to the park, the trees just then emerging out of the day's somber first light.

Zimmer pictured Steph as the kind of cook that would keep adding ingredients to a sauce, say, until he either ran out of ideas, or, "More likely," he ran out of space in the pot.

"You've got to know what taste you're looking for," Zimmer told the sauce, then tasted it. He was perfectly willing, he'd say to Steph, if he went past that objective—with the sauce, with anything—to start all over. "*That's* what I mean."

It was not entirely unlike acid-base titrations in high school chemistry, where reactions turned on one drop, period. "He could understand that?"

The bread rising, the beans and the sauce simmering, Zimmer could continue with the morning's other preparations, one of which included shaking Steph and Whomee out of their chair. And then, with a few minutes of free time, and a fresh cup of coffee, he could watch Steph stumble around the big room looking for the cot or any other place to settle for a few more hours. It wasn't so much that Steph absolutely needed more sleep, "Although he's down about five or six hours," as much as he just preferred sleep to most everything else. And Zimmer, suspicious of sleep anyway, couldn't resist watching the show in a kind of awed fascination, even wagering, at one point, "Twenty to one he crawls on top of the table."

Against all odds, Steph ended up in the kitchen, propped against the corner opposite the refrigerator.

"Good morning," Zimmer tried, pouring him a cup of coffee.

Steph grumbled a reply, and accepted the cup, kind of groped his thin fingers around it, his eyes refusing to open.

"How do you feel?" He looked lousy.

But Steph answered, "Fine," once the question circulated lazily through his otherwise empty head. And it was true, despite his hair sticking out at unnatural angles, the upholstery nap pattern speckled across one check, his eyes puffy and shut. With a sleeper like Steph, when he did get up, it really was a new day, each day virtually a new beginning, the past forgotten. So, every morning or afternoon, he was, "Fine."

Zimmer would remind him though, "All that mixing you were doing last night. Didn't you think? Whiskey sours? Sloe gin, for God's sake."

"Zimmer," Steph said, tilting his head back so that he could peer at him from underneath his eyelids. "Do we have to do this?"

"Jesus," Zimmer said, moving for the refrigerator, getting back to work. "Go take a shower."

"Fine," Steph said, turning, slowly, for the bathroom, grazing the doorjamb on the way by.

Zimmer pulled the top off the kettle to refill it and heat more water for coffee. Then he remembered where he'd sent Steph and turned off the water before Steph would start screaming. He worried that he'd be handicapped in the kitchen, so much as he would need water, as long as Steph was in the shower, and grumbled, "Maybe I should have left him sleeping."

Steph emerged from the shower cleaner, refreshed, certainly, but not noticeably more alert. He still stumbled into the kitchen, a bath towel wrapped around his waist, another one pulled over his head, hooding his eyes.

Zimmer tried again, "Good morning," handing Steph another cup of coffee.

"If you insist." Steph peered through the windows. "It's just such a waste."

"Maybe you should go take another shower," Zimmer told him, thinking he wouldn't be so careful with the water this time: shock therapy.

"All right, all right, I get the hint," Steph said. "I can be pleasant; you know I can. Just let me do this," he said, holding the coffee cup against his forehead. "Let me take care of this head. Then, you want pleasant? I'll give you pleasant until you puke," but wished he hadn't said that. His color shifted, like a rotating Christmas tree wheel, to nearly the same muted dawn colors outside. "Is there any of that bourbon left?"

"Now?"

"It's either that or a few more hours sleep, I figure."

"Under the sink."

Steph set his coffee cup down with both hands, and started plundering the cabinets. "Zimmer," he said, pulling open the three sets of overhead panels. "There's not one clean glass, do you know that."

"So?"

"Not one clean glass."

"Who needs a glass? Drink it out of the bottle."

"There's not even a bowl I could slurp out of."

"Use a straw! Pour it in your coffee, I don't care. Just do something quick, you're starting to nag."

"We have straws?" he asked, pouring a shot of Jack Daniels into his coffee. He stirred it with his finger, then sipped.

Zimmer watched the contortions from the combination work their way from Steph's face, as he swallowed hard, to his stomach, his whole upper body twitching.

Steph jerked his head, blinked his eyes fully open for the first time that morning. "Better." He gurgled another shot into the cup. "Actually, that's not too bad."

Zimmer wondered, maybe five, ten seconds, before holding his coffee cup out for some.

"Kind of a liquid omelette."

"Right."

Steph replaced the bottle and stood studying the

overflowing sink. "How did you get into *this* habit? Didn't you have to do dishes when you were growing up? Didn't your mother have you scrubbing plates right after the last bite?"

"Nope. Not me anyway. I'm a middle child."

"What's that mean?"

"Means everything I got was leftovers, even chores. Drying the dishes was one of those coveted tasks, for some reason."

"So somebody did them?"

"Absolutely."

"So what happened to you?" Steph was pulling pieces carefully out of the stack, just trying to find the sink down there somewhere, like plucking playing cards out of a Bicycle house. "I mean, how do you do this?" he said, admiring, suddenly, the engineering feat of the pile. It amazed Steph that he didn't ever foster some deadly, toxic mold on all the soiled dishes and utensils, and that he could continue to cook right up to those moments when Steph would assault the pile, despite having every single pot, pan, dish and utensil waiting to be scoured.

"What's the difference?" Zimmer answered him, pausing at the counter, chef's blade at the ready. He meant, what difference does it make if he cleans them as soon as he uses them, or whenever he needs them. "Why should I do things like your mother, or my mother, just because that's the way they did them?"

Like haircuts: Steph still dutifully went to the family barber every three, four weeks, keeping his hair trimmed to nearly the style his father had set for him as an eighth grader. Zimmer let his hair grow until it irritated him, and then got it all whacked off, starting over.

"None. Don't change a thing. It's a masterpiece!" Steph said, stepping back from the piles, finally emptying the sink, running soapy water. "Can you dry?" he asked absently.

"Now?"

Zimbarco panic: Now? Now, when he was chopping and stirring and molding and tasting? Now? Couldn't it wait, a minute, an hour. A week?

"No, no, not now," Steph said, turning him back toward his work. "Forget it."

Steph reached for the Jack Daniels again, and poured two shots into what little bit of coffee each of them still had, raising his in salute. "To masterpieces, and alternatives."

"Alternatives?"

"Alternative approaches: like families."

"To flexible absolutes, like family."

They drank.

"You know what you should do, you should start your own religion," Steph said, reaching for the radio.

"What?" Zimmer stopped, worried Steph was going to remember the campaigning from yesterday. He didn't want to have to fight that all day.

"Hah!" Steph shouted, pouring more bourbon into their empty mugs. On the radio they were playing last year's signature song form the Pirates' championship season, "We are fam-i-lee," this, the early reporting date for spring training. "Perfect."

Zimmer kneaded bits of jalapeño pepper into the dough, forming the individual rolls. Steph was whittling down the stack of dirty dishes, kind of. It got to be sort of a game, as Zimmer handed over the empty bread bowl and took the cookie sheet from Steph just as he finished drying it, to see if he could keep ahead of the cooking, could anticipate what Zimmer needed next and have it ready, lest the whole intricate process grind to a halt.

They heard a vehicle pull up next to the Bee-atile underneath them, into the only other space under the apartment. It was a big diesel sounding thing, and then they heard the horn, "Honk, honk."

Zimmer squashed a wad of dough at the noise, his rhythm interrupted.

"Frank?" Steph guessed, holding his dripping hands out of the dish water, an imitation of either a celebrant saying mass or a surgeon, either of which seemed applicable, somehow, and then turned to spy out the windows.

"Got to be," Zimmer said.

"Good old Frank," Steph said, as he came into view, waving up to them. Steph raised a window. "Frank, why are you always announcing yourself like that?"

"What?"

Zimmer, still at the counter, hollered, "The horn, goddammit!"

"Oh. Don-wanna-inderrup anyding."

"Jesus," Zimmer said. "Better have that bottle ready."

Steph grabbed a dry towel and went to open the door, finding Frank laboring up the staircase. He paused at the top, searching for a breath, then threw his cigar butt over the railing.

"Well, boys, here's the party," he said, waving a bottle of Four Roses. He unzipped his jacket to show Steph his Vegas poker shirt: a bright mural of neon marquees and dancing girls.

"Nice shirt," Steph said, waving him into Fill.

"Think so?"

Frank followed Steph toward the kitchen. He tossed his jacket over the back of Whomee's chair, then wagged the bottle of whiskey at him on the way by. Whomee yawned, then recurled himself. "You don't think it's too girly, do ya? Faggy?"

"Nice shirt, Frank," Zimmer greeted him.

"Yeah?"

"To Frank's shirt," Steph said, handing out glasses of bourbon.

"Frank's pretty new shirt."

"Fuck you, Zimbarco," Frank said, giving Zimmer a board check. "To the Wings!"

"The Wings?"

"You know," Steph told him. "Local hockey team. They almost got a playoff spot, right?"

"Damn right."

"Fuck hockey," Zimmer said, putting down his glass. "Puck hockey."

Frank put down *his* glass at that.

So Steph said, "To baseball!"

"Baseball? In February?"

"Come on, Frank. We're talking alternatives. It's the theme of the day."

"Flexible," Zimmer told him, enunciating slowly, "absolutes."

"Yeah, yeah..."

"To baseball," Zimmer said, retrieving his glass. Then, as they were all sipping, he added, "And pretty new shirts."

Steph choked.

Frank pulled at the shirt. "Think so?"

"Frank," Steph said, handing him the towel. "Can you dry?"

"Don't I always? Do you guys ever do dishes during the week?"

Zimmer said, "Not unless we run out. Why waste the hot water?" growing impatient with criticism in his own kitchen.

"And the soap." Steph was already reaching for the bottle again.

"Ain't there health codes or some shit? Doesn't your landlord check on you, his place?"

"Whomee?"

"Look Frank," Zimmer said, "you've got a dishwasher, right?"

Frank stood up from his crouch over the dishes, pushing his shoulders back. "Maybe."

"It's just about the same thing. We rinse off the dishes and stack them. When we're ready, we wash. There's very little difference."

"Except that Patty runs the dishwasher at least once a day."

"Yeah. So?"

"So you guys do dishes less than once a week, for Christ's sake."

Steph poured more bourbon for everyone. "An alternate approach, Frank."

"What? What kind of bullshit is that?"

"Not bullshit, Frank," Steph said, pushing Frank's arm, his drinking hand, closer to his mouth. "Baaassseball..."

"Get out," Frank said, pushing him away. Then he drank,

adding, "Why don't you go get dressed. You're making me nervous."

"Oh, shit," Steph said, looking down at the towel, then back up.

"Don't you guys worry?"

"About what, Frank?"

"What people think."

"What people think about what, Frank?"

"Shit, Zimbarco, you know what I'm talking about," Frank grumbled, slapping his soggy towel onto the shelving at the windows, pacing the length of the kitchen, looking through the door at Steph's progress. "Don't give me that shit."

"What do you want to know, Frank?"

"You guys ever have any women up here?"

"Uh, oh. That's right. Steph," he called. "Batter up!"

Steph came into the kitchen, buckling his jeans. "What is it?" thinking Zimmer was, uncharacteristically, calling for help.

"What about Angela?"

"Angela?" Frank asked.

"Shit."

"Angela?" Frank said again, following Steph back into the living room, the dishtowel draped over an arm, carrying a dripping spatula. Steph was searching underneath Whomee's chair for his shoes, looking around the room for his jacket.

"Frank, lis—" There was a banging at the door, like a battering ram, BANG!, pause, BANG!, pause, BANG!

Steph scurried for the door before Frank could open it, to find Bruce, carrying two stacked ice-chests in front of himself.

"You *always* act like a fucking lunatic?" Frank asked him.

"Sure Frank." Bruce stepped past. "You always carry a spatula?"

Frank waved it at him.

"Hey," Mickey said, following Bruce. "*I'm* the maitre'd," taking the towel from Frank.

Randy followed Mickey, carrying three cases of long-necks.

Zimmer came out of the kitchen to greet everyone, saw Steph still searching, guessing what he couldn't find. Steph looked up, panicked, to see Zimmer holding the keys, tossing them across the room.

Frank was groaning, "What the hell we need a maitre'd for?"

"We're going high class, Frank," Zimmer told him. "No more licking your fingers."

Bruce said, "Really?"

"Whose idea's that?" Frank asked. "Boyles?"

"Where *is* Mr. Boyles?" Zimmer asked.

Steph came back into the door, Mr. Boyles in tow, carrying a crock pot. "Zimmer, you've *got* to smell this."

They all converged on the table, where Steph set the pot, plugging it into a nearby socket.

Zimmer lifted the glass cover. "Wow."

"Soup!" Bruce said, salivating.

"Well, actually—" Mr. Boyles started to explain.

"What's all that junk floating around in it?"

"Bouillabaisse, to be precise."

"Beautiful," Zimmer said, dipping a pinky into the broth.

"Beautifulabaisse," Steph said, taking his turn.

"That will be quite enough of that, thank you," Mr. Boyles said, taking the lid from Zimmer.

"I don't know."

"What is it Frank?"

"I don't know," he said, clamping down on a new stoagie. "I don-know bout all that junk floating in there. Clam shells. Fish eyes? Never seen no soup like that."

"Frank, that's what bouillabaisse is," Zimmer said, returning to the kitchen. "Jesus."

"What kind of soup you leave the garbage *in*?"

"Frank, those things add flavor," Mr. Boyles told him, listing some other ingredients, which Frank might be more comfortable with: "Whitefish, halibut, cod, mussels, and shrimp."

"Can't you just blend it all together?"

"Bouillabaisse is different, Frank," patient Mr. Boyles told him. "Think of it as fishermen's stew."

"Stew's got meat, potatoes."

"Bouillabaisse is *DIFFERENT!*" Zimmer screamed from the kitchen, losing his patience.

"Awright, awright," Frank conceded, then continued to mumble to himself, "bowla base, bowla base: That's what it looks like, awright, a bowl a bases, with all that shit floating around in there..."

Zimmer heard him, and came through the kitchen doorway ready to strangle him, when Steph moved between the two of them, the bottle of Four Roses handy, pouring for everyone. "See there, Frank, you do know what you're talking about."

"Huh?"

"To baseball soup!" Steph said, once everyone had a glass.

The other Lumpers traded confused looks, but drank, as did Frank, and Zimmer. Bruce took the bottle from Steph, poured another shot into their glasses, toasting, "To extra innings!" and they were off, forgetting about silencing Frank, or educating him.

If Zimmer intended to ask Steph, echoing Frank, "Baseball? In February?" Steph's only possible answer would be, "Worked, didn't it?" Because he couldn't always be counted on to have fully reasoned out how and why things might work before they did, Zimmer probably wouldn't ask, yielding to Steph's back-door approach toward desired endpoints: "Worked, didn't it?"

It worked to distract and lubricate Frank, who could be disruptive if he was allowed to focus on any one irritation. They primed him, early, on dinner days. They kept his hands and his mouth busy. Once the dinners started, once everyone was seated in their respective, individualized chairs—the various styles and heights effectively equalizing their physical differences—Frank would get into the flow of the celebration, would enjoy the moment enough to forget his grievances, suspicions, forget any aggravations, as they all would.

"It worked," Steph, master at retrospection, would say to Zimmer, reaching for the bottle.

Bruce blocked him from pouring though, pleading, "Can't we please start eating?"

"We could," Zimmer said, sneaking back into the kitchen, abandoning his roommate. "Except there's someone still missing."

"Oh, yeah," Bruce said, letting go of the Four Roses. "What's her name."

"Your lady friend, Stephen."

"Where's Angela?" Mickey asked.

"That's it, Angela."

Steph was backing toward the door.

"Yeah, yeah. What's all this shit about," Frank said, following Steph. "Who's Angela?"

Steph, worried to the point of paralysis about explaining himself—both to Frank and to Angela, now that he was late—couldn't think of reasonable stories for either of them. So he said, "Batter up!" shoving the Four Roses into Frank's hands, fleeing down the stairs.

He wondered when he'd be able to quit either, the fleeing or explaining. It was then that he understood that as long as he continued to do one, he'd have to do the other as well. With Frank, of course, he could never explain things to, much like his parents. "Angela?" With her, it was different, because he *wanted* her to understand. "But how *could* she understand?" that there was an assumed cushion to his telling her that he'd be by about noon. How could he explain that being late was kind of a design of the feasts? "If I didn't live at Fill, I wouldn't understand," Zimmer's insistence that no one else thought about time, schedules, appointments, duties—even as he was killing himself in the kitchen putting together the multi-course feasts, juggling the logistics and precision of having every dish ready at exactly the same time, "*Voila!*"

He could see her, as soon as he turned onto her street, standing out on the sidewalk, waiting. He double-parked Abby at the curb, left her idling and jumped out.

"Sorry," was the first thing he said.

"It's all right," she said, patting him on the shoulder. "I was afraid you'd forgotten."

"Well," he started to say, but when any and all of the

potential follow up comments occurred to him, "as a matter of fact," as a matter of circumstance, the circumstance of Frank's belligerence, "Or my hangover," you should have seen them last night when I told them, Mickey thinks you wear gloves, but that was after Bruce was gnawing on Zimmer's shoulder, "So..." He just stood there holding the door for her.

"I'm starved."

He considered lying: Another emergency at work? "Naw." Suddenly he couldn't think of anything to say about anything, and climbed back into the Bee-atile.

Silence.

They chatted about idle things; short, forced recesses in a mostly silent trip.

He commented on the weather.

"I can't wait for summer."

"Already?"

"The park is so much prettier when it's green."

"Yeah, and the courts aren't so treacherous."

"Huh?"

He said he couldn't wait to actually sweat again, which prompted more silence, rather than less, "Of course," until they were bumping down the access drive.

"Here we are," he said, showing her the staircase.

"Please don't let there be silence," he prayed, then knew as soon as he asked for anything but, that's exactly what he'd get: A long, painfully silent dinner, everyone relying on him to reestablish the protocol that he'd fucked up. "Oh, God."

She stood at the top of the stairs smiling, her eyes darting from the doorknob to her feet, to him, and back.

"Oh, here," he said, reaching for the door, "Welcome to," perfect, nothing but silent, expectant stares, right down to the grey feline one, "Fill."

Angela stood frozen before all the attention. She knew some of the others, from the store, or from stories, as Steph introduced them. Bruce, who, as always, grinned in a way that wasn't too far removed from a leer, and Mickey, she'd seen often enough. Frank, too, had been in the store. "This must be

Whomee," she said, bending to pet him before Steph could stop her. But Whomee behaved, "That's one minor miracle."

Everyone else sort of stooped along with her, out of shock, or something, the lack of something, absence of precedent. Steph was trying to be protective. He didn't know what the others had in mind.

"This is Randy, from Lear's," he continued, nodding her into remembrance, trying to keep things moving, though aware that he was going to run out of officious distractions soon enough. "And this is Mr. Boyles."

"Greetings," he said to her. The sound of someone else's voice was so wonderful, like a long drink of ice-cold peppermint Schnapps.

"Hi," she answered, still smiling, though still trapped just within the threshold of the apartment.

The rest of them stood there smiling back, stupidly, as if smiling would cover up not saying or not doing what they didn't know to say or do. They stood there passing Frank's empty bottle of Four Roses back and forth between them.

Angela turned to Steph. "Where's Zimmer?"

"Gee," Steph snapped, "I don't know," jerking the hot potato bottle out of Bruce's hands. "Where *is* Zimmer?"

"In the kitchen, doing all the goddammed work," he yelled. "Where else?"

"Come," Steph told her, pulling her through the barricade. "The wiz."

Zimmer acknowledged the novelty of her presence with a slow, deep bow, though no hat. "*Mademoiselle* ..."

She really was an occasion. Her hair was brighter somehow, shining in the afternoon sunlight pouring through the windows of Zimmer's kitchen. And her eyes had shifted toward the greener side of hazel, as green as a sectioned lime, with little bits of brown dotted throughout. "And those teeth!" That's what Zimmer had never noticed before, maybe because of the ghostly supermarket lighting. She had big, white, "Chiclet" teeth, especially noticeable as she glided the length of the kitchen, fidgeting, smiling broadly, at everyone, everything.

"Can I help?"

"Oh, no, no, no. Wouldn't hear of it."

"I can do *something*."

Zimmer stood there, towel draped over his shoulder, knife in hand. Steph could recognize his covetous stance, as he huddled over his work. "Come on, Angie. How about a beer?"

"*That*," Zimmer said, "everyone can do."

She let Steph drag her into the other room, to the coolers.

They all congregated near the coolers, strategically close to the table, just the other side of the kitchen wall. Randy had stacked the cases of reserves in the corner. The table was set with its unmatched tableware, dishes, napkins. Everyone gravitated from the coolers, fresh beer in hand, toward a chair, awaiting Zimmer, and the food.

His was a measured absence. The Feasts were drawn out to excruciating lengths, "Because they're a tribute," more than a meal. By delaying the instance until it was completely ripe, maybe he could take some of the sting out its eventual passing. "That's the problem," celebrating the now and yet fighting back its passing, "like a linebacker fighting off blocker after blocker trying to string out a power sweep..." It wasn't so much an attempt to defy the future, but just to slow fate's tidal designs at entropy, at obscuring his presence. "It's just trying to pin the moment to its *exact* place," trying to allow potentially defining moments to become. "They're so often missed, like gulping good cognac!" He held back until he could absolutely say, "It's time," without any question.

The Feasts were a commemoration of now, both the immediate now, and all the collective nows that got them there in the first place. It was a celebration of their individual ancestry, however that had managed to keep them alive long enough to make the occasion, and their collective ancestry. "To the Romans, who gave us the arch, the oratory, and olive oil!" Zimmer said, and then amended his usual entrance speech, "And bouillabaisse."

"To bouilla--" Mickey started, then said, "to baseball soup."

"A bowl of fuggin bases awright," Frank grumbled as bowls

were passed around the table. "Cheers."

They started with Mr. Boyles' soup naturally enough, sloshed over hunks of toasted French bread. It was the meal's logical starting point, of course, but it would've been first no matter what, "Even if he'd brought cheesecake." Gradually realizing the importance of applauding effort, Zimmer could be counted on to overreact, keeping the traditional progression of courses jumbled, flexible, in appreciation of Mr. Boyles' contribution, no matter what it might have been. It was a way to both manipulate the absolutes of entertaining protocol—he thought you had to manipulate absolutes at every opportunity, "Or they'll damn sure manipulate you,"—and a way to draw attention to the dish itself. Attention to both Mr. Boyles' effort, and the ease of the process, his diminutive, "Could you use an extra appetizer?"

"That was exactly right," all that Zimmer required from any of them. He wanted only that everyone brought themselves— from Bruce's conducting the beer flow, heavy-handedly steering the events so that they all kept up with his appetite, to Frank's basic irritability: He speared an oyster, asking, "What's this?" With no answer, and not knowing, Frank left a pile of drying fish in his bowl. Angela picked at hers, though seemingly content, much like Mickey. Zimmer might worry, or balk, at risking new personalities to the feasts, afraid of tipping the balance—constantly aware of those endpoints, knowing that you had to stop tinkering with something that clearly worked— which is what his "big fucking deal" had been all about last night, whether they were talking about Angela, or Jack, or anyone else. But he was also leery of losing spontaneity, what started the feasts in the first place, and so had to trust Steph, "That unconsciousness of his," even if it bordered on the dangerous, sometimes.

"Wow," Steph said. "That's great!" reaching for another bit of bread to sop up some broth. "Spicy."

"Kinda minty."

"Saffron," Mr. Boyles told them. "Caught me. Should have realized there was no true substitute for fresh fish."

"It's wonderful."

"Absolutely."

Bruce finished first, always, and got up to clear away those preliminary bowls. Zimmer got up too, for the other courses, and then Angela stood, saying, "Let me help."

"No, no," Steph said, easing her back down. "You're the guest of honor," he said, as she blushed, nearly as red as her hair. "You sit, reign," bowing. "Must be those teeth," he decided, inducing all the genuflecting going on, following Zimmer.

"I never thought she'd be so quiet," he said, handing Steph the beans and the tray of onion rings.

"Well, she's not, really. Maybe she's just a little intimidated right now."

"Oh, of course," Zimmer said, leading them out of the kitchen. "She's not used to *real* men."

"Jackass."

"Here you go, Frank," Zimmer said, placing the platter of turkey before the boss.

Frank had assumed the responsibility of carving, whenever it was necessary. "Naturally," Steph said. Frank was a father, was used to sitting at the head of the table, was used to conducting events, "Of course he'd do the cutting," would signal the actual beginning of the meals.

Zimmer thought Frank coveted the position merely because it was a position to covet, nothing more. "So what?" that he had children. "All that means is that he sired offspring. *Fathering's* different." Zimmer would have preferred Mr. Boyles do the carving, though the old man would never even reach for the knife. "If Frank's supposed to be some kind of father figure, how come he *doesn't* ask if he can bring his kids, huh?"

"You don't really want any of us to start explaining ourselves, do you?"

"No, no."

"Besides, it's a *round* table," Steph said, rotating his arm in a wide, counterclockwise circle. "Remember how important that was?" taking Zimmer all the way back to the first dinner day, letting on that he remembered a lot more than he admitted, which halted the argument, if nothing else. "It's just his habit, that's all," Frank's wanting to be at the center of things.

As a Lumper, he was allowed habits, of course. It was something of a test, though, of Zimmer's inflexible insistence that the Lumpers bring just themselves to the dinners. Zimmer couldn't ever decide if Frank's covetousness, evident in the way he ate, even, obvious in the way he watched the bowls and platters circulate the table, watching everyone else's portions, calculating how many rolls he should take, was the result of having been deprived earlier in life or was because he now felt himself especially deserving, his authoritative, supervisory self bleeding into all parts of his life.

He had a habit, too, of passing his own definitive judgments on the meals: "This is pretty good, Zimbarco."

"Gee, Frank, thanks."

"Truly, Anthony," Mr. Boyles told him, only now that the subject had been breached.

Bruce grunted by way of compliment. He was using the rolls as bulldozers, mixing everything together into pile after pile and scooping it into his mouth. While that sight might disturb Zimmer, because it was Bruce, and because the table was round—and not one of those long banquet tables, where, if they were at opposite ends, Bruce might have been ten feet farther away, in another room, or another time zone—it was all right. "Just right."

Angela continued to peck at her food, but with a delicate hand, not the dismissiveness of Frank's selective eating. She was just sizing down the larger, typically Lumper portions Steph had given her. "It's kind of nice, though, kind of a balance all its own," Zimmer decided.

"Unbelievable!" Steph said, stopping for breath, holding his hands up. "Zimmer, where did you get *this* idea?"

"I had Frank's help."

"Hmm?" Frank said, his mouth stuffed.

"Only at Fill," Randy said, examining a forkful of turkey.

"What?" Bruce said, before pushing the last pile of massacred meal onto the soupspoon he'd retrieved, watching Randy. "I've heard of barbecued turkey before."

"Oh yeah? Stuffed with coleslaw?"

Bruce licked his lips, the corners of his mouth.

"Goddammit," Zimmer said. "What do we tell him, every time?"

Bruce doesn't pay all that much attention to exactly what's on his plate before he starts his demolition of it.

"I was hungry!"

"Right."

"And these rolls," Steph continued, rising from his seat. "A masterpiece. The delicate flavor of chili..."

Mickey challenged, "Delicate?"

"The zest of just enough jalapeno."

"Zest?"

"And still, the staff of life." Holding the bit of bread above his head with both hands, Steph lifted his face and dropped it in. "A-men."

"Ste-eph," Angela said, at his benediction.

But he wasn't done yet. He sat back down, drained another beer with a long, slow draw, and put his decidedly Lumperish punctuation on the meal. He burped.

It wasn't a forced or exaggerated burp, just a burp. It wasn't supposed to shock or disgust Angela, wasn't supposed to drive her away. But he looked at her sheepishly, aware that she was staring at him. He thought again that it might have been a good idea to explain at least a little of what went on at the dinners. But whenever he'd rehearsed the explanations in his head, they always devolved into explanations of his having to explain, "Which sound an awfully lot like excuses," a habit he was trying to get out of.

They'd tried explaining that particular practice once, in fact, after Frank had commented on how unacceptable their behavior was. Steph had tried to tell Frank that it was an ancient Chinese tradition, that if you genuinely enjoyed the meal, you showed it, "By leaning back in your chair, loosening your belt and belching, vigorously, boisterously," an unmistakable expression of how good the eating had been.

"Bullshit," Frank had insisted. "Chinese don't wear belts."

"Frank, you're missing--"

"Actually," Mr. Boyles said, rescuing Steph, "it's not a total fabrication."

It was then that they went on to discuss the gestalt of explaining things, how that robbed their actual deeds of their energy, their immediacy, and vowed to stop the practice, each of them trying to surpass the other as they took turns burping around the table.

Mickey trumpeted, "Brrraaappp!" summoning, somehow, from his small body, the definitive burp to end all burps.

He looked a little shaken by the outburst and Zimmer had to steady him in his chair.

Mr. Boyles shook his head, said, "All right, Bruce, I suppose it is time," always a little disgusted by the practice, tradition or no, and always unwilling to participate.

Still, Steph thought he owed Angela something by way of justification, so that she wouldn't think they were being animals, "At least not animals without reason."

"It's like Zimmer's speech," about heritage, the Romans.

Didn't really matter. She was watching Bruce. He was circling the table, clearing it little by little with each revolution. He balanced two picked over platters side by side along his right forearm. Plates on top of that, pushing leftovers into one growing heap for Whomee. Somehow he resisted the temptation of cheating the cat, what with the pile of food mixed together just the way he liked it. Silverware he threaded into the fingers of his right hand. Layer after layer, circling counterclockwise, three, four times, he accumulated the entire mess, everyone handing over their own plates, then fork, maintaining his order, and placing each item where he directed, with a left index finger, or a chin, or just a grunt.

Steph talked throughout the process, keeping up with Bruce's progress, smoothly handing over Angela's dishes, then his own. "We come into this world and from the very beginning the people around us—nurses, mothers, fathers, big brothers, sisters, babysitters—they're always, after every meal, burping us. And they praise us for it, Ooo, that was a *big* one! But then, all of a sudden, we're not supposed to burp anymore? It's rude?"

She didn't look convinced. She looked on the verge of shock. But then, as the rest of the table burst into applause, as Bruce managed the feat without breaking anything, "For the *eighth* consecutive Feast of St. Fill-up!" sidestepping into the kitchen with his load, she snapped out of it.

As the rest of them remained sitting, even settled into more relaxed, more expansive postures in their chairs, she asked, "Isn't anyone going to help him clean that up?"

"He's not going to clean anything," Zimmer told her.

"That won't be cleaned up for about a week," Frank said.

"You're kidding," she said, standing. "Right?"

"Of course he is," Steph said, moving after her.

"They'll be done tomorrow; Tuesday, tops," Zimmer said.

Bruce came out of the kitchen and took up his task as bartender, clearing away empties, opening refills. Mr. Boyles stood, brushing remnants of the meal from the table, and reached across to Randy. He pulled a wrapped deck of cards from his shirt pocket and handed them to the old man. Angela peeked into the kitchen, at the stacks of dirty dishes and pots and pans teetering on any available counter space.

"You sure?"

"Don't worry about it," Steph said, pulling her back to the table. "It's game time."

"Game time?"

Mr. Boyles tore the cellophane off the cards.

"Oh. Well, you know, I don't really like to..."

"Don't like?"

"I'll just--"

Zimmer jumped up as she moved for the kitchen, grabbing two bottles of beer from the table, he blocked the doorway, crossing the bottle-necks. "I *forbid* thee!"

"Angie, listen," Steph said, stepping between them. "It

would be impossible for him to play while someone was working in his kitchen."

Zimmer nodded.

"Do you want to take me home?"

Steph considered the possibility, until Bruce started, "Aw, Angie, don't go," clasping one of her knees.

"Come on," Steph told her. "We'll be partners. It'll be fun."

Mickey stood, and tried to calm Zimmer down, prying the bottles out of his hands. Zimmer was glaring at Steph, wondering if Steph had briefed her on anything.

He'd meant to; planned to tell her about the toasting, the near-orgy of food and drink, and then the poker. He didn't think, in all the commotion, that she'd mind. And if she did, "Would explanations have helped? Probably not." He'd wait, watch, find out after the fact what the effects were. "How else are you supposed to know?"

The game had become as much a part of the dinners as anything else. When the table was cleared, fresh beer handed out, the cards were cut, and Mr. Boyles dealt the first hand. "Draw, gentlemen," he said, "and lady," always the first to deal, both because he was the elder statesman at the table, and poker had been his other contribution to the dinners.

In fact, as far as the poker went, Steph would like to have had a chance, some afternoon at the bar, say, to have Mr. Boyles explain for Angela how the game had become such an integral part of the feasts, why it was so sacred to Zimmer. Then she would be as enthusiastic as Mickey or Bruce, as reverent as Randy, as adamant as Frank, as possessed as Zimmer.

"Five card," Mr. Boyles said, dealing slowly around the table. "With one-eyed jacks."

Adding to the solemnity, Mr. Boyles always played the same game, always introduced in the same manner, again, like Zimmer's, "To the Romans..."

"Life's a draw," he said quietly, to the cadence of his dealing, "but one-eyed jacks are wild."

Always, always the same. And it always reminded Steph of

his days as an altar boy, witnessing the priest's preparation and then celebration of the mass: always the same sequencing to the vestments, the same folds of the linens, the same gestures—creasing the host, raising the chalice—the same movements about the altar, the same cadences to the Latin incantations. The rigidness had bored Steph then, twelve, thirteen years ago now. His attention went elsewhere, always, yearning to wander, explore, imagine. He saw now the necessity of the ritual, agreed with Zimmer's inflexible attitude toward the game, saw now the stability and peacefulness contained within the exactness, knew the comfort of watching Mr. Boyles slowly shuffle and deal with that weightiness as if each time was the first and last time he'd ever handle the cards.

Always the same, "Life's a draw..."

Frank, of course, played a different game each time he dealt. First everything he could think of wild, then nothing at all. He had to, since he played the game for money. They all played with an ante, with money at stake. But only Frank played the game to make money, which was the opposite approach to take, according to the gospel of poker according to Mr. Boyles—who, coincidentally or not, usually took home the largest pots, one of his few sources of income.

"Do you know the different hands?" Steph asked Angela.

The table was void of everything but beer bottles, everyone's respective estates, and an ashtray shared by Frank and Mr. Boyles. The great round slab, with its unmatched surface had finally found its purpose. It could be a poker table easily enough and not have to hide beneath a cloth or canvas covering.

"It's a great poker table."

"Truly."

The Lumpers sat there, staggered in their different chairs, spreading from the feast, contemplating. Steph had his chair pushed back a little and cocked a few degrees to allow Angela to look over his right shoulder. She'd pulled up almost on top of his thigh, so that her presence, her fragrance was more than a little distracting. Mr. Boyles sat to their left, holding the remainder of the deck, rubbing the surface with his thumb. Next to him was Frank, glaring past Mr. Boyles at Steph, gnawing on one of his fowl stoagies, moving it back and forth across his mouth, grumbling. He was waiting desperately to raise again, unhappy with Steph's chattering, his holding up the bet. Mickey was next, and then Zimmer, almost directly across from Mr. Boyles. Randy was on Zimmer's left, formidable himself, but too frequently overlooked. Finally, Bruce, drunk again, lecherous, again, trying his damnest to flirt with Angela.

"Four of a kind, full house, two pair," she was reciting.

"Good, good, that's enough for now," Steph said, adding fifty cents to the pot.

"Finally."

"Too much for me," Mr. Boyles said, folding, not even waiting to see a draw.

"Have to admire a poker decision like that."

Not Frank. He plowed on, "Cos'everyonenother coin," he said, then taking the stoagie out of his mouth, "Course, you could all drop."

"You wish."

They all stayed, calling for cards. Frank took three, as did Mick. Zimmer took two. So did Randy. Bruce held up four fingers, uncalculating, and uncaring. He played as long as he didn't mind losing, and then he usually quit without complaining. Steph said, "Just one."

Angela whispered, "Why'd you get rid of the queen?"

He'd had a queen, a jack, an ace, and two sixes. It wasn't a one-eyed jack but he kept it all the same. "Can't hold bitches," he answered over his shoulder.

He heard her kind of snort, hoping it was suppressed giggling, then when she reached for the drawn card, said, "No, wait. Give it time. Watch."

Steph scanned the players. He used to think that Frank was by nature a terrible poker player, frowning and grumbling as easily as he did, "But Frank frowns at everything." Zimmer was smirking, and looked up as soon Steph was watching. "Could be a long day."

"Huh?"

He was remembering another of Mr. Boyles' commandments: Poker won't forsake the poker player who doesn't stake too much on any one hand. "There're too many variables to depend on any one hand." Nothing to do but roll with it, or fold early.

The bets came around again. No one dropped, nor raised hysterically, "An unreadable situation." Steph slid the new card on top of the other four. "Shh." He separated them, six, six, jack, ace, jack. One-eyed jack of hearts. He stifled a gasp as Angela squeezed his thigh. "Fifty more," he said, mostly composed.

Frank was frowning, of course, huffing and puffing, matching the bet. Mickey dropped, slapping his cards down. Zimmer was still grinning. Even Randy was studying Steph, which was most unnerving. Bruce, blessed, goofy Bruce, dropped a couple of cards out of his hand, spread them out on the table for everyone to see, "Anything?" and only then dropped.

Steph considered the check, thinking maybe Frank would bump the bet on his own, but said, "What the hell," tossing two more coins into the pile. "Again."

"Shit," Frank grumbled, but matched him.

"Must be Angie," Zimmer said, declining this last raise.

Steph didn't have to worry about Frank. He'd hang with almost anything through the early hands. Finally, Randy laid his cards down.

"Three sixes, Frank," he said, adding above everyone's groaning, "With a bullet."

Frank threw his cards down, reaching for his cigar. "Beats the hell outa my tens."

"Frank?" Zimmer said. "Tens?"

"Yeah, yeah, tens," he said, snatching up the deck. "Lessplay summan's boker. Stud."

"Stud? What's that?"

"No, not what. Who's that?" Steph corrected her.

Bruce screamed, volunteering quickly to explain.

She turned from Bruce, her face coloring, and slapped Steph, before reaching for his beer.

"Watch," he said, apologetically.

Frank slid the down card to everyone and quickly followed with the first up card.

"Hey!"

"No, no, it's all right. That's the game. Stud. Three cards are dealt face up."

Mickey drew a queen, Zimmer a ten. Randy, lucky seven, and Bruce got a six. Steph got another six. Mr. Boyles showed a jack, and Frank gave himself a nine. Mickey started the bet, minimum quarter, and everyone followed. Frank started all over again with another up card.

"Garbage," he said to Mickey. "Nothing for you either Zimbarco. Looking red, Mr. Tender. Boo-boo is straightening. That's nice. Another six—damn, Abrams' got em coming out his ears. An ace for old Boyles. And a king for the dealer, still diamonds." Frank played stud often, probably just so he could chatter. "Your bet Abrams."

"Why?"

"Pair of sixes," he told her, gently lifting the card in the hole: Ace. Maybe she was a charm. "Quarter."

Everyone followed, pushing the pot. Some hesitated, but everyone stayed, optimistically. That was another reason Frank played stud, for its relatively larger pots. Everyone was willing to pay for at least that fourth card, after two whole rounds of betting. Things could turn pretty quickly for the unusually lucky, plus you had a better look at everyone else's fortunes. Only a heavy handed better could kill a stud pot.

"We're concerned with those flushes, of course," Steph said, though only concerned enough to mention them. "Hard to tell with the others yet. Everyone thinks they have something, at this point, and they probably do. But we've got something showing, so they're watching us."

"Just us?"

"Well, no." He could easily lose himself in those green eyes, her breath. "Usually, it's not an exceptional hand that takes the money. But with these guys, there's so much of a blend. There are masters, or near enough, who could bust you on any given hand. And then the unconscious ones, they can be just as dangerous."

Frank cleared his throat.

"Which one are we?"

Before he could resist, he whispered into her hair, "You just keep those fingers crossed."

He heard her gasp this time, unmistakably. "You keep your mind on that money," she said, moving his hand from her lap back into his own. "I'll worry about my fingers, thank you."

Then he had to look, to catch what expression he could from her profile. But he could only see half a smirk, as she responded obediently to Frank clearing his throat again. "Jesus."

"Still garbage," Frank said, directly to Steph, dealing Mickey's card. "Another ten for Zimbarco—the whole damn apartment is blessed. The cat could win today! Parsons is still hearts. Maybe an inside straight, Brucey. Sorry, lover boy, only half a six this time. And... Another ace. Hmm. For the dealer," he said, rounding the table, "shit, a spade. Your bet, Boyles."

"Ordinarily," Steph said, quietly, "The bettor would jump at this last good chance to pile up the kitty."

Mr. Boyles hesitated just long enough, before saying, "Fifty."

Mickey dropped, not having spent too much. Zimmer bumped it another quarter. Randy stayed. And Bruce dropped, probably more because he was out of beer than yielding to the odds of filling an inside straight.

Seventy-five to Steph.

"Can I?" Angela asked, holding three quarters out over the pile on the table.

"Sure," he said, trying his best to be nonchalant. "We're in."

"Down and dirty," Frank said, after Mr. Boyles anteed up.

The players, all with their differing styles, studied the last card, by whatever ritual they thought would bring them the winner. There was silence, thick, solid silence around the table, until Bruce, behind them, restocking the cooler, burped.

"Sorry."

"Goddamm-big."

Steph peeled up his card. Ten.

"Fifty," Mr. Boyles said.

Frank decided not to squander any more money, folded, then joined Bruce at the cooler, trying to look at everyone's cards on the way by.

"Okay," Zimmer said, riding.

"Dollar," Randy said. "Steph?"

"Nope. Not me."

"Well then, let us go fifty more," Mr. Boyles said.

"Goodbye."

"Coward," Randy charged. "Another half."

"Whoa," Steph cried. "This is serious." He was pretty sure Randy had the flush, and Mr. Boyles would drop. "Good fight, but fifty more cents could be fifty cents saved."

Mr. Boyles glanced up at Steph before pushing two more quarters along the tabletop. "Well, Randall? What have we got?"

"Hmm," Randy said, breaking into a grin. "Pair of fours."

"Regrettable," Mr. Boyles told him, stuffing his cards into the deck, pulling the pile of coins toward himself. "But I thank you."

"Well?" Steph asked. "Did you have the boat?"

"Stephen, please."

"He didn't show his cards?"

"He didn't have to," Zimmer answered her.

"Why not?"

"Because he beat Randy's fours with what he had showing."

"So did we."

"But we didn't pay to find that out, did we?" Zimmer continued, though now he was addressing his comments to Steph, not Angela.

"Is that fair?"

"That's poker," Mickey told her.

Steph added, "That's life," tapping her knee.

"Well said."

When he'd first introduced the game at the feasts, Mr. Boyles had told them that all they needed to know to conduct their lives could be gleaned from the cards. "Above all else," he'd said, dealing out phantom hands at the time to illustrate his point, "don't throw good money after bad, Because there is no fairness, no balance," directly at Zimmer. As long as they remembered that rule, they could last a lot longer, maybe even long enough for a little luck to get around to them, longer than the craftiest of players who was loose with their money.

"Anyone with any sense would've dropped after his first up card," Randy said.

"Even *I* knew that," Bruce said.

"That's right!" Steph said. "It was a jack."

One-eyed jack. That had been Mr. Boyles' other lesson on poker, the one-eyed jacks. "Jack of spades," he said, holding up the card, "is for death. But of course, dying takes at least a little bit of living, true?" He reshuffled the cards, pulling out the other one, "Jack of hearts. Happiness, or at least its potential. Life, death, happiness." Then he dealt the first real hand of poker at Fill. "Life's a draw," he'd said that first time, showing them the backs of the cards, placing one in front of each player, round and round the table. "But one-eyed jacks are wild."

"Awright, awright, les'sgut-out the mumbo jumbo," Frank said, then, as now. "Les-sget on wid-it," he demanded, yelling at Mickey, "Whas-sit gonna be kid?"

"Hmm." Mickey wasn't all that fond of the game, period, and certainly wasn't endeared by any of Frank's badgering.

But he pressed on. "Come on, come on. Der ain't dat goddamm-many."

"All right, asshole," Mickey said, holding his beer up, not the cards. "Let's play baseball, Frank."

"Hah!" Zimmer said, standing, reaching to rub Mickey's head. "Perfect. Drink up shriners." He could see Angela wondering, and could only hope she was asking, "In February?"

"Explain *that*!"

Indulgence was the operative word. Actually over-indulgence was closer to the point. Mickey called the game, set the rules, had them drinking at regular intervals, whether they bet, folded, whatever. "Baseball!" It was perfectly mindless poker. Blind stud, it was sometimes called. Seven cards were dealt each player, face down. It would have been nine—a baseball team—with fewer players. Each of them, in succession, turned over their cards until they bested the previous high hand. And then they bet. Sometimes the pots got huge. And sometimes the players would go through all seven cards without revealing anything that even resembled a poker hand.

Bruce picked up on it, modified the game with as many wild cards as the table would allow, so that together, at least twice during every circuit of the deal, they'd call, "Baseball!"

It didn't matter, not to anyone but Frank. While it was true that blind stud neutralized any skills or tactics, it was poker. It satisfied those least requirements. And it was fun, so the one-eyed jacks were appeased. That had become the Lumper system of priorities on dinner days, which is maybe the one reason Angela's presence hadn't been any more disruptive than it had.

Frank tried to protest. It would be a few more weeks before he could make the killing he thought he saw the opportunity for at the poker games. After a couple of baseball hands—the whole table drinking after each player finished turning their cards, drinking after Bruce's special hands: a ten high winning hand was a shutout, "Drink!"; three aces was a triple play: "Drink!" A five card flush, or better, was an all-star team: "Drink!"—no one could be counted on for much in the way of recognizable poker. The baseball hands got to be kind of a relief. They didn't have to think, certainly. All they had to do was turn over cards and drink their beers dry whenever Mickey or Bruce told them to.

They wouldn't listen to Frank's protests, nor would they pay much attention to Angela and her misgivings. "Do I have to drink the whole bottle?" While they might have had more reason to try to accommodate her, to listen to her bargaining, "How about if I drink the first time, and Steph the next. We are a team?" it was out of their hands, really. Indulgence negated reason. "With enough guiltless indulgence," Zimmer told her, measuring his words, "there's no need for dispensation."

Bruce leaned over, innocently. "Rules is rules, don't you see? I'd like to help, honest," and then he'd forget what he was going to offer, and why.

Beyond indulgence, beyond reason.

The last hand of Feast day turned to night was another five card draw, with no limits on the betting. It got at least unreasonable, as Zimmer and Steph, the last two hanging on throughout the hand, eyed each other.

"Stephie old boy, this here's a real Mexican stand-off," Zimmer said. He'd just placed Whomee, fat, lazy, sufficiently sedated Whomee, on the table, representing the entire cat kingdom. He was raising Steph's personal ancestry, high stakes indeed—a wallet sized replica of his birth certificate. Since all their money went into a common household account, more or less, shuffling cash back and forth between them was pointless. They'd had to resort to other forms of wealth since it was just the two of them, which was also how they'd gotten everyone else to drop. Only on the last, unlimited hand would that be possible.

"I'll see your cat, and raise you," Steph said, looking around, finally scooping a handful of soil from a dying plant in the corner, careful not to get any on Whomee, "Earth."

"Oh, Steph. Nice," Bruce said. "He'll have to call that one."

"You kidding? I'll see your earth, and raise you," Zimmer said, reaching into his pocket, pulling out a crumpled candy bar wrapper, "Mars."

"Where the hell'd you get that!" Mickey cried.

"I know a guy, or two," Zimmer told him, with a double-visioned twinkle in his eye, winking in Randy's direction.

"Whoa," Steph said. "Deep, deep shit. Let's see," he paused, looking for bounty, deliverance. Looking, finally, at Angela.

"Oh, no, no, no," she said, leaning back from him. "You're not putting me up on that table."

"But you're heaven," he tried.

"Wud-dyou ged-on wid-dit for I puke."

"That's so sweet," Bruce said.

"Don't you trust me?"

"Hah!"

"In that case, I'll be forced to call," he said, placing one worn Converse on the table next to Whomee.

"What the hell is that?"

"That, my friends, is the universe, the cosmos. The ozone!"

"Well said, Stephen."

"Okay, it's okay," Zimmer told Mickey, pushing Steph's sneaker back a little and then showing his cards. "Three lovely ladies."

"Bitches!" Steph screamed. "I knew it. Bitches, every time."

"Ste-eph," Angela said, one last time, before reaching for his bottle again.

Zimmer drained his, as the victor should, but then had to squint one eye to see what Angela was doing. Then he snickered to himself, switching eyes, becoming one, and then the other one-eyed jack, until it made him dizzy, until he had to just hold the latest beer that Bruce had pushed into his hand. After that, memory faded.

For instance, he remembered refolding his trusty Mars wrapper, saving it. And he thinks he remembers trying to get Whomee into the same pocket, but that would have been stupid, right? "But where else could the scratches have come from?" He remembered selling Steph's sneaker back to him so he could take Angela home, she posting its bail. "Oh, yeah, I remember *that*!" remembered watching her arch her back and slide a hand into her front jeans pocket, looking for money. "And fucking Bruce," truly stupid Bruce, staring at her lap, asking, "Got change for a five?"

She was the only one who didn't laugh, he remembered that.

He remembered, while they all filed out of the apartment—

Bruce and Mickey still calling, "Baseball! Baseball!"—he kept trying to get up out of his chair, Whomee's chair really, trying to be a good and proper host, but falling back into it each time. He was worried some about how they would all get home. Bruce and Mickey would have to squint opposite eyes. "That'll work, right?" he asked Whomee.

Frank would be fine. "Pissed off," but fine. Randy would take care of Mr. Boyles, he could be sure of that. Who's left? Steph. "And Angie..."

He leaned back in the chair, pushing it against the wall. "Where did that smile get to?" he asked, tracing his tongue along his teeth. Either his teeth or his tongue had gone numb.

After all that, "After all the other shit," she had resorted to grocery store Angela. "Pity," that she couldn't let go all the way.

It was so simple. "Sooo fucking simple..." It was one-eyed jacks, he thought, closing his left eye. "You hide from one, from death, you forfeit the other," he said, switching eyes. "Like beer," he told Whomee, bringing his chair forward again. Whomee lifted his head a little and then settled back into his snooze. "Ah, what the fuck do *you* know."

"It's as simple as this beer bottle," he tried again, though he still couldn't get much reaction from the cat. He couldn't keep a tight enough grasp on his thoughts to make much sense to himself even. "Grasp. That's it. Bottle, grasp." He was fading.

He remembered hearing Steph stumble and bitch up the stairs, as always, and checked to see if Whomee's chair was near enough to the door, and empty. "It's gone!" he hollered, before remembering he was sitting in it. Then he laughed, chuckling softly to himself, his eyes closed, "You are a drunk motherfucking Lumper, Zim-ber," before looking to see Steph standing in the doorway, hugging the doorjamb.

He strolled through the room, either veering or dancing, humming idiotically, before falling into his chair opposite Zimmer at the table.

After a long pause, Zimmer said, "Well, maestro?"

"Well," Steph mimicked, wagging his head. "What did you

think of that?"

Zimmer considered the question a long time. "Think of what?" he said.

"Of Angela."

"Oh. Her."

Zimmer wanted to resume the discussion he'd been having with himself, wanted to detail for Steph some of the things that had seemed momentous at the time, surely, but were a blur now. He propped his elbows on the table, squeezing his half full bottle of Iron City, and finally asked, "Has she got any handles?"

Steph, his head resting on the table, couldn't make much sense out of the question, unless it was an anatomical inquiry. That didn't seem likely, but he answered, "Sure," anyway.

Zimmer sat back, collapsing, sighing, "Un-huh."

11. Easter

CHANGES of season in Tripoli were gradual and mild, even if the seasons themselves weren't. The many months of winter, if they ever were relief from the stickiness of summer, became a series of oppressively bitter days, short grey days that set in hard and fast and seemed unwilling to ever relinquish their grip. There might be solitary days, every five or six weeks, breezy days, when a reprieve might sneak through, when the temperature climbed a few degrees and everybody broke out the lightweight jackets, ready to celebrate the approach of the solstice. But winter lashed back with yet another storm, with layer after layer of continued harshness. It had a lot to do with being up in those hills, exposed on western slopes, where only the sturdiest of survivors ought to camp out—lone birds of prey, mountain goats, wandering lions.

But there was a cessation in the frosting of each northwestern storm system that passed through, every three or four days, either on short trips from the Great Lakes, or all the way from Siberia. There was a gradual ease in the extent of the chill, if not the regularity of its occurrence. The days, while still biting cold, allowed for some thawing, for a slight breach in the onslaught.

Gently, a moderate layer sifted into the brutalizing winds, and slowly took over. It was mixed in there, riding the trade winds teasing from the Gulf, and could be detected long before anything turned green. They were frequently overlooked, though, those earliest harbingers of spring, because of the customary wintertime posture in Tripoli, slouched over, protective, shoulder scrunching, an attempt to slide your ears into your shirt collar.

But if you lifted your head, cleared the passageways, beyond the cold, mingled in with the ice-picks torturing your sinuses, it was there, that sweet freshness of spring.

"Huuup..." Zimmer said, filling his lungs, arching his back. "It's there."

Maybe because he was from central New York, a few degrees of longitude to the north, he knew what to look for. There, spring was still many weeks, maybe a few snowstorms away. Inhabitants there grew to be good scouts, desperate by late March, early April, not wanting to miss a single moment of the season.

He stood at his kitchen windows, drinking coffee. "It's out there," he repeated, flinging open as many of the windows as he could. The more of this morning's sweet air he let in Fill, the more easily revived everyone would be, the more comfortable they'd feel about abandoning their warm cocoon of sleep.

Comfort, though, at Fill, was a matter of coincidence, even with factoring in what should have been inflexible absolutes.

"I mean, think of the limited space involved. Why shouldn't a supposedly comfortable space, *any* comfortable space, always be comfortable?"

At Fill, comfort was independent of the spot. The determining factor was the seeker of comfort. And at Fill, seekers of comfort covered the entire spectrum of needs. There was Whomee, who could always find a spot, even if he had to search and search for it. He'd wander around the apartment, his chair, the window ledge, behind the water heater, scouring the rooms for the likely spot. And then once found, it had to be conditioned. He'd circle and pat and scratch on it before he'd finally curl up. After all of his ritual, though, he'd sleep soundly, several times a day.

No matter what method Zimmer might employ, he couldn't seem to find an entirely restful position anywhere. Maybe he just didn't have the perseverance of Whomee. He'd flop into bed each day, not bothering to alter his routine at all, toss around for a few hours, ultimately abandoning any effort to soundly sleep and succumb to the day, rising. His pattern of work, drink, and little sleep should've reduced him to an exhausted shell of a human being, but he maintained somehow. It helped, no doubt, that he spent so much restful time at his windows, watching, relaxing. Zimmer could allow his mind to release the tension and anxiety that sleep was supposed to dissipate simply by gazing out over Dagaton Woods, and Tripoli.

And of course Steph, "Fucking Steph," could fall anywhere, anytime, and sleep any number of hours. Once he was down, he was down, and it took some form of otherwise rude behavior to rouse him again. Zimmer was finding out though, that in Steph's case, rudeness was redefined, because the only way to retrieve him from his depths of unconsciousness was through abrupt treatment. Most of the time it was passive, only quasi-rude behavior that Zimmer utilized to invade Steph's fortress of sleep. Most of the time his cooking and baking would work their way into Steph's deepest dreams. But on days when he wasn't cooking, when they had their early appointments, he had to assault other senses, other weak spots. Those days he wasn't so careful about the volume of the radio. He welcomed bright clear sunshine, or fresh breezes into the apartment.

"What the hell are you doing with all these windows open?"

"Refreshing, isn't it?"

"Like an ice cube down my back. Jesus." He stood in the kitchen doorway, clinging to his blanket. His left, leeward eye still closed, clinging sleep.

"Glad you're up."

"But not surprised, I hope."

"Coffee?"

"Sure."

"Here you go," Zimmer said, donning his customary cheeriness. "Let's get psyched, huh. Big day."

"What, big? It's Friday, right."

"Yes, yes, yes..."

"Mmm."

"But not just any Friday."

"Jesus," Steph said, turning back into the living room. That's why he had such a tough time keeping up. Just when he thought he'd figured out the schedule, Zimmer added a little extra emphasis, even if only cosmetic, a sprig of parsley on the side.

"Today's a *big* Friday. A Friday we've all been waiting for."

"Okay, okay," Steph said, slumping into Whomee's chair, pulling the blanket over his head. "Just tell me how much more time I've got," thinking he was going to snooze some more.

"No time!" Zimmer shouted. "It's already past time. We got to go check on our pregnant friend now."

"Right," Steph said, picking a shirt out of the produce box of partially clean clothes that Zimmer held in front of him. "It's always time," he said. "It's never time."

"That's right, never, never time," Zimmer instructed, tossing him his sneakers.

"Ten till, right?" Steph said, throwing off the blanket, holding his arms up like a watch in an advertisement.

"Right again," Zimmer cried, looping the sleeves of Steph's jacket around his neck, escorting him from Fill, pulling his arms back down to his sides so that he'd fit through the front door. "See, I knew you could do it."

It was never, ever time at Fill. The only clock in the apartment was Zimmer's radio, but those hands were frozen in time—"Since when,Boston? Vermont?"—frozen and shrugging ten till two. What updates on the passage of time they needed they'd rely on radio DJs. Otherwise, like the clock, they'd shrug indifferently, "Ten till."

They were established and comfortable enough with their habits that they proceeded from one station to the next as religious observers might, driven by the sequence, the momentum of their circumstances. Zimmer hardly ever slept past dinner, or any other appointments. Steph slept through everything, clock or not. Time moved the same way, whether they watched it or not, so they opted irresponsibly, choosing not to be haunted by the metronomic tick, tock...

Or worse, they chose to live completely outside time, outside of reality, in the fantasy of *Incoming Flights* every other Friday afternoon. There they could don whatever alter ego they wanted, let the characters in the show act out lives otherwise inaccessible to them. It was only about two hours a month, time wise. "A negligible portion." Like everything else in those lives, because they didn't recognize it as delinquent behavior, they didn't need that kind of rationale, those excuses.

The episode opened at the Hemispheric Airlines ticket counter.

"Audrey, honey, are you all right?"

"Sure, Hank. I think so."

"What's been bothering you lately, darling?" the older man asked. "You've missed a lot of work over the last couple of months."

"Oh," she said, biting her lip.

"She's going to say it," Steph said, leaning farther over the bar, so that he wouldn't miss anything. "We're actually going to find out officially that she's knocked up."

"Stephen?"

"Yeah, but it'll be years before we find out who the father is," Mickey said.

"All right, all right, I confess," Bruce said. "I did it."

"Right."

"I'm the proud papa."

"Shh," Zimmer hissed, before Mr. Boyles could.

The scene shifted, without any revelations from Audrey, to a hospital, and they all groaned.

"What the fuck?" Mickey said. "Is she daydreaming?"

"She's always been a tease."

The camera focused on the doors of the Burn Unit at Brighton Memorial Hospital. They swung open automatically, revealing a huddle of medical folks, all in sterile, isolation garb—gowns, paper caps and masks, footies, gloves—discussing the patients occupying the ward, four or five of which could be seen in specialized beds, wrapped and bandaged.

"The primary concern with burn victims is staving off opportunistic infectious agents while the immune system and the protective tissues are given time to rejuvenate. Multiple operative grafting procedures are necessary to replace dead tissue, hopefully stimulating new growth. And yet, they have to be kept at a minimum and closely monitored, so as not to introduce catastrophic shock to an already compromised system..."

The camera view pushed past the enclave, losing their continued monotonous narrative. It hovered near one of the beds, a mostly mummified patient. Only Captain Hastings' blue eyes were visible, opened, pleading. The beeping of all his monitoring equipment seemed to cause him as much pain as his injuries as he winced at each mechanical noise.

Then his head turned and his gaze sought out the next bed to his right. The camera followed, where only Leslie's blond hair showed, spread across a white pillowcase. Her own attendant equipment, a bleeping cardiograph, the hydraulics of her respirator, kept up a conversation with the Captain's, even drowned out the murmuring of the medical team, though it seemed slightly out of synch.

"She dying?"

"Naw, can't be," Zimmer said. Steph studied his roommate, to hear what he based such a confident opinion on. "Not unless last week's surgery compromised her already shocked system, allowing for any one of the numerous opportunistic--"

"Oh, goddammit, Zimmer, can't you--"

The sound of a descending airliner rose over the sounds of the medical machines, drowning out even their bickering at the bar, while the camera lingered on the white rumple of sheets where Leslie's legs would be, whiting out the entire scene. Then the white flashed, modulating into a blinding explosion of red and yellow, followed by the timely theme music.

"When the hell are they going to stop opening with that damn crash? It's been three damn months."

"It's the season's event, Mick," Zimmer answered.

"Well," Steph said, studying the scene, "they'd better settle the issue before they wind up showing winter background in June."

"Michael Roy Conrad," a voice rang out through the clearing

smoke and confusion on the screen, "You stand charged with sabotage and multiple counts of aggravated assault. How do you now plead?"

"What a sleaze," Bruce said. "Doesn't even use his real first name."

"Damn Hollywood types," Steph said.

Mickey raised a finger at Steph, to make some point about it being just a character's name, perhaps, when Roy answered, "Not guilty." His clear voice echoed around him in the hushed courtroom, and he seemed to follow the sound, shifting his eyes to one side then the other, finally lowering his head, away from the glaring camera, focusing on his feet.

The scene faded from Roy's shoes to another pair of feet, brown cordovans, running down the sidewalk. Then the camera backed up, preceding the shoes, until three pairs of legs filled the picture, two men and a woman's. The sound of their steps was fractionated, reverberating, modulating past the sound of human feet. The echoes made it sound like something larger, an airplane...

"I am getting *so* sick of this show."

"Sick of *Incoming Flights*?" Bruce leaned forward over the bar, spying Mickey at the corner stool.

"Yeah. Sick, and tired."

"But Mick," Steph said, between the two of them, "isn't that like saying you're sick and tired of life itself?"

"What?"

The show continued, "Why Justin? Why?"

"Look, see there," Steph said, pointing to the television screen. "There're two people sitting on a bench in the middle of an airport, talking. What could be more life-like than that?"

"Nancy, listen: Your shop will have to be closed for just a little while, until you're cleared."

"Cleared? How am I to be cleared? After they connected the stuff in my store with what Peter had brought into the country?"

"I can talk to them," Justin promised. "I can testify that you were just protecting Mark, that he's the fugitive they want."

"Oh, Mark," she cried at the mention of his name, bowing her head and leaning against Justin. "Why? Why?"

She looked off into the busy terminal, the darkened windows of her shop behind where they sat. She saw passengers running, hurrying, in one direction or another, adults wrestling with bulky luggage, children scurrying to keep up with their parents.

"See? SEE?" Mickey shouted, guessing the transition. "Why can't they let her finish, let her say why she's so worried about Mark, where she thinks he is? Why do they have to go through all this stalling shit? That isn't life," he turned and hissed at Steph. "That's suspended animation."

"She's probably just horny," Bruce tried. "They can't have her say that. This is a family show."

"Shit."

"No, no, I know. Look, see how she's twitching her legs?" Zimmer told them. "I'll bet she just has to pee, and as soon as there's a commercial she's going to run to the ladies room."

Mickey buried his head on the bar, "You fuckers..."

"Gentlemen?"

The three characters that had been running down the sidewalk were stopped, huddled around a newspaper box.

"Look, there's Mark," Steph said, nudging Mickey. "We'll find out everything, don't worry."

"Steph, these people are phony. They're fictions, bad fictions," Mickey said, standing up and peering into Steph's eyes. He ran around to the end of the bar where the television hovered, climbed up on a stool and reached up to pivot the set in its brackets, showing Steph, showing all of them the wires. "Look, there's nothing here, no people, no nothing. It's all a lie!"

Bruce got up and plucked Mickey off the stool. "Mick, you're taking this way too seriously."

"Me?"

"Here it is," Peter Jamison was saying in the show, to his sister Shirley, and Mark. They were flipping through a copy of the newspaper. "Roy Conrad's arraignment is today."

"Peter, why did we have to come back here? Especially now?"

"For the trial, Shirl. You know that. To hang this son-of-a-bitch," Peter said, slapping at Roy's photo in the paper.

"Yeah!" Bruce cheered, standing directly beneath the set, still holding Mickey. "That's real, don't you think?"

"Put me down, you jerk."

"--takes my testimony to do it..." Peter continued.

"We'll all hang," Mark said, walking away.

Peter stepped after him, grabbing his shoulder. "Mark, you didn't have to come back. I told you that."

Mark spun. "Hey, Peter," swiping his hand away, "we started this together, didn't we?"

"See?" Mickey said. "Their fucking dialogue isn't even consistent. These damn characters go through so many trait changes, you bozos could do a better job than they do," he said, pushing past Bruce, walking away from the bar.

"Hey, you know, I think he's right," Zimmer said. "Want to try?"

Shirley rushed out of the background, stepping between the two men.

"Is it just me," Steph said, studying the screen, "or does everyone else on that street look kind of bleached out?"

"Yeah, turn the sound down, Randy," Zimmer said.

"Might as well," Mr. Boyles consented. "Who can possibly hear with all this chatter?"

Randy reached over the bar's lip and tweaked the volume control down.

"Hey?" Steph said.

The three characters on the screen continued down the street silently arguing among themselves until Peter stuffed the newspaper into a trash bin. Shirley, in the middle, locked an arm with each of them and then pulled them off the main thoroughfare and down a dark alley.

"Which one of you wants it tonight?" Bruce said for her, as the shot faded.

Mickey, sitting by himself at one of the tables, with his back to the bar, groaned, mumbling, "All that lummox ever thinks about..."

Back at the airport, in the ladies room, Audrey stood composing herself before the bright mirrors. She was pale, her eyes drawn, and looking sick at heart as well as feeling the effects of her early pregnancy.

"How's that for a transition, Mick?" Zimmer called.

"What? From the street to the bathroom?" Mickey answered, coming back to the bar.

"The perfect dramatic pause," Randy said, circling back behind the bar.

"Exactly," Mr. Boyles said. "Where else would one go during the commercials?"

"But she's not going?" Steph said.

"We can't show that," Zimmer told him.

"We?"

"We," Zimmer repeated for Mick, "can only *allude* to that kind of thing," zooming an imaginary camera down on Mickey, and Steph. "Show the stall door or something."

"That's right," Bruce said. "Pregos go all the time. Everybody knows that. All we've got to do is *suggest* it."

"Wait a fucking minute..."

"Randall, could we have the sound again, please."

The sound was, of course, airplanes. The show returned to the runways of Brighton Airport, the comet sounds of airplanes either accelerating for take-off or reversing for touchdown, the screech of landing gear first bruising the runway. The camera picture was fixed onto the flight tower standing alone out on the concrete field.

"Oh, good, great," Mickey said. "They're going to show the accident *one more time*."

But the scene skipped the control room, moving instead to a private boardroom at the top of the tower, enclosed within one-way mirrored glass.

"Pennington, be reasonable."

"Reasonable? Resigning as the president of this airline? Something I built, I sweated for? That's reasonable?"

"Your sweat isn't enough anymore."

"What a line."

"You'll never convince me of that."

"Why be a fool? Why wait for certain bankruptcy? Why not try to save your airline while you can?"

"And I say the best thing I could do for my airline would be to keep opportunists like you as far away from it as I can."

"That's telling him Penningworth!"

"Penning-*ton*, you oaf!"

"If I let you take over now, what will you do in a year or so when we hit a little more turbulence? Bail out again? Hmm?"

"Let's not talk in riddles, Pennington. I'm a businessman. You have a failing business. I can help you. You need me, in fact."

"Oh, sure," Zimmer said. "The screws."

"Business-screws."

"Could we turn the sound down again?" Mickey asked.

"I need someone with a firm grip on the throttle, not a fly-by-night parasite."

"Pick me, Penningbone, pick me!" Bruce hollered, half out of his stool, with a death grip on his beer mug. "I've got a firm grip, eeeyooowww..."

"That's right, Pennington," the businessman shouted, leaning over the board table. "You need pilots! Let me help. Let me finance your restaffing."

"Never."

"Aaarrr..." Bruce growled, a sopwith camel, piloting along the bar, around the Lumpers, and away to the bathroom. "Aaarrr--"

Randy watched his progress. "That is a crazed man."

"He's just projecting," Zimmer said, glancing toward Mr. Boyles for confirmation.

Mr. Boyles shook his head, peering after Bruce's wake as well. "He's awfully grown for that."

"We're not jealous, are we?"

"Oh, right."

"You can't handle it on your own, Penning--"

"You *said* that!" Mickey screamed, standing on the foot rest of his stool.

"--line is in a shambles. Scandals are rocking your standing in the industry. You can't trust your own employees, and you're losing pilots every day."

"I've weathered worse, thank you."

"Pennington, for the last time, be reasonable..."

As the businessman pleaded, the camera backed gracefully out of the meeting room, focusing again on just the grey-mirrored windows that closed the room off, once again outside. Airplanes, or the sound of their engines filled the air around Brighton International Airport.

"Aaarrr..." Bruce continued, somehow heard from the bathroom, above the disco-hype of the Tripoli health spa advertisement on the television. "Eeeyooowww... Ke-ke-ke-ke-keeee..."

"Think it's safe?" Steph asked, standing, taking a couple of hesitant steps in the direction of the bathroom.

"I'll take care of that clown," Mickey said, stepping past Steph. "Cut that out, you goon!"

Bruce met them in the hallway, buzzing by, "Eeeyooowww... Ke-ke-ke-kee..."

"Maybe you're right, Mr. Boyles," Zimmer said. "So big. So seemingly grown, and yet..."

The commercials ended quickly, near the end of this episode. *Incoming Flights* returned to darkened windows, but not any at the airport. It was Brighton Hospital, all eight stories, parking lots, the slope of the driveway as it approached the emergency entrance, the sound of sirens wailing somewhere.

"You know what I like about this show," Steph was telling Mickey as they returned to the bar. "It's so much tidier than I could ever be. It's almost instructional, in a way."

"You're kidding, right?"

"Alpha surgery to the burn unit, stat. Alpha surgery to the burn unit, stat. Alpha surgery..."

A steady flow of green clad attendants crushed through the pneumatic doors of the burn unit. They approached a bed where a solitary nurse stood, looking up from the occupant, into the camera, teary eyes showing above a paper mask. The surgery team started barking orders, taking over the scene, "Get anesthesia up here, *now*!" gowning, gloving, working on their patient almost all at once.

The busy camera shifted scenes again. It returned, through the city of Brighton—and through time, consuming but not wasting a single moment—to the courtroom. There, the judge presiding over Roy's arraignment was debating with the opposing lawyers, holding a preemptive hand over the public access microphone, leaning over the edge of his bench to discuss the matter with the two men.

"Your honor, I strongly object..."

"Overruled, Wilkenson."

"But your hon--"

"Mister Wilkenson, you've been overruled."

"Strongly overruled," Bruce said, grounded, for the moment.

"This is just an arraignment. The charges can be altered if the court and the circumstances warrant."

"But my client has already entered his plea."

"There has been an added charge. Period. He will be asked to plead for himself again, if you gentlemen will allow me to continue," the judge told them, banging his gavel.

"Added charge?" the Lumpers wondered, turning toward each other, as the two embattled lawyers returned to their tables.

"Bailiff," the judge said to the uniformed attendant next to him. "Have the defendant rise."

"The bailiff's a part-time magician," Bruce whispered.

"Shut up."

"Will the defendant please rise."

"A polite magician."

Everyone at the bar hissed, "Shh!"

"Michael Roy Conrad, pursuant to the death of one of the victims of the crash you've been charged responsible for--"

"Whoa!" Everyone, both at Lear's, and in the courtroom,

buzzed at the news, over the insistent hammering of the judge, "Order, or-der..."

The color drained from Roy's face.

"The crimes you've been charged with now include second degree murder."

His knees buckled.

"Who?" Steph asked.

"Hastings?" Zimmer guessed.

"Leslie?"

"How do you now plead?"

Before Roy could enter his plea, the camera shifted away from the formality of the courtroom, away from the crowds. It returned to the cleansed, polished bathroom at the airport, the back of a woman bowed over one of the shining sinks.

Bruce said, "Audrey, honey?"

"Not guilty," Roy's voice was superimposed over the scene.

"This court stands adjourned, with the trial date to be set after the Easter holidays," the judge answered him, banging his gavel again over the noise at the courtroom. That sound reverberated through the empty bathroom, off the porcelain and stainless steel, while Audrey gently convulsed by herself. Finally, she raised her head from the sink. She had tear-stained eyes, and a sweat had broken out on her forehead. She seemed to be listening to the sound, as if it hurt her, her thoughts swimming in the mirror she was facing, thoughts and memories of her childhood, glimpses of the young, vibrant, defiant blond girl, along with darker images of angry, loveless parents.

The fading echoes of the judge's gavel, sounding now like someone getting spanked, and the cries of children, or the victims of some horrible accident transformed into the high whine of turbine engines. The camera blacked.

"God," Steph said.

"Thank God," Zimmer said. "Right Mick?"

Mickey was staring at the screen, the credits. "They're going to leave him in prison for Easter?"

"Damn right, the murderer," Bruce said, accepting another

beer from Randy, who then turned the volume down again, but left the picture on. "He's a goner now."

"What?"

Bruce scraped his right index finger across his throat. "Ehhhiiit."

"They can't kill him for that, can they?" Mickey said, turning from Bruce to the opposite side of the bar, Mr. Boyles. "I mean, he didn't do anything, did he?"

"If you mean, can they execute someone charged with second degree murder, I believe the answer is no, in most states, they can not."

"What's this?" Zimmer asked, waving toward Mickey. "You think he should live?"

Steph sat up straighter in his stool, looking over Mickey's head at Zimmer. "I suppose you want to axe him."

Bruce reached and yanked Steph out of the way, telling everyone, "Damn right. Off with his fucking head. Off with his balls! You crash a plane, you get the axe."

"He didn't crash the plane," Mickey said. "He didn't *do* anything. He just wanted some attention."

"He will most certainly receive that."

"I still say, off with his fucking balls."

Mickey ignored the taunt, turning again to Mr. Boyles. "That's all he was doing, just showing his worth, showing how important he was, how he should be appreciated, loved, right?"

Mr. Boyles shrugged. "Perhaps. But is that any cause to endanger a whole plane load of innocent people?"

"She walked out on him, so he crashed the plane. You heard him. You saw it. Off with his balls!"

"Steph," Zimmer said, peering over his beer mug. "We need an expert's opinion."

Steph had been sitting back in his stool, staying out of the line of fire. "About justice?"

"No. About jilted lovers."

"Aw, now, don't start on me with that shit-- What do you mean jilted?"

Zimmer laughed, then patted Mickey on the back. "Tell you what, we'll dedicate tomorrow's dinner to Roy. We'll leave an empty seat for him, maybe wear black and white striped shirts with numbers across the back."

"I could get some Army surplus tin cups," Randy offered.

"We can handcuff Whomee!"

Zimmer cringed.

"That's just a little too kinky, don't you think?"

"Said the expert."

"We'll cut off his balls!"

"We'll cut off *your* balls," Zimmer said to Bruce.

"Hey, hey," Bruce answered, leaning over Steph.

Mickey mumbled, "Does anyone know a microsurgeon?" sending Zimmer into a fit of laughter.

"What'd you say?"

"We may have to handcuff some mouths," Randy said, setting out another round for everyone.

"We *could* get some real handcuffs, couldn't we?"

Mickey turned to Zimmer. "You're serious?"

"Wouldn't *that* drive Frank crazy?"

Mr. Boyles, usually so guarded, so composed, nearly choked on his scotch.

"No, no, not the whip!" Bruce squealed, dredging up an old joke. "Anything but the whip..."

"Aaaanything?"

"We can paint bars on the windows."

"No we can not."

"Aw, Zimmer."

"But we can decorate the eggs with black stripes, and numbers."

"Eggs?"

"Yeah, eggs. It's Easter, remember. Eggs, for the hunt!"

"The hunt! To the hunt!" Bruce called, his projector gone completely berserk, galloping on his bar stool, blowing reveille through his fist.

They all stared at the rendition until he stopped, and told them, "It's the only tune I could think of."

Zimmer turned blankly toward Mr. Boyles.

"You brought the subject up, remember."

"Whatever," Zimmer said, finishing his beer. "We're off."

"And you'll be back here at precisely," Bruce started, ready to synchronize a watch he didn't have.

"Nope. Not tonight. No time. I've got work to do," Zimmer told them. "And loverboy here, well..."

"What? A date? On two-far night?"

Steph shrugged. "Think of it as research."

"Jesus," Mickey said. "What next."

Steph stood, actually pointing a finger as if he was going to answer, before Zimmer reached and pulled him for the door.

"Anthony," Mr. Boyles said, "you're not working too hard on these meals are you?"

"Never. It'll be worth it," he said, pushing Steph out into the street. "To the hunt."

"The hunt!" Bruce repeated.

The door closed on some more of his trumpeting.

After collecting their checks and stops at the retail store—to buy eggs, to confirm plans with Angela, who was just clocking out—the bank, Steph had very little time to get ready, once back at Fill.

He wasn't so very good with time anyway, so attempts at economizing only wasted more of it. He studied himself in the bathroom mirror, trying to decide between showering and shaving, figuring he didn't have hot water or time for both.

"But do I need to shave, for just a movie?"

He saved more time by not getting his hair wet, though he stood in front of the mirror for a while anyway trying to flick or push it around into some kind of shape. It would be left to fend for itself, as he stepped out of the bathroom and pulled on a different, but no less wrinkled shirt.

"Well?" he said to Zimmer, who was sitting in Whomee's chair, petting the cat.

"Would you go out with that?"

Steph frowned. "You don't have to stay home, you know. I can get her to pick me up."

"Don't worry about us," Zimmer said, exacting guilt just the same, "we've got plenty to do." He shoved his hand into his pocket, pulling out the keys.

"Thanks guys," Steph said at the door. "Don't wait up."

He wouldn't. Zimmer didn't actually have a lot to do, so much as he had a few things that needed to be done the night before. He was going to set up a sourdough starter for tomorrow's bread, and he had to soak some dried lima beans—the big white kind, "The size of Angela's teeth," he snickered: He had in mind some kind of lima bean, yellow squash, bacon casserole... And the eggs. He had them boiling away already, pots on all three eyes of the Roper, simmering three dozen eggs. Somehow he couldn't quite resist the extra twelve, sending Steph back to the dairy case from the checkout line.

"You sure?"

Even Steph knew that twenty-four hard-boiled, painted and hidden eggs were enough. Hell, half a dozen probably would've been enough, "For anyone but Bruce."

Zimmer said again, standing in the kitchen, the eggs just about done, as he'd told Steph, and Angela, at the store, "I *like* egg salad."

He was leaning against the sink, Iron City in hand, listening to the radio, an Orioles-Pirates exhibition game, this the last weekend of spring training. He was looking west, through the dark windows, thinking about last year's World Series, how he'd still been in Vermont for the first two games between the teams. Victor hated baseball; didn't think much of the sport, or the players' athletic ability. "They don't *do* anything."

Zimmer always thought he never gave the game a chance. Winter sports were king up there, high school football, skiing. Deconstructo never had any time in the summer to sit and relax and enjoy an evening's game. They worked into the sixth or seventh inning, then went home and collapsed. If Zimmer ever wanted to catch part of the game he had to sit out in the Bee-atile and try to catch a broadcast from Montreal, or Boston.

"You know, I'll bet *that's* what happened to Abby's battery."

Now he was in Pennsylvania, and baseball was everywhere, everyone still singing that song, "We are family..."

"Maybe that *wasn't* such an accident..."

He remembered the trip. "Where did I say I was going?" Florida. "Panama City Beach." He remembered Tripoli, the traffic, the cop, "That ticket!" he screamed, dropping his beer, scaring the hell out of Whomee. "I have *got* to take care of that."

He saw Whomee cowering in the doorway, and coaxed him over to where the spilled beer was, before lifting him to the counter top. "Sorry."

Then he got busy with the eggs, which were cooling in the sink. He wrapped them all up in a bath towel, like a stork's bundle, to lift them out of the sink. He spread them all out on the counter and dried them.

"Do I need to test them, you think?" he asked the cat.

He'd had to crowd them into the pans, "True." But he had a system, to get them just right. Zimmer preferred them just boiled, with the yolk still a little moist. "You turn down the heat from boiling to a low simmer for *exactly* eight minutes." Whomee's heard this before.

Exactly eight minutes in timeless Fill was usually two songs and a commercial. He was in trouble with the baseball game on, where exhibition games were especially boundless. He figured about twenty pitches, or most of an inning.

"Not to worry," he said. "There's a test."

He took one of the eggs and spun it on its long axis on the counter. If it spun true, it was done. "If it wobbles, it's gooey."

Whomee sat in the vacated sink and watched, his head shadowing the movement of the egg only eight inches away, rotating in tight little circles, his eyes getting bigger and bigger. By the third test, he couldn't resist any longer, tucked his shoulder, reached up out of the sink and swatted. The egg landed on the floor at Zimmer's feet, plop. Whomee looked over the edge of the sink to see.

"That one's yours."

Zimmer continued testing, with Whomee in the sink, contentedly watching two or three, but then losing patience, restraint. Part of the test got to be which of them could reach the egg first. They spent about an hour and a half at the exercise, sometimes batting the egg back and forth between them, wasting eight of the eggs Zimmer didn't need anyway.

And then not too many of the remaining eggs got decorated, either.

"Maybe the prize should go to the one that *is* decorated. I could leave them all white but one."

He drew magic marker lines on three, four and then promised himself, and Whomee, that with early sleep, early in the morning, they'd finish. Too much beer on a forgotten and empty stomach precluded any more serious feast day preparations.

Steph came home to a darkened Fill, but after sneaking quietly up the stairs he could hear voices from inside. "Strange voices," which he traced to the kitchen, where Zimmer'd left the radio playing, some overnight AM talk show.

He found an egg on his pillow on the cot. "See what love will get you?" was printed in a spiral around the shell. Steph had to stand at the opened bathroom door to read the message, turning the egg around and around. Whomee sat tensed and attentive in his chair, thumping his tail against the cushion, watching. Steph wondered at the message, the cat, and then tossed the egg into the chair, over Whomee's head, who had a fit trying to dig it out of the corner where it slipped behind the cushion.

"Crazy fucking cat," Steph mumbled, headed for sleep.

Whomee managed to lift the egg out of its hole, using his paw-hand like a shovel, bracing it against the side of the chair. He slept curled around Steph's egg, waking up occasionally to bat it around a little, trying to open his mouth wide enough to bite into it.

Zimmer found Whomee like that a few hours later, after he'd been up for a while already, just after dawn, when it was finally light enough in the big room to see anything, on his way by the chair, headed for the bathroom. "Crazy fucker," he said on the way back by, plucking the egg from Whomee's grasp.

Whomee followed him through the swinging door, intent on that egg.

"All right, all right, don't get bitchy," Zimmer said to Whomee, down at his feet, clawing his pants leg. Zimmer gave him back his prize, rolling it into the corner.

There was no space on the counter for Whomee to jump up on to anyway. The one uncluttered spot, where they could have played a little egg hockey, was reserved for the cooling rack, for the bread, after it finished baking. Zimmer checked its progress, and then stood back from the opened oven, amazed, as always, that he could fit both the roasting pan and the long baguette pans into the cavernous Roper.

"What a beauty."

Whomee was in the corner, lying on his side, pummeling his egg with both back feet.

"But everything's a beauty this morning, isn't it?"

Sometimes all of his planning fit together so perfectly, like the stove, that it maybe scared him a little, "Like it's *too* perfect," easier than he should allow. "Bullshit." He would not talk himself down. He popped the cap of his first bottle of beer of the morning, toasting its success, knowing, "It's just plain *working*."

The turkey was near done, "Long time drunk, already," on a gallon of Ernest and Julio's rose, stuffed with oyster dressing. Zimmer tasted the two casserole dishes, the squash, and a sweet potato souffle, which only needed to be reheated. "Perfect." He inhaled the cloud rising above a pan of brussels sprouts steaming in Sauterne. All that was really left to do was the rarebit, and the double-broiler sat on its own surface eye, "Ready..."

He'd even finished the eggs. "Well," most of them were painted. He pickled four of them in an empty mayonnaise jar, and had already made a small batch of egg and olive salad. Other than the one Whomee was still torturing in the corner, there was just one egg left unaccounted for. Zimmer stood there holding it. He could paint it, "True." He could peel it and munch on it himself. "A shake of salt, a pinch of pepper, a slug of beer."

Whomee was watching his pantomime. "Oh, Jesus, you pig. Here," Zimmer said, rolling it in his direction.

The pupils of Whomee's eyes got about as big as the egg wobbling toward him. He swatted at it, pushing it under the kitchen door, then struggled to reach after it.

"Come outa there!" Zimmer shouted, getting down on all fours behind Whomee. "Come on outa there."

Zimmer pulled the door open, Whomee squeezing through the tiniest of gaps. He pounced on the egg on the other side, bouncing it along the carpet in the direction of the table.

"Whoa," Zimmer said, as together they circled the table chasing the egg, batting it back and forth between carved feet. Whomee grabbed at it, to try and lift it into his mouth, to carry away, but only tore off a bit of shell before it rolled toward Zimmer. He used his hands like hockey sticks, batting the egg into open space, on a breakaway for the goal. Whomee easily retrieved the prize, but Zimmer cross-checked him with a back-hand. The cat rolled over with a growl, the egg rolled underneath Steph's cot. It was a sprint to the corner. Whomee bounded over the top, only lightly clawing Steph. Zimmer, right behind him, took the direct route, plowing into the cot.

"What the..." Steph cried.

"Good morning," Zimmer said, next to him, on his back, his legs draped over Steph, Whomee stretched across his forehead, scratching for the egg trapped beneath Zimmer's shoulder.

"The fuck?" Steph finished.

"A little hockey."

"Thought you hated hockey."

"Yeah, ice hockey. This is egg hockey."

"This is a fucking nightmare," Steph said, pulling the blanket over his face.

To reinforce that notion, Zimmer cried, "The bread!" and jumped up.

"A nightmare."

Zimmer yelled from the kitchen, "Goddammit," and then louder still, "Perfect, fucking perfect!"

Steph held the cot on top of himself, trying to filter out reality with the fine mesh canvas, while Zimmer grunted from the kitchen, "Ooo-ooh."

"Shut up!"

"Ooo-ooo-ooh."

He got up, dragged himself to the kitchen and found Zimmer shadow boxing with the stove, Whomee cowering in the corner by the refrigerator.

"Of allll tiiiime..." Zimmer said, raising his arms, still shuffling, the whole kitchen trembling, threatening to crack from its joists and fall to the ground.

"This," he said, changing tacks, changing voices, "is my finest hour."

Steph looked at Whomee. "What the hell is he talking about?"

"I'm talking about dinner, about feasts, about ritual and celebration. I'm talking about pre-cise-ness: the dinner's ready. The kitchen's *cleeean*. And I'm ready, ready for Lumpers, ready to celebrate."

Steph opened his mouth, to answer maybe, or ask another question, or maybe it just fell open, waiting for his mind to wake up, absorb, somehow comprehend. A rapid banging at the door filled the silence.

"Yes, YES!" Zimmer shouted, dancing again. "Bring on those Lumpers. Bring on Frank. I'll take em all on. One at a time. All at once. It don't matter." He followed Steph out into the living room, but lost ground as he circled and paused every few steps, jabbing at the wall, Whomee's chair.

It wasn't any of the Lumpers but a uniformed delivery man. "Tony Zimbarco?"

"Well, yeah, kind of," Steph said, signing for the telegram.

"Someone's been trying pretty hard to find you, pal."

"Uh-huh," Steph mumbled, closing the door, still considering the possibility that he was dreaming.

Zimmer worked his way to the door, backwards. "Ooo-ooh."

Steph studied the cable, its three different addresses. "Who's Koogan?"

"Koogan's an asshole," Zimmer said automatically, a reflex learned a long, long time ago.

"You'd better take a look at this, Zimmer."

"Koogan," Zimmer repeated, coming back to reality, ready to explain it to Steph, scanning the short note, turning it over, then back, all the play and color draining from him, "Is dead?"

He stood there staring at Steph, squinting, as if he wanted to tell Steph something, but had to have it explained to him first. He just repeated, "Dead," and shook his head. He handed the telegram back to Steph, turned and stomped back to the kitchen.

He broke off most of one of the loaves of bread and pulled a six-pack out of the refrigerator. He grabbed his jacket off a dining chair on the way back by.

"I gotta go," he said. "Take the turkey out in about an hour. And don't forget that Whomee likes to help carve."

Half out the door, he turned and said, "Oh, the eggs aren't hidden yet," standing there thinking about the hiding places he'd had in mind, then thought how trivial that now seemed, everything now seemed. "Who cares?"

Steph didn't have an answer.

"Shit. See you."

Steph was still standing there a moment later when the door opened again.

"Keys?"

"Oh, yeah," Steph said, retrieving them from his jacket. He tossed them across the room. Watching their flight, he focused on something for the first time that morning. "Something's real wrong here."

Maybe it was the character swapping, the projecting. "Maybe I can't do it," not like Bruce. "Maybe not at all."

But he tried. He pulled the turkey out of the oven in what felt like sixty minutes, "Or a month." He guessed it was done, poking it and sniffing it like he'd seen Zimmer do. He carved it without too much mutilation—Fran being late, which was maybe another bad sign, "Or not,"—and picked the carcass clean of scraps with Whomee, both of them hunched over the skeleton on the kitchen counter.

When the Lumpers showed up, he had to switch back and try to explain Zimmer's absence, which he couldn't. He passed around the telegram, with a lingering sense of fault, thinking *for* Zimmer at least, how he could amend his Romans speech, "Who brought us the arch, olive oil, and the sport of killing the messenger..."

All they could guess from the telegram was that Zimmer was most likely headed toward its address of origin, Salyne, a town in New York that none of them were more than vaguely familiar with. They had a geographical location, and a name, Alice. That was all. The telegram ended up sitting in the middle of the table, within everyone's reach throughout the meal, but remaining untouched.

They all tried filling the void, ceremoniously setting up Whomee in the chair Zimmer would have occupied. Even though the cat refused to pass the brussels sprouts—he alone knowing the sauce had never been made, perhaps—the dinner didn't break down completely.

Out on the road, Zimmer cranked up the radio in Abby just about as far as he could. He both welcomed the song, Lennon's "The Walrus," and hated it. He could sing along, "I am you, as you are me... as we are all together..." and whistle or hum or beat the dash in time, making enough noise to maybe drown out the Bee-atile's engine clacking away at high speed, but that didn't mean he could forget anything, that he was out there, headed north, and why.

The song had been popular during basic training, in San Antonio. He and forty other airmen were bound together, scared and bullied into a common corner. They'd rallied themselves around rock-and-roll, surviving six weeks of non-reality, where they'd look at themselves in the mirror forty-two mornings in a row and ask, "Is this really happening?" It felt like he somehow hadn't heard the song since those days, maybe because those were his last good memories of Richard Koogan.

Koogan had been the nexus. From that very first night turned morning of military life, where they'd been huddled into an ante-room attached to their barracks, suffering six hours of haranguing by a ball-busting west Texas training instructor, who spoke out of the side of his mouth, who promised them a couple of hundred times that they were going to regret opting for the Air Force, regret, especially, the bad luck that had landed them in his charge, "For the rest of your goddammed lives." He discovered Koogan's name first among all of them, maybe smart enough to recognize Richard as the requisite smart-ass, bad example that every platoon of recruits needed so that they could be beat into better examples, into soldiers. More likely, "He was just plain lucky, as we all were."

"Who's Koogan?" he'd asked sometime about two in the morning, drawling out the first syllable. "Who's Kooo-gan?"

It was Richard who answered, "Koogan's an asshole," stealing the T.I's thunder, ensuring their own personal six-week battle.

"Shee-yit, Kooo-gan, you gonna need you a new one by the time I get done kicking you around."

Later, after lights out, with about three hours of potential sleep, if any of them could manage to shut out the fear and the dread, before, "The *real* fun," started, Richard said into the dark, "Who's Kooo-gan?"

From the next cot, Zimmer answered, "Koogan's an asshole."

Someone else in the room called out, "Got that new asshole yet?"

"Nope," Richard said. "And I only got forty-two days left."

Each day everyone else in the outfit laughed and shook their heads at Koogan's nerve. They sang rock-and-roll songs and smoked cigarettes on breaks, increasingly fearless and confident, Zimmer thought, because each night Koogan would start, "Who's Kooo-gan?" and then he'd wrap up that day for them, "Only twenty-two days left."

Tripoli's radio station, TPY, was playing their customary weekend blocks of music. "Eight days a week," Zimmer sang, tweaking the radio up some more, trying to hold the fading signal.

Frank tried to cooperate with the subdued mood of the dinner, checking his irritability, even though he was the brunt of plenty of needling for being late. He said nothing about Whomme being at the table, and then on the table, and nothing about them playing black-jack instead of poker, a game Angela understood well enough to play by herself, a game Frank hated. He didn't complain, even ate his vegetables, even the bland little cabbages, which would've disappointed Zimmer, at least. He might have worried about Frank's shift in character, might have suggested Frank see the company doctor or something.

But without Zimmer, Frank's restrained behavior was what the Lumpers needed the least. If Frank had been his usual contrary self, they might have started the day with a proper toast, might have proceeded with a more normal Feast day. But in the total absence of protocol and direction, who, of any of them, knew what to do?

Zimmer pushed on the accelerator, but he couldn't escape. He couldn't leave behind the memories of those last weeks of basic training. When he looked into the rearview mirror, despite the stubble on his face or the length of his hair, he saw a skin-headed, green-clad recruit, "A pinger," column after column of pingers, waiting, at ease, at the base firing range.

"You ever fired one of these?" Zimmer'd whispered over Koogan's shoulder, in front of him.

"Where in hell would I get an M-16?"

"*Any* gun."

"Naw."

"Aren't you worried?"

"About what?"

"About doing that."

"Naw."

"I am," Zimmer admitted. He felt the panic, an eighteen year old's dread at having to follow through on all that acting and posturing, all over again. "I'm not sure I even want to try."

"That's your first mistake, Z. To try is to fail," Koogan told him, and then risked drawing attention to their conversation by turning and giving Zimmer a look he'd later imitate. "You either do it or you don't."

Those first months in the service, thanks to the buddy system they'd both pre-enlisted for, were a lot like the idle time they'd spent between graduating high school in June and leaving for basic the next February, "A fucking gas." Together they managed to stay above the military's best homogenizing efforts. Zimmer, at the time, more short sighted then he'd ever admit to now, was contented with the experience, counting down the days, cruising along. He never planned or worried about anything beyond what he was going to do on his next weekend, his next furlough. He had a best friend, a steady girl—Koogan's sister, Alice—a guaranteed job, and a new car.

When they were separated after basic—an apparent forfeiture of their recruitment contract, which they couldn't do a damn thing about—they had no plans for how to handle that twist. The different technical schools they were sent to were roughly the same length, and Zimmer, more trusting than he would ever again be, figured they'd just hook back up after that, contented to wait another twenty-four weeks, even keeping up with the ritualistic, "Only a hundred and sixty-six days left," for a while. He managed to accept the intervention as something entirely out of his control. "Or didn't think about it enough to question it."

Koogan wasn't so resilient. For reasons Zimmer never found out, he suddenly couldn't accept any of the military's manipulation any more, "And he damn sure wouldn't try." Without anyone's counsel, he got out, claiming an old knee injury. They let him go, before six months had elapsed, so they didn't have to give him any benefits. The two inseparable teenagers, whose entire young existences were understood and envisioned through two sets of interdependent eyes, were now at opposite ends of everything.

Zimmer tried some antidotal measures, "We all *tried*," but the results were never less than disastrous. He tried returning to Salyne, on leave, as if he could fall back into his former life. But that world was not standing still waiting for him, and not really improving on its own. He tried implanting himself into the Koogan family, marrying Alice. All that meant was that he took Alice away from Salyne as well, leaving Koogan alone, "Not just *unencumbered*," free to get himself going, "Supposedly."

Then, when that damage became evident, they tried relocating Richard with them, creating a travelling Salyne, "Since he wasn't doing anything at home," he could be their cook, their housekeeper, their gardener, "Anything!" They'd have kids. He could be a nanny. They'd name the first child after him, boy or girl, "Didn't matter."

The schemes sucked the life out of all of them. "And now, Richard's dead." And Zimmer, who thought he'd left behind his own rapidly decomposing corpse a few years ago, "And feeling good and guilty again," was headed home.

Angela, maybe because she was the one outside of the usual Lumper circle, most unfamiliar with what was missing, tried the hardest to fill the emptiness around the table, inside the apartment. She chattered almost non-stop, in the absence of everything but the most cursory of conversation between the others.

No one blamed anyone else, but they admitted early that it just wasn't working. There could be no celebration without Zimmer, or at least without some more clearer instructions from Zimmer as to how they were supposed to proceed.

It was well before dusk when they gave up the attempt, finally realizing that the harder they tried, the worse it felt, and the more they questioned the whole idea to begin with.

As they stood in the doorway, gathering coats, aimlessly waiting to see who the first to leave would be, Mickey asked,

"Think he'll be back?"

The question seemed to spur them into some kind of action, at least. Frank grumbled, "Goddamn better be back," gnawing on his cigar, stuffing his hands into the pockets of his Regency coach's jacket, "Or I'll gan-isass," stomping down the stairs.

The other Lumpers skulked off in their own separate directions, Bruce, commenting of Frank, "He just doesn't get it, does he," but speaking for all of them.

"Never has, I'm afraid," Mr. Boyles answered, holding on to Bruce's steady shoulder as he navigated the stairs.

That left only Angela's blue Mazda underneath Fill. She stayed, listened, as the exchange crystallized all the thoughts Steph had been having during the day, and they finally fell out.

"Do any of us get it? I mean, we can't answer that question, can we. Why don't we know?" he asked. "We don't know anything. Can't do anything. Hell, Angie, what if... Why don't I know?"

She listened, mostly. "How could you know?" she said at one point, gathering the beer bottles, the last dishes, running water in the kitchen to work on the mound of dirty dishes already there.

Steph followed, but stood against the counter, looking out over Dagaton Woods, glowing orange in the sunset. "Makes me wonder what the fuck I've been doing all these months, what I've been paying attention to, if anything, if I don't have any more idea than this about where he's going, or why."

Angela said, "He'll be back, don't worry. He won't leave all this, will he?"

"You don't know Zimmer," he said, and then had to laugh at himself. "He won't be back because we want him back or because we need him back, or because he *should* come back. I really think he'd be perfectly willing to forget all this," waving around the kitchen. "And start over somewhere else."

"Really?"

"Yeah. Really."

"Why? After he's put so much into this."

"That's the thing about Zimmer. I'm not sure *this* has

anything to do with *here*, or with us." Having said such, he wasn't at all comfortable with the implications. "You saw what happened today."

She stopped, turned, and held him by the shoulders. "Then what makes you think you can do anything about that, about his willingness to forget this, forget us?"

"Nothing. But I'd like to know. Don't you see?" He didn't want or wait for an answer. He didn't really want to hear any indictments of Zimmer, didn't want to make him the target of their anguish. "This is about more than that," more than what he would decide to do or not do, and why. "It's about what binds one person to another," for however long, under whatever circumstances, how tentative those bonds really are, "*Everything*, really is." This was about how, all of a sudden, Steph was damn sure decided that he didn't like this helpless feeling, the *clueless* feeling. "It's not enough to just play the part, Angie. You've got to pay attention, so you can know, so you have a chance to *know*."

He rambled on and on through the evening, never venturing too far from that theme, "You should know," know those people around you better than that, you should pay attention, you should find out, "However you can," adding at one point, "I would've gone with him."

Except for a slight hitch at that last, she nodded, listened. He kept moving in a continuous stream of not always jointed thoughts and revelations and questions. She listened, and stayed.

12. Resurrection in Lear's

IT had been dusk of that same Saturday evening in central New York as Zimmer reached the southern limits of Salyne, still feeling himself drawn inexorably back to his birthplace, back along International Drive, the main thoroughfare of the city. He waited and waited all those hours, all those long, lonely miles, for some kind of feeling of anticipation, some pocket of warmth and yearning inside of him, but it didn't come. The road stretched before him like a hard black scar, keloided over years and years ago, insensitive to any stimulation.

At the very best, International Drive was like a dark, stagnant river reeking of undesirable familiarity, coursing the city, Zimmer's mind.

"You missed the funeral, Tony. What took you so long?"
"I came as soon as I got your telegram."
"Where were you?"
"This isn't easy, you know."

International Drive was a misnomer. It wasn't cosmopolitan at all. It was local. It was just another north-south main drag. It was international only in the aspect that, like thousands of other average sized U.S. cities, it was the citizens' point of focus for too much of their lives, whether hoping for salvation to come rolling down the street, or deliverance from following it away, away. It was intersected a hundred times, and occasionally detoured, but it remained the central route for most traffic, was the well-trodden path about which the city had been formed.

International Drive was Salyne's past preserved. It had been one of the preferred trails used by the great northern Indian tribes to both gain access to the foothills and lakes and secretive forests of the Adirondack Mountains, and it was the route down which they'd recede again from the winter harshness up in those elevations. Though presently, International Drive snuck out of the local remnants of those Indians—the Mancussa Indian reservation, which abuts the southern border of Salyne. It collided briefly with the interstate just after that and then carried its travelers on into the valley of Mancussa County, New York. It was an ominous beginning for International Drive, arising out of the collected deprivation of once proud lives, together mired in controlled poverty. But the buckshot riddled sign said, Welcome to Salyne, nonetheless. Welcome to Salyne: The nation's leading salt producer until 1922. Ominous and fitting, most members of the populace, former members, especially, might say.

"I don't like funerals anyway, Al. You know that."

"Exactly. You don't like saying goodbye under any circumstances. This was different, Tony."

"Think he'd have felt better knowing I was there praying for him?" He wished he could retrieve the words as soon as he heard them, but they were gone. Then, with no more feedback than her breathing, he said, "Hey. Sorry. Let's lighten up, okay?"

"Why are you so defensive?"

"Why wouldn't I feel defensive when I'm being interrogated?"

"Who's interrogating you?"

She was right. If it was really happening, he was doing it to himself. She's always been able to see right through his words.

"I'm not interrogating... Why would I-- Oh, Tony. You didn't kill Richard."

"Oh? *Feels* like I've killed just about everything around here."

The south side of Salyne was not immediately distinct from the reservation, at least not subjectively. The houses may have been sturdier, standing erect, side by side. And the toys scattered about the patchwork lawns might have been costlier.

But there existed between the dissimilar lifestyles a shared, barren complacency about the homes of lives settled short of expectation. And there was the same blank compliance in the faces of both peoples, despite the hidden cheekbones, the paler complection of the ancestors of the Europeans who'd instituted the objective segregation between them some five hundred years ago.

The south side, with cohabiting blends of Italian and Irish and Polish and German neighborhoods, was the matronly section of the city, void of any adolescent vigor, continuing on with its routines, still dusting off each yellowed day, relinquishing any other control to inevitability. The outcome could be seen in some of the buildings. What used to be small family businesses, an antique shop, a grocery, a dry-goods store, were struggling, or had already surrendered, vacated of merchandise and of customers. They could find all they wanted or needed and more in any one of a number of sprawling shopping malls that circled Mancussa valley, popping up around the perimeter rim faster than anyone could count, like young virile Mancussan braves might have, long, long ago.

But long ago was forever gone. "Even not so long ago," Zimmer knew, gazing down his own street, bordering between the south side and downtown Salyne, was equally altered, lost. The props might endure—a tree fort rotting up in the branches of the huge elm tree in back, the fenced yard of the neighbor who never relinquished kickballs or Frisbees that strayed onto his manicured lawn—but the players, even the script, were gone, or just modified by circumstances not nearly reversible. What was left to miss, "Or come back to?"

"Maybe," she said into the quiet, "you're being a little too self-indulgent."

"You tell me how else to be then. I feel like a fucking hun, an invader."

"Have you considered how we feel? How we've felt all this time?"

"No, see, that's the thing. I forgot everything else when I

heard about Richard. Everything. I didn't think of what I'd find here, or what I was leaving behind. I either should have told some people what I was doing, or I shouldn't have come back at all."

"Why?"

"Because things change, Al. You know that. You remember. It's a trap to come back here. I didn't ever want to believe that, but it's always been true. Every time, there are those few minutes when I want to believe that there're people who want to see me, they'll interrupt their lives because I was coming home, can't wait to see me, hug me, shake my hand, find out how I am, what I'm doing... Things change. People change. I mean, I can't even call it home anymore, right? I don't live here. Why *would* they care? It's crazy to think life could ever be like some goddammed television commercial."

"Why is that so crazy?"

"Why? Because that shit doesn't happen. People don't spend their precious time thinking about you unless you're there, all the time. I thought I could come back here, after all this time, what..."

"Almost four years."

"Yeah," Zimmer said, hesitating, that she could answer so quickly. "Almost four years: and we're all guilty of the same damn thing, aren't we? Four years, and we're all acting as if nothing's happened during that time, but it has. Everything's happened. We've loved and lost and fucked and been fucked, and now we've died too. I'm not the same person, and neither are you. So why are we acting this way?"

He heard her laugh. "Who's acting which way?"

He remembered her smile, a slow, crooked smile that she would only let out reluctantly. She'd close her eyes when something amused her, trying to hide the effect. When she would open them again, there'd be a light that wasn't there before, and the tiny lines around her eyes would shift, as a grin spread across her face, and she parted her lips to reveal bright, but imperfect teeth.

On the northern edge of Salyne's downtown district, finally, there was some semblance of life, of robust, earnest living. There were alive things happening, but they had to be qualified, like too much else about the city. It wasn't an internal renaissance at work.

Sometimes, sure, downtown Salyne was teeming with traffic, people scurrying to and from the half-emptied office buildings, between appointments, beneath the grey and threatening skies that most usually hovered over the city; or pigeons, either filling those skies, but more probably waddling about the feet of the pedestrian traffic, hordes and hordes of babbling pigeons, the only permanent inhabitants of the buildings.

Neither the part-time office tenants nor the birds could sustain life downtown by themselves, though. Some of life had to be trucked in, so that the grey people shuttling between sodden granite buildings could glimpse and smell and taste a more Technicolor, more varied world. Bordering the business blocks of downtown, on both sides of International Drive, serving as stark contrast, not as transition, was the farmer's market. Within the block or two of transplanted rural New York, lawyers and MBAs could suck on a soft pear, heedless or not of the juice trickling down the sides of their mouths. They could buff up and crunch into wine sap apples, or bag up a couple of pounds of baking potatoes that still had clods of black fertile earth ground into their eyes, or select a half dozen ears of silky yellow corn from overflowing bushel baskets. And if they tried real hard, they'd see that captured within the makeshift stalls, gathered together with the produce on the back of the pick-ups, was the smell of the hayloft in the barn out back. There was the sound of chickens scratching and clucking about the entrance to the barn—as near their cousin pigeons as they'd ever be, scurrying about underfoot. In the distance, out in the fields, lulling cattle, hustled from the confines of the building by a busy retriever, meandered, munched. Riding the breeze rippling those grasses was the penetrating aroma of manure, and the sense of lifestyles that were not so much hardship as they were hard won self-gratification, a sense too tenuous for any of those business folks to catch. Hardships for them were obstacles put in their way by some cruel god, delaying what they saw as an inevitable and justified reward—justified, mostly, by virtue that they wanted it badly enough. They wouldn't ever accept a negative transaction—an early frost, say, or a summer's drought—as integral to the process. But then, dealing with the stresses of common denominator, bottom-line living, was no kin at all to mending the same section of fence again and again, replacing splintered loft planks or pounding out a bent tractor axle. In the city, hardships were either bought out, or diluted. A lot like Tripoli, Salyne had far more bars than churches, or barns.

Off of International Drive, down a side street, hidden from the farmer's market, was Phillipi's, a popular subterranean cavern full of downtown Salyne's supposedly happy hourers at dusk on the Friday evening the week after Zimmer had arrived in town. He was by himself, huddled in a corner phone booth, away from the noise.

"So what are you doing?" Alice asked.

"Chasing life. Chasing death. Can I see you?"

"No, really. What are you really doing now?"

"I don't know. I've been roaming around the city, visiting old haunts, looking, watching. In some ways everything's real strange; but in others there's a familiarity that's kind of spooky. I'll get lost, for instance, and not have a clue where I am, but then end up where I wanted to get to anyway, or someplace better, that I hadn't remembered until I was there. It's a real strange feeling. Sometimes I think it's Richard's ghost, you know. Then I think *I'm* the ghost, but don't know it yet."

"I meant where you live. What are you doing?"

"Oh, I'm a Lumper. I work night shift at a grocery store warehouse. It's inhuman. I spend every day, all day, trying to go to sleep, or trying to wake up. I drink coffee until I can't hold the cup steady any more. And then I drink beer until I'm bloated, drunk, or unconscious. It suits me though, I think, that constant flux. No dust, right? I've spent the whole week just waiting to get back to that. Crazy, huh."

"So you're going back?"

"Well, that's what I'm trying to figure out."

"And?"

"Can I see you?"

"Why?"

He didn't have an answer for that. He didn't think he'd *have* to answer.

"I'd just like to see you."

"To see if you still... If we could..."

"Maybe. Why not?"

"I can't do that again, Tony."

"Okay."

"I can't. It's too late. I've spent all this time getting used to your leaving. I can't do that again."

"Aren't you skipping a couple of steps?"

"It's too late."

"All right, all right," he said, thinking to himself, Then why'd you send me the fucking telegram? trying to remember, suddenly, if it had been her, searching his pockets for it, remembering he'd left it, finally, deciding. "All right. Listen, I don't want to upset you, okay. I got to go. I'll drop you a line sometime, okay?"

"I'm sorry, Tony. It's just too late. Don't you see?"

"No, Alice. I don't," he said, and let the phone drop, leaving the phone booth with it swaying back and forth, leaving Phillipi's, Salyne

He didn't continue along International Drive. He knew what lay beyond the farmer's market, north of downtown. Out there in the midst of the industrial complexes, was Mancussa Lake, which, typically, was devoid of any life. The mills and plants and forges and the salt refineries, the sole source of the city's pride, were abandoned now. They were transformed into only latent toxic threats once everybody realized they were strangling every living, swimming or growing thing in the lake, once that threat crawled out of the fetid waters and advanced upon the captive inhabitants of North Salyne.

Zimmer didn't need the further suffocation the sight and putrid stench Mancussa Lake held waiting for him. He turned south, not even along International Drive, but for the interstate, the federal roadway that truncated Salyne's main drag, and he sped back to Tripoli. He had to get out fast, just as he had to leave the phone dangling. He had wanted to tell her that Daylight Savings time was still two weeks away, "It's not as late as you think..."

"Asshole, asshole, asshole," he said, pounding Abby's dash, as he found the entrance ramp and traced its curve up, and away. "She's right." He's always known that. But did that mean she had to tell him, he had to be reminded. "Facts. Fucking facts. Yeah, I'm an asshole," he repeated. "Shit. Me and you, Abby-gal," Zimmer said to the car, then turned on the radio. "Let's go home."

"Wherever that is," he had to say a little bit later. He didn't want to follow all the implications of that question, but he couldn't exactly escape them either. "Shit."

At the southern border of Mancussa county, five miles past Salyne's city limit, past the sprawling reservation, Zimmer looked into the rearview expecting to see all those ghosts of his past gathered, galloping after him, hurling invectives like hand-ground spearheads. There was nothing but the night, so he cursed himself again, "Asshole."

It became the central theme about which the ride, his thoughts, the conversation he carried on with the night and the Bee-atile all revolved. "Fucking asshole." The conversation was more continuous than the bits and pieces he'd let out might make it seem, more connected than it would ever sound to any passenger.

"I just wanted to see... I had to leave."

He'd sing along with the radio for a while, to try and rinse that bitter defensiveness out of his head, but then say, "What the fuck was I supposed to do?" answering some new charge, from another corner of himself that had suddenly stood up and voiced its objection.

That's what it felt like, all the way past Binghamton, and on to Scranton: a heated congressional debate about pay raises or welfare funding, on the verge of complete disorder, parts of him shouting accusations, parts defending themselves, and parts just regretting the whole unsavory episode, wishing, as always, that he could just be taken for what he offered, and "What's so wrong with just trying to rescue a few moments out of this whole fucking mess? That's all I wanted. I wouldn't ask for more, wasn't suggesting anything else..."

If Zimmer had been any less drunk, or any less tired, he might have known not to trust those voices, not to even listen to them. He'd have remembered that they were as fantastic, as unreliable, as unlike reality as dreams, "Or commercials." He might have seen that all the voices said what he wanted them to say, asked the exact question needed to further the dialogue along its predetermined track. And just like in dreams, he never hit the ground. He never died.

But he didn't. He listened almost exclusively to the scripted argument in his head, to the extent that he couldn't remember much of the ride at all. He felt the same rush of adrenalized panic as when, on other trips, after driving too many hours, mesmerized by the night, the lights, the painted lines of the highway, after nodding off for the briefest of fractions of time—but what felt like minutes upon minutes--he realized, for that interval at least, how out of control he'd been, how he could have killed, "Or died." His whole trip back to Tripoli seemed that way, as if, jerking awake as he exited the interstate again, he had to wonder, cruising down 13, "Did anything *happen*?"

And then another chunk of time would be lost trying to figure that out, remembering, instead, "Again," the debate, so that he couldn't swear, because Rt. 13 had been mostly deserted, to stopping and waiting at all the traffic lights, that he wasn't still a broadsiding, unyielding hazard on the road; he couldn't even testify with any conviction, sitting in his customary stool at Lear's, where he'd parked Abby, hell, whether he'd parked her at all, hadn't just jumped out, and she was still cruising, headed south, to Maryland, or Florida, since she's obviously got some kind of auto-pilot, or it was that same ghost-pilot, that he didn't know about before, or else, "How the fuck did I get here?"

He remembered the discussion, though, or at least the integral parts of it, the parts that made him feel somewhat better about himself. Slowly, in the presence of another human being, finally, he came to realize how jaded the dispute had been, though, how his objectivity had been forfeited from the very beginning, which, in the twisted, obsessive, circuitous track of the tempest that the whole episode seemed to him now, had become one of the other major themes of the debate."It seemed to me," he recited for Mr. Boyles, perched on his bar stool next to Zimmer, pulled up very close to the bar, limiting the motions he'd need to make. "That the most burning fucking questions, when you boil the son-of-a-bitches down, deal, ex-clus-ive-ly with responsibility. Are any of us, ever, really without an option? Is any decision final, forever? Is there any fucking forever? Is it worse to break promises than to try and promise things you probably cannot deliver? Or doesn't one just chase the other around and around and around."

Mr. Boyles held him to specifics, though, even reached and patted Zimmer's hand. "You loved her at one time, true?"

"Yes, yes, I did. Or thought I did. I'm guilty, yes. But, how independently objective is guilt?"

"Well..."

"Ah-hah!" Zimmer yelled, pouncing on the hesitation. "If it isn't, how can we ever be guilty or guiltless unless we want to be? And if we want to be guilty, meaning we choose to do what we're doing, guilty nor not, what's the point of guilt at all?"

Mr. Boyles just stared at him.

It was beginning to feel like the road all over again. "Ah, never mind. With you, here at Lear's, I'm guiltless again. One-eyed jacks, right?"

"Precisely."

As Randy refilled his beer, Mr. Boyles' scotch, who used the interval to draw out another cigarette and light it, Zimmer looked around the mostly empty bar.

"Where is everyone, anyway? It's Friday night, isn't it? Two-far night?"

"No, actually, that's next Friday, I think."

"Yeah," Randy said, adding, "we just had Easter dinner."

"Wow. Seems a lot longer than just one week." Then Zimmer said, "Still, I expected someone to be here."

"Well, it is a little late, Zimmer."

"What late? Why the hell is everyone talking about *too late*? It's not as fucking late as you think!"

They just stared at him.

"Sorry. Old joke. We're talking about Lumpers here, my dear Randall. Where's Steph?"

Randy looked from Zimmer to Mr. Boyles and back. "We haven't seen much of Steph this week, actually."

"What's he doing, moping up at Fill because I took off? Or is he too lazy and spoiled to hitchhike anymore?"

"I think, perhaps, merely busy."

"Un-huh," Zimmer said, chugging down his beer. "Well, we'll see about that. Busy, huh. You just set us up for two-fars, Randy, a special two-fucking-fars for my homecoming. I'll be right back with our Stephie," he said.

"Understand, Anthony," Mr. Boyles said as Zimmer pushed himself from his stool. "It happens to everyone."

"What?" Zimmer said, almost leaning into his lap.

"Well, I believe we were just talking about it, as a matter of fact. That things change."

Zimmer turned for the door of the bar, just kind of peeled his attention from Mr. Boyles and clomped toward the exit. Then he turned back, in a wide, halting circle, eventually ending up back at his stool. "Are you, like, getting ready to tell me one of your stories or something?"

Mr. Boyles hesitated. It had become a habit of the old

man's, late into the night, those nights when Zimmer or Steph would hang around till closing, to loosen up and allow them glimpses of himself, his history, by telling long, detailed stories out of his past, with or without any immediately recognizable relevance. They were just stories that he seemed to need to tell more than anything they needed to hear, although, later, when they thought about them, when Zimmer relived the telling, unraveled the facts and details, it would have more personal significance than just something Mr. Boyles wanted to get off his chest.

Mr. Boyles lifted his glass, drank, kind of tilted it at Randy. "Randall, would you mind? And maybe something else to smoke," as Randy pulled a joint from the pocket of his vest, which comprised his bartender's uniform. "Very well."

Zimmer could see, even if he had to squint one eye, then the other, Mr. Boyles considering exactly what he wanted to say. He pulled on the joint then offered it to Zimmer. He hit on it, the effect calming, and focusing, more than anything else. Zimmer could then almost sense the old man's dilemma, the mental debate he was going through. "It's always a problem of where to start, isn't it," he finally said.

"Begins at the beginning," Zimmer said, another of those automatic answers he's collected over the years.

"Yes, but you see, we don't know beginnings all that well, do we. Let's pretend, though. Let's go back and alter your history. Let's say you're still married to ... I'm sorry, what was her name?"

"Alice."

"Yes, Alice. Let's say you're an older man and a younger man all at the same time, hmm?"

"What?"

"You're living your life on the road. You're in a band, or some other kind of performer. Or you're a traveling salesman, say, with a circuit you must travel, to earn your living and it keeps you away from Alice, from home, for long periods of time."

"Is this one of those farmer's daughters jokes?"

"Zimmer?"

"Sorry."

"But it isn't quite working out. The days are always too long. Your take, or commission is never enough. Your expectations, those of Alice, are never realized. So you quit. You give up that endeavor—sell the franchise, drop out of the circuit, admitting that it just wasn't working out, trying to tell yourself that you gave it a good try, but just came up short.

"Because there is always going to be a point, isn't there," he said, turning to Zimmer, "when no matter the circumstances, there has to be a point where you have to look at whatever potential your situation might possess, and realistically, you have to look at the level of actualization, do you understand? Despite all the disclaimers, the second guessing, despite whatever truthfulness there might be in second guessing, in hindsight, no matter if you've done everything right at each step along the way, sometimes you have to step aside and give up *your* potentials, for the sake of another's."

He talked right through Zimmer's incomprehension. "You agree to stay home with Alice, to establish that home, changing careers, attending a trade school, utilizing whatever veteran's benefits you have remaining. You set up a meager household, as diametrically opposed to your former gypsiness as could be, and the two of you even start discussing a family, having a baby, something she's always wanted but was delaying until now."

"I don't know, Mr. Boyles. This doesn't sound like me. This sounds more like Steph. Don't you want me to go fetch him?" Zimmer asked, half upright from his stool, pointing across his body with his left hand, at the door.

"No, actually, I'd prefer you to stay," Mr. Boyles said, facing the bar, handing the joint back to him.

"But..."

Randy held Zimmer's right wrist against the bar, saying, "Listen, Zimmer. Shut up and listen," sliding a fresh beer into that hand.

Mr. Boyles sat bent over his glass, the vestiges of a frown

showing in the side of his face Zimmer could see in profile, the corner of his mouth tucked in, his jaw muscles taught. That picture of the old man underscored Randy's admonishment, so, willing or not, Zimmer shut up.

He continued without lifting his head, speaking down to the bar, his glass, rattling it, only half full of scotch now, with a few eroded ice cubes. "You're trying, nonetheless, to dedicate yourself to this new scheme, this new plan the two of you have. You're trying to accelerate through the curriculum, overloading most quarters, taking night classes, if that's the only time you can get the required credits. And you're trying to bring in whatever supplementary income you can, at the same time, doing odd, seasonal jobs. This puts an equal burden of support on Alice, necessarily. Because, you see, even if your previous occupation hadn't been as successful as you'd hoped, it brought in a considerably greater amount of money than five dollars a lawn. But she agrees, agrees to hold her job for the nine, ten months it will take, agrees to all the plans. What you come to find out is, that she agrees *to* them, but not *with* them."

Mr. Boyles raised his head again. "See, Anthony, it's a bitterness that surfaces only once you've started, indeed, are well into your studies. Who can really tell when it began? You think, well, naturally she's going to feel neglected, faced with your progress while she stagnates in the drive-thru booth at a neighborhood bank. But you have plans, together, plans that are graduated, progressive."

He leaned in closer to Zimmer. "Listen: While at one point it was true that you and Alice fell in love with each other just for each other, just by virtue of some physical or even psychological compatibility, that love required nurturing, growth. Forward growth. But the union cannot grow if *all* the parts do not, right?

"Wrong. See, even as one part grows—in a perfect union— the other benefits, if it *chooses*. Which it must," he said. Then he held his hands out over the bar, palm upward, though he couldn't quite fully extend all of his thin fingers, and they trembled, noticeably. "The support one gives to another is so much more involved and complicated than merely monetary, which is what commitment is all about, true."

Zimmer couldn't answer, though it seemed obvious. Like other little parts of the story seemed crystal clear, absolutely pertinent, though he couldn't begin to say why, even if he could well enough guess why not. "I wasn't exactly at my lucid best."

"Let's say you, or Alice, have decided not to, or at least have come to resent having to support each other's endeavors. You no longer feel your situation together is worth that effort, which has to be a possibility, doesn't it?" He left that question hanging as well, turning back to his glass, now mostly empty. "We are always so conscious of couples parting, of divorce, and we keep exquisite statistics on our domestic relations, when it has to be at least as likely that two people will decide that they don't want to share their lives with each other as decide it might be worth a try. Why *should* a fifty percent divorce rate surprise anyone? The error is in not allowing for change, in not recognizing that the whole institution is only an *attempt* at happiness, at fulfillness. The error, I think, is in not considering the idiocy of such things as vows, promises."

Zimmer's right eyebrow shot up in another of those moments of recognition, but he squinted again, trying to trace his way from the recognition to its referent.

"One night," Mr. Boyles continued, sitting back in his stool, straighter, crossing his legs, speaking levelly, and a little faster, holding his refilled glass, balancing it lightly on the edge of the bar. "Alice drops you off at class. If nothing else, the logistics of coordinating school and work with only one vehicle adds stresses that you shouldn't have had to handle, couldn't possibly have anticipated. She's on her way to an appointment of her own, which is the result of a militantly enforced parity, you know," he confided, chuckling in a raspy, smoker's way. "It's that, Well, if you're going to be so busy all of the time, I've got things I can get involved with too, which is the first explicit signal that the gears are grinding rather than meshing—behind all the *implicit* moods and dissatisfaction. Maybe a less patient person than you are now," they both laughed at that, "What with your schedules and your assignments, it doesn't really matter to you that she goes off, so long as she returns in two hours to pick you up. But maybe she wasn't always thrifty with her time. Perhaps, she spent it idly chatting, or chasing what seemed to you meaningless goals. She has never felt the urgency, wasn't concerned with the finite world closing in around her. She wouldn't have been able to make the decisions you've made, in fact, to abandon one tack, to recognize diminishing returns: those are exclusively your manic concerns. When she isn't waiting at the drop-off point after class, you're not too surprised. And you have other things to think about, your books, and a lecture fresh in your mind. A new bit of homework. You spend your time pacing back and forth along the sidewalk adjacent to the parking lot where you're supposed to meet, stepping in and out of the yellow conical glow of the street lamps. At one end of your circuit, you can see the road which Alice will have to use to approach the lot, and you scan the empty street at the end of each cycle, before you turn and head away from it again. And when you reach the opposite end of the sidewalk, that closest to the classrooms, you turn to face the lot and the street beyond. Each time, you tell yourself that she'll be there, or coming. And each time that expectation is followed immediately by disappointment, which grows, and grows as you approach the street, eventually reaching a crescendo of whirlwind emotion succeeding emotion, until all curricular concerns are pushed from your mind.

"You realize you've been waiting, and pacing for nearly an hour. What could have happened? you wonder, and systematically list the possibilities. It's possible that she's still talking with someone," Mr. Boyles said, counting on his fingers. "And it's possible that she forgot, and headed straight home. But surely she'd remember, once there. It's possible she's gone to the wrong rendezvous spot.

"In any case, there's not much you can do about it, but

check the three or four other parking lots on campus. You jog down the main road, between the two entrances, scanning the principal parking areas, and then back, taking about fifteen minutes, not finding any clues. Then at the north entrance you find a telephone. A call to your house goes unanswered. After some investigation, a call to her meeting place unearths only a sleepy, irritated voice that tells you, curtly, that the meeting had been cancelled. You hang up, step outside the booth, and figure, she's been busying herself otherwise, or missing, for more than four hours."

Mr. Boyles paused, to sip his drink, switch his legs. He cleared his throat.

"Back inside the phone booth, you call the police. No, they haven't had any reports of an accident in the area. You're soothed very little by that news, knowing that it could mean that she just hadn't been found yet. Or, and here is where your mind really starts to move into a dimension you hadn't anticipated, she *has* been found. She's been found and accosted. Or abducted. You make one more phone call. You call one of Alice's close friends, who lives nearby, and ask her for help. She arrives minutes later, hysterical, crying, asking all sorts of questions, the same kinds of questions that you've been asking all along, that she thinks you have answers to, as if you are somehow responsible, or know more than you're telling...

"That, Anthony, plants an ugly little seed in your mind. Ugly," he said, and then paused, for a long, long time.

"Together, you driving her car, you trace all the likely routes that Alice might have taken, between campus and the meeting place, there and home, home and campus, tracing, tracing, sure that at the next bend, or behind a dark and isolated convenience store, you'll find your abandoned, blood smeared car. Or worse. But you don't find anything, and the only plan you can settle on is to head back to campus, back to the point of origin and work it all out again.

"You're thinking of a time when you were a little boy, how you got lost in a department store once. You'd panicked, racing all over the store trying to find your parents, heedless, thoughtless. When they finally find you, hours later, your father, the most stern, most direct, and most impressionable you can ever remember him being, tells you that if you ever, *ever*, **ever** get lost, cut off from them again, to stay in that place. Don't move! They'll find you. You believed him, without question. Still do. It's one of the two or three things he's ever told you that you will always consider credible, and just then you realize that's not a bad goal to aspire toward, being able to furnish another person two or three items of good advice, two or three good memories. Trying to be everything, all the time, is too much to ask."

Zimmer had started leaning toward Mr. Boyles, watching his mouth closely, watching the words come out.

"You deposit Alice's friend—let's call her Renee—at the phone booth, pushing a handful of quarters into her hand to call anyone who might know anything, and trot up the road through the campus again, slowly, looking around you, talking to yourself. You find that you're speeding up, sprinting across lawns, hopping fences, and yet not concentrating on that effort, but thinking about how sure Renee had been, with her soap-operatic flare for the dramatic, that something awful has happened to Alice. Death, at least. And in that state of adrenalized agitation, with everything functioning wholly independent of anything else—your legs racing through the darkness without the strain of unrehearsed exercise, your eyes peeking into corners you couldn't have known of—your thoughts are sneaking too, as untethered as anything else, into corners usually kept dark. You think about your car, and its loss, the *inconvenience*! You think of Alice in a hospital, or dead, and the insurance associated with either. You never worry about insurance. What you're doing is trying to think ahead, extending your life from what appears to be happening, so that you can be ready, somehow, so that you can maybe keep functioning. You consider the possibility of being alone again, all alone.

"Then you stop. In the middle of the dark campus you stop,

and think, allowing that thought room to flex, about how preferably uncomplicated your life would be if you were alone. You don't necessarily *want* anything to have happened to Alice—although, if Renee could think that you have somehow contributed to Alice's absence, as she seems to, how would Alice had to have characterized you for that to be true, and what does *that* say about your marriage in the first place, Do you see where that thought has sprouted?—but you are comfortably past that. You're alone again. You want to live by yourself again, and your mind, with your legs, as you resume the search, flying across the campus races with those possibilities.

"And then you see your car. It isn't wrecked, or burning, or damaged in any visible way. It isn't even moving. It's parked on the opposite side of the business building, not particularly hidden, and you wonder how long she's been sitting there, in the dark, but that's not what comes out of your mouth.

"Where the hell have you been?

"Her answer, of course, is the same question.

"I've been looking for you, you say.

"Looking for me? I've been here for hours. I was just about ready to give up on you.

"You've been here since six?

"Just about."

Zimmer was fascinated by Mr. Boyles' rendition, the way he kept turning his head, answering himself. He could almost see two people having the exchange.

"You continue like that for quite a while, neither of you saying anything about being worried, or concerned, or relieved. And you know, even while its happening, there's no accident in that."

It wasn't until a little later that Zimmer considered the story as being autobiographical, rather than the fictitious fables he usually unfolded for them. But being a few hundred miles and ounces of alcohol past the point of being able to unravel riddles, as he drove through Dagaton Woods, he still couldn't correlate the story. He almost forgot, tracing the curving, shadowy roads, through a misty drizzle that had started, what it was he was trying to figure out. He just cruised the park roads, adhering to the official, but widely ignored fifteen mile an hour speed limit, letting the rest of Mr. Boyles' story play through his mind, hoping for clues, in the intervals between the slap-whack of the Bee-atile's windshield wipers.

"Through the anger that the misunderstanding between you and Alice precipitated, you can't possibly summon the conviction to perpetuate what is suddenly revealed as the biggest lie of your life. At that moment you decide that you no longer want anything to do with the woman, nor she with you, and no convention of morality or civility or tradition can obscure that fact. All either of you want is solitude, and a chance, maybe a last chance, to do something satisfying with your lives. A chance to get it right, once, or once again. That is the *bitch* of life, Anthony, you get to a point where you have to try to get it right, because you felt it was right, some time, and if you let go of that feeling, you let go of too goddamn much..."

At the time, Zimmer remembered sitting up straight suddenly, raising his hand, pointing a finger, to make some point, but not, thinking he was only reacting to Mr. Boyles' sudden and unprecedented use of profanity. "But no," that's not what he had wanted to say at all. He wanted to tell the old man, "Exactly. Exactly. *That's* how all this started!"

"But it's you who leaves. You don't take anything that she wants, and don't leave anything she doesn't. You end up with a fraction of what eight years of marriage can accumulate, with the entire load of guilt associated with breaking up those kinds of things, and a five year bill to pay for the decision. But you also end up with yourself. And you can defend yourself to all those who would accuse you of breaking what their god had joined together, breaking vows or promises.

"*Look*," Mr. Boyles said at the last, his voice hardly a whisper, "look at how much better you are, you can say to her, to them, now that you're paying attention to the present moment, not living in terms of forever and ever, amen. Surely, you can understand that!" he said, straining to hold Zimmer's attention for just a little longer. "Maybe if you had done that all along, any of the current messes could have been avoided. If we noticed the subtle little changes as they're occurring, noticed and incorporated them instead of always reacting *against* change, resisting wrinkles in the routine—when changes are going to happen whether we like them to or not— we wouldn't be creating these huge lies of denial which is what's really destructive; we might live our lives a little more honestly, whether we stay together or not."

At times, Zimmer slipped under the speed limit, Abby chugging along just fast enough to keep from stalling. He wanted to allow all the time he could for recalling how nice it always felt in the park. This was a sense of welcome he had anticipated upon returning to Salyne.

"But home," he said, creeping along in the dark, leaning with his elbows against the steering wheel, "does not necessarily have anything to do with family. Home changes."

He very nearly plowed over the curb and through the underbrush, dangerously close to two large pine trees.

"That's it!" he yelled, regaining control, composure, accelerating toward the park exit. "Sure. No car. No cook. He went back home. Oh, Steph..."

Zimmer thought it through, pretty much making the theory fit with what he'd been told at the bar. "He probably went home for Easter, and that went well enough, so they asked him back. They sat around watching television the next night, and the next."

Zimmer sat up straighter. "Why should that worry, or bother me? Is that what Mr. Boyles was talking about? This has all been a lie?" But what's the lie, he had to ask. "*What's* this? And what the fuck does '*It* happens to everyone' mean?"

Steph just took the easy way out again, Zimmer figured, "Which is fine, as long as the motherfucker likes T.V. dinners."

In a full drunken rage, Zimmer charged down the access road behind Fillingim, swinging wide into the parking space beneath the apartment, only to smack solidly into an automobile already occupying the space.

Zimmer sat there, grinning stupidly, mindless of any damage. "The son of a bitch went out and bought a car!" he said, tickled at the thought of them being a two-car family.

But there was a nagging familiarity about the car. He got out of the Bee-atile and circled the blue Mazda, wagging his head, trying to figure out what it was.

He heard, "Snn, snn..." the only other sound from either upstairs or down in the garage, other than the rain, and tried to figure that out too. "Snn, snn..."

He realized both answers as a shivering grey cat crawled out from under the engine compartment. "This is Angela's car." Then, "Whomee, buddy, why are you out here? You'll catch a cold. Jesus, Steph."

Zimmer curled up in the Bee-atile, huddling with Whomee for the remainder of the late, chilled morning, shivering against each other, and slept.

Angela found them like that, Whomee curled into the crook of Zimmer's arm, sneezing, his nose running, Zimmer's legs draped across the gear shift.

"You're back!" she said, startling both of them. "This is a good morning."

In the process of trying to untangle himself, and trying to keep Whomee from clawing him to death, Zimmer wasn't thinking of civility. He was thinking, actually, that he now knew what Steph meant when he complained about being so cheerful so early in the day. He turned and squinted over his shoulder to look up at her, at all that red hair, those teeth.

"Good morning."

"Angela."

"Hi. Glad you're home."

Home? Zimmer thought, still trying to disengage himself.

"Listen, I hate to bother you, but could I get my car out? I've got to get to work."

"Sure, sure," Zimmer said, still too groggy to question anything. He just pushed Abby out of the way. She drove off, saying, "See you later," and Zimmer waved.

"I know one thing," he said to Whomee as they circled the garage and thumped up the staircase. "If he ever accuses *me* of being too cheery in the morning again I'm going to slap him."

13. Gone To The Bears

ZIMMER stood in the kitchen, as coffee water heated, looking out over Dagaton Woods. He'd seen all of its seasons from those windows now, all of its changes. Back in the winter, early winter, before any snow, it'd seemed like the bright gay colors that had welcomed him to Fill, to Tripoli, were gone forever, that the trees were stripped bare and relegated to some environmental concentration camp, never to bloom again. The whole park had been so barren, so naked, malnourished looking—even from this vantage, some of the limbs, the peeling maple branches, especially, looked like an old man's arthritically knarled and knotted hands and knees. He could see through the foliage, the muted, barren ground, which only helped to reinforce his sense that Dagaton Woods had shriveled and died. Zimmer had looked out over it every morning a little sorry, but always hoping. By the time the snow came there wasn't enough left to the trees to support any accumulation, so that it all sagged and fell to the ground. Everything stood out in relief, the dark limbs against the white ground covering, instead of being blanketed in a winter showcase.

But then Dagaton Woods sprouted again. Little by little, aided along by those frequent spring washings, the brown gave way, the park woke up, stirring and green. So now, in the throes of summer, Dagaton Woods was wild and wonderful again. This was the personality of the park that Zimmer liked best, of course, this unsculptured, unconstrained green bursting through one shade then another, and another, refusing to follow a pattern, to take any shape except its own.

All around the park, Tripoli yielded to civil engineering, "Chamber of Commerce," plans. It followed a strict order. It reminded Zimmer of aerial views of Manhattan, with its park, stubbornly in the midst of all that business. Looking past

Dagaton Woods, farther west, farther into the valley, he could see the patterned outlines of the housing tracks along Knollwood Road and Bellows Lane, 13's parallels. He couldn't see much detail of the model homes, but he could see the patterns, "Tree, house, tree, house, tree, house, corner." He didn't want to see any more than that. "That's enough."

"Who are you talking to?"

It was the second time this morning that Zimmer's ruminations—something perfectly normal for him—had been challenged. But Steph didn't wait for an answer.

He had the sheet off the bed draped haphazardly about himself. His hair was standing up in four or five places. He wore only one grey basketball sock. His skinny legs were otherwise bare, as were his arms, both of which clung to things. In his left was a pillow. In his right, a cat: Whomee hung from Steph's forearm looking more confused than uncomfortable. And his eyes were still militantly shut.

"Goddammed disrespectful insomniacs around here... I just don't know what's wrong with you. Why can't you respect sleep? You have all these other lofty, high-browed ambitions and attitudes, all your inflexible absolutes... It *is* still morning, isn't it? What time is it? Why are we awake?"

Zimmer looked instinctively at the clock radio, then shrugged along with it. He could answer those questions, he really could. Especially the last two.

"Isn't this Sunday? Don't you know that Sunday is the absolutely most delinquent day of the week, every fucking week? They play games all over the world on Sunday. Movie tickets are at a premium on Sunday because people are always in search of idle entertainment on Sunday. Networks save their best programs for Sunday. They serve booze for breakfast on Sundays! Why are you desecrating this fine, lazy day? What's happened to sleep? Why is this cat in bed with me pawing at my face? Where's Angela?"

"Gone to work," Zimmer said, jumping at any legitimate pause, though that was also part of all the answers.

"Oh yeah, that's right."

"You knew?"

"Sure. She told us. Don't you remember?"

Zimmer was stumped, though Steph corroborated the story as she'd told it a couple of hours earlier, when she'd caught him grumbling to himself, "It's not even light out yet! What the hell time is it?"

"Who are you talking to?"

She stood there in a robe, drying her hair with a towel.

"No one," he'd said, busying himself with pots and pans, since he was up.

"I don't know what time it is, since you assaulted the clock. But it would have been about 5 when the alarm went off."

"What are you doing?"

"Getting ready for work."

"Today."

"Yeah. I switched. Don't you remember?"

"Switched?"

"Zimmer, I told you last night. I'm working weekends now. I'll be off Monday and Tuesday."

"Oh."

But he didn't remember. He had to try and reconstruct the memory, backwards, starting with the clock: "I was sleeping." He'd been in bed, tossing and turning on the cot he'd inherited since she'd moved in, but mostly sleeping, "Until the clock went off, that is." He'd had to track the damn thing down, in the dark, with Whomee's help, creeping around the bamboo partition, ambushing the offensive little appliance off her nightstand, clawing for the socket behind the couch to rip its life-line out of the wall, strangling the thing until the glowing red numbers faded and blinked out. Then Angela leaned over the mattress and shushed *him*! "You'll wake up Steph."

Zimmer knew the improbability of that. "Are you kidding?"

He remembered her going to bed early last night, Frank pleading her to stay. "Son of a bitch was lucky beyond belief. Beyond possibility." He remembered Bruce offering to tuck her in, and the two of them giggling away behind the partition for a few minutes before Steph thought to interrupt. He remembered bidding her good night, like everyone else. But he doesn't have any recollection of a reason why she had to sleep, doesn't remember any discussion that she had to get up early. "Hell, I'd've kicked everyone out." None.

"Coffee?"

"Oh no, I'll not be party to this horrible breach of sanity. I refuse to wake up," Steph answered, trailing back to bed, forsaking Zimmer's offer, even leaving his cat behind. "I just don't understand how you can treat such an important part of your life, the one ab-so-fucking-lutely vital part," Zimmer had to lean, and then step toward the doorway to hear the rest of his speech, "Because they can synthesize food; they can process water. But they'll never, *ever*, simulate sleep!"

Steph stopped at the partition, and turned back for the kitchen.

Zimmer was sure there was more, and stayed leaning into the doorway, listening, when Steph almost bumped into him, asking, "What's that you're cooking?"

"Oh, shit," Zimmer said, pushing the coffee cup he still held on Steph. "Sauce," he told him. "For Frank." Then, "Jesus, look at this place. Angie's going to have a fucking fit."

Zimmer stirred down the molten, spitting sauce, flipping the heat off, glaring over at Steph, like it was his fault.

"I thought you said she went to work?"

"I thought you were going back to bed?"

"Yeah, well," Steph said, waving at the stove. "Tough to concentrate on snoozing."

Zimmer looked at him a little disgusted, squinting his eyes. "Why *is* she changing her schedule, anyway?"

"I don't know. She just wants to take Monday and Tuesday off for a while. Change of pace," Steph said, hovering around the stove, sniffing the red smudges on the counter, then rubbing one off, licking his finger. "Can I get in there?" he asked over Zimmer's shoulder. "Can I taste?"

Zimmer blocked him away from the pan.

"Couldn't we eat a little?" Steph said, retreating, but poking around for other evidence of Zimmer's cooking, lifting the towel off the French bread, inhaling the yeasty fragrance. "Just a little barbecued omelette, say, while the bread finishes?"

"Get out of there," Zimmer yelled at him. "Go get dressed, would you. By the time you're ready, it'll be time to go."

"I'm going like this," he said, stepping to the windows, rearranging the sheet. "Mrs. Frank'll love it, don't you think?"

"Maybe," Zimmer said. "But we're not going to Frank's house. We're going right to the ballpark—what's it, Lucas Field?"

"Stadium."

"Frank wants to have a tailgate party."

"At a baseball game?"

"It's Frank, remember."

"Well then, that settles it. We'll have to eat now," Steph said, moving in on the stove again.

"Why?"

"Because Abby doesn't have a tailgate."

"Get *out*!" Zimmer said, shoving Steph toward the door. Then, watching Steph trip and stumble over his train, offered, "I will pour you a beer though."

Steph leaned back into the kitchen. "Already?"

"Game time is sooner than you think," Zimmer told him, before stooping into the refrigerator, pulling out a bottle of Iron City, pouring some into two recycled olive pimento jars. "It's a double header."

"Then pour away master Zimbarco," Steph called. "Since we won't be visiting Pineapple Estates, who cares?"

"That's it!" he said, turning back to the windows. Suddenly he remembered something Steph had told him, about *deja vu*, how Steph usually felt like he was living out someone else's *deja vu*. "Not living out someone else's life," but serving as that spooky reminder, of brushes with former lives, past actions. "And you know what I wonder, Zimmer? I wonder what the rest of his life is like."

Frank lived in the housing track west of Dagaton Woods. "Pineapple Estates. That's not the *real* name, is it?" Zimmer called.

"Naw, don't you remember?"

Zimmer was getting sick of people accusing him of that. "I remember!"

They'd been to Frank's house, down in the subdivisions, earlier in the summer, much earlier. It was before the alarm clock had materialized in Fill, before Angela cared much at all whether she was on time for work, before she started calculating, maximizing, "Why else the change in schedule?" It was before Zimmer ever would have concerned himself with how messy his cooking was, "In my own goddammed kitchen!"

They'd gone to Frank's for a backyard cook-out, winding through the neighborhood of identical houses and near identical street names, Cherry Lane, Cherrypit Court, Cherrystone Avenue.

"What are we looking for again?"

"It's supposed to be easy to find," Steph said, from the back seat of Abby, halfway quoting from his notes, supposed directions, jotted down on a bar napkin at Lear's the night before.

"Then where the fuck is it?" Zimmer yelled, his frustration boiling over. He was veering back and forth across the gently curving, *always* curving roads, between alternately parked station wagons. "Where are we?"

"We're in Cherries Jubileeland!" Angela said, beside Zimmer, starting the ridiculousness, Zimmer laughing, his other emotions spent, worn out and exhausted from the anxiety and the effort and the futility of this first travelling Feast day. His laughter sent Abby into her own convulsions, tossing Steph around in the back seat with the basketball, while he tried to save the food.

"Fruit Cocktail Acres," he said, leaning forward, between the seats again, until Zimmer snorted, stomping on the gas, throwing Steph back against the seat, screaming.

It was then that Angela'd whispered, "Pineapple Estates."

"Give me those directions."

Zimmer reached back and snatched the napkin from Steph,

tossing it out his window.

Then, around the next loop—there were no square blocks within Pineapple Estates—Steph shouted, "There! There!" pointing between Angela and Zimmer, through the windshield. "There's Mickey's car. We did it!"

The three of them had talked and snickered, later that Saturday afternoon turned Sunday morning, about the horrors of being lost in Pineapple Estates for the rest of their lives, cruising the meandering roads, braking for school buses come fall, at crosswalks and speed bumps, turning into and then backing out of one cul-de-sac after another, hoping for an exit, escape. That was a Sunday much earlier in the summer.

Although, when Frank greeted them as they pulled into the parking lot of the ballpark, "Iss-bout goddamm-dime you do showed-dup!" and Steph looked over at Zimmer, mirroring his I've heard that line before look, maybe they both were thinking of that day so long ago, when Frank had yelled just about the same thing, "At least that's what it *sounded* like," over his four-foot redwood fence. "And wasn't he wearing that same `Kiss the Kook' apron?"

"Naw. That's too spooky."

Zimmer shivered against the premonition, afraid that their lives really were overlapping, and tried to change the subject. "So, this is the famous Lucas Field, huh?"

"Stadium," Steph corrected, irritably, knowing Zimmer was doing that on purpose. "Great, isn't it."

Before Zimmer could inquire after Steph's reverent gaze up at the old park, Frank hollered, "Where the hell's my sauce?"

Steph *would* have told Zimmer how great the stadium had been at one time. To look at it from the outside, it was one of those perfect baseball stadiums, that didn't try too hard to confine the game to the playing field. No dome, no concrete saucer. It wasn't a multi-purpose complex. It was a baseball park. The tall, arching girders still showed, painted, supporting slanted tiers of bleachers, where you could see—approaching the gates, queuing up with hundreds of other anxious fans—

sunshine peeking through the legs of those in attendance and the gaps left in the construction of the seats. But that would have been a long time ago, too. Without the fans, it was a different picture. Lucas Stadium now looked cold and empty and grey, the paint peeling off the girders, showing splashes of rust here and there, the color, to Zimmer, not that different than the sauce he hurried over to Frank's lonesome tailgate party on the mostly empty parking lot.

"Greetings," Mr. Boyles said to them, perched on a fold-out canvas chair, drink in hand.

Randy was nearby, setting utensils and other necessities onto a cloth covered card table. Frank was camped at the opened rear end of his truck, turning, returning pieces of chicken on a portable gas grill.

Zimmer handed Frank the pot of sauce and the foil wrapped bread. He asked, "Where's Bruce? Mickey?"

"They should be orbiting back through shortly," Mr. Boyles said, pursing his lips, as if Randy had squeezed a lemon into his vodka tonic instead of a lime. "They're playing a rather hybrid game of catch."

"Hybrid catch?" Steph said.

"You know how Bruce gets."

"But--"

"Buttonhook! Buttonhook!" Bruce yelled across the lot.

Mickey came streaking across the faded yard markers into the circle they'd created with their cars. He stopped as best he could and spun to his right, holding a gloved left hand in the air. The baseball shot over the awning Frank had erected, far too high for Mickey to reach, who backpedaled furiously to try and catch up to the missile, brushing past Steph.

"There's more," Mr. Boyles told him, unmoved in his chair.

"Hey!" Frank yelled, guarding his grill, jamming his cigar back into his mouth and glaring around his truck at Bruce. "Wash-it-wid-dat-shit!"

"Double," Bruce called. "Ground rule double. Man in scoring position, nobody out."

"What?" Steph started.

"What do you mean double?" Mickey said, returning with the ball. "That was interference."

"That's what ground rules are, damnit. Play ball!"

"Bullshit," Mickey said, but gave up the ball.

"Ready?" Bruce asked. "Slant left, fast ball, on two. Hut one, hut two," he said, shuffling back five, six paces into the pocket, watching Mickey go through his route, around an empty station wagon, cutting behind it sharply to the left.

Bruce stopped his fade, leaned forward on one bent leg, fingering the baseball behind his back. He nodded and went into his windup just as Mickey was clearing the free safety Chevy. As Bruce's kick reached its zenith, Zimmer burst into the backfield, waving his arms and hollering, "Blitz! Blitz!"

Bruce halted his delivery, leg up, arm cocked, frozen like a bubblegum card, his eyes bulging, as he watched the charging Zimbarco.

When Mickey saw the hesitation, he started jumping up and down, slapping his bare hand against the gloved one. "Balk! Balk!" he cried. "My ball. Go on, punt."

Zimmer was making his own rules, and kept charging. When Bruce realized he actually intended to sack him, he started to scramble, begging, "Somebody blow the whistle! Drop a flag, signal the bullpen, anything, quick!" as Zimmer chased him around and around the table, Mr. Boyles' chair, the cars.

"Travelling!" Mickey shouted. "Fifteen yards!"

"Stop!" a familiar voice shouted, "Stop!" though none of them could remember hearing it at that volume before. Mr. Boyles coughed, pulled his baseball cap down over his eyes some more and he hung his head. "Sorry. I just couldn't stand this lunacy any longer."

"Slobs," Steph said. "You guys are real slobs."

"What?" Zimmer said, bent over, holding his knees, panting from the effort.

"What happened?" Mickey asked, returning from the field.

Bruce in nearly the same position as Zimmer, not five feet away, answered, "Third down, man on second; some crazy fan decides to blitz."

"*That's* not what happened, you assholes. This stupid game of yours happened," Steph said, taking Mickey's glove from him.

"I'm sorry," Mr. Boyles said again, looking around at the winded players.

"No you're not," Steph argued.

"What?" Zimmer said again, to Steph this time. "I don't get it, what's the fuss?"

"No fuss," Frank said, from a million miles away. "No muss. Just barbecued chicken!"

"I'm just a little over-sensitive," Mr. Boyles said, getting out of his seat. "I'll wait inside."

"By yourself?"

"Over-sensitive? About a parking lot?" Bruce asked the others, looking around, tossing the ball into the air, catching it barehanded with a slap.

"Not the parking lot, jackass," Steph said, thumping Mickey's glove against Bruce's chest before stepping after Mr. Boyles. "The stadium. The Bears!"

"Let's eat," Frank called. "That'll make everyone fat and happy."

"I'm not eating out here," Steph called over his shoulder.

"What do you mean you're not eating out here?" Frank asked.

Steph spun and shouted at him, "I'm not eating out here with this freak show. Just what I said. I'm eating inside."

"They won't let us bring all this stuff in there."

"I'll eat a hot dog, like you're supposed to."

"Hot dog?"

"Precisely," Mr. Boyles answered, though no one could hear him but Steph. They were almost to the closed gates. "Thank you, Stephen."

"They just don't know."

"And how did you?"

"I knew as soon as I saw your cap."

"Oh, this," the older man said, taking it off, wiping his forehead with a handkerchief.

Steph had recognized Mr. Boyles' cap as an original Bears cap, before they started putting that fiberglass meshing in the crown to keep it rigid, before they'd jazzed up the logo. His was the faded chocolate brown version, caved back against his forehead, just the stitched outline of a bear. The button at the peak was a metal one, rusted now, like the stadium. Steph recognized the cap because his father had one very similar to it. He'd always coveted that cap as a child, and now wondered if he didn't just covet those Saturday afternoon games with his father. He figured Mr. Boyles for one of the loyal fans his father always spoke of, who went to all the games, who were part of a very tight and diverse family at the stadium. Steph's father used to tell him not to worry about how few people were at the games with them, that they were real baseball people. But even knowing that, Steph couldn't have guessed at all the reasons for Mr. Boyles' sensitivity.

And Zimmer couldn't have guessed at any of it, never having heard of the Bears, Lucas Stadium. Randy could have told him some, but he sat at the table, only half outfitted, watching Mr. Boyles and Steph. The rest of them stood around without any clue as to what to do. Mickey slipped his glove back on and flexed it vacantly. Bruce stood there with his mouth opened, still tossing the ball. And Frank stayed back by his truck, stuffing his mouth with chicken.

Zimmer shook his head and trotted after the two of them just as they turned away from the gate. When he got near enough, he asked, "No show, huh?"

"You kidding?" Steph said, stepping ahead of Mr. Boyles. "We can get box seats if we want. We can get press box seats. We can cart the whole business inside if we want and enjoy the aura of the stadium with our meal."

Mr. Boyles caught up to Steph, pulling his raised arms back down to his sides. "No glass containers, though," he reminded Steph, without tempering his enthusiasm.

"Wow," Zimmer said. "How'd you swing that?"

"They all know Mr. B," Steph said, pointing back at the stadium. "You should have seen them. Henry? Henry Boyles?

It's *great* to see you! They called the offices, the clubhouse, announcing his presence!"

"Henry?" Zimmer said.

"I'd appreciate it if that didn't get too far," Mr. Boyles said to him as the three of them approached the cars.

"How did it get out at all?"

"He's a regular here, I'm telling you," Steph said, leaning across Mr. Boyles, who was in the middle. "A fucking hero!"

Mr. Boyles elbowed him. "Used to be."

In fact, Mr. Boyles worked for the Bears, as clubhouse manager, back in the forties. He told them stories about some of the real heroes of the team, early Pittsburgh stars, when they were learning their craft at this minor league level, how they spent their whole lives in the clubhouse, learning, listening, practicing. He told them about a few other players that he'd known, who'd had more talent, "Unmistakable prospects," but who had been called into service, who never played again.

"It was such a strange time to be both a baseball fan and a patriot. There was no question, then, of course, but one wonders now. After the war, other realities caught up with the team, the integration of baseball, for one. There's no doubt that was the best thing for the game, but it changed the tenor of things around the stadium certainly. Those were difficult times."

"Is that what happened to attendance? Why they were sold?" Steph asked.

"No. In fact, attendance went up for a while. It was clearly better baseball, more exciting baseball. No, minor league teams were hurt most when the game went national, I think, with the move to the west coast, and television. Or, some folks think, the area will always be football crazed," Mr. Boyles told them, nodding past Randy and Zimmer, to Bruce. "I mean, look at the major league teams, the difficulties they're having these days," meaning the Pirates and the Phillies, "even with their success."

It was a truly sparse crowd at Lucas Stadium that day. The

Lumpers occupied a whole row of seats in the section adjacent to the third base bag. They were eight rows up from the field, and the only other fans in that section were three kids down near the corner of the dugout. Other fans were scattered about the park, maybe a hundred and fifty of them. They could have literally sat anywhere they wanted, but Steph picked those seats. Frank had lobbied seriously for seats behind home plate, the nearest he could get to a televised rendition of the game, but Steph had been adamant, belligerent, almost.

Those seats commanded a view of all the action of the field except for the interior of the third base—"The home team"—dugout. They were the seats preferred by Steph's father, who too would pass up better, closer seats to sit up alone in section seven, if he had to. Frank sat in the A seat, closest to home, grumbling about being so goddammed far away. Steph had promptly taken the seat at the opposite end of the row, an attempt at not annoying Frank further.

Not that anyone was allowed to sit *directly* next to Frank. "Loog-gat all dese empty seats, would ya? Don't get so close," he'd growled at Mickey.

There was an empty seat on each side of Bruce, likewise, who'd stashed much of their picnic in and around himself, serving as both bartender and waiter. Zimmer was to Bruce's left, and had helped him with the food, held the cups while Bruce poured contraband beer—smuggled into the stadium in gallon milk jugs Bruce kept stashed in the trunk of his car for reasons he never explained. Randy was next, then Mr. Boyles, and Steph.

They'd finished their meal and most of the beer before batting and infield practice was over, then sat there relaxing, waiting for the first pitch. These were the moments when Steph's father would talk the most, keeping young Steph busy looking around the park, watching the different player routines—some doing a last few wind sprints, some playing cards in the dugout, chatting with fans, how they tested their legs jogging in the outfield, how they sat on the grass and stretched. He would tell Steph to look at all the different shades of brown he could find, as an exercise, starting with the three shades in the home uniforms. Steph would find the dirt of the infield, the leather of their gloves, even the tan lines on exposed arms, or the black-brown juice of chewing tobacco as he watched players lean over the lip of the dugout steps and spit.

When he searched for colors like that, other senses would become just as attentive, and he could hear all the sounds mingling behind his father's voice, umpires making calls, infielders encouraging their pitcher, or the vendors, whose hawking was a steady, almost eerie plea which would reverberate in and out of his consciousness throughout the entire game, as would the aroma of the steamed hot dogs or roasted peanuts they carried.

Lucas Stadium wasn't built to contain those aspects of the game either, which may have secured its inevitable doom. It was built for baseball, would live or die with baseball. "But how could you die by baseball?" How could you go wrong at all?

"Every single time we came, my father would say, This game is the greatest, sounding, every time, like he'd just had the thought. And then he'd tell me why, talking about how baseball was the only game where the defense had the ball, how it wasn't stopped for penalties or fouls, how errors themselves were part of the continuous process of the game. And," Steph said, leaning forward, down the row, as they stood for the national anthem, at Zimmer, "there's no clock!" shrugging, ten till.

"I always knew your father had to be a better person than you ever give him credit for," Mr Boyles said as the scratchy recording started.

Steph waited for the end of the song before answering, but then just kept his answer, "Like you said Mr. B, that was a long time ago," as they sat again, cheering the Bears taking the field.

He sat perched forward in his seat during the early innings, both to see past their row, to spy the crowd, and to chase down any stray balls. The others relaxed, Frank crossing his legs into the aisle, Zimmer and Bruce draping theirs over the seat backs in front of them.

"Why did you and your father stop coming to games?" Mr. Boyles asked.

"He used to go with guys from the plant during the week, and take Jack and me on Saturdays. When the Bears were sold that first time, what, twelve, fifteen years ago, the other guys from work quit going and I guess he just fell out of the habit too. And then, when they were sold again in '77, he said he didn't want to see some Canadian team playing America's game," Steph said. "Besides, who ever heard of a blue bear?"

Zimmer perked up at that. "Canadian team?"

"They're a farm team for Toronto now. To Jack Sr., that's Canadian enough."

"They just sold the team, right. The players stayed the same."

"Most of them."

"You had to know the fans back then," Mr. Boyles said. "They were truly fanatics. It was the original sale, the one that took them out of Pennsylvanian parentage, that did it. By '77, they were just looking for an excuse, I'm afraid."

"Even you?" Zimmer asked him. "You never even talk about them, or read box scores, shit like that."

"I suppose I got out of the habit, too," Mr. Boyles answered during a break, while the Bears brought in a relief pitcher. "I made excuses, just like everyone. Claimed I was too busy. Who can remember?"

"We used to listen to the games at the bar for a while, remember that?"

"Never was the same, somehow."

"Nope," Steph said. "Nothing like a live Bears game."

Each of the Lumpers assented, in turn, grumbling, nodding, a wave of sentiment down the row, until Frank.

"Except they're getting their asses kicked."

"Doesn't matter," Steph told him.

"Nope, not with these bums," Frank agreed. "They'll be gone next year, no matter what they do."

"What?" Steph said, leaning across Mr. Boyles' legs.

"Yup. Been sold again."

"Really?" Steph said, scanning the faces back down the row, past a different collection of shrugs and ticks, not altogether decided consent until Mr. Boyles sat slowly nodding confirmation.

"Yeah," Frank snarled, "really," stuffing his stoagie into his mouth again. "Dongew read de goddammed-bapers?"

Steph sat back in his seat finally, and tried to concentrate on the last few innings of the game.

No, he didn't read the newspapers, at least not with any regularity or thoroughness. Newspapers never seemed designed for their lifestyles. They rarely cared about news in the morning, more concerned with drinking some beer and stealing a few hours of sleep. Afternoons were always filled with whatever they'd hoped to accomplish in the remaining hour or so of light, whether basketball or shopping.

Except for every other Friday and most Saturday afternoons, the sound on the television stayed down at Lear's. There wasn't a set at all in Fill, despite Angela's recent protesting. WTPY didn't cover much in the way of hard news. "Who needs more information?" Zimmer had always claimed.

It made for isolated lifestyles, by design. As he sat and watched the last of the lopsided game, Steph thought about what other gaps lurked in the design. And he had to wonder about the desirability of that on a permanent basis. During the last three, uneventful outs, Steph looked around the mostly empty stadium, his arms folded, his glove tucked under his seat.

To his left, all the way to the foul pole and around into the bleachers in left field, there were but the three kids, just this side of the outfield wall, there for souvenirs more than the game, roaming all over the park. He watched them, scanned the sea of empty seats around him, all the way up to the overhang, down to the playing field, and wondered about the future of Lucas Stadium, wondered about his history with the place, as a restless kid himself.

Between games, after he'd scampered underneath the sun-drenched bleachers with the rest of them, for the bathrooms, for some concession beer, Zimmer found Steph up at the top row of their section, looking back out over Tripoli. "Has the beer always been this bad?"

"How would I know?" Steph said, leaning with his elbows on the metal railing. "Part of the charm, I guess. Did you get a look at the burgers?"

"Crispy critters?"

"No, un-uh. Just the opposite. In a hurry to get you served, I suppose, they leave them bleeding."

"Wonderful place, Steph."

"Like a lot of things in this city, Mr. Boyles'll tell you, it really used to be."

Zimmer stood with his back against the railing, looking down at the row of contented Lumpers.

"Have you ever seen that?" Steph asked him, pointing back up at the hills behind Dagaton Woods. "The quarry?"

Zimmer turned around. "Where?"

"That shelf of white rock on the other side of the interstate."

The rock, glistening in the afternoon sunlight, stood out against the grays and browns and greens around it like some kind of monument.

"Nope," Zimmer said, wondering, at the same time, how he could have missed it.

"I guess you can't really see it through the trees and all. I'd almost forgotten about it, actually. It's not really a quarry, though, not any more. Not since they put the interstate through."

"They're *still* putting the interstate through, Steph," Zimmer quipped, never missing a chance to comment on Pennsylvania highway construction.

"They're waiting on your money."

"Oh, goddamn--"

"Me and these two other kids, Timmy Reed, and Phil... Phil something... We used to go up there all the time, like every day in the summer. Packing lunches, hiking up the hill, climbing over the boulders, up the facing, into the caves. We'd play up there all day." He turned to Zimmer. "I mean hours and hours."

"Let's go up there some time."

"No, I don't think so."

"Why not?"

"It's different. The pit's a road. The caves are probably filled in. It's different."

"What about the other two kids?"

Steph turned around as the P.A. man started his announcements. "I don't even know what happened to them. Gone, I guess."

"Married. Two and a half kids. Hair thinning."

"That's bad?"

"You tell me."

"At least they got out of Tripoli," Steph started, but then had to add. "I think."

"Maybe."

"Really. I don't actually know." He shuddered at the reminiscence. "Weird."

"What?"

"I don't know, spooked, like I know I've forgotten something, just can't figure out what."

"More beer?"

"Naw. Something else. I mean, did you ever have friends like that? Kids you knew when you were growing up, you were going to be friends forever—hell, I was closer to them than I was with Jack! And now, I don't have any clue what they're doing, can barely remember their names."

"Sure, everybody does," Zimmer told him.

"Koogan?" he guessed.

Zimmer winced. "Well. Yeah. Kind of."

Steph scuffed at the planking with the toe of his sneaker. It was hardly a useful comparison.

Zimmer added, "But even if, you just can't answer to all the ghosts."

"Ghosts?"

"Yeah, you know," he said, waving up at the quarry, and then widening the gesture to include much, must more.

"Is that what happened in New York? Too many ghosts?"

"Hah."

"Don't you have to answer some of them, at some point?"

"Well, shit, Steph. How are you going to do that"

"By paying more attention."

"Really? And how are you going to do that?"

They were summoned by the starting line-ups.

"Here's the best you can hope for, right: a few defining moments. Everybody's got one, a situation where every time you think of it, you think of that person."

"That's the best?"

"It's not bad, when you think about it."

"You know," Steph told him, as they started back down the stairs. "We really didn't think you were coming back."

"How could you?"

"I mean, we've never talked about Alice, any of that."

Zimmer stopped. "Yeah. I know."

"Why *did* you come back here to this shit hole after that?"

Zimmer grinned at him. "To see a goddammed baseball game," he said, over what little crowd noise there was, starting back down the stairs, "What else?"

"Jesus," Steph said, concentrating, short step, long, back to their seats. There was more to the question, of course, and Zimmer knew it.

At their row, they saw Frank buying beer, Bruce portioning it out, moving along the row, singing, "One, two, the-ree strikes you're out at the old, ball, game!"

"Please?" Mr. Boyles pleaded with him as he got to their end.

Zimmer stopped again, before squeezing past Mr. Boyles and Randy for his seat. "To get one right," he told Steph.

"No more beer for Zimmer."

"Fuck you."

Retreating before Zimmer, Bruce tried to explain. "Honest,

Mr. Boyles, I'm not defiling anything this time. I'm serious. I'm reverent, really, I am."

"But he's *not* clean," Mickey said.

"What?" Bruce turned and asked.

Zimmer knew the reference. "He's definitely not thrifty."

"But he's the bravest Lumper I know," Steph said, raising his cup to Bruce.

"All right, all right," Mr. Boyles conceded.

Bruce continued, "We just got to get into this game. They're going to do it this time," he said, sitting too, more positioning himself, like the Bears defense. "All they need is a little home town support. So, *everybody* sing, Take me out to the ball game, take me—"

"Stop!" Mickey yelled at him this time, slapping him, pulling his tee-shirt over his head even.

"All right, all right," Bruce said, easily regaining control. "No more singing. Somebody give me a glove."

They all feared he might actually climb down onto the field and bastardize the game as a tenth fielder, a short fielder. But he only stuffed his big hand into Steph's glove and pounded it, cheering the defense on, hooting, whistling, even biting off a hunk of one of Frank's cigars to get the requisite wad of tobacco in his cheeks at one point, anything to aid the Bears.

And it worked. The Bears held the visitors scoreless through the top of the inning.

"See?" he said to the others, but with the tobacco, it sounded like, "She?" He spit the wad out, passing Steph's glove back to him as well. "Nice mitt. Musta played some ball."

"Sort of."

"Why sort of?" Randy said, as he handled the glove.

"Well, I was on the team, but I didn't play much."

"One of the scrubs."

"That's right Frank. Weak wrists. Too slow to the hole. Just not a natural."

"Natural?" Frank croaked. "You didn't work hard enough."

"Oh no," Bruce said. "These guys are born jocks. They may not look it, but they are."

"My father always thought it was a strategist's game."

"Isn't it?" Mr. Boyles said.

"Well, that's why he kept me playing. But they're naturals too."

"True."

"I mean, do I strike *you* as a strategist?" He leaned down the row, asking Zimmer, the only veteran he knew of. "Imagine me, a general."

"But he kept you playing?" Zimmer answered back.

"Yup."

"Now that sounds more like Senior."

"But see, I think that was just part of his love for the game, wanting me to feel the same way he did, taking me to those games, telling me all that stuff—how to watch good infielders position themselves, how to react to the swing of the bat, as well as the sound."

"He showed you a harsh game, though, it sounds like," Zimmer said, thinking at the same time that his father hadn't done even that much, hadn't showed him too much of anything. He wondered about the consequences of either, squinting back at Steph.

"It's a game, period," Bruce said, doling out another round of beer. "And we're going to have fun because the Bears are going to kick some ass this time. Give me that glove back," he said, trading a brimming cup of beer with Steph for it, then stepping back along the empty row in front of the Lumpers, his bar, slamming his fist into Steph's mitt. "Dee-fense! Dee-fense!"

Mr. Boyles tugged at the bill of his cap.

Zimmer encouraged him, though not *just* because he was feeling more than a little belligerent. "It's a game!" he firmly, absolutely believed. "It's just a game," some people might want to say, which was not the same sentiment. Not quite. "Thank *God* it's a game," that we have things like games, that they never had to stop watching, attending, playing games. It's true, he was feeling argumentative just to be argumentative, but that's part of what the others now recognized as his just becoming more Zimbarco-like. This was absolute Zimmer, again. "Now you're talking," he said to Bruce, taking up the chant, "Dee-fense!"

The two of them persisted until the rest of the Lumpers joined in on the cheer, or at least pumped their fists into the air to the cadence. Mr. Boyles finally started rocking his drinking arm to the rhythm.

And then they extended themselves past merely chanting. When the Bears' lead-off hitter was called out on a check swing third strike in the bottom of the second, Bruce exploded out of his seat, "Bullshit!" and had to be grabbed, Mickey a leg, Zimmer about his waist, to keep from toppling over the seat in front of them.

The top of the fourth, with the left fielder and the third baseman chasing a lazy foul pop-up, running toward the Lumpers' section, Bruce, Mickey, and Zimmer stood and followed their progress until the faster left fielder slid into the fence, cradling the ball. The Lumpers jumped and slapped palms as the umpire signaled, "Out!"

In the bottom of the fifth, when the Bears scored two runs, on two sharp singles sandwiched around a sacrifice bunt, and then a double to the gap in center field, they all played third base coach, windmilling the second runner all the way home from first, Bruce getting carried away by the momentum of the gesture, crashing over the seats.

When Mickey, Bruce, and Zimmer, the middle of the row, got to rollicking and waving like that, the others didn't have much choice but to join in. It was either participate, or get trampled. To the rest of the crowd, many of whom watched the Lumpers with as much fascination as they watched the game, it might have looked rehearsed.

In the top of the seventh, the Bears nursing a one run lead, but in trouble—two Chiefs in scoring position, nobody out, the infield in tight—Bruce stepped over into the next row, pacing, leading his "Dee-fense," cheer, urging not just the Lumpers but all the fans, waving down toward home plate, all the way up to the press box.

The crack of the bat brought Bruce's attention back to the field, sent him reeling toward the action, in fact, down the aisle. The third baseman knocked down a line drive with a dive to his left, and then scooped up the ball.

Steph was out of his seat too, the old infielder, skipping a few steps down the aisle on his side of the row, positioning his feet, hollering, "Look him back!"

The third baseman showed the ball to the lead runner, and then threw a bullet to first. Out.

Bruce, who stumbled all the way down to the fence, leaning over what would have been a press or television camera area, just to the side of the dugout, echoed the first base umpire, "Out!" and then threw his arms into the air, exalting the third baseman, "Yeah!" He danced back in the general direction of his seat, greeting the next batter, "Dee-fense, Dee-fense!"

Zimmer had moved into Bruce's serving row. With Mickey and even Randy handling the interior of the Lumper row now, and Steph still jitterbugging along the steps of the aisle, they effectively had an entire section rocking, "Dee-fense, Dee-fense!" jumping up and down on vacated chairs, skipping along the concrete steps.

The batter, his concentration rattled by the noise in section 7, perhaps, struck out, after fouling off two grooved fast balls on a dramatic full count—the runners starting, then returning to their bases after each. Bruce, circling back down the aisle, sweating out each pitch, chanting louder and louder, climbed up onto the Bears' dugout after the third strike, announcing, "Sweeeeng an-a-miss..." greeting the pitcher with his arms raised, his fists clenched. "Yeah!"

A security guard stuck his head up over the lip of the dugout and motioned Bruce down. He climbed off in time to see a weak dribbler to second base for the third out. He stood in the aisle leading a stadium wide standing ovation as the home team left the field.

Bruce then ran up the steps, two at a time, to catch the beer vendor, pumping his fists, crying, "*That's* how you do it."

He resumed his duties as bartender, handing out more beer,

so that everyone had at least a couple of cups they were working on at the same time, saying, "That's all these guys needed."

"Some real fans," Mickey said, still standing on his seat.

"We ought to come to all the games."

Steph asked, "Think we'd last?"

Zimmer sat down in a seat in the lower row, drinking a beer from each hand. "Someone's got to inspire these folks."

"They can't even stay up for the stretch," Mickey said, looking around the park.

"Even the bear," Zimmer said, pointing at the mascot, who was hanging out in the left field bullpen, watching the Lumpers now, with his head off.

"Maybe they'd pay us," Mickey said.

"I certainly would. *That* was quite a performance."

"Bruce'd be a better bear," Zimmer said.

Randy leaned over and told him, "Bruce *is* a bear."

"I'd be a better bear."

"Why don't you buy the team back, Boyles," Frank said. "See what it's like to have these idiots working for you."

"Why don't *we* buy the team?" Mickey said, crouching over, almost whispering so that the secret wouldn't get beyond the Lumpers.

Frank looked up at him. "What?"

"Why don't we buy the team."

"Ged-oudda here..."

"That's a great idea!" Bruce said, climbing over into their row, looking up to Mickey.

"Can I be the bear?"

"Forget it," Frank grumbled.

"Why? I'd be a great bear."

"I mean forget buying these losers."

"What a perfect birthday present," Steph told them. "I'd love you guys forever for buying me a baseball team."

"I thought your birthday was in December?" Randy said.

"Bears don't need love, just a good hard tree to scratch their behinds on," Zimmer said, sliding against the wooden slats of his seat.

"I'm serious," Bruce said. "It's a great idea. We all got credit, right?"

"You're drunk," Frank said. "Forget it."

"We could all sit up in the owners' box, sipping wine," Steph said to Mr. Boyles.

"Not me," Zimmer said.

Mickey climbed down off his chair, asking, "Why not?"

"Forget it!" Frank tried again.

But even Mr. Boyles said, "That is one way we could keep them in Tripoli, isn't it?"

Zimmer stood, a little wobbly, stifling a burp, and answered Mickey, face to face, "Because I'm the Bear, and the Bear's place is down on the field, that's why."

"FORGET IT!" Frank stood up on his tippy-toes, shouting over Zimmer's head, Mickey's. He sprayed the whole row with tobacco spittle.

Zimmer climbed up on his seat, towering over Frank, growling, "Don't nobody shout at the Bear!"

"You're crazy Zimbarco," Frank said, sitting back down. "You're all crazy. You clowns couldn't afford to buy one lousy pair of cleats, much less a whole team."

"Frank and his fucking whistle," Zimmer said, climbing over into his seat, settling down with the rest of the silenced Lumpers. The continuing game—top of the eighth, two out, no threat—reoccurred to them. "You're a lot of fun, Frank. You know that? You and your fucking stop signs."

"You guys are just dreaming, wasting your lives," Frank said, pivoting, crossing his legs out into the aisle, but snickering back over his shoulder, "Buy the goddamn Bears, shit."

They watched the rest of the game, subdued by the reality that it was probably the last Bears game they'd see. And then, to complete their agony, the Bears held their lead through the top of the ninth, cheating everyone out of one more half inning of baseball.

The Lumpers filed out of the stadium with the rest of the fans, slowly passing through the creaking, almost protesting turnstiles, and walked to their cars, worn out by the long afternoon of baseball, roller-coaster adrenaline, and too much beer.

"See you tonight, boys," Frank called cheerily, firing up his truck, the first to vacate the scene.

"Not me," Zimmer hollered after him. "I quit. I'm going to be the goddammed Bear, Frank."

Zimmer growled again after Frank's truck disappeared among the rest of the traffic exiting Lucas Stadium.

The rest of the Lumpers growled at each other in parting, Mr. Boyles and Randy heading back to Lear's, the others for home, to rest up for work.

All the way back to Fill, Zimmer grumbled about the Bears, Frank, stop signs in general, and all the other signs in particular, that he was suddenly aware of as they drove. "Yield; Walk; Don't Walk; Do Not Pass; Do Not Enter; No Parking; No Standing.

"Shit, Steph, I might as well be a bear, the way the world treats you like an imbecile, putting up these fucking signs for everything."

"I got another one for you."

"Where?"

"This is one we need, don't have yet."

"What's that?"

"Don't feed the Bear beer."

"That's ri-ight," Zimmer sang, and pulled into the Quick Stop for a six-pack, "Since there aren't any signs to the contrary," shrugging his bearly shoulders.

For once, Steph had to help Zimmer up the stairs to Fill. It didn't help much that Zimmer wanted to scale the narrow flight on all fours. "It's the only bearly thing to do."

He occupied the entire landing, wagging his head back and forth, pacing, growling, sniffing, as Steph tried to reach over and unlock the door.

Zimmer reared up on his hind legs, snorting, "I smell a cat," almost knocking Steph back down the stairs. "Bears like cats."

Clinging to the weak railing, Steph said, "I thought bears

were vegetarians."

"Hmmph," Zimmer said, then, "Fuck. Another sign."

"No. That's right. They eat fish, don't they?"

"I mean this," Zimmer said, his nose pressed against a note pinned to the door.

Regaining his balance, Steph saw it too, and asked, "What's it say?"

"Says: At the laundry, love, A."

"Angela."

Zimmer stood and started down the stairs. "Let's go see what she wants."

"What are you talking about?"

"She wants us for something. She must. Why else the note?"

Steph didn't exactly understand the logic, which didn't surprise him, but followed.

Zimmer backed Abby out from under Fill, muttering, "Fucking signs."

They found Angela at the brightly lighted, noisy Laundromat at the bottom of the Turnpike.

"Hi there," Steph said.

"Well, well, what's this?"

"We're here about the sign," Zimmer said, snarling his lips about the last word.

"Sign?" Angela asked, turning to Steph.

"Your note."

"Oh. That. I just thought I'd tell you where I was."

"No Loitering," Zimmer read from the wall behind her.

"Did you guys come to help, by any chance?"

"Sure. Why not."

"Attendant Does Not Carry Change."

"Now this *is* a surprise."

"Do Not Leave Machines Running Unattended," Zimmer read, big, red stencilled letters in three or four places around the room. "Applies to everything, you know," he said to no one. "Do Not Leave Machines Running Unattended."

Angela chatted with Steph, glancing at Zimmer from time to

time. "Wouldn't it be nice if you guys got regular jobs and we could always spend this kind of time together."

"Regular jobs?" Steph said, folding a towel.

"That's okay, Angie, we quit our jobs."

"Really?" She turned from Zimmer to Steph. "I mean normal, day jobs."

"Yes. Really. Zimmer quit, anyway."

"Gonna be the Bear," he said, wandering off.

In response to her puzzled look, Steph said, "Don't ask."

"What about you?"

"I like what I'm doing."

Zimmer was over at the snack machine, shaking it, trying to reach a paw up under the door. He hadn't eaten anything all day, never able to bring himself to eat anyone else's cooking.

"Always?"

"No, probably not *always*. I don't know."

The attendant came over to Zimmer. "Hey, what the hell do you think you're doing?"

Steph went over to rescue him. "Zimmer? Need some change?"

"Do *Not*," Zimmer said, allowing himself to be led away from the machine. "I repeat, Do *Not* Leave the Bear Running Unattended."

"What's with him?" Angela asked, as Zimmer snorted at the detergent she was using.

"Nothing," Steph said, grabbing Zimmer before he could get too close to a couple of kids tracing Matchbox cars through some spilled powder.

"Nothing?"

"Just another alcohol induced fuck-you-world rage."

The other patrons in the busy, loud room kept a wary eye on Zimmer, moved their children out of harm's way as he wandered down the aisle of dryers, wagging his head in tandem to the rotation of the big drums. Steph caught him again, steering him for the door, finally.

On the way past Angela, Zimmer leaned very close, asking, "Do you know what this is?" giving her a prolonged, Boyles one-eyed jacks wink.

"D.T's?"

"Come on, Zimmer," Steph said, not laughing, stepping between them. "Let's go get ready for work."

"That's," Zimmer said to him, answering his own question, giving Steph another forced wink, "the only sign we'll ever need."

It wasn't nearly time for work yet. Steph had in mind some basketball, suddenly, for his own benefit, as much as Zimmer's. Zimmer, he hoped, would sweat out some alcohol. And he felt enormously frustrated, for reasons he couldn't exactly say.

It had something to do with Angela, her questions. At a time when he was genuinely concerned with how quickly, and thoughtlessly he had moved from station to station to station without enough consideration for *how* he got there, she was asking him to change again. It wasn't her fault, of course, but did she know well enough, "Do any of us?" what she was asking him to leave behind? "It's all so tenuous."

He felt a need to pay stricter attention to the in-betweens. It's the transitions, "Just like in basketball," that can make or break you.

He could be contented with that. But it wasn't working. Oh, sure, the basketball served as a useful model for Steph to try and figure out what was nagging at him, but only normal basketball would allow him to test those theories. Zimmer wouldn't allow that. However much the game might have appeared to be the best thing that they could do, in an effort to sober Zimmer up some, Steph wasn't entirely sure that he wasn't making matters worse, as if the exertion, the increased circulation was keeping the alcohol coursing through him, keeping him drunk. Where Zimmer'd grumbled about the idea when Steph had first suggested it, he couldn't be persuaded to stop now, despite the lousy basketball he was playing, getting beaten, easily, and then trounced, and then shut out by Steph.

"One more," Zimmer said, holding the ball on his side, leaning over and panting.

"Come on, Zimmer. Let's go to work." They were almost a

half hour late by that time.

"What work? I'm quitting. One more."

"You can't quit. You're a Lumper. Once a Lumper, always a Lumper. Remember? Let's go."

"Nope. One more. That's why you've been beating me. I made a tactical error. I've been playing like a goddamn Lumper when I'm not anymore. I'm the Bear."

"Okay. All right. Not a whole game though. Just one basket. If I score, you're a Lumper, and we go to work. If you do, well..."

"Okay," Zimmer said, grinning. "To show you how confident I am, here," he said, handing over the ball without really handing it over. He kind of held both Steph, and the ball.

Steph tried to dribble anyway, starting to his right. Standard stuff. Zimmer rode him, pawing, growling, eventually shoving him out of bounds. He kept working on him like that until he'd pushed him right up to the bushes, twenty feet or so off the court.

"Stop, STOP!" Steph cried.

"The Bear is here," Zimmer roared, beating his chest, not at all like a bear. "Give me ball."

"Oh, no, un-uh. Bears can have fouls called on them, can't they?"

Ordinarily, they played traditional school-lot basketball, no harm, no foul. Or they played a slightly harsher brand, which only good friends should play: no blood, no foul. That didn't mean that someone couldn't call a foul. It meant that they typically passed on the opportunity, ignoring those errant elbows, those extra shoves, then either reciprocated the attitude, or the offense itself. Steph was exercising his only reasonable option, considering Zimmer's bearness.

"I should tell you a little secret, though," Zimmer said, as Steph took the ball out of bounds, only to be picked up in a Zimbarco hug and carried back to the bushes. "Bears can not foul out."

They continued, Zimmer playing his bear defense, Steph trying his damnest to play real basketball, to get free, just once, just to launch one solid shot at the basket. Zimmer got as rough as he needed, determined to deny Steph that shot.

Steph tried every manner of break-aways, being at least two steps quicker than Zimmer, especially now. But Zimmer would just reach out and grab whatever he could in time to prevent Steph from getting a shot off cleanly. He had to be a little cautious, at the same time, of not getting sloppy with the ball, of settling for the fouls and starting over again, of making sure *he* didn't foul Zimmer or turn the ball over. Considering Zimmer's bear defense, "I'd hate to see what his offense looks like."

But after Zimmer had collected something like twenty-five fouls, and Steph had yet to loose anything that got very close to the basket at all, he finally said, "Okay, that's enough."

Steph knew that Zimmer was granting him a step, lazily, relying on bulk, and reach, to stop him. Zimmer gave him that step once more. But Steph didn't make his usual beeline for the basket, not another failed attempt to sidestep the strategically placed Bear. He didn't merely fake one way in order to angle in the other direction either—a move that hadn't worked a dozen times already. He continued to fake, one side, the other, then the other, spinning faster, and faster, widening the arches he turned back through, and faster, left, right, left, right. Zimmer had to shuffle farther and farther along his horizontal line of defense, had to be ready to react for what he was sure would be Steph's move to the basket, surer and surer with each turn he made. But Steph kept turning back, and back again, taking a step, spinning back around to his other side, step, spin, step, spin, until he looked like some weather vane or helicopter gone berserk, until Zimmer got so tangled up that he landed flat on his ass from trying to keep up.

Only then did Steph advance, stepping past the prostrate bear, laying the ball up and in. "Game."

"What the fuck was that?" Zimmer asked, from the ground.

"My one shot."

"What? I've never seen you move like that."

"Been saving it."

"Well, damn. That's a game winner, all right," Zimmer said, sitting, but sounding more reasonable, finally. Then he asked, "Want to try it again?" with all the charm he could summon.

"No," Steph said, collecting the ball, Zimmer, loading them both into the Bee-atile, now over an hour late.

"I guess you're pretty proud of yourself," Zimmer said, after they'd ridden along in silence for a while. "Here we are, riding to Regency," he said, to the night, the dark shoulder of 13, "a conquered bear, a Lumper hero."

Steph just smiled, driving straight, and tall.

"I'll tell you what," Zimmer said, slouching down in the seat, tired, sober, "it never really comes down to just one last shot. There's always someone looking over your shoulder. I'll see that move often enough. Then I'll stop it."

"Maybe," Steph said, turning onto Warehouse Drive. "A Lumper might stop it," he continued, pulling through the gates to the Regency parking lot. "But a bear *never* will."

Zimmer tried to climb over the gear shift handle and nuzzle Steph like a cuddly new cub, but Steph ground Abby to a halt, only half way into a parking space and jumped out of the Bee-atile.

"There they are," they heard as they strode into the spotlights.

"If Frank asks," Zimmer said, "I don't want you making up stories and lying for me. If he asks, you tell him I was going to quit tonight, and would've, if not for that fucking whirlybird shot of yours."

"Well, well, well... Is-bout goddamn-dime," Frank greeted them from the top of the stairs. "Good evening, gentlemen. Or should I say good morning."

Steph stopped Zimmer short of the first step leading up to the platform, with Frank glaring down at them, the other Lumpers off to the side, laughing. "You could leave all this?"

"Shit, yes."

14. Bronco Willie's

STEPH surfaced from the tangled cave of linens one part at a time. First an arm groped out, toward the nightstand—slapping at Angela's resurrected clock, the top, sides, the facing, searching for an off button. He had mistaken the murmuring chatter which had invaded his sleep as originating from the clock, that it had somehow grown into a clock-radio overnight, and was tuned to one of those news/talk AM stations his father always listened to in the car.

Half of his face surfaced and he opened one bleary eye, not that it helped much. He stared at the digital numbers for a long time, a further attempt to make some sense out of it, even though he now remembered it couldn't broadcast anything but the time. It showed 11:14. He kept watching until it blinked to 11:15. "Damn," he said. "I've slept all day."

He received that news rather blandly, considering. 11:16.

"Shit!" He bolted all the way out of bed, but then had to sit back down against the sickening inertia. Then a few nagging questions slid into focus behind the swirling lights and black dots before his eyes.

"Lights," for one. Which meant, "Why the hell is it so light around here?" if he had slept all day and was late for work.

"Alaska?"

Zimmer, for another. "Where's Angela?"

"You are still, and always will be one of the world's foremost sleepers," he said, the source of the low register mumbling which had worked its way into Steph's sleep. "Isn't there some club, or award, a world's record or something we should be training you for?"

"Like you'd ever be qualified to coach anyone on sleeping," Steph said, sliding back into the covers, awake enough to have sorted out the puzzles, but not wanting much more to do with them.

"Come on, Champ, you can do it," Zimmer said, yanking the blanket off Steph. "Up, up! You don't need any more practice."

"False."

"Steph, you were sound asleep and snoring like a pig when I came in last night."

"So?"

"So, that's been about ten fucking hours ago. Get up!"

"There're an awfully lot of clock watchers around here lately," Steph said, and rolled away from Zimmer, from the open and brightly lit bathroom where he stood glaring down at him.

Steph wasn't late for work, but Zimmer almost was. "Too many goddamn changes, period." Steph was still a Lumper, and as such, still didn't work on Saturdays, even if it had been almost midnight—not noon—as he'd first feared. What's more, it was the Saturday after Thanksgiving, so Steph'd been off for three nights already. He didn't have anything but the parade of parties and dinners and nights spent at Lear's to blame his disorientation on. "Doesn't mean I'm any happier," about being awake at 11:21 in the morning.

"Up, up, up," Zimmer reminded him, padding by and depositing a cup of coffee in front of the clock for Steph, before stepping into the bathroom, dropping his shoes, loudly, on the naked linoleum floor.

"Not shoes," Steph reminded himself, sitting up to sip his coffee, spying them: Boots. Cowboy boots. Steely toed, shiny tanned, tool died, slanty heeled, "Fucking boots."

Zimmer stuck his head out of the bathroom. "What's that?"

"Them."

Zimmer stepped all the way out of the bathroom. Through a mouthful of toothpaste, said, "Would you knock it off about the boots already?"

Zimmer was the side cook at Bronco Willie's, a new country and western place that had opened up near the mall. "It's just part of the costume." Bronco Willie's had been a bar, until the present ownership purchased the building and layered their Texan decor over the usual bar trappings.

Steph had asked, "Is Bronco Willie really from Texas?" when they'd first discussed the job back around Labor day.

"No, Steph," Zimmer said. They were playing basketball at the time, a cool September Saturday morning, about two in the morning. "That's just the name of the place."

Bronco Willie put pegs on the inside of the front door for hombres to post their six-shooters, bleached out Georgia O'Keefe steer horns over the archways, western movie posters on the walls, piped Waylon and Willie throughout the bar, and had a menu full of just about anything that could be barbecued.

"They hired him for his sauce," Steph informed the other Lumpers, later that Saturday—Zimmer's first night at the new job.

"Good and spicy and half an inch thick," Bruce recited, gnawing on Mickey's shoulder, still having fasted, but now at a loss for what to do with his hunger.

After a few weeks, they decided just to change venues for the feasts, trying to keep some continuity. Because even though they dictated what Zimmer wear while he was on the premises—a ten gallon hat, a roughneck bandanna and peg leg bell-bottomed jeans to go over the godawful boots—they let him cook and they paid him for it. There were a couple of pool tables in the place, so Bronco Willie's was near enough Lear's to be near enough Fill.

It was nearer Fill than Fill was, what with all the modified living arrangements there, "All the goddamn changes," everyone's divergent schedules. Zimmer had Sunday and Monday off. During the week he worked from four in the afternoon until around midnight. That bridged the gap between Steph's and Angie's hours well enough to manage all the comings and goings. But Saturdays were different. Zimmer worked from noon until nine or ten Saturday nights.

"So get the fuck up, Steph," he yelled from the bathroom, as Steph had dozed off between sips of coffee.

Steph blinked back at him.

"You do want Abby today, don't you?"

They nodded to each other.

"Then you'd better get your ass ready to drive me to work," he said, glancing into the mirror for a reflection of the clock that hung on the wall behind him: 13:11. "Clock watching, indeed," he mumbled.

But then Steph's face eclipsed the numbers. "What are you doing?"

Zimmer turned, white foam clinging to about a third of his face. He pointed his razor at Steph. "Sha-ving."

"You shave for this job? You want it that bad? I can talk to Frank, you know."

"Jesus, Steph, where have you been?" Zimmer said, finishing. "Listen, shaving's not bad, once you get used to it." He rinsed off, then looked at Steph in the mirror again, grinning. "But you wouldn't know anything about that, would you, baby face?"

"This isn't a baby face," Steph said, pushing Zimmer away from the mirror. "This is the next step up the evolutionary ladder."

"Right. Get dressed, would you," Zimmer said, chasing Steph from the bathroom.

"Savage."

Steph tumbled over the bed, settling among the pillows again, while Zimmer stood over him and snapped his Bronco Willie's pearl button plaid shirt over a Buster Keaton tee-shirt.

It was only every other Saturday that Steph had to forego sleep to drive Zimmer to work, only those Saturdays when the Lumpers would gather at the bar for dinner. But each time he wondered how he'd managed to get talked into that, though they'd all agreed to the changing dimensions of life at Fill.

"See, if I take this job, you and Angie'll have a ton of time together," Zimmer'd said, on the basketball courts that morning. "You can do all those things she wants to do," only loosely guarding Steph.

Steph, backing into the key, threw an elbow. "I thought you were taking the job so you could cook?"

"Yeah, well."

"Yeah, well, what?"

Zimmer stopped. "Sometimes," he said, raising a finger to Steph, "you have to give up your potentials."

"What the fuck are you talking about?"

In truth, there was already a recipe for the sauce used at Bronco Willie's, an inviolate recipe brought all the way from west Texas. There was a recipe for the slaw, too. And the bread, baked in volumes to serve scores and not just the handful of diners Zimmer was used to, stayed relatively immune from what touches he could add to it, kneading away all by itself in giant rotating stainless bowls with scalloped dough hooks for hands.

"I'm just trying to figure out how all this can work, without anyone moving out, say."

"Moving out?" Steph hollered, spun and shouldered Zimmer toward the basket, tossing up a shot. "What the hell's wrong with you?"

"Guilt," he almost said. "Good guilt," Koogan'd called it, but only later. "Trying to avoid it, actually." He was trying to figure a way where it all could work, as if life had become one of his grand feasts, and dinnertime was always approaching. And just like cold turkey or a gooey casserole or failed bread, he knew the kind of seething damage that could accumulate within those kinds of living arrangements, "If you let it."

Or he was trying to remove himself from the equation, without having to disappear. He just wanted to be part of the choir, he told himself. Not the maestro. And he almost believed himself. That's what he wanted the message of Mr. Boyles' story to be, that anyone foolish enough to depend on him, or anyone, for that matter, hadn't done their homework. "Just look at my history!" It was their fault, not his, which he never believed for a second, wound up feeling more guilty rather than less.

For what, though? "Quitting Regency?" That wasn't even a choice altogether his. Frank had been threatening to fire him anyway, more than usual, since the night of the Bears game, "And earlier," since Easter. "How long has that been?"

Every other Saturday, Zimmer tried to explain it all for Steph, "I quit for the exact same reasons you won't," except the explanations always reminded him of the guilt, so he'd end up explaining that. He was tired of starting over. Or, he knew now, walking away from unfinished business didn't make *it* go away. Only makde it unfinishable, shifting agency, getting awfully close to responsibility.

As the undeniable architect of the Lumper structure, he didn't want anyone else thinking he was declaring it defunct, just because he was leaving Regency. He hoped, secretly, beginning with Steph, that they could preserve it, with or without him, if they chose. Abandoning things, people, was unavoidable. "Right Mr. Boyles?" Things change.

But working Friday afternoons, and evenings, and then Saturdays, made it tough to keep up the Habits. He had to con the rest of the Lumpers into coming to Bronco Willie's on Saturday nights, so they could have dinner there. And for once, he needed help—help convincing the Lumpers, for one, and Mr. Boyles, that they should come to Bronco Willie's; and then help driving Mr. Boyles, since Randy would have to stay and tend Lear's. He even needed help with the guilt, which wasn't abating, though he wouldn't admit that, "Not yet." It was tough enough, outlining his intentions every other Saturday, an attempt to objectify them, through Steph, as if a conscience was ever really assuaged by sharing.

"You know better than that." Even if Zimmer believed in absolutes, both flexible and inflexible, he was no Christian, not even the part time Christian of convenience he'd seen too much of in Salyne. No, he'd always believed Koogan, who delivered his pearls of wisdom and conduct with the jive accenting he'd picked up from playing basketball downtown near the projects.

"No, man. You either did it, or you didn't do it. What you *meant* to do don't mean shit."

Steph understood, though, or at least he didn't challenge Zimmer when he would explain to him, "This isn't for me," relocating the dinners, arranging for the Lumper's presence in Bronco Willie's, reserving space for them, providing free meals. "It's for everyone."

"I know, I know," he said, from the passenger side of Abby, cruising through the park. "That's why I have to get up early, right?"

Unlike Zimmer, Steph just assumed it would work, as it always has, "Until it doesn't," of course. Such a zero-sum calculus might not have been any more comforting. It was finite, though. He never suffered much from constant, gnawing guilt.

In fact, Steph would only brood over the entanglement enough to try and improve on the dilemma, to get something like a definitive answer: Doable, or not?

"Right, so you can figure out a way to get more sleep."

"That's not true."

Sometimes, it was really for the puzzle, as if that's what he liked about it, "Three people, three schedules, two cars," as if he would sacrifice the little bit of sleep *only* so long as there was a puzzle. "Twenty-four hours, eight hour shifts, Sunday to Thursday, Wednesday to Sunday, Tuesday to Saturday." He sat there figuring, permutated clusters of fingers pointing up, down, every which way. "There ought to be a way."

"Forget it."

Steph looked over at Zimmer, the puzzle showing up in his facial contortions, only one of its matrices.

"There're two dependent variables."

"Dependent or independent?"

"What?"

"It makes a difference."

"Whichever."

"Right."

"Angie," Zimmer said, holding up just one finger. "She can't."

"What's the other?"

"She won't."

"Right."

"And that leaves only you," Zimmer said, sliding out of the Bee-atile at the back entrance to Bronco Willie's, the smoke from the hickory grill pit already billowing out of the kitchen's chimney.

Steph, still trying to find a way, regardless of the real domestic tension, said, "What about Whomee?"

Zimmer frowned at him, then stalked off in his boots. If he ever envied Steph, his attitude, his approach, he only did until he remembered that it couldn't last. "It just *looks* easy," that least resistance of his. "The ghosts'll catch him sooner or later." That realization angered him, a little, though not from the envy, "No," at a world which couldn't allow for people like Steph.

"Later," Steph drawled to Zimmer's receding figure, "partner," slipping his foot off the clutch, pushing on the gas, as Abby skipped forward, squealing a little on near bald tires. "Whoa there, hossy, whoa!" Zimmer could hear as he dipped into the kitchen entrance.

By himself, and only by himself—he'd never attempt to convince Zimmer—Steph'd say, "She tried, though."

Retracing the journey back through downtown Tripoli, through the sparse Saturday morning traffic, he told himself again, "She really tried," and that was good enough for him. It was good enough all by itself. He knew Zimmer's argument, "To try is to fail," which was another Koogan decree, not strictly Zimmer's—though Steph didn't know that, and recoiled enough at the Old Testament sounding judgement to allow that it was good enough for him, for Steph.

Angela had tried to learn how to drive Abby, so that the revolving door that Fill had become wouldn't get jammed, wouldn't be forced to reverse itself, depending upon which car was there.

Mondays were the days the three of them did any scheming. It was a Monday evening, after Zimmer's interview, that they'd gone shopping together at the mall for his requisite boots, when they planned the shuttling that would get everyone to work on time.

"Let's see, it'll get tangled on Wednesdays, right," Zimmer'd said, himself accepting the challenge as if he were trying to bring a twenty-course meal to the table all at once. "Steph takes the Mazda Tuesday night. Angela, you'll have Abby Wednesday morning."

Steph kept count, on the other side of Angela, as they walked down the crowded corridor, mothers dragging kids to back-to-school sales.

"Wednesday afternoon, I'll take the Mazda. Steph takes Abby that night. Angela's back in her car Thursday morning."

"You take Abby," Steph said, accelerating the formulations, just pointing to drivers, "Mazda, Abby, Mazda," down the row, himself, Angela, Zimmer, "and we're all square by Saturday morning," meaning that Angela could start the weekend driving her own car again, until the following Wednesday.

"Yeah," Zimmer said. "If you want to do anything early on Saturday," he said, looking across at Steph, "you can drive one of us in."

It was a master plan.

When they got back to the parking lot, Zimmer clomping across the asphalt—the clerk had told him he'd need to break the boots in some before standing all night in them—and climbed into the Bee-atile, Angela sat watching Zimmer work through the gears as he searched for the exit, before saying, "I can't."

Steph leaned up into the space between the front seats. "What?"

She looked up from Zimmer's feet.

"Drive a stick?" he guessed.

She grinned.

"Hmm," Zimmer said, as Abby coasted across the parking lot, trading looks in the rearview with Steph.

So, the Monday morning after that, Steph just off work, on the empty Regency supermarket parking lot, Angie and Zimmer traded places, and she tried.

"Now, just ease off the clutch and gently press down on the accelerator," Zimmer patiently told her, from the navigator's seat. "You'll feel the gears engage and the car will start to move."

"You should look up to see where you're going, Ang," Steph suggested, on the edge of the back seat, his elbows on their backrests, working on his first beer.

"How do I know if I'm doing my feet right if I don't look at them?"

"It'll get to be a natural feeling after a while, honest. The clutch is under your left foot, and the gas pedal is under your right, just like your car."

"How do you brake?"

Zimmer turned and looked over his shoulder at Steph. He'd tried to convince Steph earlier that only one of them should be in the car trying to teach her. Steph, of course, insisted, that it'd be fine. "It'll be fun."

"Don't worry about braking now, Ang, not while you're accelerating."

"Right, and then once you're up in gear, you won't have your foot on the clutch," Zimmer added.

Steph patted her shoulder. "Go ahead. Try it."

Angie eased down on the gas farther and farther, but Abby stayed firmly grounded.

"Okay, up on the clutch."

Angie sat, eyes riveted forward, a death grip on the wheel, and slipped her foot off the pedal. Abby lunged forward, choked on all the gas, and slammed into silence.

"Whoa, hossy!" Steph said, picking himself off the floor of the back seat, splattered with beer.

"A little less gas," Zimmer started, "and the smoother you release the clutch, the less it will jerk like that."

For the next five, ten minutes, Zimmer reiterated what he'd already said about the transition. He described the workings of the flywheel, the clutch plate, the different gears while Angie stared down at her feet, the floorboard. Then Zimmer got Abby started for her again.

And it helped. "Yahoo!" Steph hollered this time, a newly opened bottle of beer pulsing like a geyser, unable to do much about it, as Angie actually got Abby bucking and bouncing across the painted lines of the lot.

"Good, good," Zimmer said, trying to find something to grasp. "Try second."

"Second?"

"Watch it," Steph said, as Abby lurched toward a lamppost.

Zimmer yanked the wheel and Abby cleared the obstacle. "Second gear. It's just about the same maneuver, in reverse," he said, wrapping her fingers back onto the wheel. "Just ease off the accelerator, down on the clutch. Pull the stick down into second. Off the clutch, accelerate. Okay?"

"Okay," she promised, but by the time she got around to attempting the feat, disengaging first gear, bringing the higher gear to work, Abby was barely moving, idling, mostly, unable to support the demand.

Zimmer hastened everyone out of the Bee-atile again, shoved her into motion, trotting along, then jumped in and popped the clutch. He turned around slowly, heading back to where Angela and Steph stood.

She was trembling.

He was saying, "You're doing great."

Zimmer yanked up on the hand brake, got out, panting, and Angie took command again.

He would end up exhausted by lunchtime. Abby would end up with her gears ground to dust and the clutch burnt to a crisp before Angie was doing well enough to try the road.

And then, after all that, after surviving the trip back to Fill, everyone wearily climbing the stairs, readily agreeing that they all needed a nap, Steph, silly from too much beer, not enough sleep, actually thought the adventure had been a success, wanted to toast, wanted to drive some more, back to the store, for some champagne, so they could celebrate. He was coming back from the kitchen with just beer, finding Zimmer spread-eagled in Whomee's chair, Angela readying the partition for them, and he thought he heard her say she didn't want to drive Abby.

"No, no more driving today," Zimmer told her.

"No, I mean at all," she said, disappearing behind the bamboo.

"What?" Steph said, for Zimmer, for all of them.

"I don't think I'll ever get used to it," she said, a disembodied voice. "Besides, how would I get it started?" a slightly more defensible excuse.

"But?" Steph said, again, to Zimmer more than her. "Angela, what about?"

She retreated to the bathroom, closing the door, the discussion.

Subsequent mornings, Angela gone to work, Zimmer and Steph would ponder the equation some more. Leaning against the kitchen counter, maybe splitting an omelette, looking out over Dagaton Woods, Steph with a beer, Zimmer with coffee, Steph would always start, "We ought to be able to figure this out."

That was about as far as Steph would take it though, those mornings after work, before he'd start gravitating toward the bed, and sleep. Zimmer had the rest of the day to think about it, would often consider the problem nearly every night at Bronco Willie's, when he expected to be in an organizational mode anyway. According to his sometimes exclusive absolutes, it had to work, or they'd be forced to abandon the whole idea, "And start over." Ought to work was not nearly close enough to working, though, as Zimmer has learned all too well. That's maybe the *only* thing he'd learned at Bronco Willie's.

He set the day's first big batch of bread dough going in the vat and the whine of its motor joined in with the other noises of the kitchen. Pitman was stoking up his grill. Zimmer had tried to find out what his name was, but Pitman was all he'd allow, and all he'd answer to.

"Pitman. I am what I do," he told Zimmer. "Works."

Pitman worked all right. He was a big, somewhat rounded black guy, with a doughy face, a greying afro, and a long, long goatee that he wore braided. He shunned the rest of Bronco Willie's costume, wore just a tank top tee shirt that was already soaked through, and tennis shoes. Zimmer'd asked about that once, too.

"Shit, how'm I gonna work with all that motherfucking shit on?" Pitman'd answered. "I don't never come out front anyway, so it don't matter. Them folks out there think Waylon Jenning's back here cooking, not some fat, old nigger. Or they think you cooking," he said, eyeing Zimmer's dress. "Works, though."

That's all that mattered to Pitman, what worked. Zimmer found out, too, that he was the only aspect of the place that was authentically Texan, and much like the first Texan Zimmer'd ever known, Sergeant Brister, Pitman laid it out for Zimmer, early on. The slaw had to be blended together in batches small enough so there wasn't too much left over, but large enough to last the rushes, for consistency's sake. The base for the sauce was kept in big plastic gallon containers in the walk-in refrigerator. All Zimmer had to do was cook and add the veggies, and keep the simmering pot at the proper temperature.

"Not burnt."

The bread was at least a constant task, since the rolls needed to be as fresh as possible. So, like everyone else in the kitchen, his work was dictated by the frantic hours around each meal that the bar was open, trying to keep Pitman's sauce pot full, trying to be ready, as each plate was passed from Pitman to one of the three waitresses in front of him, to tuck two rolls and an ice cream scoop of slaw onto vacant corners snuggled around the slab of ribs or pieces of chicken or chops. In-between peak hours, they restocked what had been used up— a Lumper enough approach: Zimmer would recycle the sauce, add to the slaw or start a new batch of bread kneading.

That's when they got their breaks. Zimmer washed the caked flour off his hands, wrists, pulled the apron from around his neck and slipped out the back door, wishing he had a beer.

"Big motherfucking crowd today," Pitman said, already outside, toweling off. "Almost got me, the fuckers," he added, lighting a joint. "Coupla chickens went on the rack still frosted. You kept up."

That was all Pitman would give by way of compliment or acknowledgement.

"I tried not to waste time breathing," Zimmer told him.

"Uh-huh."

Zimmer shrugged. Sometimes he considered comparing cooking theories, organizational approaches with Pitman, but always decided, "Not now." Maybe not ever. He just wasn't as sure, these days, how well they—his theories or approaches—worked in practice anymore, the only thing that mattered to Pitman. Or he just felt outclassed there in the sprawling kitchen of Bronco Willie's where the fluctuation between supply and demand could sway by thirty, forty people at any one meal, versus the meager-seeming complications at Fill, "Three people, three schedules, twenty-four hours..." Zimmer was considering the possibility that his theories only worked when he was the only person attempting to apply them, meaning, once he started spreading his plans out, allowing for multiple principals, like at Fill, the situation grew more complicated rather than less. "Isn't that the point where you have to abandon everything, start over?" Preserving what, an unworkable theory?

"What do you do if it doesn't work, Pitman?"

"Shit, what else. Fix it."

"No, I mean, what if--"

"Shit, man, you think too damn much," handing Zimmer the remainder of the joint.

"Jesus," he said, as Pitman left, stubbed it out after dragging on it and headed back to work.

On those rare good days, Zimmer wanted to hug Pitman, maybe take him back to Lear's, buy him a drink, make him a Lumper.

On not so good days, Zimmer considered stuffing his apron in Pitman's sauce pot and screaming at him, "It's not that simple, motherfucker!" maybe wishing it was, or maybe just hearing too much of himself in Pitman's proclamations.

And then he'd have to sit back, pause, try to reason with himself, before the tension and frustration from both the job and the bullshit at Fill drove him crazy. At some level, it had to be that simple, didn't it? There had to be some point in the construct, some weight bearing point, where you could definitively say, "This works," or it doesn't work, allowing you the chance to either continue, or tear it all down. "Had to be, right?"

He knew what Pitman would say. "Shit man, you thinking too much."

He knew what Mr. Boyles would say. "If we lived our lives a little more honestly."

What would Steph?

"What difference does it make?"

Last Tuesday night, Wednesday morning, Zimmer'd come home from Lear's, where he usually ended up after his shift at Bronco Willie's, and found the Mazda parked under Fill.

The interim plan—"Interim to *what*?"—had been that Steph took the Mazda to work, Zimmer got up and gave Angie a ride to the store, and then Angie either got a ride home from a friend or Steph went and got her.

Zimmer squinted one eye at Angela's car so he could concentrate. "Angela's got Tuesday off, right? So Steph drives the Mazda," he said, standing between the two cars in their slots beneath Fill. "Unless he called in sick?"

Then, tracing the steps up to the apartment, figured, "We don't have a phone," pushing open the door. "Could've called from Lear's."

He tiptoed into the kitchen, leaving his boots by the door, still trying to figure it out. He returned with a long neck in each hand unable to resist the urge to peek into their bed on the way by, to the bathroom.

"Could've been two bodies," he told himself. "But no snoring. And Steph makes a lot of fucking noise when he sleeps."

When he came out and stood there in the light shining over his shoulders, onto the bed, he saw that Angela was alone.

"Where's Steph?" he asked, out loud, uncaring of the hour.

Then he repeated the question, determined to wake her up. "Where's Steph?"

She squinted against the light, pushed her hair back from her face. "Work."

"How?"

He stood at the foot of the bed demanding answers, not letting her dodge any of his questions, not letting her settle back into the warm bed.

"Said he was going to hitch."

"Why?"

That was a question he asked repeatedly, ignoring claims about insurance liability or complications from her family or her ex seeing Steph driving her car.

"Why?"

He shifted his weight, standing at the foot of the bed, for about the hundredth time, still clenching a beer bottle in each hand. The right one was empty, the left half-full. Angela sat all the way up at last, leaning back onto the collected pillows of the bed, hugging her knees to her chest.

"You know Zimmer, that's what I want to know, too," she said at last. "Why won't he even consider another job? Why won't he even look? Do you know how tired I am of sleeping alone?"

"Jesus, Angie, what are we talking about here, some time-table of yours? Steph *likes* working nights."

"He thinks he's got to stay at Regency or else there won't be anyone else to keep up your Lumper crap, now that you've left."

All week he'd had that nagging feeling that she was more than a little right. That, honestly, he'd set things in motion, unthought of things, unaccounted for things, whether or not he took responsibility, felt guilty.

Zimmer slept about two and a half hours that morning, and then with more beer, was waiting for Steph under a bright spotlight in the parking lot at Regency when the Lumpers' shift, the Lumpers' week ended.

"Greetings," Steph said, having to wake him up. He pushed him over into the passenger seat. Then, rolling down 13, with Zimmer using a cold beer bottle as a compress—against his sleep deprived, not quite sober, not drunk enough headache— Steph told him, "She'd lined up a job for me at the store. Stocking, I think."

"Jesus. Same job, just different hours, right."

"I guess."

When he'd revived a little more, in the park, Zimmer said, "You know, she thinks you're only staying at Regency to keep up my *Lumper crap*."

"Yeah, I've heard that."

"That's not your responsibility, you know." Then, to make sure, Zimmer added, "You should only stay there as long as you want to."

"Yeah. Right."

They passed through the park, up the Turnpike hill to the access road, and into the empty space beneath Fill. "So?"

Steph didn't answer until he was at the top of the stairs, checking his pockets for the key. "Listen to you."

"What?"

"Of course I'll only stay there as long as I like it. If it means hitching once in a while, so what?"

Zimmer almost asked, "What about sleeping?", knowing it was a sensitive subject with Steph, but then he wondered what he was trying to do, wanted to ask himself, "Why?"

Why would he do that, knowing he would only be challenging Steph, pushing for a resolution, just like Angela. That's when he knew it really wasn't working, he'd crossed into Pitman territory.

What had Mr. Boyles said about decisions, resolutions, diminishing returns?

"That they never really come as a surprise."

But it had. Zimmer'd maybe expected this feeling, this gone but not yet going feeling back in Salyne, in Vermont, in every other place, "But not here." Not as a Lumper. "How much of a

Lumper can I still consider myself though?" He cranked up the processor, chopping cabbage and carrots and green peppers for that one, last, calculated Saturday night batch of slaw.

"Once a Lumper, always a Lumper," Steph would tell him, not just a Zimbarco imitation anymore.

Steph would take up more and more of the absolutes—hitching to work once, twice a week, "If that's what it takes." He'd miss the sleep. All because he liked what he was doing, was willing to like it and keep doing it against other advice. Not because he'd decided, so much as he was just a natural Lumper. He was a natural something, "Finally," which maybe accounted for some of his determination. "Who better?" than he, to take on the task of maintaining Zimmer's *Lumper crap*.

Steph genuinely believed, "Once a Lumper, always a Lumper." Though he would tell Angela, "If I didn't work at Regency, I wouldn't be the same person. Is that what you want?"

"But people don't *really* change."

"Right. Situations change."

"And they usually work themselves out."

"Oh? If the situation changes, the definition changes. You don't know your role anymore."

"Right. That's what you work out."

And Steph would try to make it work out, try his damnest, past the point where Zimmer saw it was worth the effort, even, which brought on more guilt. "A whole lotta good guilt," he remembered Koogan saying.

But the effort was showing, and the strain. It wasn't natural, anymore, dragging Mickey and Bruce and Mr. Boyles to the hokey Bronco Willie's. But he would, and they'd all be sitting there waiting for Bronco Zimmer at the end of his work week, being as obviously contrary as they needed to be, Steph initiating that goddammed chant of his, "Zim-mer, Zim-mer, Zim-mer!"

"Cut that out, Steph," Zimmer said, sneaking out of the kitchen, making his way to their table, trying to be a lot more inconspicuous than he's ever really been. "Cut it out or I'll have you gagged the moment you come in here," untying his costume bandanna and waving it in front of him.

"Yass, sir," Steph said, throwing his hands up, surrendering, causing a commotion at even that.

"Maestro, please, sit, sit," Bruce said, jumping up and dragging over a chair, aiding Zimmer down into it.

Someone at the table where he'd borrowed the chair asked Bruce what the fuss was all about, which was all the encouragement he'd need.

"That, gentlemen, is the sauce master of Bronco Willie's," he announced, while Zimmer pulled his hat down over his eyes. "And the bread? *Manifique!*" he squealed, kissing the tips of his fingers, bowing in salutation. "A beer for the master, *vite, vite,*" snapping those fingers now at Mickey.

Mickey scowled, but poured.

They all frowned, feigned attempts to moderate Bruce, maybe, but Zimmer was genuinely squirming, from the attention, from the idea of the attention. He took off his hat and hit Bruce with it, even gave it to him to wear, "If you promise to shut up." Zimmer had yet to feel comfortable out front in Bronco Willie's, seeing all the patrons he was supposed to look like. He hated boots, combat boots, cowboy boots, didn't matter. His feet would never adjust to the damn things, he knew, no matter what that fool had said at the western wear store, his toes all squashed together, pushing against the leather. He stretched his feet out under the table, maybe just to distance himself from them—though they were more than a little ubiquitous, "Like Bruce": they made noise when he walked, clomping along, not to mention that with their size, 13's, they looked something like pontoons. And they were insensate, as he clogged Mr. Boyles, sitting opposite him.

"Jesus, sorry, Mr. B."

"Quite all right, Anthony," he said, adjusting his chair. "By all means, put your feet up. You certainly deserve it."

Which got Bruce started again, "That's right, make some room under there," he said, waving Steph and Mickey back, underneath the table, refereeing.

"Dammit, Bruce," Mickey said, then explained to Zimmer, "Don't mind the ape, he thinks he's hot shit, thinks he's solved the cr--"

"The mystery of Hemispheric Airlines flight four-o-four!" Bruce said, surfacing, bouncing his voice off of the corral walls around Bronco Willie's. "Hey," he said to the table, calmer, "I knew who was going to win the mayor's election didn't I?"

Steph piped up, "You had at least a twenty percent chance of getting that one."

"But I was one hundred percent right."

Zimmer took his hat back, held it low over his forehead, shading his eyes.

"Don't you want to know who won?" Steph asked him.

"No."

"I'll give you a hint," Bruce said, anyway. "Ground swell."

"You really don't care?"

Zimmer lolled his head back over his chair.

"Nobody really cares," Mickey said. "It was Hast--"

"I'll handle this," Bruce said, jumping to his feet, "if you don't mind," holding up silencing hands.

Zimmer could see, just under the brim of his hat, a ceiling fan over their table. If he rotated his eyes against the direction of the fan, individual blades appeared out of the blur. That made him think of helicopters, rather than airplanes. Then he thought he heard that sound that helicopters make, beating the air, "That noise you can hear a long way off," you can't ever really get out of your head.

"It wasn't the former judge," Bruce said, folding down the thumb of his right hand. "And it wasn't the real-estate hotshot."

The sound was getting louder, closer.

"It wasn't the crooked school super."

Zimmer thought it might be blood rushing to or draining from his head, because of his posture. He could feel the sound in his temples.

"And who does that leave?"

"Whom?" Zimmer mumbled, uncaring. He could feel himself

slipping, either dozing off, or passing out.

"Angela!"

"Who?" Zimmer said, snapping his head up, then holding out his hands as if to steady himself, while the black spots dissipated, the blood returned to his head.

"Hi," she said, standing over the table, across from him.

"Hi," Steph said, reaching for her, sliding over into Bruce's chair so she could sit between them. "What are you up to?"

"I was going to try to get to the mall before it closed," she said, checking her watch.

"Ready?" Bruce said.

Everyone stared at him, uncomprehending. Someone at the next table called out, "Is that Angela Ward?"

She looked over, squinting. "Oh, God."

"Ward?" Zimmer said.

"My maiden name."

"Maiden name?"

"Couldn't be."

"Do you mind?" Bruce said to both tables. "A-hem," he cleared his throat. "The next mayor of the fair city of Brighton, New Jersey, Captain Arnold Hastings, retired Hemispheric Airlines pilot!"

"What?" Zimmer challenged while Bruce borrowed another chair from the neighboring table. "He won campaigning from a hospital bed?"

"Oh yeah," Bruce said.

"Why don't y'all join us?"

Bruce ignored them. "Political history making stuff, actually. A real flair for the dramatic. Press conferences from intensive care. Kissing premies. Beautiful."

"Angela can, at least."

Zimmer glared past Bruce at the table, then said, "He can't stand witness at a trial but he can run for mayor?"

"Shit," Mickey said. "They're going to drag that trial out for years."

"That's right," Steph said, "Roy's got to ghost write his book first."

"*Cleared for Landing,*" Mickey sneered.

"Now that he's had his religious experience."

"Religious experience?"

"Yeah, see, and his priest is smuggling out tapes to be transcribed."

"Isn't that illegal?"

Angela turned to Steph. "I've got to go."

"Okay, in a second, all right?"

"What illegal?" Mickey said to Zimmer. "There're no laws on that show."

"Actually, there are laws," Mr. Boyles reminded him. "They're just a little more flexible than in real life."

"Oh?"

"For instance, it looks as though they're maneuvering to have Roy's charges dropped altogether."

"Who, they?"

"Mr. Pennington—remember him?"

Bruce went, "Eeeyowww..." as a reminder.

"On the counsel of Captain Jamison, and Mark."

"Can they do that?"

"Certainly," Mr. Boyles assured him. "It was the airline that brought the criminal charges in the first place. He'll still lose his federal job, of course."

"But why?"

"Wait a minute, wait a minute," Mickey said. "Zimmer, remember what we're talking about, okay? It's a new season, they don't have a new story line yet, so they've got to keep milking last year's plot. They'll do anything. Roy could wind up his own lawyer, his own judge, for Christ's sake. Hell, they spent so much time in the hospital, they screwed up and forgot to introduce any new characters."

Angela stood.

"Except one," Steph said, getting up with her.

"It is," the call came from the other table again. "It is Angela Ward."

One of them got up and came over. "I can't believe my eyes, Angela Ward."

"Phillips, actually," she said.

"Oh, married?"

"Separated. Getting divorced."

"The *ba-by*," Steph bent and whispered to the table, before turning with Angela.

"You're not leaving are you?"

"Yes. Have to."

"I can't even talk you into a game of pool?"

"Sorry."

"Not as sorry as I am," he said, tipping his own ten gallon hat, bowing, his studded shirt opened three buttons down, layers of gold chains swinging around his neck. "Some other time."

"Maybe," she said, blushing, turning for the door.

"Jesus," Zimmer said, "What was that all about?"

"You don't want to know," Bruce said.

Mickey said into the silence, "The baby's not really a character. All they ever do is talk about it. You never see the kid."

"How much can you talk about a baby?"

"Want to guess how many weeks they devoted to who the father might be?"

"I thought it was that businessman? The guy going to New Orleans the day of the crash."

"Wrong."

"I almost had that one worked out, too," Bruce said.

"You did not."

"Didn't I almost guess John-John's father?" he asked Steph, as he returned to the table with a fresh pitcher.

"John-John?"

"You weren't even close."

"Oh man," the guy at the next table called again, "You let her get away? Bruce, what's the matter with your friend?"

Steph just stared back, blankly.

"Who *is* that guy?" Zimmer asked.

"*That*," Bruce said, "is Booth Dumas, football he-ro."

"Bruce, Bruce, mind the rep, huh," he said, coming back to

their table, standing behind Bruce, squeezing his neck.

"What's new, Dumb-ass?" Bruce asked him, slapping the hand away.

"Traveling. Meeting clients. I'm just in hick town for a little celebration."

"Celebration?"

"Thirty days to thirty," he announced. "The first baby born in Pennsylvania in 1951—12:01 New Year's day." He punctuated the statistics by popping smoke rings out over the table, torquing his jaw, sending tight, thick spiralling rings. "Maybe y'all'd like to join us?" he said, waving back at his table with a pool cue. Then he said directly to Steph, "Tell me, how's Angela?"

"Fucking Dumb-ass," Bruce said, standing. "Still don't know when to shut-up, do you?"

"Hey, I just want to celebrate," he sang, letting Bruce steer him to the pool tables.

"So who the hell is Booth Dumas?" Zimmer asked, taking his hat off, frowning as he tried to watch their game.

"High school quarterback," Mr. Boyles told him, also watching the pool. "Bruce might have played with him, I suppose," he said, directing the question toward Mickey.

"Beats me," he said.

"Second string high school all-American, I believe. Scholarship to Penn State."

"Come on Bruce, be a man," they heard Booth say.

"Nope," Bruce answered, returning for his beer.

"Shit, man, you wouldn't bet fat meat is greasy, you know that."

"Same old cocky Booth. Wants to play for twenty bucks."

"Oh my," Mr. Boyles said.

"What?"

"He thinks he's a hustler."

"He's a guppie," Zimmer said. "Bruce, did he do anything at State?"

"Naw. Never made it through the first year," Bruce said, looking over his shoulder as Booth sank shot after shot.

"Flunked out, then played one mediocre year at some Allegany junior college."

"Come on, Bruce," Booth called. "I'm feeling generous. I left you a shot. Hurry up and miss, and have that green ready."

"Maybe you could say that a little louder, Dumb-ass."

"Bruce," Zimmer stopped him to ask. "You're not really playing that asshole for twenty bucks are you?"

"Naw. Told him a pitcher was my limit."

"Good man," Mr. Boyles said.

Bruce walked up to the table, took one lame shot. Booth laughed, then finished the rack.

Mr. Boyles said, "Maybe we could leave now?"

They stood, readying, willing to leave undrunk beer, even, until Booth said, from the pool table still, practicing his English on the lone cue ball, banging it against one rail, and another, spinning it through tight angled banks, lazy obtuse ones. "That's it? That's the best you can offer? Come on..."

Zimmer shook his head, saying, "I work here. It wouldn't be fair."

"Shit. What about you other guys? Maybe the old man. I seen you watching." He winked at Mr. Boyles. "I'll go easy, promise."

Mr. Boyles broke into a grin.

Zimmer looked at him. "Fucking guppie," he mumbled, unzipping his fatigue jacket. "I guess I could try one game."

"All right," Booth said. "Listen, we won't tell anybody."

"Aw, don't worry about it. I'm not sure I care about this job anymore," Zimmer told him, racking. "It's getting so they'll let anyone in, you know?"

Booth laughed, then moved to break.

They traded shots, each sinking one, maybe two a turn. It looked to be a pretty evenly matched game.

"Is he any good?" Steph asked Mr. Boyles.

"He's not that good."

"Then why is Zimmer struggling?"

"I don't know."

"What's the matter?" Steph asked Zimmer when he came

back for some more beer.

"Son-of-a-bitch won't shut up. Why is he fucking with me?"

"Anthony, remember. It doesn't matter."

"Oh?" Zimmer snapped, guzzling. "Who the fuck does he think he is?" he asked Bruce.

"He *thinks* he's New York Fats," Mr. Boyles said. "But he's not. He only *knows* the vocabulary. You can prove that."

"Yeah, Zimmer. Finish him."

Zimmer looked over at the game. "It may be too late."

"Remember our friend. He never let Fats *outplay* him."

Zimmer squinted at Mr. Boyles a moment before returning to the game.

"I thought it was Minnesota Fats?" Steph said.

"That's true, but only after they made the movie. Originally, he called himself New York Fats. Then he became famous. When anyone mentioned billiards, they thought of Fats. They staged all those dreadful television exhibitions."

Zimmer and Booth traded misses on the eight ball.

"Who's your friend?"

"Willie Mosconi."

"Oh yeah, I remember some of those games," Bruce said. "Didn't Fats win any of them?"

"Oh, certainly. But Willie always said Fats couldn't outplay him. He could only talk him out of a game."

Then Zimmer got lucky, perhaps. Booth just missed a bank shot, cursing the table as he did, and leaving the eight ball very near the side pocket. Zimmer finished the game and put up his cue.

But Booth followed him away from the tables. "Aren't you going to give me a chance to win my money back?" he asked, dropping the two dollar charge for beer on their table. "You know I should have won that one."

"No, Booth," Zimmer tried to say levelly, gathering his jacket. "I'm not going to take your money, either. We've got to go, really."

"Thank you, Anthony," Mr. Boyles whispered, as Zimmer helped him with his coat.

"Oh, I get it, babysitting. Maybe you could come back?"

Mr. Boyles closed his eyes, sighing, then sat back down, sparing Zimmer the need to ask.

"Well, maybe one more."

"Anthony," Mr. Boyles said quietly, holding on to Zimmer's arm. "If he pushes, ask him to play one pocket, a truly respectable game. Then you'll know."

Zimmer strode over to the table, not even taking his jacket off, just pushing the sleeves up some.

"Great. Maybe we could make it really worthwhile then, since we may not get another chance?" Booth said, as he racked.

"Sure. How about some one pocket?"

"What's that?"

Zimmer grinned. "What'd you have in mind?"

"Eight ball. For fifty."

"How about a hundred and fifty?"

"Sure," Booth said, but looked over to his table of friends. He lit up another cigarette.

"Oh, and another thing," Zimmer said, leaning over the cue ball, readying to break. "It's my table now, so keep your butts off of it."

"Thought you were the cook, not the manager."

Zimmer shook his head. "That's true. I just bake the bread. Use an ashtray."

"The baker, huh," Booth said, moving past him, to tap his cigarette into an ashtray on his table. "Boy howdy, now that's some job."

Zimmer looked over and grinned.

"What an asshole," Steph said.

"Precisely, Stephen. That's the point. It's supposed to agitate you out of your game. Fats was most effective."

Zimmer stroked his cue stick a few more times over the rail, then sent the cue ball crashing into the rack. One of the corner balls dropped as did another from out of the set. The eight ball skidded over against a side rail, flirting with a pocket, the break had been that good. As Zimmer watched the game open up before him, he paced around the table and felt all the frustration from the past few days, or weeks, "Months?" drain right down through his arms, his hands, through the stick.

"What is this shit? You dancing with somebody?"

Zimmer laughed at him, chalking the cue, starting his run. "Six." And then he felt the restraint drain as well. "You hear this guy? Somebody who looks like he just stepped off the disco floor with all that fucking jewelry? Three ball."

"Hey, man," Booth said, moving closer. "Sly Stallone wears jewelry."

"Oh, that's right," Zimmer said, bending over his next shot. "Two. Well, John Lennon bakes bread." He stepped past Booth for a sip of beer. "We've just got different heroes Booth."

"Least mine's a man."

Zimmer stopped drinking. "You know something Booth, I'd drag this out a little longer," he said, re-chalking. "One ball. But I don't think I can stand to hear that voice of yours any longer. Seven. I just wish I'd hooked you for a thousand bucks while I had you. Eight, in the corner."

Again, Zimmer slid his stick into the wire rack in the corner. He brushed baby powder and blue chalk from his hands and left the ghostly-lit pool area for the Lumpers' table.

"Hey," Booth said, following him one more time. "You're not going to just leave, are you? You think you can sucker me and just take off?"

Zimmer said to the Lumpers, without turning to face Booth, "Now isn't that a strange question from someone who was conceived on or about April Fool's Day?" sipping the last of his beer.

"Asshole," Booth shouted, and threw what remained in his glass at Zimmer's back.

It was mostly ice. Zimmer looked over his shoulder, at the wet spot, then at Booth, farther back, gauging the distance. Booth gave him the finger.

Zimmer wagged his head. Steph tensed up on his forearms, "One of the all time dumbest fucking guppies I've ever seen." Then Zimmer moved, ducking his left shoulder, motioning in that direction with his empty beer mug. Booth's hands moved to cover his face, which made Zimmer grin, as he pivoted in the other direction, his left hand clenched, his reach good enough, with maybe a half a step, "To knock the motherfucker's jaw out of joint, so it'd be a long, long time before the bastard was blowing smoke rings again, that's for damn sure..."

But Steph knew the move, thought to say "Earl the Pearl!" as he vaulted out of his chair, onto Zimmer's back, wrapping himself around his shoulders. "He's baaack!"

Mickey and Mr. Boyles steadied the bucking table and its contents as Bruce, just a fraction of a moment later, got to his feet. Leaning back against Zimmer, he said to Booth, "You like living, don't you Dumb-ass? Why don't you shut up for once, and get the fuck out of the way."

Then, with Mickey steering them, like a little tug boat, and Mr. Boyles gathering their coats, Zimmer's hat, they wrestled Zimmer from Bronco Willie's, though not before Zimmer could kick Booth's table over on him, where he sat, lighting another cigarette.

"Welcome home," Steph said, still riding, as they squeezed through the door.

"All right, all right," Zimmer bellowed, after the Lumpers pinned him against the Bee-atile out in the parking lot. "Let me go!"

"You sure?" Steph said, slowly climbing down.

"Yeah, yeah, I'm okay," Zimmer said, straightening himself. "What do you think? He's going to come out here?"

They laughed at that.

"Oh, but hey," Zimmer said. "He forgot to pay me, didn't he?" lunging for the door.

Steph reacted instantly, again, leaping onto his back, riding the careening cook around the parking lot, bouncing off other cars.

"That's what this place needs," Bruce said, following them, then standing over them after they'd collapsed. "One of those broncing bulls, like Gilley's."

"Why you..." Zimmer started, disengaging himself from

Steph's entanglement.

"Oh, God. Help me, Mick. Help!" he screamed, clutching Mickey to his chest.

"Couldn't we please just leave?" Mr. Boyles said.

"Yeah," Mickey agreed, his feet dangling down around Bruce's shins.

"Come on, Zimmer. Let's get the hell out of here," Steph said, pushing him toward Abby.

Zimmer climbed into the back seat of the Bee-atile, something he couldn't remember ever doing before, allowing Mr. Boyles the front seat beside Steph. He wrestled out of his fatigue jacket, then the obnoxious shirt. It reminded him of Booth all of a sudden, or worse, maybe. John Travolta. He shuddered, pushing off the hot boots, massaging his feet.

"So tell me," he said, stretching his legs between the bucket seats.

Steph glanced up into the rearview, then over to Mr. Boyles, wondering what Zimmer wanted to know.

"Anything," Mr. Boyles said.

"Who's the father?"

"Hah!" Steph roared, as Abby swerved over the mid-line of 13.

"Who would you have guessed?"

"I don't have any fucking idea if it wasn't that Cajun."

"It was Hank," Steph told him.

"Hank?"

"Yup."

"Hank? The old black guy?"

"Precisely."

"Hank?" Zimmer said a little louder, pulling himself up between the front seats. "The porter?"

Steph watched him in the mirror.

"The one and only."

"Hank? Who hustles tips from rich old ladies who carry ugly little dogs onto the planes with them?"

Steph smiled over at Mr. Boyles. "The proud papa."

"I'll be goddamned. I love it!" Zimmer said, pulling his jacket back on, as Steph slid into a space at the curb outside Lear's. "That man is an instant, honorary Lumper!" he told Mr. Boyles, who held his seat up for Zimmer.

"Hey, don't you want these?" Steph said, standing in his opened door, out in the street, holding up Zimmer's boots.

Zimmer frowned over Abby's roof at him. "Hell, no. Does this look like Bronco Willie's? I can't wear those things in here," he said, turning and padding his way into the bar, an arm across Mr. Boyles' shoulders, still saying, "Hank? Really?"

15. Keep Fried

"LET me take you down..."
Chink.
"Cause I'm going to..."
Chink.
"Pineapple Estates..."
Moments like that.

Zimmer sat self-absorbed, more or less forced into the posture from having had to defend himself. "Where nothing is real..." But now, now he was ridiculously self-contented, Chink, because he could toss Iron City bottle caps across the big room of Fill, from the table to the front door and into a goal there, "And nothing to get up about."

"*That's* what I've been trying to tell you," he said, as if the feat proved anything, really, waving an arm to no one, unless Whomee was just feigning sleep over in his chair. "Nothing is real: life is only a metaphor for living." He raised an oratorical finger to hammer home the point, but suddenly wasn't sure he believed himself. "Listen..."

He listened to the radio playing softly in the kitchen, and the thought that came to mind was, "Why Lennon?" Why had he chosen Lennon as his hero last week at Bronco Willie's? More importantly, "Is he really any match for Sly Stallone?"

Zimmer laughed. He only knew Lennon baked bread from last month's *Playboy* interview. They'd asked him what he'd been doing, these last few years of obscurity. "Babysitting. Baking bread." And then there were the requisite inquiries about a Beatle reunion. Seemed like the subject came up whenever any of them did any new work, showed up anywhere in public. "What a curse." But what else should they expect? "Once a Beatle, always a Beatle..."

"What are you going to do?"

"I'll cook."

"Uh-huh."

"And play basketball," he said, raising his hands for another bottle-cap jump shot, Chink. "You know, in this star-studded, sports-crazed country, where you have to be who you are, every minute of every day, where you're identified by *what* you do, basketball players are the best equipped to deal with that pressure, don't you think? I mean, rock-stars, politicians, where are they without their stages? And movie stars, sure they can look good all the time, can deliver practiced, proven lines, but what good is it?"

"I mean for money."

"I'll paint houses."

"In December?"

"Indoors?"

He threw another bottle cap. "Basketball." Chink, where almost any object is throwable and nearly any receptacle constitutes a goal.

"I'm doing it," he said, holding his hands up meekly, answering Angela's question again. "Again and again and again." He thought of Pitman: "I am what I do."

"I'm doing it, so what am I?" he asked, the bottles scattered about the tabletop, his cat sleeping over in his chair, Steph, snoring, on the other side of the partition.

"She should never have to ask me what I'm going to do again," he said, reaching to his left, into the cooler, for another beer.

"Besides," he thought, settling back in the chair, stockinged feet propped up on their trusty basketball underneath the table. "What the hell would someone who has to have the gears of her car automatically changed for her before she can drive, someone who has a job where some machine reads the prices she's apt to misread, what the fuck would she know about absolutes?"

"When are you finally going to grow up?" she'd said, at the last, before leaving.

That's when he'd thrown the first cap, at the door, as an answer, "As the only answer," to that question.

Ca-thunk.

"Shit."

That first one had banged off of the door and fallen into his boots, left by the door, "Always. Absolutely. Always." He searched around for another cap, among the clutter on the table, in the melted ice in the cooler, on the floor beneath his chair. "Well fuck." He thought of opening one of the few remaining beers even though he was no more than a third through the one he'd just opened. Then he thought he'd just throw a bottle, reminding himself, "Any throwable object..." when he saw Steph over in the corner, bent over his boots, examining the scene.

"What the fuck are you doing up?"

"That noise," Steph said, then moved away from the doorway with a puzzled look on his face.

"What noise?"

"That noise, like the nets at Dagaton Woods... I was dreaming about it."

"Oh," Zimmer said, grabbing a new beer, opening it and handing the bottle to Steph, launching the cap, Chink. "*That* noise?"

"Wow." Steph drank, out of habit, shivered after the path of the brew, then took another sip. "Better. I was killing 'em, hitting anything I threw up."

Zimmer sang, gleefully, "I read the news today, oh boy..."

"Then they went and got this knight-in-armor to chase me around the court, Chink, chink, chink..."

"About a lucky man who'd won the war..."

"Raised hell with my concentration."

"Why don't they play something new?"

"What's new?"

"You know, *Double Fantasy*."

"No, I mean you," Steph said, waving at all the bottles. "What's new?"

"Oh. That. Got fired last night."

"So we didn't have a party?"

"Shit no. We haven't had a party in-- Don't you want to know why?"

"Why you got fired?"

"Yeah."

"No."

"No shit?"

"No shit."

"Son-of-a-bitch screwed me."

"Man, what a dream."

"He tells me he doesn't want my friends coming in and busting up his place any more, so I told him it was me that kicked the table over, that you'd tried to stop me, in fact."

"So he fired you?"

"No, not for that. I was already fired. He says you can't come in anyway. Where's the justice in that?"

"No loss there."

"Justice?"

"Bronco Willie's."

"Really?"

"Really."

Zimmer fished the last two beers out of the cooler. "Angela just got done telling me," Zimmer started, waving toward the door. How long ago was that? "She just got done telling me that she liked it there, that she preferred it to Lear's, that she was happy I'd found the job, proud of the way I'd been *applying* myself. Christ, Steph, she was so upset, I thought she was going to start crying or something."

"Nah. She never cries."

"I mean she--" Zimmer stopped. It seemed like so long ago, suddenly. "What time is it?"

Steph shrugged, automatically.

"No, not that." Zimmer got up and went into the kitchen. "What's everybody doing today? Do you know? Is it too late to have a feast?"

"Never."

"There must be something around here to cook," Zimmer

said, rummaging around in the refrigerator, the freezer, pulling out a large bag of leftover turkey. "Naw," he said to it, thinking of sandwiches, soups, casseroles. "That's no fun." He tossed the bag onto a lower shelf and investigated the two crisper drawers. In there, in the various plastic bowls of half eaten concoctions and bags of fistfuls of chopped veggies, other meat not used in one recipe or another.

"Got any ideas?"

Steph'd never had to answer that question before.

Waiting, Zimmer spied the Samson tucked away on top of the shelves. "That's it!" he said, bending back into the refrigerator. "Why didn't I think of that?"

Steph peeked over the door to the icebox, at the source of the racket, and the grumbling, Zimmer squatting down, pulling things out of drawers, shelves, redistributing, adding to the pile at his feet, "Yes, you'll do. Yeah, perfect." He looked up. "You got any money?"

"Sure, some."

"Some?"

"Yeah," Steph said, retreating to the living room, the nightstand, retrieving his wallet. He came back into the kitchen, counting. "Some."

Zimmer looked at the bills he held. "Hmm."

"Why, what do you need?"

"Forget it," he answered, pulling a few more bowls, bottles of sauce from the refrigerator, hoisting the montage up to the counter. "All we really need is beer. You can get that at Lear's when you pick up Mr. Boyles and Randy."

"Okay," Steph said, trying to keep up. "What are you doing, anyway?"

Zimmer backed around the swaying door with his last armload of leftovers. "What's it look like?"

"Cleaning out the refrigerator?"

"Exactly," he said, opening lids of the containers and sniffing what had taken up residence inside, to see how virulent it might be. "I've decided," he started, and then laughed. He'd decided he was going to let everyone assume what they would and not argue with anyone anymore. I am what you think I do, he thought, and chuckled again.

Steph couldn't decipher the laugh, and when Zimmer didn't elaborate further—just kept inspecting the refugee food, talking to the eggplant Parmesan batter, or the blue cheese dressing—he went back to the other end of Fill for his sneakers and a flannel shirt, to start on his mission.

Zimmer peeked around the kitchen doorway. "You know what to tell anyone if they ask?"

"Ask what?"

"You tell them it's fry-day!"

"Of course," Steph answered.

Then, sitting on the bed, lacing up his Converse, he thought, Wait a minute, I'm the one that's supposed to be confused. I'm the nightshifter...

He walked to the kitchen, taking short, wide steps, so as not to trip over his untied shoelaces. "It isn't Saturday?"

"Eggs-actly!" Zimmer said, letting out another of those demonic chuckles, standing back from the counter, holding a broken eggshell in one hand, a dripping fork in the other. "And so, it's fry-day!" he said, motioning with his head back down at the mixing bowl, where the egg had gone, and the fork had been. "Fry day."

"Ah, *fry* day, not Friday."

"Exactly."

"Deep fried day."

"Right again."

"What?"

"I don't know yet. Anything. Everything."

"Anything?"

"Maybe even ice cream. Or hot dogs. But I need beer!"

"Coming up," Steph said, finishing his shoes, pulling on his jacket.

"Beer!" Zimmer bellowed, as Steph was sliding through the front door.

"And more beer," he yelled out an opened kitchen window as Steph was climbing into the Bee-atile. "And those fucking

Lumpers!"

He returned to the batter, adding the last few ingredients, some melted butter, a pinch of brown sugar and a mound of finely grated Romano cheese. Then he set it aside. It was the eggplant batter, "Recycled into an onion-ring beer batter." It had to bubble itself out some.

He cleared space on the counter—lofting egg shells toward the trashcan in the corner, "He shoots..."—rinsed off his fork and reached for the next largest bowl from the cupboard above him. "For the tempura," to dip the mushrooms and the florets of cauliflower which were soaking in milk. He stood over the bowl, a pinch of baking soda poised over a puddle of red wine vinegar.

"Would have been nice to have gotten some shrimp somewhere."

Whomee was in the sink, covetously eyeing the bowl of lumpy milk.

"Aw, what the hell," Zimmer said, sprinkling on the soda, watching it fizz out before adding flour, and then just enough ice water so that the batter dripped in little globs instead of chunks, but didn't pour. "There's going to be a whole bunch of food before we're through," he said, moving the cauliflower out of harm's way, then setting the tempura next to the onion ring goo, reaching for another bowl. "In fact, there probably won't be any *un*-fried food left when we're done. Or any clean dishes, either."

He poured flour into the bowl straight from the bag, no longer in any mood for measuring. He added cornstarch, a few fingers of mustard powder, three tilts on the garlic powder, and one, two, three, "Four, five, sixseveneight nine, ten," shakes of soy sauce. Then he lifted the cover of the egg carton.

"Uh, oh," he said, counting, pointing to one bowl or another spread around him on the counter, and the four lonely eggs.

"Seen this movie," he said, remembering a past critical egg situation. "What do you think Master Who? What are our immediate priorities? Pickle batter for the Lumpers, or Sunday breakfast? What if we don't survive the night?" He shrugged.

"Of course, we could use the other batter for the pickles." He drank some beer. "Pickles in an onion ring batter? Naw," cracking that first egg on the edge of a clean bowl, then another of the remaining eggs. The last two were reserved for deep-frying some hunks of chicken. "Sorry," he said to no one, everyone. Sorry he couldn't be what they wanted, couldn't even moderate how much he wasn't so it at least wouldn't look so obvious. What?

"Cut that shit out." He tiptoed to the refrigerator and pulled out a half-gallon sized jar of Kosher dills. He sliced *all* of them, into five or six crosswise section, throwing the sliver of one end to Whomee, and eating the other himself. "We're so sorry," he sang, as he arranged the slices on a large cooling rack on top of a cushion of paper towels, sprinkled them with table salt and then more towels.

Potato slices soaked in more vinegar under their own towel. The sliced white onions sat piled on a platter ready to be dipped. Separate wet and dry ingredients stood ready for the chicken. Normally, on a feast day, he'd be hustling to finish as much of the cooking as he could before anyone showed up. The trick on those days was to greet them with the product, the finished dish, ready to be portioned out.

"But fried-days are different." On fried-days, the presentation was the process. Zimmer rehearsed, pantomiming, dipping, dunking, turning, dipping, waving a pair of tongs around like a maestro's baton.

He stepped back up to the counter to put together the chicken marinade. He poured some of the cauliflower milk into a bowl, along with the last two eggs—then poured a little more of the milk into a dish for Whomee. He added a couple of squirts of Worscestshire sauce, some sherry, and whisked it all together. On another plate he piled flour, more garlic powder, oregano, basil, pepper, and a cascade of Progresso Italian Bread Crumbs. "Stranded on a desert island," he told Whomee every time he used the ingredient, "this is the one absolute necessity I'd have to have." Every time.

"Why?" he said, holding the carton.

"I don't know. *That's* why."

He'd gone beyond not answering. "The non-answer *is* the answer. What am I going to do? Nothing. I'm not going to do a bloody thing all day," he sang.

He reached into the refrigerator for the chicken, stashed away in the back in a long Tupperware container, with Angela's loopy script on the label: Chicken parts. He couldn't remember suddenly when he'd last cooked chicken, and scolded himself for not checking the condition of the meat before using up the eggs. He flinched at what was inside. Then he sniffed it. "Cheese," not chicken. "Mozzarella." He set the container down, staring at it. "Fuck." He almost let the frustration get to him, that feeling of, Just when you're going good, something like this has got to happen. "God has decided." He almost tossed the cheese at the trashcan, uncaring.

"Decided what? To ruin my day? It's really only your fault," he said to the Tupperware lid, "you fucking liar," tossing it out the window behind him. He took the cheese out and set it on his cutting block, telling Whomee, "Trust me," then threw the rest of the container after the lid.

He reached for a paring knife, but held it poised over the cheese. "If this doesn't work, there's a zucchini, I think," he said to the cat, cutting.

Looking for a colander to drain the potatoes, he ran across more Tupperware, a set of graduated—"And unused"—pale pink bowls. "Oh, no, no, no," he said. "I'm on to you fuckers. Out," he commanded, sailing them through the window one after another. Then he went looking for more, banishing each item from his presence in turn, yellow measuring cups, green spoons, and a bright orange fruit peeler. "Who thinks up this shit? Out!"

He was searching for more Tupperware, sure there was more hiding somewhere in his kitchen, plotting a take over, self-replicating, when Steph called from the front door, "Hey, Zimmer!"

"What?"

"You all right?" he asked, coming all the way into the

kitchen, holding a case of beer and some of the Tupperware he'd had to carefully drive around to get into the garage.

Zimmer took the plastic off the top of the case of longnecks and tossed it out the window a second time. "Now I am."

"Hey, watch it with that stuff."

Zimmer craned his neck out the window to see Bruce standing down there, a cooler in his arms, another case of bottles on top of that, and a two quart mixing bowl on his head, jauntily skewed.

"Sorry," he offered, watching Mickey scavenge around Bruce picking up other pieces. "We're so sorry..."

Steph stood in the doorway, questions lingering about his face, and eyes. Zimmer pulled the beer from him, hoisting it, saying, "Success!" preempting any comments.

As the other Lumpers filed into the kitchen, they all carried with them both random pieces of the Tupperware and the same silent looks of wonder. And Zimmer repeated the same censorial routine, receiving the gadgets and containers, exchanging them for a cold beer and throwing the plastic back outside.

The silence he created with that gesture wouldn't go away on cue, though. When everyone was assembled in the kitchen, Mr. Boyles parked on his stool in the corner, Randy in the doorway, Mickey, Bruce, Steph, and finally Zimmer over in the other corner, he tried, "Greetings. Ready for fry-day?" He stepped up to the stove and turned on the burner beneath a large skillet full of olive oil. He had some lighter, safflower oil in the Samson, already heating.

He searched through the drawer for a second pair of tongs, thinking that would speed things up somehow, but only found a plastic ice-gripper. He showed it to them, said, "Where do they all come from?" and tossed it out the window.

The Lumpers gazed out the windows.

Zimmer asked, "Get it?"

Mr. Boyles sat petting Whomee. "Certainly is curious."

Steph asked, "More of your war with Angela?"

Bruce grabbed Steph's shoulder, "War?"

Zimmer shrugged.

"She fussed at him for getting fired. Right?"

"Fired?" Mickey said. "Now what?"

"Now? Now we cook. And eat."

"I mean what are you going to do about a job."

Zimmer shrugged again, then tested the oil with a glob of batter. It sank to the bottom and bobbed back up, hissing, rotating in the hot oil. "I'm just watching the wheels..." He slid three large platters off the shelves, layered them with paper towels and handed them to Steph, who moved into the space in front of the refrigerator.

His job was to receive the fried foods as Zimmer pulled them dripping and spitting from the oil. For now, what with Mickey's question hanging over them, he was just glad to be out of the line of inquiry.

"Now, I'm going to do now, Mick. I don't know what else to do. You?"

"Say no more," Mr. Boyles told them. "Shall we toast?"

"Damn right," Steph said, setting the platters on the window shelf, gathering fresh beer from the refrigerator. "Keep fried."

Zimmer took his and clanked longnecks with Mickey. "Keep fried."

"All I want to know is," Bruce said, stepping between Zimmer and Mickey. Zimmer had plunged his hands into the onion ring batter, up to the knuckles. He hesitated then, waiting for Bruce's question. "What's under the green towel?"

Zimmer grinned. "What's it look like?"

Bruce struggled with a guess.

Zimmer volunteered only, "Trust me."

A relative silence settled back over them as Zimmer busied himself at the stove. He dunked eight, ten onion rings into their batter, held them up to let the excess drip off and then set them in the heavy olive oil. On the other side of the stove he repeated the gesture with the mushrooms, frying them in the safflower oil. In between he slid to the sink to rinse off his hands. More ingredients went into their respective batters, and then it was time to turn the initial batch. It took four waves of onion rings to fry them all, but only two doses of mushrooms, before he could tempura fry the cauliflower. He fried potato slices between different foods to clarify the oils as much as he could.

Even with that constant motion, always dipping, dripping, dunking, rinsing, turning, dipping, he could feel the silence, and asked Mickey, "What is it Mick? What is it you think I'm going to do? What have you decided in that little head of yours?"

Bruce snickered.

Each time Zimmer needed more onion rings, he had to reach over the draining pickles, teasing Bruce, who would lean with him. They were all caught up in the action at least a little bit, straining to see what went where next if they weren't actually bending or shuffling or reaching along with Zimmer. That would have accounted for the silence, and would have been acceptable. But not this morning. Zimmer knew better.

"Huh Mick?"

Steph wanted to say, "Let it go," and thought he saw the same words shadowing Mr. Boyles' face, and Randy's.

"I think you've already decided, Zimmer," Mickey told him.

"Decided what?"

"Decided that you're out of here."

Zimmer busied himself with the cheese. It had to be double-coated: dunked once in the egg goo, rolled in the Progresso crumbs, dunked again and then sprinkled with more crumbs.

"If you think I'm gone, Mick, I'm gone."

"What else can you do?"

Steph took up the argument. "He's not going anywhere."

"Nowhere."

"Nowhere?"

"Nowhere, man."

"Precisely."

With that, Zimmer resumed his cooking, dunking, rolling, dunking, sprinkling and then gently settling the cubes of cheese into the hot oil without burning his fingers. He had to nudge each chunk with the tongs so they wouldn't adhere to the bottom of the skillet and disintegrate; and he had to turn them almost constantly to keep an even heat on all sides.

"See there Mick," Steph called past Zimmer, "he's doing it."

But Steph had used an onion ring as part of his evidence, and then bit into it, so he sounded like, "Eb's boing nit."

Then he tossed a piece of evidence Mickey's way, who bit into it, and truly seemed to forget his argument long enough to exclaim, "Wow."

"Need I say more?" Steph asked, tossing an onion ring to each of the other Lumpers. Then he held one out for Zimmer to sample.

"Sometimes I get the feeling that you fuckers haven't paid any attention at all."

"What?"

"No catsup?"

"Catsup!" Steph said, handing the platter over to Mickey, who passed it to Bruce. Steph reached into the refrigerator for the bottle of catsup and more beer, passing them along. Mickey threaded bottles into the fingers of Bruce's free hand, who made his way into the other room.

Steph passed the mushrooms and the cauliflower next, to Mickey, who sampled one of them, to Mr. Boyles, then Randy, and out the door to Bruce, followed by the cheese, and then the chips. It was slow moving, this ad hoc assembly line, antithetical to its original intention.

It kept Bruce busy, though—as he had to clear away the empty bottles still on the table, and then set it as they passed out dishes, napkins, Zimmer's sauces—and out of the room long enough for Zimmer to fry the pickles in his absence. He wouldn't know what they were until he'd eaten several of them, which was best.

Without any cues or benedictions, without any of the usual fanfare the fry-day feast had begun. There was very little distinction between the cooking and the eating, which is exactly what Zimmer preferred.

At times it was like any other feast, where they all sat at their seats, passing the platters and the saucers of dips around, clockwise, observing a kind of social etiquette, even if no platter could be successfully passed without sampling. They took turns beer-tending, Mickey, Randy, then Steph volunteering to get the next round. But every once in a while, when Bruce mixed the horseradish and mustard sauces together on his plate, say, one or all of them would have to get up, investigate, reach over his shoulder, grab a pickle and test the combo. That would set off a round of testing and tasting, like they were having some kind of food fair in the apartment, and they'd end up sitting back down into different seats. Except Zimmer. He just sat back and watched, "Just watching the wheels go round..."

He played referee more than anything else, flinching at some of Bruce's experimentation, and then finally calling a halt to the orgy, afraid someone—again, Bruce, most likely—might hurt themselves, remembering Mickey eating himself sick that very first feast day, "Enough."

"Enough," he cried above the clatter, hoisting his beer.

The others responded, "Keep fried, keep fired," and pushed the massacred plates and a virtual mountain of soiled napkins to the side, where they'd sit until Bruce could stand.

But, picking up one more cheese square, he had to know, "Tell me again why the cheese didn't melt."

"The bread crumbs," Zimmer answered groggily.

"How did you know that?"

"Zimbarco karma."

"*Instant* karma."

"I mean, I thought, sure as shit, he's going to have this floating gooey greasy cheesy fucking mess--"

"Jesus, Bruce."

"How did he know?"

"Here's what he knew," Zimmer answered. "He knew that Progresso Italian Bread Crumbs would never fail him. Never."

"How did you know that?" Mickey asked.

"His grandmother told him."

"When? Where?"

"Somewhere in--" Steph started, but Zimmer cut him off with a wave of his hand.

Then he rested his head back against Whomee's chair, almost reciting, "In a little town in northern New Jersey, when he was about eight years old. He was standing in a chair in her kitchen watching her put together one of her unbelievable Thanksgiving Day feasts for the whole Zimbarco clan." Then he closed his eyes. "She made the best oyster dressing ever. Know what the secret was?"

"Progresso Italian bread crumbs?"

"That's one," he said, holding up a finger.

"Finding oysters, I should think."

"Nope."

"What?"

"Capers," holding up a second finger.

"What's the third?" Steph asked.

"No third. Two secrets, that's all."

"There has to be a third."

"Why?"

"Equilibrium? I don't know."

"Two. That's what she did. She didn't teach him how to cook. She just let out a few choice secrets."

"What about these?" Bruce asked, holding up a pickle.

Zimmer lifted his head, opened his eyes. "Those? Now that I picked up in a sleazy catfish house off base one night. They had picnic tables inside this place; and they kept all the silverware in a bucket on the table, all bent and abused and unmatched. Great food though. They put out dishes of pickles for chum. Figure that?"

"Which base?" Steph tried.

Zimmer grinned over at him, what seemed like hours, his eyes all puffy and red. "Down south somewhere, near the Gulf."

"Goddammit," Steph cried, throwing a cauliflower across the table at him.

Zimmer covered, letting the barrage bound off his forearms, shoulders.

Bruce crouched down by Zimmer's chair, reaching for rebounds, eating every other one or so.

Mr. Boyles cleared his throat, reaching for a deck of cards and unwrapping them. They pushed more of the carnage from the meal aside, as he announced, "Draw," as always, "with one-eyed jacks."

They tried to settle down and play decent poker, with difficulty. They thought it was because of the dishes, or Zimmer's relaxed attitude toward everything. It wasn't until the third hand that anyone figured out the problem, why they couldn't quite ease themselves into any studied reverence.

Bruce caught it, at least in theory, on his first deal. "Something's missing."

"No shit," Steph said, examining his cards. "Thank God for the draw."

"No, not that."

"You haven't lost all your money?" Mickey tried, having a pretty good start himself.

"No. That's not it either."

"Frank," Zimmer said.

"Yeah, Frank," Bruce said. "No grumbling, no chatter."

Steph almost said, Thank God for that too, but didn't. No one said anything, just kind of sat there.

"Can we get on with the game?" Mickey asked, holding a queen high straight—having drawn to an inside one, the hand of the year, of the century.

Bruce wagged a finger at him, not finishing dealing out everyone else's draw cards. "You got to mumble more. And spit a little. Can we ged-don wid-de goddamn game?"

Zimmer stood. "I can fix that." He went into the kitchen and came back with a package of cigars, handing one out to everyone.

"Where'd you get these?" Randy asked.

Zimmer shrugged.

"He is blessed," Bruce said.

"He's been saving them," Steph told them.

"Case we have any babies around here."

"Jackass."

Everyone lit up a stoagie, except for Mr. Boyles, who stayed with his Camels.

"Now try it," Bruce said to Mickey, still holding up the game. "Come on, ya fuggin-goon."

Mickey got to spread out that hand of his for all to see. And he got to rake in the pot, however diminished by the interruptions. That would be as serious as they could get about poker though.

A couple of hands later, with Zimmer and Steph the last holding cards, they raised each other food instead of coins. In the blue haze that quickly accumulated in Fill from the five cigars, Bruce was able to reach in and sneak out part of the kitty, quietly munching on a fifty-cent mushroom.

That was about the time Zimmer gave up any pretenses at legitimate poker, unable to think of what game he wanted to play, unable to even shuffle or deal the increasingly grease coated cards. "Indian poker," he called, "no draw," dealing just one card to each player.

They took their cards and pasted them against their foreheads, face out, where they stuck, thanks to the mingling oils. They really looked like six Indian braves sitting around a campfire. Steph had a ten of clubs feather, Mickey an eight. Bruce tried to roll his eyeballs up to see past the shelf of his brow, to catch some glimpse of his lowly four of hearts, against all rules of the game. Randy had a six of spades, Zimmer the nine, and Mr. Boyles the king. No one would've bet too heavily against the king, not with Mr. Boyles holding it. But they weren't betting money. They all anteed up food, so the bets went around the table twice until Zimmer called it. That first hand of the game might not have precluded any additional poker if not for Bruce's exuberance, who kept betting only so he cold keep eating. Mr. Boyles scooped the pile of now soggy onion rings and limp potato chips toward himself then sold the currency out to the table again for the next hand.

Zimmer passed the deck to Mickey, and got up for fresh beer. When Mickey reached for the six cards they'd used, a couple of them stuck together, and the card Bruce had looked momentarily like a five of hearts instead of the four, thanks to a slightly off centered catsup smudge.

"Jesus," Steph said, reaching for the card. He ripped it in half and threw it at the door, repeating the gesture with the other five.

Three opened longnecks in each hand, Zimmer watched the torn cards sail through the air, remembering his boots somewhere over there in the fog. Then he remembered the bottle caps, the long morning, remembered everything. "Nothing is real," he sang, dolled out the beer, and launched a few bottle caps in the direction of the door, Chink.

They played eight more hands of Indian poker, adding the wild jokers back into the deck, actually bluffing Bruce into folding with one of them. After each long and arduous hand they saluted, "Keep fried!" draining their beer, hurling torn cards and slightly bent bottle caps at the door of Fill. Even Whomee got his own beer, so that Bruce would have an additional cap to throw.

After the last hand, they threw everything left on the table, cards, the last few remnants of food, anything, cheering, "Keep fried," in Zimmer's case, vowing, "Keep fired!"

They were sufficiently fried by that time not to have noticed the shaft of daylight filtering through the thick, blue haze in the apartment. When the front door was fully opened, they just sat there awed by the phenomenon until they heard a faint whimpering coming out of the light.

"Angela?" Zimmer guessed at last.

"Angie," Steph said, getting up to meet her, maybe guide her into the room. "How was work?"

But she didn't wait. She cleared a space in the debris at the threshold of Fill with the toe of one polished white buck. She set a bag of Regency groceries there, and the few pieces of Tupperware she'd held. She moved to the side of the room, pulled the partition out and disappeared behind it, openly crying.

Steph hesitated before following her, long enough to look back at the table.

And enough people there understood the look well enough

to respond. Mr. Boyles stubbed out his cigarette, as well as Steph's abandoned cigar. Randy gathered empties and Bruce reached for the platters and saucers. But Zimmer took each bundle from them in turn, suggesting he'd take care of everything, not to worry, they should go on ahead to Lear's, that he'd no doubt be vacating the premises himself shortly. "I'll see you. In a while, huh?"

As Zimmer was closing the door behind the last Lumper, Steph came around the partition, saying, "Thanks."

"Yeah, well, I'll get out in a minute too, just let me clean a little."

"You don't have to do that," he heard Angela say, from the bed.

He stood there, his ears ringing, unable to decide which thing he didn't have to do she meant. He shook his head, said, "I'll be in there," waving at the kitchen, walking in that direction, none too steadily.

When he got there and saw the damage of Fry-day, he surprised even himself. "Did I do that? This could take a week." Dried streaks of batter laced across the stove and counter. Oil speckled the walls and cabinets. Salt encrusted paper towels on cooling racks supported a mountain of dirty bowls.

Zimmer opened one more beer, tilting it toward Whomee, who sat cowering on Mr. Boyles' forgotten stool in the corner, telling him, "Might as well make a celebration of it," drank, and reached to turn up the radio.

Ricki Lee Jones sang, "Dow-wow-wown stairs in Danny's all-star joint," as Zimmer filled the sink with water.

He sipped at his beer, pushed a pile of dishes into the suds and picked up the lyrics again, jiving at the sink, up to his elbows in Ivory. "You can't break the rules until you know how to play the game, but if you just want to have a little fun, you can mention my name..."

Zimmer clapped his hands at the line, sending bubbles exploding through the kitchen. "Hah."

He shook his head, resumed the task, and chuckled, both at the lyrics and thought of a crowd of kids on American

Bandstand, suddenly, "Try dancing to *that*!"

He knew they'd try.

"And fail?" thinking back to his own high school dances, trying to find steps to go along with *Sgt. Peppers*, say, or doing a *Norwegian Wood* waltz—practically the only ones on the dance floor making the attempt, where he might have to apologize to his partner, in his oblique way, "Blame it on Mick Jagger."

He remembered the endless, endless refrain of *Hey Jude*, and he remembered the rule he'd had, telling Katy Klein, or Peggy McDonald, or Myra, "My-my-myra," that he'd only dance to Beatles songs, and only that as a counterpoint to Koogan's love for the Stones. "Not that I could dance at all, mind you," just carving absolutes. "You got to have absolutes," he knew, even then, otherwise ignorant of dance steps, ignorant of love, really, just enjoying their feel, their closeness, the way his skin reacted when it brushed against theirs. "And those fruity wine highs," he remembered, and life was perfect, then, at least for the duration of whatever song was playing. "Three-and-a-half minutes of utopia. You got enough 45's stacked up, life would be perfect."

It was perfect until he got home, anyway. "Hours late." His parents, "Never got it," never understood that he wasn't being pointedly belligerent, wasn't challenging their authority. "I just wanted to preserve the moment." He remembered thinking even then, Why can't this last?

"They thought it was a waste of time," he said. "Imagine that. Imagine there's no heaven..."

They thought he was squandering his future, thought he should be concentrating on that future, on what he wanted to do with his life.

"I was doing it," he said, and just as suddenly the memories brought him back, brought him to the day, to Mickey's, and Angela's questioning.

He turned to look out the windows. It was just dark enough not to be able to see what was left of the Tupperware fallout. He had to wonder, if people were still questioning his actions, were still challenging *him* about what he was going to do with his life, "Have I made any progress? Should I even worry about that, them?" Should he be accountable for the last ten, twelve years? If not, were his ideals, his "fucking absolutes," still applicable?

"I've done plenty," he answered himself. And he could argue, with himself, with Whomee, his bored, drunken, snoozing cat. "That was then. That was another time, another song, another dance, another girl in another place, and none of it even exists anymore for all I know, not even the goddammed band!" He remembered another Lennon interview, from another, angrier time, explaining that the Beatles were "Just another rock-and-roll band."

"You see," Zimmer said, drying his hands, "That was then."

Zimmer leaned over his cat, swaying gently. "You're just a cat, right? And I'm just a Lumper. And this is just a puny little kitchen. But that's all we're likely to get, right? And that's what rock-and-roll's about, right? What have you got right now, that's all that matters. Don't even bother washing the dishes, mother-fucker, because if there isn't anyone around to eat off of them tomorrow, they won't mind that they're dirty, now will they?"

Zimmer stood up and leaned against the doorjamb. "Besides," he said, "there aren't any more eggs. Remember?"

Remember. He'd almost forgotten Steph and Angela were still there. He listened to Steph's "Shh, shh, it's all right," and Angela's, "I just didn't know there was going to be a feast today. Why didn't he tell me?"

Zimmer flinched at the line and then wobbled in the direction of it.

"I would've stayed away if that's what he wanted."

Zimmer mumbled the last of the line, "...if that's what he wanted," and had to wonder, Who? Then it occurred to him, who.

"Oh, goddammit, nobody knew there was going to be a feast today," he answered, through the partition, not really meaning to be so loud. "It just happened!"

Steph looked around the barrier to find Zimmer doubled-over, grimacing, slapping the sides of his head for interfering.

"Zimmer? You all right?"

"Yeah, yeah. Sorry. Guess I'll head for Lear's. Anybody want to join me?"

Angela sniffled, then blew her nose.

"Jesus, Angie," he said, reaching and pulling himself up on his tip-toes to get his chin over the top bar of the partition, to look at her sitting balled up in one corner of the fold out. "I meant all of us!" Trying for that precise amount of emphasis, "Together," he couldn't keep his balance, and came toppling over onto the mattress.

Angela drew her knees up a little closer, sniffed again, but was smiling at least. "I'm not sure I want to go anywhere with you right now."

"I mean it," Zimmer said to her, trying to get himself untangled.

"Right," Steph said, watching as Zimmer tumbled off the bed, onto the floor near the bathroom with a thud. "You're in complete control."

"That's right, I am," he said, pushing himself up, with the aid of the wall, but then slid back down, the slightest of altitude compounding his condition suddenly. He finally understood how Steph felt at the top of the stairs of Fill those first nights long, long ago.

"I think it's time to call it a night, Zimmer."

"Okay, for tonight," he said, allowing Steph to help him to his feet. "But I do mean it. We're all going out together, as soon as you're ready. A road feast."

"Right," Steph told him. "You just work out the details."

He had to half guide, half carry the stumbling Lumper bear-cat, who was quickly slipping out of consciousness.

And then he would just as quickly slip back, momentarily, "The quarry!" he said. "We'll have a fucking picnic," squinting to focus on Steph's face for approval.

"Sounds good," Steph said, lowering Zimmer onto his cot.

"A double date," Zimmer persisted. "You and Angie. Me and

Abby-gal." Then he snorted.

"Shut up and go to sleep," Steph said, and put Whomee into bed with him.

"I love you too, honey," Zimmer mumbled, speaking to no one, with his eyes closed, wrapping an arm around his cat.

16. The Quarry

FOR someone who ordinarily had so much trouble sleeping more than four hours at any one stretch, Zimmer made up for his last year of restlessness since he'd come to Tripoli, all at once. He slept through the night as dead as he'd often accused Steph of being. He slept through Angela's early morning preparation—her shower and hair drying, the aroma of coffee escaping from the kitchen while she fixed herself some lunch—and departure.

When Steph got up a few hours later, he was overcome by an attack of the same kind of anxiety Zimmer usually felt. He leaned close over Zimmer's motionless body, worried for the absolute worst, until Zimmer stirred, some: enough to prove he was alive, at least. Then he was back out, gone to whatever nether land he'd been occupying going on twelve hours.

When Steph finished cleaning the kitchen and straightening the mess that Zimmer had caused behind the partition, Zimmer still didn't wake up. Not all of him, anyway. Parts of him returned from their retreat to take care of things he was otherwise neglecting. Custodial things: his bladder woke up about noon, as did his feet, to carry him to the bathroom. And once he was safely sitting again, he dictated to Steph, who was sitting on the foldout, reading, one of the details of their picnic.

"Eggs," he said, groggily, starting the grocery list, even in that state, the organized cook.

With that taken care of, he could return to the cot for a few more hours of sleep, hours he'd missed back in July, maybe.

"And pickles," he said, the next time he visited the bathroom, just before Angela got home from work.

Steph was still sitting on the bed, still reading, both an old *Sports Illustrated*, and a dog-eared paperback loaner copy of *Garp*, from the stash of material he always kept under the bed. He thought there was hope, when Zimmer finally responded to external stimuli, to Steph and Angela talking in their bedroom. "And a nice bottle of wine."

"Hi, Zimmer," she said, lying next to Steph, flipping through a *Cosmo* she'd brought home from the store, still wearing her Regency uniform.

He looked, nodded in her direction. Then he headed back to the cot.

At about twenty-four hours, after Steph and Angela had had a chance to enjoy the rest of the afternoon and early evening coming and going from Fill, shopping, and then out to eat at a new bar Angela'd heard about, at the mall—one of those new fashioned, gimmicky bars, with bicycles hanging from the ceiling and a menu that sometimes read like a comic book: they ate a platter of "the nastiest nachos north of the border"—just as they were beginning to worry, wondering if they shouldn't call in some professional help, Zimmer passed by his cot on his way back from the bathroom and joined them in the kitchen. They were standing and gazing out the windows, sipping Irish coffee. He declined a cup, intent on taking care of another little chore.

He reached under the cabinet and pulled out the biggest pot in Fill. Above, from the shelves, behind the plates and the coffee mugs, he pulled out a bag of dried kidney beans. He dumped the bag into the big pot, the clanging of the beans on the dry metal the loudest sound there'd been in the apartment all day.

Zimmer laughed at the sound, imitating, "Ping, ping," like he really was finally awake, admitting that the sound reminded him of another of those forgotten moments from his past. He promised Steph he'd tell him what it was, maybe the next time he was up. He poured water into the pot until the beans were submerged, whooshed them around, under everyone's curious nose, rinsed, repeated the washing and set the pot to the side, the beans soaking.

"Good for the heart," he told them, grinning, leaving the kitchen for the bed again.

"Don't worry," Steph said to Angela, as he readied for work.

She was showing signs of the anxiety, commenting on spending the night with a corpse, or the converse, spending it with a wide-awake manic Zimbarco.

"Really," Steph assured her, the expert in the field. "Now he's got to sleep off the fatigue of sleeping so much."

It could have been a vicious cycle, sleeping off sleeplessness and then sleeping off sleep. Zimmer could have spent the rest of his life tacking back and forth between one or the other objective.

But he didn't. Thirty hours proved more than sufficient. He was fully awake, waiting in the kitchen when Steph returned from work the next morning, Monday. He'd already gone through most of a pot of coffee, in fact, spending the last few hours of the night quietly waiting for sunrise. He'd just turned out the dull yellow light on the face of the stove that he'd used to navigate the dark kitchen in anticipation of the dawn creeping over the mountains behind Fill, stirring the darkness below, when Steph guided Abby into the space under the apartment.

"Eggs?" Zimmer asked, peering over his coffee cup as Steph reached the kitchen doorway.

"He's alive!"

Zimmer frowned, traded a cold beer for the groceries Steph held: the eggs, a jar of pickles, three clanking bottles of Angela's favorite wine—a California Chardonnay—a bag of doughnuts, some potatoes, stew meat, etc.

"How was your night?" Zimmer asked, but was intent upon the doughnut he couldn't chew fast enough, a soggy, coffee stained, sugar doughnut. "When was the last time I've eaten?"

"Rough," Steph told him, sorting through the bag. "Frank's pouting."

"No shit," Zimmer said, but through the doughnut sounded, "Nosshwit."

"He's pissed about being left out of a feast."

Zimmer looked up, remembering, calculating the time lapse.

"Don't look so innocent. It's all your fault."

"My fault?"

"That's right, your fault. It never would have come up if Bruce hadn't taken up that toast of yours, Keep Fried!"

"First of all, I have never had any control whatsoever over what Bruce will or will not adopt," Zimmer said, reaching for another beer for Steph. "And it seems to me you were the first one to use *that toast*." He spied floating chunks of bloated doughnut in his coffee, then pulled out a bottle of beer for himself.

"Yeah, well, Frank didn't have too much trouble figuring it all out, and then flogged himself all night demanding details."

Steph found himself playing all sides, offender, instigator, "They thought it was all my idea!" defender and apologist.

"You do that so well, though."

"So when Frank figures it all out—fucking Bruce raving about the pickles—he starts cutting the breaks short so he won't have to be reminded of what he missed."

"He wouldn't have eaten those pickles anyway, you know that."

"That's not the point. And those two assholes just kept aggravating him, Mickey chanting, Keep fired, keep fired!"

"If you ask me, it was worth it, if the Mick finally gets it."

"What about Frank?"

"Steph, you know we didn't purposefully leave him out. Did you tell him about the cigars?"

"No," he laughed. "Somehow I'd forgotten that."

"Did you try to convince him that it just happened? That nobody had planned anything?"

"Sure I tried. But I already knew that wasn't going to work. I've seen that movie. I could've closed my eyes and it could've been Saturday night, all over again. All this *deja vu* shit; I don't need any more of it," he said, moving for the refrigerator. "I keep repeating myself enough."

"Isn't that a sweet thing to say," Angela said from the doorway, pulling the sash of her robe tight around her waist. "Now I remind you of Frank?"

They both spun in her direction, Zimmer wincing.

"No, Ang," Steph said, reaching for her. "Frank reminds me

of you."

"Oh, good," Zimmer said, looking for some place to hide in the tiny kitchen. "That's better, great Steph."

Angela laughed. "I disagree. Not only do I not look like Frank," she said, showing off, moving to a space at the counter between them. "I don't sound like him, or smell like him, or feel like him," rubbing against Steph, "or taste like him," she finished, kissing Steph, smacking. "Do I?"

"Oh boy," Zimmer said, turning back toward his cooking.

She took a step after him. "Do I have to prove it to you too?"

"No, no," he said, backing up, holding out a sacrificial cup of coffee toward her. "I'll take his word for it," pointing at Steph.

"Naw. I'm too tired. You two work it out. It's sleep, in a matter of seconds," Steph said, wandering from the kitchen.

Angela took the coffee from Zimmer, and the jelly-filled doughnut he offered as further defense, and followed.

Zimmer went back to work on the picnic menu. The beans simmered away. On the other burner, in the next largest pot, eggs and potatos boiled together. The cook had been dreaming about more than just grocery lists and preliminary necessities.

"Killer potato salad," he told Whomee, who was watching him test the doneness of the eggs. Zimmer couldn't know how much he sounded like a waiter for Summits, the place Angela'd taken Steph to.

In Zimmer's case, though, it wasn't hype. Sometimes he just had trouble, when creating his sauces or salads, sticking to the ordinary, tested methods. "I could never have gotten along with Pitman."

He did things like adding cole slaw dressing to pasta salad or sneaking a little hot pepper sauce into his cole slaw. He's taken to adding a little brown sugar and catsup—"Shit!" he cried, realizing the possibility that they were out of catsup after Saturday, but they weren't—to his vinaigrette recipe for spinach salad.

"That's the dream," using that mix, of olive oil, red wine vinegar, basil, together with an herbed mayonnaise for the potato salad. "What d'you think?" The potato and egg quarters tossed with some salad olives, "Maybe some Progresso olive salad instead?" some sweet pickle bits, or relish, crispy bacon crumbled up...

"Stop!"

He bent and scrounged around in the cabinets below for something to save the potato water in. "Isn't there one of those ice cream buckets somewhere?" Anything.

"Hell, after Saturday," all the leftover containers should be empty.

"Maybe Steph doesn't know where they go?"

Then he remembered what he'd done with all the Tupperware. He stood to look out the windows.

"Looking for something in particular?" Angela asked from the doorway, wagging a plastic scrub brush at the opened cabinets, and him, a pail in her other hand. "You could have told me you didn't like this stuff, you know."

"Is that?" he started, but not needing to know, grabbed the bucket and brush and threw them out the window.

"Hey!"

"Aw, Angie. You won't miss it, you know."

"It's useful," she said, looking out the window.

"They just want you to believe that. It's evil."

"Evil?"

"Yeah, evil. You've seen those brochures and commercials where the whole refrigerator's full of Tupperware; cabinets and countertops controlled by those variously colored tins, all lined up according to size and shape, little armies readying to take over the world!"

"Then it wasn't a personal thing?"

"Personal? Why?"

"After what we'd said that morning. What *I'd* said."

"That? No. What did we say? What day was that?"

She stood there smiling at him.

He reached for one of the bottles of wine chilling in the refrigerator, "Ready?"

She looked up to the clock, instinctively.

"Ah, ah," he said, twisting in the corkscrew. "Ten-till, right?"

"Right."

"Let's make some bread," he said, pouring her a glass, saving just a cup of the potato water before pouring the rest down the sink. "First the yeasties."

"Yeasties?"

"Yeasties," he repeated, bending low over a bowl where he'd just sprinkled a tablespoon of coarse yeast granules onto the water. "Treat them right, they'll treat you right."

"Sounds like more Lumper stuff."

"Partly," he said, refilling her glass. "Get used to it."

"This is what you're like when you're rested?"

"I'm not going to hear that as a challenge. Because I'm not going to spend any part of this day defending myself. You hear?"

"I'm sorry."

"No, see, Ang," he walked to her end of the room, clanging his bottle against her glass, "don't do that. Be sassy, like earlier. That's the only way this can work, don't you think?"

He walked back the length of the room, to allow her to ponder that. At the refrigerator, on the bottom shelf, behind the beer, behind a forgotten head of cabbage, he pulled out a large mason jar, clamped tight, and another bottle of beer, singing, "So they say it's your birth-day..."

"Zimmer?"

"Hap-py birthday to ya."

"What's that?"

"Sourdough," he whispered. He'd forgotten about the starter too, had only seen it again Saturday morning when he was cleaning out the rest of the refrigerator.

"You sing to it?"

"Sing to everything on their birthday."

"Birthday?"

"It's a year old. Year and a week, actually."

"That stuff's been in there a whole year."

"Year and a week," he said, showing her the masking tape with the date pencilled on it, 12/1/79.

"Yuck."

"Yuck?" he said, pulling the jar back from her. "No, not yuck. Watch," he said, loosing the metal retaining clamp.

Angela started to move away, started to say, "No, no, don't," but was knocked silent, knocked almost the rest of the way off her stool by the alcoholic fermentation that escaped from the jar. "Wow."

"Not bad, huh?"

"What's it for?"

"For the bread. Sourdough pumpernickel."

He ignored her scowl, her "unqualified," scowl, and went to work on the bread. He added some starter, salt, molasses, caraway seed and a couple of cups of dark rye flour to the bowl of dissolved yeast. Next, he stirred whole wheat flour into the blend, then a little more of the rye and finally some heartier, glutinated bread flour, stirring, scooping, and flipping the blob around in the bowl. Then he scraped it out and onto the countertop, rubbing out the flour and dough clinging to the sides of the bowl, before dropping it into the sink. He stepped back, sipped his beer, and said, "Now for the fun part."

Zimmer moved back up to the counter, hitching up his jeans like he was getting ready for an arm-wrestling match. He grabbed a handful of flour from the canister and sprinkled it over the countertop. Then he started kneading the dough, pushing, then folding, rotating the brown blob a quarter turn. He sprinkled more flour over the board and repeated the sequence, push, fold, rotate, sprinkle, a kind of elegant dance step, once he was up to rhythm, push, fold, rotate, sprinkle, five, six, seven, eight.

"That's fun?"

"Oh, yeah," he said, in cadence. "Great, fun."

Even as sweat started to glisten on Zimmer's brow, and an ache seeped into his forearms as he worked on the ever-stiffening dough, he told her, "The most, relaxing thing, I do," push, fold, rotate, sprinkle.

Flour was everywhere, from the sides of his head, where he'd pushed hair out of his face, to the back of his pants, where he'd wiped his hands either before or after he pulled on his beer, or both. It was all over the floor, spread like a halo around where he stood, knees flexed, working the dough. If Angela had ever wondered why that particular part of the kitchen floor was always sticky and gooey, she now knew.

"Maybe it's time I got to work," she said, staring at the spot.

"What?" Zimmer gasped, finishing the kneading, setting the mound aside and covering it up with the bowl.

"You know, the floor."

"No, no, no. No work today. Not on picnic day."

"What do you call what you're doing?"

He didn't answer. Cleaning the bread bowl, greasing it, he set the bread aside to rise, before saying, "Chili," reaching for the beans.

"Oh!" she said, and stomped out of the kitchen.

Zimmer grinned, and did not feel bad. "What she wanted, right?"

He drained the beans and added them to a pot of stewing Rotel tomatoes. On another burner, he started cubes of stew beef browning, meanwhile chopping up some mushrooms, peppers, and a couple stalks of celery, adding it all to the meat once it had been seared and colored on two sides. He was in full four-part orchestration now, his cooking moving from a simple waltz to a symphony, what with the strokes of his chef's blade against the cutting board, Chock, Chock, and the bubbling sauce, the sizzling meat and sauteing veggies, with Zimmer's vocals, "Oh, yeah. That's nice."

Angela could have snuck around unnoticed, could have dusted the woodwork, or polished some brass, hell, she could have run the vacuum cleaner, but she just changed into a sweatshirt and jeans and returned to the kitchen, Mr. Boyles' stool, and Zimmer's performance.

He was bringing the concert to a close, spooning the meat and veggies into the pot, de-glazing the skillet with a generous pouring of tequila, a spitting and crackling crescendo of pungent steam.

Angela coughed, rubbing her eyes, both from the tequila

and the peppery tomato breaths burping out of the chili pot.

"You sure I can't help a little," she said, motioning toward the nearly full sink.

"Help how?"

"You know, clean some dishes, sweep the floor."

"No. Not on picnic day."

"So what am I supposed to do?"

"Whatever you want."

She sat there and thought. Or rather, he figured, "She tried to think." Nothing would come to mind, he knew, putting the question in that stark manner.

He reached for the bowl of rising dough, slipping the towel off, tested its doneness: poking a finger halfway into the dough and then studying the imprint.

She got up and looked over his shoulder. "What's wrong?"

"Nothing," he said, finally punching down the dough, letting a pocket of sourdough and rye and caraway and molasses waft through the kitchen.

"Just got to be careful with how long you let it rise. Cause," he said, rolling the ball up and inverting the bowl back over it. "You have to make the yeasties start over, without discouraging them, or pissing them off. If you're too rough," he turned around, leaning against the counter, "the bread won't rise a second time. You get a brick. But if it rises too much, you get those holes in the loaf."

"What's left?"

"Yeasties," he said, turning back around, retrieving a couple of loaf pans from under the counter, and a rolling pin. "You let them tell you what they want, when they want it. Something we could all learn, when you think about it," he said, pausing, rolling pin raised like a pointer.

"Now that," she said, hugging him from behind, "I can understand."

They stood there motionless for a couple of long moments.

"What I want," she said, releasing him, "is some more of that wine."

"At your service, me-lady," he said, reaching for the bottle.

"It's your day."

He finished flattening out and then rolling up the loaves, setting them aside to rise again, the towel draped over both pans.

"What else?" he asked her.

"Let me do something for you."

"Like?"

"Whatever you want."

He frowned, at first, then, moving for the refrigerator, said, "All right. Lend me your palate."

"My tongue?" she asked, smiling wickedly.

Zimmer actually blushed. "Your exquisite *taste*," he corrected her, but smiled back.

He pulled out two bowls. One held the French dressing, that he blended back together. The other had the herbed mayonnaise. He whisked a little of the vinaigrette into the mayo, then a little more, trying just to cut the mayo taste, not its firmness.

"Taste," he said, holding the bowl out to her.

She reached for the silverware drawer.

"No, no. Use your finger," plunging one of his own into the dressing, demonstrating.

He watched her sample, then asked her expressionless blinking, "More zing?"

He retrieved the catsup from the refrigerator and the mustard powder from the cabinet. After a few more exchanges, after Angela got used to the methodology and started contributing to the process instead of staring blankly, Zimmer arrived at his dressing and set it aside.

But Angela took one more sample. "You really should be cooking," she told him.

He shrugged. "I am."

"No, I mean like at Willie's."

"That again?"

"It's what you do best, isn't it?"

"Except I'm not a very good employee, like I wasn't a very good soldier, or a very good husband."

"Maybe you were just in the wrong environment? The right situation could make all the difference. You've got so much to show, Zimmer, to teach."

"Ha. I don't think we need any more assholes in the world. There're plenty of those already, aren't there?"

"You're too hard on yourself," she said, sampling the dressing one last time, before he moved it to the other side of the counter, away from her.

He knew one thing, if he ever did teach anyone to cook, a wife, a friend, a child, he'd sure discourage that sampling as you go approach... Then he felt like an asshole again for thinking that. "I think, rather, that I'm not hard enough."

"Oh?" she said, the wickedness returning to her face.

"Cut that out," he said, checking to see if the oven was up to temp.

Once the bread was baking, he slid the cooled salad onto that cleared space on the counter to stir in the dressing. He took a big wooden spoon out of the drawer and vigorously blended in the dressing, bits of potato and bacon and egg spilling over the edge of the bowl occasionally.

Angela sat behind him and watched, even stooped to try and catch a few of the large chunks, before whining, "Zimmer!"

"What?"

"Look at the floor."

"Yeah."

"I just cleaned that yesterday."

"And it was supposed to stay clean?"

"For a while, yes."

Zimmer stood paralyzed, holding the spoon.

"Oh, you're just like Steph, just another man."

"Ah, Jesus, Angie, what's that got to do with anything?"

"A lot."

"How? What good does it do to break things down along those lines?"

"What other lines are there?"

"Individual. Can't we just be ourselves?"

"Said the Lumper."

Zimmer wagged his head.

"Sorry. Must be the wine," she tried, showing him her empty glass. "Just gets a little lonely sometimes."

"With yourself?"

"I guess."

"Well, what do you want?"

"I want a home. A family."

"To know who you are?"

"No. That's part of me."

"A missing part?"

"Maybe."

"And Steph fits that part?"

"Hah," she said, stepping next to him to reach for the wine. "He doesn't think so."

"I'd have to agree," Zimmer said. "I don't know if he could do a family yet."

"I beg your pardon, he's a wonderful lover!"

"Not that."

"And you?" she asked, pulling a bit of dough, or potato out of his hair. "Ever thought about having a couple of little red-haired girls."

"Now *that's* a frightening thought."

"Why? That's what he says. Why does the very thought scare you two?"

Zimmer busied himself, backing away from her, reaching for the potholders off the top of the refrigerator. He opened the oven door, pulling one pan out and testing the bread, thumping it, a second, and third time, before deciding they needed a few more minutes. "It's just that--"

"Goddammit, Zimmer!"

"It's just that," he said again, making her wait before she went to see what Steph was screaming about. "I've always been part of one family or another—can't really remember it ever being otherwise; and I've yet to get it quite right, you know. So, yeah, the thought of starting another family scares the hell out of me."

He got busy again with the bread before she could answer,

not that Steph was going to allow for any thoughtful consideration anyway.

"How the fuck am I supposed to sleep with you cooking?"

"You're not!" Zimmer yelled back. "Get up."

"No."

"Hi."

"No. More sleep."

Steph held a pillow on top of his head and fell back on the mattress.

"You can sleep on the way to the quarry."

"The quarry?"

"For the picnic," Angela reminded him, sitting on the bed.

"Picnic?" Steph lived so decidedly in the present, it only seemed like he was repeating himself, from others having to constantly remind him what his name was, what day it was.

"Are you getting ready?" Zimmer called into the silence, as he finished slicing up sandwich ingredients. "Don't distract him, Angela. Let's go."

He gathered their feast and started loading the Bee-atile, first stomping through the room with an ice-chest containing the salad, some beer, the wine, checking, "Steph?"

"I'm coming, I'm coming."

Angela guided him through his weary preparations, scrubbing his face, coaxing him into some clothes, as Zimmer made a second trip with supplies.

Once in the car, Angela was in charge of guarding the pot of chili on the passenger side floorboard. Steph stretched out in the back seat, still clutching his pillow, still seeking more sleep.

"Just go up the turnpike. Wake me up at the overpass," he said.

Only a few minutes later Zimmer was craning around in the driver's seat, the interstate overpass in view, yelling, "Steph!"

"All right, all right," he answered, rubbing his eyes. "There should be an old trucker road off to the left, if you can still get down it," he said, leaning into the space between the front seats. "There."

Zimmer pulled off the turnpike, onto the road, which was

just two overgrown tread gullies.

"Well, like I said, if we can get there, this road'll take us up to the top. Take a right at the fork, if it's still there. Hell, Zimmer, maybe we should just go to Dagaton Woods."

Zimmer frowned into the rearview mirror before slipping Abby into first gear.

The road was still there, as was the fork, though they weren't so easily navigatable as they may have once been. The city had tried to block the road with a few old concrete drainage conduits bridging the embankments and sitting low over the gravel road. Off road bikers had worn paths over the coarse brush to the right of the roadblock. Zimmer steered for it, keeping the left wheels grooved in the track, the right spinning, clawing over rocks.

Angela couldn't begin to both hang onto her door handle and keep the chili steady and shifted it to the back seat for Steph to wrestle with. He flopped around back there, cradling the sloshing black pot, sacrificing his body, his clothes.

Zimmer finally found the spot, the shelf of rock. It was an area of scrubbed, lusterless granite about the size of Fill's living room, with only patches of moss occasionally hiding on the shaded sides of larger boulders, two spindly bushes that had forced themselves through the rock.

They got out of the car, Angela shuddering. Zimmer mumbled, "Jesus," at the almost moonscape starkness of the place.

He held the door while Steph crawled out of the back still balancing the chili.

"Isn't this great?"

Zimmer stepped to the front of the Bee-atile, only about six feet from the cliff's edge. He could see that they'd found the steepest, highest shelf still intact along what remained of the eroded and forsaken quarry's rim.

Steph joined him at the front of the car to unload the cooler, sacks of food, two blankets. "Some trailblazing, Abby-gal."

"You're surprised?" Zimmer asked, moving back to the

clearing that Angela'd staked out.

By the time Steph had unpacked the trunk and he and Angie had laid out the blankets, anchoring them with smaller rocks, Zimmer had managed to get a fire started, sparks popping out of a tight pile of twigs, dried grass, nursing it into a larger and larger fire.

"I'm not even going to ask you where you learned how to do that," Steph said.

But Zimmer stood, at semi-attention, saluting Steph with three spired fingers, intoning, "On my honor I will do my duty-"

"Naw."

"Honest."

"No. You?"

"What?" Angela asked.

"Brave, clean, reverent..."

"Stop," Steph told him.

"Courteous, thrifty..."

"Stop! I believe you."

"What?"

"And, obedient," Zimmer finished, nodding to everyone with a satisfied smirk, dropping the pose.

"Really?" Steph asked once more, narrowing his eyes.

"Really what?"

Zimmer folded his fingers into the salute again. "Really."

The trace of doubt stayed on Steph's face, though, until he realized what bothered him about the picture. "That's the wrong hand!" he yelled at him, another southpaw attempt at rearranging the world.

Zimmer insisted, "I was too! I still got my merit badges. I can prove it," he said, fumbling around in the pockets of his painter's pants.

"They wouldn't let people like you in the boy scouts," Steph said, looking for something to throw at him.

Zimmer ducked, reaching into the cooler for two beers, a glass for Angela. Then he straddled the cooler with the sandwich ingredients before him. "I used to have those badges somewhere, I really did," he said to the turkey.

"Wher--" Steph started, then stopped himself, but not before Zimmer knew what the question would have been, giving him just a tiny little shrug.

"What's the big deal?" Angela asked Steph, pulling bowls from the bag.

"I was a Boy Scout," he told her. "I was proud of that."

"Sorry," Zimmer said.

They passed the food around, the salad, chili, spooning generously into separate bowls.

"No paper plates," Zimmer had said. "If we can't bother to bring the dishes home and clean them, we'll just throw them over the cliff."

He assembled the sandwiches as soon as the bread cooled a little more.

Steph and Zimmer traded Boy Scout career stories, lies mostly, telling Angela about camping trips where bears fell onto tents trying to get at the emergency rations of Twinkies and Cracker Jacks tied up in the tree, that mothers always sent into the wilderness with their pioneer sons; about raids on Girl Scout camps, or sabotaging the tents and latrines of rival troop sites.

"Latrines?"

"Outhouses."

"What'd you do?"

"Harmless, kid's stuff."

"Like snakes."

"Or firecrackers."

It was a calm, humid evening. By the way the sunset lingered, they might have mistaken it for a slow summer evening, not a night in December, safely in standard time again, only two weeks from the shortest day of the year. But the weather in Tripoli, as usual, could be a tease, and everyone knew it could be bone-chilling cold within twenty-four hours. They knew, too, to enjoy this reprieve, settling into a quiet, relaxed dinner, taking in the view from their unobstructed vantage up on the rocks, which probably accounted for the sustained sunset more than their being transported through the seasons.

After dinner they sat at the edge of the cliff in the dark, dangling their feet over, munching apples, watching the parade of lights along the interstate below.

"This is really a nice place," Zimmer said into the quiet.

"Should have seen it before."

"So peaceful. Quiet."

"Romantic," Angela said, making Steph frown, squirm.

"So romantic," Zimmer echoed, lying back and gazing up into the dark sky.

"Still not what it used to be."

The timbre of Steph's voice stayed further teasing. It was the same tone he'd used when he'd first showed Zimmer the shelf they were sitting on, from the upper railing of Lucas Stadium, back on that authentically summer afternoon.

"Can be tonight," Angela said, taking her turn as rotating bartender, moving to the cooler for two more beers, half a glass of wine. "Can't it?" she said, stepping back to the ledge, using Steph's shoulder to ease herself back down.

"Careful," Zimmer said, reaching from his prone position to steady her hand.

"Worried?" she asked.

"I think our bear's got a thing for you, Ang."

"Just had a spooky thought, is all. A memory, really."

Steph looked down at him, pretty sure he wasn't grinning.

"One of those memories you wish you could change, you almost see yourself changing the events."

"Another Boy Scout story?"

"Ha. No. There was this park we used to go to on church picnics, stuff like that, up in the hills east of Salyne. There was a dried river bed, a dried waterfall we used to climb. One year, somebody fell, a girl from school. Nancy something. I didn't know her. I was climbing when she fell, was about halfway up, saw her fall."

"Did she die?" Angela asked.

"You never have time to really *do* anything in those situations. Only when you're remembering them."

Steph laid back into the same position as Zimmer. "You sure are telling a lot of stories lately."

"Yeah. I guess."

"Does that mean the Mick was right? You leaving."

"I don't know. Not tonight, anyway. This is too nice."

"Then that settles it," Angela said, settling down between them. "We'll stay."

"Yeah. We'll build a cabin. Right here."

"Start a family," she said, nuzzling up to Steph.

"Kids?"

"Ha."

"We'll name the first one Zimmer," she said, to make the idea sound a little better.

"That's all I need, another one."

"Thought you were going to have little red-haired girls?" Zimmer said.

She sat up and poked at his side.

"That uncle Zimmer can save from the edge of the quarry."

They were quiet for a while, Angela settling back into Steph's arms. Zimmer had his hands behind his head. He could sense the ghosts stirred up by the stories, the conversation, but they didn't feel threatening, not at that precise moment.

Finally, Steph said, "Sounds like I'm going to have to work some overtime."

"Speaking of which," Angela said, sitting up again. She glanced at her wrist, but wouldn't have been able to see the face of her watch in the dark, even if Zimmer hadn't forbidden her wearing it to the picnic.

"I don't suppose either of you Boy Scouts can tell what time it is?"

They stared into the sky.

"That was one of my badges."

"Right."

"Tough to do with all these clouds."

"Excuses, excuses," Steph said, getting up.

"Let's see, where's that moon?"

"Where're the keys?" Steph asked, standing over Zimmer.

He moved to the Bee-atile to turn on the radio for the time. Angela got up too, to start gathering things.

The radio wound up on the last lines of a Lennon song, "Strange days, indeed..."

Zimmer laughed.

The dee-jay voiced over the fading refrain, "John Lennon, dead tonight, at age 40."

Angela, unhearing, called, "Steph, can you turn on the lights so I can see?"

"Shh."

"Let's go back to New York for an update on tonight's tragic shooting."

"Shooting?"

"--peating what was confirmed just minutes ago by Roosevelt spokes-persons: John Lennon, brutally assaulted nearly forty minutes ago in the doorway of the Dakota, has died of gunshot wounds to the back."

"Zimmer?"

He'd heard, was up and moving away from the car, the radio, its news, "... gunshot wounds to the back."

Angela came over to Abby. "What happened?"

"Tonight's tragic shooting," Steph repeated for her cryptically, or maybe just not wanting to process it any further yet.

"The suspect was arrested without incident, but the investigation is continuing."

Zimmer had backed his way to the farthest reaches of the clearing. "Why the fuck would anyone shoot John Lennon?"

Steph looked across the darkness, barely making out Zimmer's white pants. "Zimmer?"

"We have a report that the Lennons were returning to their residence and the accused approached, reportedly calling Mr. Lennon before assaulting..."

"Can this be true?"

"Got to be one of those war-of-the-worlds bullshit radio gags. Got to be."

"Why the fuck--"

"--the bullets entering approximately here..."

"Have they said who?" Angela asked.

Zimmer moved toward the question.

"Is there any indication of a motive yet?"

"Doesn't matter."

"Was the assailant an acquaintance?"

"He reportedly had been hanging around the apartment building most of the day. He said he was a fan."

"A fan?"

"Doesn't matter."

"Couldn't they have stopped him?"

"Doesn't fucking matter!" Zimmer screamed, reaching into the car and punching the radio quiet. "If it's true," he said, waving into the car, "what else could possibly matter?"

Angela said, "Let's go, huh?"

Zimmer walked to the edge of the cliff. "What the fuck. I tried, you know. I've been trying."

Steph got out of Abby and moved closer. "Trying what?"

Zimmer threw his bottle of beer down into the darkness and spun away from him. "Trying. Everything. Sure, I know that's failure," he said, not speaking to Steph any longer, if he ever was. "But I don't what else to do, but try. I tried. I tried to believe that it was just another rock-and-roll band, that they could just as easily break up or stay together and the world wouldn't change one tiny little fucking bit," he said, tracing around the Bee-atile, "but I *needed* them. Yeah, I needed them." He sat, releasing the hand brake, slipping the gearshift into neutral. "Or I needed to believe that they *might* get back together some time, because that's what we do, isn't it? We keep hoping we can get back together with all those better times, right?" He stood again, facing Steph.

"Right."

"Let's go home," Angela said.

"Home?" Zimmer snapped. "What the fuck is home? Who cares? Who wants anything to do with any of this shit if that's what's going to happen?" he said, waving at the radio, pacing again, slamming the trunk. "I don't want any of this," he said, stepping to the rear end. "None of it," pushing his shirtsleeves up.

Steph had seen that gesture maybe five hundred times over the last year, was pretty sure what Zimmer was up to, and moved to the front of the car, bracing one shoulder against the trunk just as Zimmer lowered against the engine compartment.

Angela stood over him, asking, "What are you doing?"

"None of it."

"Zimmer, wait."

"No. Get out of the way."

"Zimmer?" Angela said, trying to peel one of his arms loose, but not slowing his progress much, as he inched the Bee-atile toward the cliff. She skipped to the front, "Steph!" pulling on his arm.

"How'll we get home?"

"Fucking fly. Who cares?"

"What about Whomee?" Steph tried.

"Fuck him. Cats land, remember?"

"Stop it!"

"Why here?"

"Where the fuck else?"

"New York."

Finally, Zimmer hesitated.

"We'll take Abby to see the Dakota first."

Zimmer didn't answer, but he stopped pushing, and stood. He moved to the other end, next to Steph, and together they pushed Abby back away from the ledge, to the top of the clearing. Zimmer got in and turned the key. The engine actually cranked, and caught, without them having to jump-start her. He turned her so that the headlights illuminated their picnic area, left her in neutral, idling, while they gathered the rest of the dishes, the blankets, and the cooler.

17. Third Year's Eve

ZIMMER turned the radio back on by the time they were halfway down the Turnpike hill, halfway to 13. They had a name of the assailant by then, were putting together his history as fast as they could. And they had the testimony of eye-witnesses, suddenly, bystanders, neighbors, talking into the radio. They said Chapman had gotten John's autograph earlier. There were different, even conflicting reports of exactly what had happened, how many shots were fired. Zimmer punched another button on the radio each time one of those descriptions came on. Somehow he couldn't listen to the views of people who were so close, but not close enough. Another station would be playing Beatles music, "Help," or "Day in the Life," but always eventually broke in, with more news, more information. Zimmer kept pushing.

"--could've gotten away, but he just stood there, holding his gun, and some book."

Zimmer punched off the radio. But then, as they were pulling into the Regency parking lot, he turned it on again.

He stood to let Steph out.

"You going to be here in the morning?"

Zimmer stared back, nodding a little. "Sure."

He didn't realize until later that Steph meant both at Regency and in Tripoli. It would be several days before Zimmer would be able to recognize those subtle distinctions, before he was paying much attention to anything other than the news of Lennon's death.

He was there to pick up Steph Tuesday morning. They didn't stop at the retail store on the way home. Zimmer had beer in the car for him. They went downtown, to a newsstand, so Zimmer could get a copy of the *Times*. Radio stations all over the country, the world, played nothing but Beatles music all day. Zimmer stayed in the kitchen most of Tuesday, reading, listening.

Chapman's arraignment was Wednesday. An op-ed column bemoaned a situation where a former mental patient could buy a .38 special for a hundred and fifty bucks, carry it around for six weeks, contemplating suicide, murder; could hang around the Dakota for days and finally empty the thing at the back of John Lennon. Specialists discussed the likelihood of this kind of thing happening, what with the thoroughness of pop culture idolization.

Thursday they printed some of the reactions from around the world. Russian newspapers blamed capitalism. There was to be a memorial service in New York on Sunday, in the park, with ten minutes of silence that afternoon at two.

By Friday the story was off the front page, even though mourners were keeping up their vigil at the Dakota.

At Lear's that night, Steph asked, "You going?" meaning the Sunday service.

"I don't know," he said. And he didn't. Part of him wanted to, of course. Most of him did. But part of him didn't want to go, because everyone would be going.

Zimmer thought about it all night, and everyone waited to hear what his decision would be, left in a kind of suspended existence until he decided one way or another.

Saturday they went shopping. Angela wanted to get another space heater for the apartment. Zimmer drove Steph all over town, knowing all the second hand shops, chauffeuring him from one to another, staying in the car while he checked it out, listening to the radio. Steph half expected to come out of any one of the stores and find him gone. But that didn't happen. Zimmer actually joined him in one place, but didn't help in the search for a heater. He looked at television sets, used black and white sets, buying a small portable one for forty bucks.

Angela took that for a positive sign, a signal that he was committing himself to Tripoli. "He's not going now," she told Steph when she got home from work, watching Zimmer set up the television on top of the table.

Steph wasn't as convinced. He spent the most restless night

he'd ever had in Fill, listening each time Zimmer stirred. And he was awake only minutes after Zimmer was, well before sunrise, joining him in the kitchen for coffee.

"They're saying there could be half a million people there today," Zimmer told him, looking out over Dagaton Woods. "Or more."

"Should be one hell of a sight."

"I just heard a guy talking about how John's death could be the salvation for the generation, a reprise of activism. Most, though, think it's the death of the sixties."

"What about you?"

Zimmer shook his head, grinning. "Another guy says, listen to this: that John's seclusion over the last few years was emblematic of what had happened to the movements of the sixties, that even *Double Fantasy* was an extension of that domestic introversion. But now, because he's dead, people will take to the streets again, for a few days at least."

"Wonder what John would say to that."

"Said it a long time ago," Zimmer told him, then sang, "They're going to crucify me... But mostly, he'd probably just say, *rubbish*. These people are full of shit. I mean, they even found some jackass theorizing the coded entendre of *double fantasy*. Jesus."

And then the original "Ballad" came on the radio.

"But it makes me wonder if I'm doing the same thing," Zimmer said, turning off the radio in the middle of the song. "You know?"

"Naw, you're only trying to get you some peace," Steph sang.

Zimmer smiled.

It was then that Steph knew he wasn't going. He didn't know exactly what would happen, but sensed with a kind of unnameable confidence that Zimmer wasn't going to abandon everything just to be part of that scene.

He went to wake Angela for work. She seemed to sense his relaxation immediately, and started talking about an idea she had, for a party, a New Year's party. "Ring in the new," she said.

Steph stayed in bed, napping, considering the idea, snoozing through Angela's preparations, barely rousing enough to bid her goodbye. He didn't wake up again till after noon, to the foreign sound of television commercials in Fill.

Zimmer was watching the service from New York, drinking a beer. Steph saw him stand with the rest of the crowd at the appointed hour, bowing his head in silence. After the ten minutes, and then minutes upon minutes of the crowd singing, "All you need is love," over and over and over again, Zimmer switched off the television, pulled on his fatigue jacket, and reached under the table for the basketball.

"Feel like a game?"

"Absolutely," Steph said, scrambling to find his sneakers, a jacket.

He took that as the surest sign yet that Zimmer was achieving some kind of resolve with what had happened, was becoming himself again. That was a mistake Steph would spend most of the rest of his life trying not to repeat. It was unfair of him to sit back and wait for Zimmer to return to some former self. The universe, his universe was different now. "So why shouldn't he be?" And it was doubly unfair for him to suspend life, like some referee, until it seemed more normal, more safe. Zimmer was changed. "Grief changes you."

When Zimmer stayed in that same distracted, preoccupied mood through the afternoon's basketball, Steph realized all this, that the grieving process changed you, that you couldn't just return to old habits, old attitudes, now that the pieces were irretrievably scattered. Zimmer would have to become a different, changed person, now, and Steph watched the painful process.

The weather didn't help. The balmy, spring like weather of the night of their picnic had lasted a full two days, but Arctic temperatures and frigid winds were back by Wednesday night. When it warmed up a little in the winter like that, and rained, instead of snowing, it was possible to disappear in Dagaton Woods. The low December sky and the lingering mist cloaked everything within the park's borders, a patchwork, layers of fog filling gaps between bare tree limbs and bushes, spreading across the access drives, hovering over fields and courts. Everything was suspended within the condensation, rootless and indistinct. The only thing possible on those days, in fact, was disappearing. Sometimes Zimmer thought that was the best thing he could do, though, wrap himself in a comfy cocoon and just be blind and ignorant to what might lay beyond his outstretched hand.

And then winter came back, whipping down on the jet stream, as always, Mother Nature reminding everyone not to expect any change with the New Year, another winter, locking Dagaton Woods in a crisp, crystalline stiffness in which nothing could hide, or escape.

"You can even see your breath," Zimmer said, exhaling a cloud. He didn't much like being so conspicuous, so public. But everything was conspicuous, the trees standing out boldly against the postcard blue sky. Words, sounds took on a visual, trackable trait, as if because of the cold everything was conducted in slow, achy motion, suspended before ever watchful eyes. Zimmer couldn't breath enough air, move or think fast enough when it was this cold. Maybe that's what bothered him so, made him feel exposed, in danger.

"Steph," he said, hands in his pockets, not defending as Steph dribbled around him. "What's that called when they freeze people?"

Steph stopped short of the goal, just kind of flipped the ball up and in. "What?"

"You know, before they're dead."

"Cryogenics?"

"That's it."

Steph came back to the top of the key, tossing the ball for Zimmer to check. Zimmer watched it thump against his stomach and fall to the ground.

"How cold is that?"

"I don't know," Steph said, trotting after the ball. "Absolute zero?"

"How cold is that?"

"Minus two-hundred, something like that?"

"Hmm."

"What are we talking about Zimmer?"

For some reason, he'd been thinking that what he should have done ten years ago was have himself frozen when the Beatles broke up, not to be revived until they got back together, or there was some other good news out of the decade. Instead, he bought the Bee-atile, "Which doesn't have *any* goddammed heat." Another half-assed attempt at what now seemed like a pretty good idea.

"You know when you freeze to death, you fall asleep first, so that you don't really feel much pain."

"You all right?"

"I don't know. Feels like I'm stuck or something," he said, taking the ball, stepping outside the key, traveling, though Steph wouldn't call the infraction. "Iced over, kind of, you know, like windshield wipers, that just keep accumulating snow and ice and get slower and slower, until they stop." He stood there aiming the ball at the basket from almost thirty feet away.

"Only *your* windshield wipers do that because Abby doesn't have any defrost."

Zimmer let go the shot.

Dumbfounded, Steph watched it sail through the chains, Chink. "One in a million," he said, chasing down the ball.

Zimmer let go another shot from downtown.

"Jesus. Two in a million? Don't move," Steph instructed, retrieving the ball again.

But Zimmer said, "You know, I should get those fixed," dropping the ball and turning for the Bee-atile.

"Are you nuts?" Steph would have fed him the ball all afternoon, to see how many of those shots he could make.

Zimmer got in Abby and tried the key. Nothing. "I should get that fixed, too."

"What's the matter with you?" Steph said, helping him push.

"Nothing makes sense all of a sudden. I mean, some clown

carrying *Catcher* says Mr. Lennon? and then Bang, bang, bang. Leaves kind of a gap."

"For you?"

"I guess."

"That was then, remember?"

"You know," Zimmer said, leaving Steph at the rear of the Bee-atile to jump in and start her, "that's a pretty irritating habit you've picked up."

"I'm just trying to figure out what's wrong with everyone."

"What everyone?"

"You, living in the past all of a sudden. Angie making plans."

"It was a pretty big deal, you know?"

"I know, I know. I'm not saying it wasn't."

"What plans?"

"House in the hills. A party. Little red-haired girls."

"I thought that was the wine talking."

"So did I."

"What party?"

Steph started to tell him about Angela's idea, "To celebrate the New Year, everyone's renewal, hers, ours, America's," but Zimmer shushed him, listening to Abby.

The Bee-atile shuddered as he took her through the gears, groaned as he turned the steering wheel. Out on the road she rattled and backfired, and struggled up the Turnpike.

"Jesus, I've got to fix this car."

He scrounged around in the glove department, under the seats, for the owner's manual. He couldn't remember the last time he'd seen it, if he'd ever really looked at it thoroughly, then asked Steph, "Is there a library somewhere?"

"Sure."

"You got a card?"

"Used to. What do you need?"

"I've got to fix this car."

At the Tripoli Public Library Zimmer found a book called *How to Keep Your Volkswagen Alive.* He spent that night and the next couple of days flipping through it. He bought tools at a hardware store in town, and Steph would wake up in the afternoon to the sound of Zimmer cursing, under the apartment, *fixing* Abby. He'd stomp up the stairs, face in the book, make himself another cup of coffee, then turn and head back downstairs to work on the Bee-atile. He had a mechanics light strung from the rafters, parts and tools strewn around on the gravel parking area.

If Steph ever got himself some coffee and attempted to join him, sitting on the back seat of Abby, say, pushed over against one wall, asking, "How's it going?" all he'd get by way of response would be more of Zimmer's groaning and cursing, "Goddamn this fucking piece of shit!" from trying to maneuver in the confined space, with not always exactly the right tool. Steph knew to leave him alone.

For the next week, ten days, *any* response they got out of Zimmer had that same kind of flavor. He'd either be cursing the car, its faults, his attempts to fix them, or he'd be reading the book, cursing his own stupidity, as he found out things he should have known sooner, should have known or investigated before he'd even bought the car, according to the book, which was subtitled, *A Manual of Step by Step Procedures for the Compleat Idiot.*

One weekend night at Lear's, sitting away from the bar, reading at a table over near the game room to catch some light from the pool tables, he cried out, "Jesus, all this time I'm thinking I can't use jumper cables because it would fry my fuel injection, when Abby doesn't even *have* fuel injection! They didn't start that until '72," addressing no one and everyone at the same time. Only the other Lumpers answered.

"Didn't you ever look under the hood, Zimmer?" Bruce asked.

Mickey was crueler still. "Don't you know what a carburetor looks like?"

"That's what a guy told me once, that I couldn't use jumper cables."

He'd bought the car for reasons that hadn't required any automotive understanding. All he really remembers of the transaction with the car dealer was the guy's pitch that Abby's particular model year boasted a new and improved heater, which turned out to be a lie—or irrelevant, at best: Is nothing an improvement of anything? And, flipping through John Muir's book, Zimmer found out that supposed improvement would date Abby as a '69, not a '70.

"Jesus, you were right," he said, but would give no other explanation. If the book was designed for the "compleat idiot," Zimmer was discovering how thoroughly he fit the bill.

It was helpful, though, and Zimmer was able to make several successful repairs and adjustments. As a cook, he figured, "I ought to be able to follow step by step procedures." He fixed the clunking in the rear end by pouring in an additive. "Sometimes masking a problem is as good as fixing it, when you factor in cost/benefit," he read. He relubricated the axles, repacked wheel bearings, and changed the windshield wipers. He even tuned Abby up, so when he *could* start her, she purred. The proud papa was fond of letting her idle behind Lear's, or out in the access road beneath the kitchen windows, jumping out and tweaking the timing or adjusting the fuel mix, more and more comfortable with his new role as a grease monkey. He even said he could work on Angela's car, once he finished his overhaul of the Bee-atile.

"Except," he couldn't fix Abby's disinclination to start by herself. He tried, through a long series of trials and errors, even fixing related nuisances along the way. But he kept coming back to the original problem. He filled the battery cells with distilled water, cleaned the connections, even replaced the cables. Still, after wrestling to get the battery back under the rear seat, he turned the key, Click.

"Fuck."

He checked for shorts in the electrical system, tracing wires, pulling fuses. He used most of a roll of black electrician's tape, shoring up any exposed leads, but that didn't solve the problem. He tapped grit out of the solenoid. Nope. Which left him with a faulty starter motor.

When he read about the procedures for dealing with that,

sitting in Lear's the next Friday afternoon, the last Friday of the year, he called out, "Jesus, you compleat fucking idiot," slamming the book to the floor. The other Lumpers, sitting along the bar, watching *Incoming Flights*, paid no attention to the outburst, more than used to it by now. "The way you test a bad starter motor is to push the car backwards, to get it unstuck," and then try the key, which is why Abby started the night of their picnic. "All this fucking time."

He was disheartened when he read that rebuilding starter motors was something, "Best left to experts," and worried that he'd reached the end of his capabilities without really improving the situation much. All that time and energy, he sat there thinking, sipping at his beer. "For what?"

But the next day, he was underneath Fill, tightening the motor mounts, which the book said might be the cause. He threaded the stick into third gear, pushed Abby back out from her parking space, jumped in and turned the key. She started.

"No shit."

Then he drove to the library, to turn the book in a day early. The test would be when he came back outside. She started again. He turned the car off and tried again. "I love it!" He was so pleased with himself that he drove around town the rest of the morning running errands he hadn't even thought of for the last two weeks, just so he could stop, park, browse and then return to the Bee-atile more and more confident that it would start up for him. It was a flawless morning. He bought doughnuts, a dozen glazed Dunkin' Doughnuts, went back to Fill to get Steph, then hustled him into clothes, out the door, for Lear's.

"She starts. See."

Hours and hours later they stumbled out of Lear's to Abby, parked at the curb like any other automobile, and she started, first time. Zimmer left the radio off, commanding Steph to listen, as he went to second, then third gear. "Listen," as he turned into Dagaton Woods. "Listen to this," as he tached the Bee-atile up to a roar, climbing the Turnpike hill, even passing a truck on the way.

Abby started all day Sunday, and Monday, and Tuesday. Zimmer was *so* pleased. When he picked Steph up Wednesday morning, he didn't have to leave the Bee-atile idling while he sat and waited. He no longer had to endlessly top off the gas tank because he could turn off the car and not worry about having enough gas. All that night, New Year's Eve, he was actually proud of the grease still embedded under his fingernails, eager to show them around the bar at Lear's. He was so pleased not to have to look for hills to park on, or spaces that would allow for their push starting the car. It was obnoxious, the way he kept referring to his success. "I can drink so much more now," or, "Do you know how much more sleep you can get?"

It was a load lifted off his shoulders, so he really could return to form. He was magnanimous again, paying attention again, to the people around him, what they were doing. After Lear's, during the little bit of basketball they decided to play, he stopped and asked Steph suddenly, "Hey, I thought Angela wanted to have a party? What happened?"

Steph stopped his dribble. "What do you mean what happened?"

"It's New Year's Eve, isn't it?"

"Yeah."

"And she's working, isn't she?"

"Right."

"So what about the party? How can she work and have a party too?"

"She can't. The party's Saturday."

"Saturday?"

"The third."

"Third year's eve?"

"You don't remember me telling you?"

"About the third? No."

"Or the guest list? The menu?"

Zimmer lifted the ball from Steph's hands and dribbled to the basket. On his way down from banking in a soft lay up, he said, "It's at Fill?"

"Of course."

"Who's cooking?"

"Jesus."

Steph took the ball and practiced his free throws.

"One more question."

"You swear?"

"What am I cooking?"

"What else?"

"A whole turkey?"

"The works."

"Do we have it yet?"

"You're out of questions, pal."

"She hasn't bought it yet?"

"You're the cook."

"Jesus." Zimmer started pacing around the court, pulling at his hair. "That thing's got to thaw, Steph. We got to get busy. Tell me more."

Steph stood on the foul line, outlining the rest of Angie's plans. Zimmer fed him. "Tell me again, why Saturday?"

"For you, and the Lumpers. Feast of St. Fill-up, remember?"

"Well. That's nice."

"For her news, too."

"News?"

"Divorce'll go through on Friday. It's all part of her new beginning, ringing in the new with news. She's got it all planned."

"And that's the ring?" Zimmer asked, pointing to the band Steph wore on his right hand.

Steph tucked the basketball under his left arm, slipped off the ring. "Christmas present."

"Uh-huh."

"Fuck you," Steph said, giving him the finger with the same hand.

"Sorry. Did you know she was married?"

"It never really came up."

"Never came up?"

Steph shrugged.

"Okay, I'll shut up."

"Now there's something new."

"What the fuck does that mean?"

"Nothing."

"Steph," he said, walking the ball back to him. "What is all this fucking talk about new?"

"I don't know. But it's all she talks about. How wonderful everything's going to be."

"You should tell her that *nothing* changes New Year's Day."

"Oh, I don't know. Plenty's changed. I'm not so sure about new, but plenty's changed." Steph took up his shooter's stance.

"Think so?" Zimmer said, turning for the basket. "Name three." He stood under the basket waiting for the ball, watching the chains. And watching. Finally, he turned back toward Steph to find him staring off at the treetops. "Steph?"

"I'm thinking."

"About?"

"Three things. There're so many. Can you name three that *haven't* changed?"

"Fuck you."

"See? See how much easier that is?"

"I give up," Zimmer said, stomping toward the Bee-atile.

"This isn't easy, you know."

"What, being an idiot?"

"A complete idiot?"

"A compleat idiot."

"An absolute idiot."

"Yeah."

"No."

"What?"

"I mean, don't you wonder if there're *any* universals? Any *real* absolutes? Something, anything—three things: that'd be proof, right?—that *never* changes."

"I could name three million," Zimmer said, turning the key. Abby cranked, and cranked, and cranked, but didn't start.

"I'm beginning to see what you mean."

"Fuck you."

"Already counted that."

"No problem. This is no problem," he said, getting out. He pushed Abby backwards a few yards, thinking the starter motor had slipped somehow. He got back in and turned the key. Again, it cranked, and cranked, but didn't start. Zimmer kept turning, kept trying, until it became obvious he was wearing down the battery, on the verge of undoing almost everything he'd done over the last couple of weeks. "Shit."

He stood, pushed his sleeves up, said, "Ready?"

But Steph was bent over the hood on his side of the car, sniffing at the gas tank. "When's the last time you got gas?"

"What?"

"Gas-o-line."

Zimmer stomped over to his side. Steph was quick to get out of the way. Zimmer pushed on the car then listened for any sloshing. Nothing. He sniffed too. He stood back upright.

"This is new."

"Shut up, Steph."

"The great mechanic runs out of gas!"

"I'm warning you."

"This is priceless."

Zimmer hurled the basketball at him, and then charged. Steph ducked and then spun away, laughing, skipping backwards, feigning one direction, before angling off in another, always just out of reach. Zimmer chased him across the courts, around the goals, up the hill, around the retreat house, and most of the way out to the back entrance to the park, on the Turnpike.

"Stop, STOP!"

Zimmer doubled over, panting.

"Truce?" Steph tried, imitating the posture.

"More like a time out. I'm still going to kill you."

"At least that hasn't changed."

"Time in," Zimmer yelled and chased him out into the road, in front of a station wagon full of high school girls. They screeched to a stop, Steph bracing his hands against the grill, posing as Superman.

"Are you all right?"

"Sure."

"What are you doing?"

"Hitching a ride. Thanks for stopping."

"Jesus," Zimmer said, watching Steph highjack a ride for them.

That much had changed, at least. "A year ago, he never would have done that." Zimmer sat sprawled out along the rear bench seat, listening to Steph, in the middle of the front seat, "We're talking absolutes; you can go *anywhere* in the world and this gesture'll be understood," he said, shamelessly folding both hands into the gesture.

"Jesus."

They let them out at the corner of Fillingim, calling, "Happy New Year!" as the doors closed.

"Happy *Third* Year," Steph reminded them, waving a finger.

"Jesus," Zimmer grumbled, walking toward the Moseley's. "What's changed?"

But he'd try. He'd try to adjust his personality to suit the situation. He'd try to give Angela full rein with her party plans. Unless she consulted him directly, he wouldn't comment at all. The only item he added to her shopping list was a gas can, so they could rescue Abby early the next morning.

"It's your party," was all he'd say.

She wasn't necessarily being a tyrant about it. She just wasn't approaching it the same way he would. "And why should she?" Why would anyone choose to do things the way he did? He wasn't all that sure anymore if he wanted to.

When she said she wanted casseroles on the side, he said, "You're the boss."

She wanted a buffet table, new dishes, furniture. She had a guest list of twenty-five people, at least.

"Your party."

That distancing, and his own doubt, carried Zimmer through the intervening days. He'd concentrate on the cooking. He'd hide out in the kitchen, wearing an apron. He'd serve, "And shut up."

At first he groused some about her presumptiveness. But then, cruising the aisles of the grocery store, New Year's day, not hungover, "For a change," he knew he wouldn't have allowed them to have the party anywhere else. "So what was she supposed to do about food?" Cater? Have someone else cook? "Buy bread?"

"So quit your bitching, and shut up."

He agreed to the turkey, the mashed potatoes. Agreed with the squash, although he couldn't resist doctoring the dish. He agreed to the cloverleaf rolls, and the sweet potato souffle, the beans and the wine. It was her party, and he would just shut up and abide by her designs, which were clear: She wanted a dignified affair. She wanted people mingling. She'd invited co-workers, single women. She invited Frank, Steph's brother Jack. She mentioned inviting his parents as well, but Steph'd managed to dissuade her of that.

With Steph mostly sleeping in the car, Zimmer ran errands for her all day Friday, stopping in at the store on the way home from the warehouse, and then checking back in with her at regular intervals, as she kept remembering one more thing that had to be done. He bought candlesticks, an old candelabra. He bought a coat tree, and finally found himself one of those chef's hats. He was her go-fer, her chauffeur, her chef. He liked the roles, he said, even considered a future as someone's domestic someday.

"Get out of here."

"I can think of worse things."

Angela sent the two of them out that night on one final errand. She needed more chairs, as the party threatened to burst all confines. They returned to the second hand shops, to find them closed. They stopped at Lear's, figuring they could just tell the Lumpers to bring a chair each.

When Zimmer refused a drink, claiming he had to be up at about three to start on the turkey, and then turned up the Turnpike instead of continuing to the park, Steph said, "This is getting to you, isn't it?"

"What are you talking about?"

"I'm not sure. I can't tell what it is you're trying so hard to do."

"I'm just trying to give Angela what she wants."

"Which is?"

"A nice, responsible party."

"Right. How are you going to do that?"

"What do you mean how am I going to do that? I'm doing it, like everything else. I'm doing it."

"No, not like everything else. You're not doing anything like you usually do it."

Zimmer looked over at him and grinned.

"Ah," Steph said, "I get it. The *new* Zimmer."

Zimmer nodded.

"Never work."

"It already is."

"Won't last."

"Bet?"

"Bet."

"How much?"

"This," Steph said, taking the ring out of his pocket and slipping it on. "You?"

"I can match that."

"How?"

"I'll be your domestic."

"My gofer?"

"Absolutely."

"No, better. You'll work for me. Be my research assistant."

"Research assistant for what?"

"And you don't get to ask questions."

"You haven't won yet. Research assistant for what?"

"For the third."

"Third what?"

"Third thing that never changes."

"What's the second?"

"You are."

"Fuck you."

"And *that's* the first."

"*When* I win, you and Angela cook breakfast for me. And I mean the works."

"You'd actually let us do that? You'd eat it?"

"Every bite."

"Now that *is* different!"

"Fuck you."

"No, no, no, no, no. How many times do I have to tell you? *That's* the first."

"Jesus..."

Zimmer was up and busy in the quiet apartment, tooling around in the kitchen by about four, he figured. Behind the closed kitchen door, wearing the floppy hat, he smeared the Butterball with oil, drenched a dishtowel with melted butter, layered it over the bird and then slid the roaster into the warm oven. He started a couple of things boiling, the yellow squash, the green beans and the sweet potatoes on the three burners he could coax to life. Less than an hour later, still forty minutes before sunrise, he broke open a gallon jug of Gallo's Hearty Burgundy, and started basting. That's what took all the time when he roasted a turkey, glug-glugging a couple of cups of wine over the bird every twenty minutes or so. And of course, he'd have to sample the wine himself, pouring some into an olive pimento glass, hoisting it to the windows, christening the day, the feast. That much would never change, he knew.

But he would change. "And why shouldn't I?" Angela was right. Irresponsibility was only all right so long as you didn't effect anyone else's life. "The golden rule, right?"

Not even Whomee was up yet, though he could hear some stirring from the other room. "Angie," he guessed. "The anxious and worrisome hostess." He moved the squash aside—testing its doneness—to make her some coffee. He ran some hot water for the bread dough, sprinkling yeast over a cup of it as Angela came into the kitchen. "Morning."

"Good morning. How long have you been up?" she asked, pushing her hair around, rubbing her eyes.

"A while. You ready?"

"I guess," she said, smiling. "You need any help in here?"

"Naw. The kitchen's taken care of. Pretend I'm not here."

"Right," she said, accepting the coffee from him.

He went back to work, starting the dough—shaking dill weed into the yeast broth, mixing the flour, salt, sugar—basting the bird again, slowly progressing with the veggies, when she came bursting into the kitchen again.

"The toilet's broken!" she cried, her hair pulled back, soap on her face.

"Broken? What's it doing?"

"Nothing."

Zimmer went to check, lifting the tank lid, reattaching the pull chain.

"Try that."

"Thanks."

Half an hour later she couldn't get the small window outside the bathroom opened, trying to dissipate the bleach she'd been cleaning with. And then, half an hour after that, she tripped a circuit breaker—running the vacuum cleaner, with the iron already on. Zimmer had to pull his coat on and trudge under the apartment to reset it, but the emergencies didn't interrupt his flow much—they fit in rather well, in fact, between the basting, whipping together the different casseroles, punching the roll dough down between rises.

He had an emergency himself when he turned the faucet on to wash out the mixing bowl between the squash mixture and mashing the potatoes: no water pressure.

"Oh, great. What the hell are we going to do with twenty-five people and no water?"

"Turn off that fucking water!" Steph screamed.

Then, a moment later, appearing in the kitchen, shampoo still in his hair, he said, "Do you mind?"

"What are you doing up?"

"I'm supposed to sleep with all this shit going on?"

"Well, as long as you're up, I've got a mission for you."

"Anything," Steph said, reaching for the sink. "Just leave this off for five more minutes."

"No problem."

Zimmer went to work on the rolls. He had four separate muffin tins spread out on the counter before him. He was going to divide the dough into 144 supposedly equal little balls, to make four dozen cloverleaf rolls.

"Her party," he chanted, working out the fractions: "Two, four, eight, sixteen..." Then he segregated half of the blobs, working on two dozen rolls at a time, since only two of the pans would fit in the Roper while the turkey was cooking. Then he had to pull the dough into thirds, twenty-four, seventy-two. That's where the distortion came from, how the rolls got lopsided, trying to divide the gooey dough into three equal parts.

He stood counting all the different combinations, to be sure it would come out right.

"Eight, sixteen, seventy-two..."

"See, nothing's changed," Steph said, looking for coffee, buttoning a shirt. "You're as loony as ever."

Zimmer looked up, losing count.

"What do you need?"

"Need?"

"My mission."

"Oh." He stood there with his floured hands raised. "See if you can find some real cranberries for me, all right. And a pint of oysters would be nice, too." Steph squeezed past him as he rolled the individual blobs into spheres, dropping three each into muffin cells. He reached into the refrigerator for a beer, forgoing coffee. "Get some more of that, too."

"Oh?"

"What?" Zimmer said, stopping. "I'm not supposed to drink?"

"Just seems like the same old Zimmer to me."

"Shut up," Zimmer told him. He was too occupied to keep track of their bet.

Steph backed his way out of the kitchen, plucking the keys to the Bee-atile off the countertop.

When Angela saw him, fully dressed, she panicked.

"Oh my God," she cried. "What time is it?" She rushed into the kitchen, still wearing one of Steph's pajama tops, dirty jeans, still barefoot.

"Don't worry," Zimmer told her, at the windows, showing her the early morning light. They listened for Abby to start. "You got lots of time."

"Zimmer," she said, staring at the counter. "I forgot about appetizers. What are they going to do when they get here?"

"I thought they were going to mingle?" he shrugged, but when he saw the look on her face, offered, "We could get some nuts." By that time, though, Steph was disappearing down the access drive.

"What are we going to do?"

"We?" He poured her a glass of the burgundy. "Don't worry," he told her again. "I'll think of something. Go get ready."

But when he finished the bread, buttering the tops of the rolls, and looked into the refrigerator, he wasn't so sure. He pulled out an armload of ingredients—raisins, ricotta cheese, a package of cream cheese, some shelled pecans, a jar of jalapeno pepper slices, an old jar of cocktail onions that Mr. Boyles had never used, half a brick of cheddar cheese, grape jelly, and most of a loaf of raisin bread. He spread the ingredients out on the counter, rearranging, pairing them up, like he was trying to solve a puzzle. He put the jelly and the bread back and found a jar of stuffed green olives hiding in the back. When he set those on the counter, he lifted the raisins, said, "Now I think we're getting somewhere." He pulled the ricotta from the picture too. "Yes, yes..."

He started to work on a frying batter, intoning, "Yes," feeling devilish, in a way, but released, too; finally entrusted with managing a portion of the party, allowed to add his own touches, "Not just drafted into service."

Angela finished her cleaning, finished pushing the furniture around. She had the partition down, the bed folded up and pushed against one wall. Across the room, she had the chairs spread out in a fan, facing the couch, four on each side of Whomee's big chair. She had a sheet draped over it, in a calculatedly haphazard way, trying to cover the worn spots, the stains. Whomee himself had been banished from the apartment while she stood at the top of the outside stairs thumping his fur from the seat cushion, the couch sections.

Steph returned and she took the groceries from him in exchange for the cot, which she wanted stored underneath, out of the way. She waited for him to come back upstairs, so he could help her move the table out from the wall, and then they both walked the groceries into the kitchen.

"What's this?" Steph asked, when he saw what Zimmer was doing. "The famous Zimbarco onion ring batter?"

"Onion rings?" Angela said, doubtfully.

"No, no. Trust me, all right," he said to her.

"Now that's different."

"Shut up."

"Do I have time for a shower?" Angela asked.

"Go right ahead," Zimmer told her, then reached for the bag. "What'd you get me?"

"Cranberries. No oysters."

"Shit."

No matter, he thought. There wasn't much time for changing the dressing now anyway. "But if I'd been asked earlier..."

Steph stood there, one dark eyebrow raised, grinning.

"Get out of the way," Zimmer said, elbowing him toward Mr. Boyles' stool in the corner. "Don't you have anything to do? Where's Whomee?" he asked, once he'd figured out what that look reminded him of.

"Just tell me what that batter's for."

"A surprise," was all Zimmer'd say. "Something *different*. Now get out of here."

Zimmer had the olives and the onions draining in the sink, out of view. "*Not* onion rings..."

In another bowl he mashed the cream cheese, grated cheddar, crunched up pecan pieces and chopped jalapenos.

"Just a surprise."

Angela didn't have as much time as they all thought, as the first of the guests arrived. Frank, standing in the still opened door to the apartment, grumbling, "God-dammed if dis-blace dudn't look spig-an-span for once." He pulled his cigar out of his mouth as he reached the kitchen. "First time ever, eh Zimbarco."

"It's the new Fill," Zimmer told him, for Steph's benefit. "The third."

"Shit," Steph said, opening beers for Zimmer, Frank. "The third my ass."

"Wad-der-fug-er-u..."

"Happy third year's eve, Frank," Zimmer said, clanking longnecks with him. "How've you been?"

"Yeah, yeah," Frank started, his usual impediment smothered beyond any recognition as he sipped on the beer.

"Frank?" Angela said, coming into the kitchen, still drying her hair. "You're early, I hope."

"Yeah?" Frank answered, looking first at his wristwatch and then at the clock radio.

Steph and Zimmer shrugged. "Ten till."

"Frank's always early, Angie," Steph told her, giving his beer to her, opening another one.

"Here's something *else* that's new," Zimmer said, as they all repositioned themselves in the small room, so Zimmer could get back to work. "A no smoking policy, right?"

"Oh, yeah. Frank, do you mind?"

"No sweat, no sweat," he said, stepping to the windows, taking a few last hits on the stoagie before tossing it outside, talking between drags, through clouds of thick blue smoke. "I need to give the damn things up anyway."

"What's this?" Zimmer asked him. "A third year's eve vow?"

"Yeah, yeah--"

"Why the hell is it every time I come here you're throwing shit at me?" Bruce yelled from below, standing beneath the windows, carrying his cooler, a case of replacements on top of it, a ladder back chair threaded up his forearm.

"It wasn't me," Zimmer said, leaning out one window.

"That's right," Steph said poking his head out another. "He's *changed*."

"Right."

"Would you knock that shit off for now," Zimmer said, reaching around the window frame for Steph's neck.

A car was creeping up the drive, five of Angela's friends from the store. They guessed they were near the right place when they saw Bruce standing there with all that beer, and he was only too eager to offer his assistance, whether they needed it or not.

Angela looked out the window and gasped. "Steph, you've got to greet them, I'm not ready yet," she said, pulling him from the room toward the door.

He let her drag him backwards from the kitchen, smiling, shrugging back at Zimmer, rescued from the mad chef.

Frank hung around in the kitchen, getting in the way, mostly.

"What ya frying there, Zimbarco?"

"Nothing Frank. A surprise," Zimmer told him. "Go mingle."

Zimmer knew why Frank and Angela sounded so sensitive when the question of onion rings or other deep-fried foods came up. He didn't think he could ever atone to either of them, much less both at the same time.

"Hey, hey, Angie," Bruce said at the door, his chair, the beer, Angela's friends and Mickey in tow, "you are hereby appointed permanent Lumper social director!"

"Accepted, accepted," she called from the closed bathroom.

Steph stood to the other side of the doorway, mumbling, "Greetings, greetings," taking coats.

Bruce was playing Houdini, trying to shrug out of his coat while still holding the beer and the chair.

Mickey, stuck behind him on the landing, nudged him, "Do you mind?"

"Wait, wait a minute," Bruce said, pulling the chair up to his shoulder, one arm out of a sleeve, the sleeve inside out. "I think I got it now."

"Christ," Frank said, watching from the kitchen doorway. "This is going to be a freak show, Zimbarco."

Zimmer hovered over the Roper, layering his batter-coated little bundles into a skillet of hot olive oil.

Frank turned around and watched him. "Whad're those?"

"A little treat," Zimmer told him. "Take these out, would you," handing him the tray of jalapeno-cheese balls.

The throng from the door was headed toward the kitchen, Angela leading the tour.

"Oh, Angie, this place is so cute," one of her friends said.

Bruce, Mickey, and Steph, behind the others, traded looks. Cute?

Frank stood at the table holding the tray, sampling the bite-sized cheese balls.

Angela introduced him to her friends. Before he could chew enough to talk through his mouthful of food, the pepper hit him, finally sneaking out of the smooth cheese, the subtle pecan.

"Got-damn!" he said, then blushed.

Zimmer saved him, some, hollering, "Pick up!" like he was Pitman working his grill back at Bronco Willie's.

Frank put down the tray, so that the others might try some, and stepped back into the kitchen for a tray full of the fried nuggets. He peeked around the corner, to see everyone munching quietly, and snickered to Zimmer, "Any second now..."

Zimmer said, "You better start opening beer, don't you think?" but knew Frank would try the new appetizers first—the pickled cocktail onions and briny stuffed olives, wrapped in the beer batter, deep fried to a golden brown—knew they would engage more immediate taste buds.

He heard Frank, just the other side of the door, exclaim, "Ho-lee shit!" losing all sense of decorum.

"Success," Zimmer said to himself, toasting with the turkey, pouring wine, drinking straight from the bottle, then calling again, "Pick up!"

That precipitated a crowd drawn to the small room, both to

see what the source of that food was, and what might be next.

Zimmer meant only to pass out the beans and his first batch of rolls. "Trying to make some space is all." They caught him with the bottle raised to his mouth.

Mickey clanked his beer bottle against the burgundy, started to say, "Keep--"

Zimmer held up his other hand, quieting him, correcting the toast, "Happy third year's eve, Mick."

But the dinner had already started its irretrievable turn from the ordered banquet that Angela had envisioned into a more Lumperish grab-bag affair, despite Zimmer's concerted efforts to the contrary, wincing in her direction.

More guests showed up. Zimmer urged Steph and Bruce to set the table, still trying to preserve some kind of protocol. When Jack showed up, calling from the doorway, "Happy New Year," Bruce called back, "It's happy third year, Jackson," holding up the last of the olives, "open up!"

He flung it across the room. It sailed out the doorway, between Jack and Angela. Color drained from her face as she turned back to Steph, her mouth ajar, slowly blinking. Steph steered Bruce back to the kitchen.

Randy dropped Mr. Boyles off at Fill, with his scarf, a houndstooth pulled down over the tops of his ears, an obligatory tumbler of scotch—all to fend off the chill of the New Year. He traded time between his stool in the corner of the kitchen watching Zimmer cook, and sliding through the crowd to the outside staircase for a smoke.

"Damn zoo in there," Frank said to him on one of those occasions.

"Interesting, though, don't you think, Frank?"

"I spose. I ain't playing cards with all them loonies, though."

"I shouldn't think you'd have to worry about that. Not today, at least."

Whomee, who'd been hiding down in the garage, would only be coaxed back upstairs into the crowded apartment by the soothing voice of Mr. Boyles. Even with that, he wouldn't leave the old man's grasp, or his lap, once they all got back inside.

"Thought you gave up smoking, Frank?" Steph quizzed his boss, from across the kitchen, after the two older gentlemen and the cat congregated that way once again.

"Yeah, well, maybe next year," Frank grumbled.

"Next new year?" Zimmer asked. "Or next third year."

"Third year?"

"Third year's eve," Zimmer told him, hoisting the wine, opening the oven door, the aroma from it wafting through the kitchen, out into the other room, enticing everyone's attention.

"What's all this third shit?" Mickey asked.

Steph was in the corner opposite the door, supposedly helping. "Exactly Mick. That's our problem. What's the third?" he said, holding up the middle finger of his right hand.

"Today's the third," Zimmer said, against everyone's silence, then called, "Cranberries!" trying to keep Steph busy, off the subject.

Steph reached into the refrigerator for the cellophane covered bowl, repeating, "Cranberries."

But Mr. Boyles asked, "Third what, Stephen?"

"Pick up!" Zimmer called.

He handed the cranberries over, to Mickey, who gave them to Mr. Boyles, who handed them to Frank and then out the door to Bruce. Zimmer just then realized how the party had segregated itself, wondering what the scene looked like on the other side of the wall, wondering how Angela was faring. "Parties always do that, though, right? Nothing new about this," looking around the kitchen of exclusively Lumpers.

Steph was telling Mr. Boyles, the rest of them, "This is the first," showing that finger again.

Shit. "Pick up!" Zimmer called, a little louder, handing over the sweet potato. He turned a scowl toward Steph, hissing, "Don't," before turning back to the counter to finish mashing the potatoes, sprinkle breadcrumbs over the squash.

Mickey picked up Zimmer's chant, saying, "Drink up!" after passing the dish along. He took a sip of his beer, and passed that along the chain too. That was enough to draw any lingering attention from the other room not already attached to the Lumpers.

Bruce urged Angela and her friends to join in, not moving from the threshold, holding the tray in one hand, beer in the other. Most of them did help, except Angela and Jack, passing the dish to the table, chasing with the beer. Bruce opened a beer from the cooler and started a reverse drinking line, passing the beer back into the kitchen, creating a constant flow of beer that the food would ride out of the kitchen on, like driftwood.

Mickey handed the beer past Zimmer to Steph, calling, "More wine," as Zimmer obliged with another, "Pick up," handing over the mashed potatoes.

Steph stood from the refrigerator with another bottle of beer, opening it, taking a sip before passing it on, saying, "And the second is--"

"Get the wine," Zimmer said.

"I just did."

"No, the *real* wine," Zimmer said, waving the cork screw at him, repeating, "Don't do it."

Steph handed over two bottles of Chablis, eyeing Zimmer's weapon. He stood there trying to twist the middle finger of his left hand into that curly-cue shape.

Zimmer watched a beer trace its way back to Steph, before calling, "Pick up!"

They continued like that, getting faster, more efficient, until the last item, the gravy boat was passed along the chain.

Zimmer pulled the turkey out of the oven, stopping everyone. A crowd gathered in the doorway. Angela poked her head into the kitchen, asking, "Ready?"

Steph was still in the corner, still twisting his fingers. She asked him, "Steph, what are you doing?"

Zimmer had his long carving knife out, was sliding it back and forth along a sharpening stone. "I was just about to cut that thing off for him," he said, which emptied the kitchen.

"Everybody hungry?" Angela asked.

Frank grumbled, "Bout goddamn time," squeezing past

Bruce, who was on his way into the kitchen with the cleared appetizer platters.

Mr. Boyles stood, setting Whomee on his stool, following Frank, as did Mickey, and then Steph.

The throng gathered around the chairless table, looking at the spread, chattering nervously, waiting while Zimmer carved the turkey back in the kitchen. After several minutes, they grew quiet, anticipative. Angela called out, "Zimmer? You ready? We're about to say the blessing," reaching for Steph's hand on one side, Jack's on the other.

"Go ahead. Be right there."

They all bowed their heads, and after a few more quiet moments, Angela urged, "Steph?"

He thought she meant for him to go check on the missing Lumpers, broke the chain and disappeared into the kitchen.

She'd really intended for him to start the meal, to give some blessing to the feast. She looked around the table. "Frank?"

He choked on a roll he'd been sampling, and looked over at Mr. Boyles who only shook his head, one side, then the other.

Jack spoke up, "I'll do it, I'll do it."

In the complete silence before he started, they heard sounds coming from the kitchen, guttural, animal sounds, of lip smacking, bone crunching. Different looks of recognition and reaction passed over the faces of those around the table, from Mickey's snickering, to Angela's shock, as she traced the sounds to their source.

Stepping through the kitchen doorway, she shrieked, at the sight of the four of them, Steph, Bruce, Zimmer, and Whomee, all crowded around the turkey carcass, picking at fragments of meat still clinging there or bending to knaw on an exposed bone entirely. Whomee paused only long enough to look up and see what that noise was before continuing. The others knew they'd better get themselves cleaned up, better join the rest of the civilized animals on the other side of the kitchen door, which Angela tried her hardest to slam on them.

"Uh-oh," Bruce said, wiping his mouth, plucking the platter of carved meat off the counter and sliding through the door.

"That should just about do it," Steph said, he and Zimmer rinsing their hands off at the sink.

"What?"

"Prove me right. You heard that shriek," he said, holding his dripping hands out.

"So?"

"So, towel please, Mr. Assistant," Steph said, grinning.

"Forget it," Zimmer told him, but draped a hand towel over his hands anyway.

The others were serving themselves, settling into chairs around the room. Jack had moved back to Whomee's chair. Angela fixed herself a small plate, put it in the seat of the chair off his left shoulder, where she'd been sitting before, then went back to the table to supervise, host. Bruce found an empty space for his chair next to the couch, while most of Angela's friends followed her lead and picked out seats on either side of Whomee's chair.

Steph walked past the table and plopped himself down in the middle of the couch. Zimmer watched him, in amazement, before asking, "You're really serious, aren't you?"

"Bet's a bet."

"Yeah, but Steph..."

"Hey, we're talking science," he answered, waving the middle finger of his right hand at him.

"All right, all right," Zimmer said, starting on a plate for him, still trying to keep him off the subject, but by this time, he was getting tired enough, lubricated enough, satisfied enough, as he looked at the food spread around the table, not to care too much, to find a way to enjoy the game, chuckling to himself, at the thought of his being Steph's valet for the day, the rest of the new year.

He delivered Steph's plate to him, then backed away from the couch, bowing, to almost everyone's delight. Zimmer grew to like the role so much he started waiting on all the others. He fetched Mr. Boyles' bar stool from the kitchen—pausing only long enough in there to take one last sip of wine and turn the turkey carcass over for Whomee—so that the old man might feel most comfortable. He went and got rolls from the table and walked around the wide semi-circle of people offering more. He followed with the wine, topping off glasses here and there.

He spent the rest of the meal standing by the door, arms crossed, holding the wine in one hand, a beer for himself in the other, listening, watching, ready to jump whenever someone needed another slice of turkey, a scoop of potato. He tried to compliment Angela on the party, to turn some attention away from himself, back to her, but she wouldn't relent in her obvious irritation. She kept her back to him, turned sideways on her chair, listening to Jack.

She wouldn't give any attention to Steph, either, not that he really noticed, which worried Zimmer. Not that Steph wasn't paying enough attention to her, her wrath, "Though you'd think he would, at least a little." Worried that if Angela's ire went unnoticed, "It can't vent." So Zimmer worried, and tried his best to bring the fractured party back together.

What happened was that he became fractured from the effort, of trying to pay the proper homage to Angela, since he hadn't been able to keep his touches off her party; trying to serve as the bridge between them; and still trying to keep Steph off the subject of his research, though he found it harder and harder to remember why he should do any of that. So he drank more, and didn't eat, "So I won't remember *any* of this," hopefully.

He would listen to Steph's side of the room, hear Mickey ask about the third and then interrupt Steph to call across the room, "*Today's* the third, Mick." When Bruce asked about the second, Zimmer would hop to service, asking, "Seconds? Of what, potato? Beans?"

Steph eventually got around to answering Bruce's question, telling him, "Zimmer's the second."

But Zimmer deflected that well enough, saying, "That's right, I'm his left hand man," and felt pretty good about his apparent agility, at being able to push and nudge Steph off the subject, like it was a game of verbal basketball.

But then, turning back to the other side of the room, hearing Jack go on and on about the changes coming to the country, with the new administration just a couple of weeks from Reagan's inauguration—the new tax system, reprivatization of the country, deregulation—Zimmer added, "You really think anything's going to change, Jack?"

"Oh, I'm sure of it. You can feel the optimism, the excitement, can't you?"

"Naw. I don't expect much difference. Nothing ever changes with those guys."

Which prompted Steph to pipe up, "Name three," effectively uniting the party again, even if on the wrong subject, prompting questions, more questions than Zimmer could control.

"Three what?" Maryanne asked, standing with her finished plate.

Zimmer rushed to take her dishes from her, trying, "Today's the third," which didn't make any sense, only caused her to repeat the question, "Three what?" crossing the room to sit on the couch.

She sat on the end nearest Bruce, who told her, "Three things that never change," before slipping off his chair, sitting on the floor, resting his chin on the armrest near her elbow, staring up into her blue eyes.

"That's right," Steph told her. "We've got two, and me and my trusty assistant here," waving at Zimmer, "we're going to find the third."

"What's the first?" another of Angela's friends asked, likewise standing with her plate.

Zimmer took it from her and disappeared into the kitchen, but not before looking helplessly over at Angela, who had a piercing glare fixed on him.

Stephanie pulled her chair across the room and sat cross-legged in front of the couch.

"It's hopeless," Zimmer said, peeking back out the door in time to see Steph demonstrating the gesture, to hear his explanation, even some new comments about how other hand gestures meant something completely different in other parts of the world, in other cultures. "But not this," he said, holding up both fingers. "This never, ever changes."

"And the second?"

Zimmer pulled the door to. "Hopeless."

Whomee had finished his meal and was at the edge of the counter, contemplating jumping, but seemed wary of the effort, after gorging himself. Zimmer picked him up and set him back on sturdier ground. He walked kind of funny, like he really had hurt himself, and pawed at the door.

Zimmer stood leaning against the counter beneath the windows, asking, "You sure you want to go out there?"

Whomee turned around with a panicked look in his eyes, so Zimmer finally pushed the door open for him, and then tried to sneak behind the chairs on that side of the room, to the front door, to let Whomee out. He couldn't help but notice the quiet, but didn't realize everyone was watching him, and couldn't have known that he'd just been the topic of all conversation. It was a conversation that had turned into a bit of an argument, between Steph and Angela, though he had begun it by merely relating some of his empirical data, "He even *tried* to change, for this party."

Angela hissed toward Jack, "I suppose we'll have to give him an A for effort," while Steph was asking them, "But why should he change? Would we feel the same about him if he were suddenly different?"

Angela answered, "God forbid we should expect him to grow up and *do* something with himself," Steph maybe just then realizing the extent of her anger, surprised at the viciousness, initiating the silence, almost demonstrably, which surprised everyone, that anything so decisive should come from Steph.

Zimmer turned from the opened door, from watching Whomee side step down the staircase and met everyone's gaze, wincing, what might have grown into an apology.

Steph would not have it though. "It's time," he said, standing.

Zimmer shrugged, not the reflexive shrug of Lumper habit, but an honest-to-God "I give up" shrug.

Mickey missed the distinction, automatically saying, "It's never time!"

Steph was adamant, a change *no one* was prepared for. "Nope. Not anymore," he said.

The comment seemed to wound Angela even more, and until that moment no one there would have thought Steph would ever do that intentionally.

But any comment any of them might have made at that juncture would probably have hurt her, as decided and unforgiving as she seemed. Right? Zimmer tried to mediate, saying, "Yes, it's time, time to discuss our research strategy," hoping only, really, to clear the apartment, so that maybe Steph and Angela could talk alone.

But Steph said, "Lear's?"

"Yes, Lear's," Bruce cried, thrusting his right arm into the air, his middle finger extended.

"Not for me," Frank said, stepping by all the others standing around, crossing the threshold, inserting a new cigar into his mouth. "Danks fer de grub, Zimbarco."

"Could I ride with you?" Mr. Boyles asked Zimmer, standing before him, holding his stool.

Zimmer had lost all control. "Why not?"

Angela, seething, said, "I think I'll just stay here, thank you," turning for the kitchen.

If Steph had any thoughts of protesting, he didn't entertain them long. He stepped to the coat tree, dismantling it, handing coats back out, grabbing his ski-coat, Zimmer's fatigue jacket.

Bruce had his cooler, his chair, standing in the middle of the room, waiting for the crowd at the door to decide what they were going to do, to get out of the way.

Steph moved things along, saying, "Thanks for coming, Jack," reaching a hand out to his brother.

He said, "Thanks for the invite," shaking Steph's hand. "I'll go say goodbye to Angie."

A couple of her friends came to life at the mention of her

name, said they were going to help clean, and followed Jack.

The party fractured again—though Bruce had managed to convince Stephanie and Maryanne to join them at Lear's—the Lumpers exited Fill.

Whomee had only made it to the bottom of the staircase, was lying on the dead grass underneath the second step, kind of moaning.

Beneath the kitchen windows, Bruce and Zimmer had to push Jack's car out of the way of the garage doorway, where it was blocking Frank's truck, and the Bee-atile.

"Thought I was through pushing cars," Zimmer said, but didn't bitch any more than that. He just thought again how nothing *really* changes, and held up his three Boy Scout fingers at Steph, once they had the Toyota out of the way.

He was standing out in the drive, looking up at the windows, watching the bodies move back and forth in the kitchen.

18. Lumper Research

THEY moved down the access drive like a caravan. Frank in his little truck took the lead. Bruce had Maryanne beside him, Mickey and Stephanie in the back seat, his cooler and chair in the trunk, his pockets and the cooler stuffed with as much of the food he could smuggle out for Randy. Steph was in the back seat of the Bee-atile, his legs stretched out along the bench, leaning against the passenger's side, looking out the rear window. Mr. Boyles sat beside Zimmer. There was still no heat in Abby, so Mr. Boyles sat there huddled up, his head down, but trying to carry on a conversation anyway. "How serious are we about this research project?"

Zimmer glanced up at the rearview, answering, "Ask the boss," but Steph wouldn't comment.

"And where do you think it'll take you?"

Zimmer looked over at Mr. Boyles, realizing too late the actual intent of the question. He wished he could be that subtle, could ask those multi-leveled questions that wouldn't pin anyone against a wall, into a corner. "They can answer whichever question they choose," freeing everyone of the responsibility of exposing more of themselves than they could withstand.

"That's a real good question," was all he could think to answer.

At Lear's, Bruce pulled into the last metered slot on the curb in front, but then jumped out of his GTO and stood in the intersection of the block just before the bar, directing Zimmer up onto the sidewalk. Zimmer stopped alongside the Lumpercop, rolled down his window, reminding him, "Bruce, I don't have to park there anymore."

"Don't give me any shit, buddy," Bruce said, waving him on vigorously. "Nothing changes, remember."

"Name three," Steph grumbled from the back seat.

Mickey yelled from the sidewalk, holding the door, Stephanie and Maryanne huddled in the doorway, "Come on, will ya."

"Nope," Zimmer said, easing Abby over the curb, "nothing changes."

Inside, sitting around the bar, once the chill wore off, once they'd digested some of their food and Randy'd eaten his, had a few more drinks to loosen them back up, Steph said, "New York."

Mr. Boyles asked, "City?"

Steph thought about answering, "Somewhere in New York," but said, "Where else?"

"Where else for what?" Randy asked.

"For something new, obviously."

Bruce said, "Oh, I know, I know: The first annual Lumper's third year's eve resolution research project."

"Exactly. Where else but the hub of internationality?"

"Home of the United Nations," Zimmer said.

"And Ellis Island," Mickey added, to add something.

Steph had to detail the project for Randy, with more than a little help from Bruce and Mickey. Zimmer didn't bother trying to waylay the conversation, or even correct what sounded like more of Steph's fabrications—"*Refinements*," he called them, sarcastically, telling Randy that Zimmer had spent his whole life trying to find people to fit in with who wouldn't expect him to change to meet their needs, "From his family, to the military, even to some of us here in Tripoli," he said, unfolding three fingers. "And the beauty of it all is that he's never changed. Any of the rest of us would have, if we're honest with ourselves," he said, looking around the bar. Zimmer just sat there, shaking his head.

When Maryanne leaned over and asked, "You're not from Tripoli, are you?" Zimmer laughed out loud at the thought of explaining all that.

But he tried, admitting bits and pieces over the next hour or so, as he got drunker, and tireder, starting, "No, I'm from New York, originally."

"City?"

"Upstate," Mr. Boyles answered for him, leaving space for as many possibilities as he sometimes did with his questions.

Steph was busy explaining his theories to Bruce, Mickey and Stephanie on the other side of the bar, or he would have been most interested in Zimmer's answering Maryanne at all.

"Listen, Bruce, it's simple," Steph repeated, struggling to keep his attention, to keep his own concentration. "Thesis," he said, holding up a bar napkin, "antithesis," tearing it apart. "And synthesis," he told him, piecing it back together, but in a different, supposedly superior way, "Closer to its true sense." Then he tried, "Have you ever heard of the logic of fallacy?"

Bruce whispered, "Steph, there are females present."

"What the fuck does that have to do with flipping somebody off?" Mickey demanded, either not hearing or not heeding Bruce's sensitivities.

"It doesn't, necessarily," Steph said, jumping up and pacing the floor behind them. "It has to do with methods, ways toward the truth."

Zimmer sat back in his chair, glancing to his right, to Mr. Boyles, then turning his attention to Steph, recognizing that he was getting wound up with his ideas. Bruce and Mickey groaned, some, and leaned farther over their drinks on the bar. They'd been captive to enough of Steph's lectures and tirades to know he was just beginning to froth. They knew that they'd pushed some unnameable button within Steph, but, as always, they hadn't known what they were doing until it had been done, and he was off, instructing them on the scientific method, outlining data gathering and correlating techniques.

"Who knows statistics?" he asked, holding his hand up as an example. "We must be certain," he told them, "that we canvas an unbiased, random sample," he continued, and continued.

He moved to dialectics. "The law of the *union* of opposites, not the tension between them. It's the *relationship* between ideas," he said to Mickey, holding his arms out at his sides. "See, there's no harmony in polar opposition," bringing his hands back together in front of himself. "Oh, sure, sure, you may get an occasional balance, but no *real* harmony. That takes three," he said, somehow returning to the subject.

Then to application, on the move again, longneck in hand: "This isn't going to be just another nugget in Lumper lore," he started, pacing the entire circumference of the bar. "We're talking international implications," thrusting a finger into the stale air of Lear's. "We're talking Nobel laureate stuff here. Hand gestures pre-date language, or the wheel, or fire!"

Steph lapsed into that peculiar seizure of his, agitatedly flailing his arms and pacing, talking, addressing the Lumpers, the other patrons of Lear's, or himself, mostly, the whirlwind of thoughts and rethoughts inside his head.

"As far back as digits, just after we crawled out of the primordial soup, *that's* how old the problem is."

Any discussion of antiquity, or prehistoric man, of Neanderthals and evolution, was enough to revive Bruce, who could grunt and groan and scratch himself, who could pull on another characterization for himself like he could pull on a rubbery Halloween mask.

Even if not everyone noticed, this wasn't, as Steph'd said, just more of their "Lumper crap," not just another isolated opportunity to be foolish. Zimmer and Mr. Boyles could see, or could sense, that he was speaking to more than that. Because only Steph could permute and expand the idea, the goof, really, about flipping someone off, to something that he could act on, giving everyone the same option, just like he would have been Zimmer's campaign manager.

That was Steph's natural niche. He could take ideas—or manufacture them, in the absence of any other likely candidates—and milk them, nurse them, until they became full-fledged, bona fide opportunities.

"That's what an opportunity *is*," for Steph, something that was discovered, through the constant and chaotic chasing of ideas upon ideas. It wasn't something that was handed to you. "Look it up in the fucking dictionary," he could tell Angela, or Jack, any of his goddamn family.

"A   favorable   or   advantageous   combination   of

circumstances," he quoted Webster.

"No guarantee there, no goddammed guarantee at all," he might elaborate, to any and all challengers of his whimsical way of living.

And what's more, you can't make it happen. "It just does, or it doesn't." It occurs through a willingness to let it happen, like learning to play pool, like fried-days: Favorable combinations of circumstances. "Search, and research."

But Steph didn't necessarily need to argue the point, didn't need to be convinced, or convince others. Least resistance. He preferred to just live his life as he did, willing to be a disappointment, if that's what it took to free himself of their expectations and their suffocating notions of what his potential might be. He wanted to remain a Lumper, until, of course, a better idea presented itself, "A better combination of favorable circumstances." As a Lumper, he could entertain any ideas he wanted to, could, like Bruce, cloak himself in whatever costume or guise that suited his present attitude or situation. He could, like Bruce, climb over his stool, pound his chest, chew glass. He could pretend he was commander Perry, or Steph Lewis, with his Zimbarco-Clarke.

But he really wasn't pretending at all. The others might have thought so, seeing him work his way over to the other side of the game room partition, signalling to those pool tables that their preliminary work was through. Even when he moved to wedge himself into the space between Zimmer and Mr. Boyles' stools, asking his assistant, "Have you been taking notes?" they might have figured a whirlwind excursion to New York City, that he'd be back by tomorrow night for work.

Not Steph. Zimbarco-like, he'd decided, and listed some items they'd need to start their field work. "Tape recorder."

Then he initiated another Lumper sign, symbolic of their quest, a longneck toast, crossing bottles, "Sis," and then, "Trans,"—he would have been happy to explicate, but no one asked—like crossing sabers, *repartee*, antecedent to the duel which faced them.

Bruce loved that, mutating instantly into a poor man's Errol

Flynn, skipping through the bar, jousting with shadows, with an even poorer accent, "*Touché! Touché!*" his left hand high in the air behind him, "*Entrechat,* mother-ere fuck-ere..."

"Questionnaire. Camera."

"I suppose that answers my question," Mr. Boyles said to Zimmer, while Steph stood between them, head raised, eyes closed tight in concentration.

"Sounds like," Zimmer said, huddled over his list, turned into his wrap-around posture, pencilling the items onto a bar napkin. Zimmer stopped, and looked over at the old man, squinting. He thought back to all the things that Mr. Boyles had told him over the months, knowing now how much he must have missed. Hell, if he had to start over again, "I could do worse than this stool right here in Lear's." He stood, knowing an instant later, "Wouldn't work." He wadded up the napkin and stuffed it into one of the pockets of his fatigue jacket.

"And him?" Mr. Boyles asked, looking up at Steph.

"Who knows," Zimmer said, draping Steph's parka across his shoulders.

Steph said, "Do you suppose we could get a grant from National Geographic?"

They toasted once more around the bar, clanking beer bottles. Randy looked up from his bar chores in time to say, "Great food, Zimmer. Thanks."

Mr. Boyles raised his tumbler to the two of them, "Indeed, thank you."

They might have supposed that outside, in the cold and the dark of the early morning, out of the haze and the stuffy glow of Lear's, that Steph would consider postponing their trip. After all, given the nature of their research, if he was even half right about the historical roots of his thesis, it surely wouldn't suffer from waiting a few more hours, from a little sleep.

Zimmer considered the argument, or he considered confessing to Steph that he was in no condition to drive or do anything else until he got some rest. When he saw Steph snuggle into his cat-like fur ball on the cold passenger seat he didn't think he'd have to. He was sure Steph would have a change of heart once they got up into the warm apartment, once the trip up those stairs had their usual effect on him. But when they turned onto the access drive, Zimmer had to stop short of the garage, stop before a collection of mixing bowls and utensils and cutlery strewn across the drive, littering the space beneath Fill's window, gleaming in the Bee-atile's headlights.

"Aw, fuck," Zimmer said, guiding Abby through the mess. "How about I just drop you off?"

Steph peeked out his window. "Maybe she's trying to be funny?"

"Right. Remind me to tell you my theories about *that*."

When they came around the rear of Fill, Whomee was still lying at the bottom of the staircase, snoozing. They tiptoed up the stairs, hoping that Angela was sleeping too, shushing themselves as they fumbled for their respective sets of keys, trying to guide one or the other quietly into the lock. Zimmer couldn't find the right key, in the dark, so Steph pushed him out of the way. He only had two keys on his chain. When he leaned against the door to steady his hand it swung open all by itself and banged into the coat tree on the other side of the wall. They stood in the threshold grimacing for a few agonizing moments, neither of them relishing the thought of a confrontation with her.

As they tried to sneak by the partition, for the kitchen, she said, "Are you just going to disappear and not even say goodbye?"

"Aw, Jesus, Angie," Steph said, retracing his steps back around the partition.

Zimmer stood in the middle of the apartment, listening, his ears ringing, swaying a little bit.

"You were, weren't you?"

"What do you mean disappear?"

She means *disappear*, disappear, Zimmer thought.

"You said it yourself, he's never going to change. He's never going to quit drifting through life, fucking up everybody else's. He's never going to do anything with his."

True.

"Jesus, Angie, why do we have to keep having this conversation? He's *doing* it."

"And that's what you'd prefer to do, isn't it."

"What's that mean?"

Zimmer thumped his chest with his left index finger, banged it against his sternum, *Mea culpa*, twice, then a third time. He was missing some parts of the conversation when he took time to consider responding. He thought he was keeping up with it well enough, though.

"Why are you taking up for him after he ruined my party?"

"Ruined your party?"

"Yes, ruined my party," she shrieked. "Just like he's going to ruin my life."

"Ruin your life?" Steph repeated. He knew that was irritating, but he honestly didn't know what she was talking about.

"But I do." Zimmer shook his head a couple of times, shrugged, then went and got his duffle bag from one of the low cabinets in the kitchen, and another beer. When he came back through the kitchen doorway, shaking the old sack open, Angela was standing in the middle of the living room, wearing one of those long tee shirts she sleeps in, her fists balled up on her hips.

"You're leaving, right?"

"Right."

"Tonight?"

"Now," he said, turning back into the kitchen for his clock radio. He checked the remaining utensils in the kitchen, to see if there were any left that he wanted to take with him, then emptied the boxes he kept his clothes in into the bag.

"And you're going with him?" she asked Steph, who was likewise stuffing a backpack.

"Yes."

"You coming back?"

"Probably. Why not?"

"Because he's not."

"What difference does that make?"

"It makes a big difference, to me. I had plans. *We* had plans."

"What plans, Angie? We were just trying to make each day work. That's all."

"So what now? What about me, and my life. What about us?"

Zimmer slipped behind them for the still opened door.

"Come with us," Steph said.

Zimmer stopped on the top of the stairs, listening for her answer.

"No! I can't do that anymore. I don't want *you* to do that anymore." She saw Zimmer listening, which enraged her further. "You're really enjoying this, aren't you, you bastard."

"No, Angela. I'm not. I'm just trying to get out of your way."

"Great. But when are you going to start thinking about all the damage you leave behind?"

"Damage? Goddammit Angela, what the fuck is it that you want?"

"I want my life, the way I had it planned!"

Zimmer stepped back into the apartment, screaming back at her, "That's what everybody wants. That's what *I* want. But it just doesn't happen, Angie. It just doesn't happen. Get used to it."

When she didn't answer to that, he waved around the room, "Fine. It's yours. Everything's yours. The apartment, the deposit, if you can find that asshole Moseley," knowing somehow she would. He hoisted the duffle bag over his shoulder, turning for the door again, saying, "I got nothing going for me around here anymore, I'll just go--"

"Jesus fuck-ing Christ fuck-ing Jesus. I'm so goddamned sick of listening to you, and you, and you bitch and bitch like you've been robbed, like you *deserve* better! Let me tell you something, life don't owe you a fucking thing, not one fucking thing."

Steph stood there heaving, as some of the blood drained back out of his face, through the throbbing veins popping out on his forehead. Zimmer would always wonder who the third You was supposed to be. "Life don't owe you a fucking thing." The line was maybe the final distillation of his theory about ideas and opportunities.

Steph stomped past Zimmer, out the door. Zimmer considered trying to explain, as if she, any of them, could somehow understand, if they could once see things from Steph's perspective, whether they agreed with him or not. But she was past listening. When Zimmer met her eyes, she hissed, "You bastard," moving to grip the opened door. "Get out."

"You're right."

"Get out."

He stepped through the door, saying, "But so is he."

She slammed the door. "Life *don't* owe you a fucking thing," he repeated, to the door, to her, himself.

Steph was underneath the staircase standing over Whomee, who was still comatose from the dinner. He wouldn't be moved, no matter how much urging either of them tried. "Come on, Whomee, it'll be great. We'll play in the park. Go to the zoo. Eat pretzels in Times Square!" But Whomee's distended belly anchored him to the spot. All he could manage was to lift his head and pant contentedly at his master.

Steph finally said, "Let's go," not yet thinking that Zimmer really meant what he'd said about leaving it all to Angela, just wanting to distance himself from the episode, as far as he could, as fast as he could. They got into the Bee-atile and backed their way down the driveway for the Turnpike.

After cruising up the hill in silence, seeking the interstate, arching up the entrance ramp under the shadow of the quarry, Steph turned to Zimmer and said, "Sorry."

"No you're not. We're the ones who should be sorry."

Before Steph could counter that, Zimmer pulled to the side of the highway. "You sure you want to do this?"

"Yeah."

"Why?"

Steph looked at him, frowned.

"Why not, right?"

Zimmer started up again, but after a few more minutes, he pulled to the side again, and then arched Abby all the way through a U-turn, heading back toward Tripoli.

"She's right, you know," he told Steph. "I'm not going to change."

"Nothing changes."

"Shit."

"Who wants you to?"

"She does."

"Exactly. What she needs to figure out is that you can't have it both ways."

"Jesus, I hate cliches."

"Yeah, so do I. But in this case, it's true."

Zimmer thought about that, thought for the first time how wrong he'd been about Steph. "Resilient doesn't mean malleable." Steph was speaking for himself, he now knew. "*He's* the one who's spent his whole life trying to find some one, some situation, where he wouldn't be weighed down by expectations beyond what he was prepared to give, or do, naturally."

He stopped the car again. "You know, I wasn't even really going to New York."

"So. You lied."

Zimmer laughed, making another U-turn, "An O-turn," wondering if that canceled out or compounded what moving violations he'd already made. "No matter," he said, thinking one last time about his outstanding reckless driving ticket. "They've got a big old book they're waiting to throw at me."

"What?"

"Nothing."

He wondered if he even remembered to pack that citation.

Then, once they were safely distanced from Tripoli, Zimmer said, "Let me tell you a story," though he didn't quite know where to begin. Begins at the beginning, right? "Ever been to New York?" he asked.

"Once, when I was a kid."

"The last time I was there was with Koogan, about eight,

shit, ten years ago now. Ever heard of the New York Dolls?"

"No. Don't think so."

"They were this raunchy rock-and-roll band out of the city that never got much notoriety anywhere else. They were a Stones rip-off, mostly, so Koogan loved them. He absolutely loved them. About two weeks before we were supposed to go into the Air Force, they were playing in New York. How he heard about it, I never knew.

"Anyway, we decided that we'd have our own kind of farewell blow-out, take a trip to New York, see the Dolls, waste as much time and money as we could. See," Zimmer looked over to see how attentive Steph was. He was hanging on every word, of course. Zimmer could tell him, "That's the reason I never tell stories." Not because he wanted to keep things secret. He was just never very sure how much anyone would care. "We wouldn't need any money, not after we left for basic, so we took off, just the two of us, not even telling anyone. And we didn't plan on returning until it was time for our more official send off. It was a great idea," he said, thinking all over again about his feeling at the time, the height of independence and secrecy they both felt. "We left early in the morning, at a time when no one would have expected us to be moving at all, much less screaming along in his lemon yellow Challenger. His beloved Challenger," Zimmer recited, grinning.

He navigated an abandoned interchange, hooking up to an East-West connector, nothing but the Bee-atile cruising through the pale funnel of yellow light cast onto the stark concrete from lamps out of view, forty feet above the road surface; nothing but Abby's own headlights tracing the banked concrete retaining walls. He eased his seat back some, once on a barren straightaway again, empty of any other traffic beyond an occasional eighteen-wheeler.

"You know, usually, a trip, a long trip, like this one, like that one, is just a blur. All you remember are the high points, because it's so otherwise dreary getting from one to the next. But I think I remember every little bit of that Dolls run. I remember stopping in this hicky little upstate town to buy shades, because the sunrise was killing us after we'd turned East, for the Catskills. I remember all the stops, for doughnuts, and then beer and chips, all the garbage accumulating in the back seat. I remember singing along with Koogan's tapes, Elton, Dylan, the Dolls, of course.

"I mean, the trip seemed so short to me at the time. Still does. It was one of the finest times I can remember with Koogan, though there were plenty. It only lasted five, six hours. And I know he felt the same. He wasn't as clumsy as I am, spoke in theories, a lot like you. He'd say, This is 87 percent fine."

"I like that," Steph said. "Like that a lot."

"He worried that when things were going really well, if you pressed, pushed things over their threshold, bad news was lurking, to bring you back down. Whereas," Zimmer said, grinning, from using one of Koogan's favorite words, "Whereas, if things were shitty, there was never any help to be found, nothing to do but ride it out. I believed him. I worried, wondered if we weren't pushing it, lighting that last joint, playing that last game of basketball, worried that he wasn't keeping track.

"Before I knew it, we were at the zenith of the Tappan Zee bridge, parked to the side, where it says Emergency Parking Only, taking in the sights of the city, the Hudson, digging the vibrations of the bridge as the perpetual rush hour traffic zoomed by. Koogan says, Wouldn't it be great if the bridge collapsed?" Zimmer chuckled. "He said the Challenger would save us. We could jump in, roll the windows up, closing out the carnage, freezing time. We'd be sealed in—what's that called?"

"Hermetically sealed."

"Yeah. Then once we hit bottom, some huge, mutant fish would come along and cart us off, in little plastic bags with air in them. We'd spend the rest of our lives in a bowl on some two-ton catfish's television set.

"And then we were in the Bronx, poof, looking for a nice safe neighborhood to park the car in. He was worried about where we'd park in Manhattan, and what would happen to the

Challenger if we did. I ragged him about being scared of the traffic. He wouldn't take my shit, parked his precious car. We jumped on the Lex, headed downtown."

Steph sat there listening, hardly noticing the collection of small towns they approached, and then passed, all within just a few moments: a hodgepodge of burgs and villes and fields, the only distinguishing characteristics being which gas station franchise was closest to the exit ramp. "They might as well be called Sunocoville, Shellfield, Mobilburg."

He paid only slightly more attention to the larger cities they began to encounter as they pressed eastward, those with multiple exits, lodging and restaurant advertisements to go along with the gas stations. The larger cities would have mileage markers, too, for New Jersey, the city.

Zimmer took even less notice of their surroundings, or so it seemed. He only surveyed the signs once, so far, seeking a spot where he could be sure the gas station was opened at that time of the day, and week. He slowed a little as they approached the Delaware Water Gap, but didn't stop, unwilling, or unable to be distracted, or interrupted. Steph craned his head out into the biting air to see what he could, which wasn't much, the sun still an hour away.

"We detoured off the train, though, with plenty of time before the show, hopping off at 161st, Yankee Stadium, just to revel. The trains there are elevated. It's noisy and dirty as hell, but he loved it, the pulse, the people. We found this deli about a block from the stadium. Koogan orders liverwurst, and bacon, with Colby cheese, a tomato slice—provided it was ripe. On an onion roll, a fresh onion roll. He drove the poor guy nuts. God, that was the best fucking sandwich.

"We talked about hopping on the 8, but he didn't want any part of Times Square, too many tourists, assholes hustling between their posh jobs, the *theatre*," Zimmer said, slipping into Koogan's imitative accent. "We stayed on the Lex. After Grand Central, the freaks came out. Did he love that. He was getting psyched for his Dolls, talking to strangers, singing. We had to get off early, around Astor Place, I think, because he couldn't stand the idleness any more, wanted to walk the rest of the way to the club where they were playing. Hell, I didn't care. I trudged along with him. He knew where we were going, he'd given the whole event his peculiar purpose. I wasn't going to question him."

Lost in Zimmer's quick maneuvering, as he sorted out another complicated interchange, checking for traffic in blind spots around the Bee-atile as he slipped out of disappearing lanes, or darted across traffic for the ramp he needed, was any clear indication that he was just telling a vacation story any longer, just filling in the idle time of their trip.

That last little bit seemed beseeching somehow, "Confessional," though Steph couldn't yet see why. "Those details," were things people only remembered if they've played the events over and over and over again.

"And then, in Washington Square, or near it, these guys jumped us," Zimmer said, pausing at the toll booth for the Lincoln Tunnel, before descending into the dark tube.

The noise of the Bee-atile, reverberating off the tiled walls, and the rest of the growing traffic, along with Steph's fascination, halted the story.

And then on the other side, at the base of that famous skyline, once he found a space, Zimmer pulled to the side of the road near the intersection of 42nd Street and 8th Avenue, undecided about which direction to head. South, to the village, or uptown.

"They dragged us into this alley, waving their knives. They took everything," he said, squinting in that direction, before some delivery truck honked at them, the driver screaming obscenities in garbled Brooklynese.

Zimmer eased back out into traffic, sliding from one vacant curbside space to another, only to be routed by a cabbie, another delivery van, then a cop.

"They took all of our money, of course. They took Koogan's keys, actually asked where his car was. 'You'll never fucking find it, assholes.' So then they took the Doll's tickets. He couldn't believe that. 'What the fuck are the five of you going to do with just two tickets? Where's your car? Fuck you.' So they passed the tickets out amongst themselves, said, Guess we're just going to have to ruin your date, princess. Koogan went nuts. 'I don't fucking believe you're doing this,' he hollers, pushing, tugging on those guys, out of control. They had their knives, though. It only took a couple of swipes, and then a few punches once he was cut, to quiet him back down. Then they left us there, still laughing, 'Believe it, motherfucker.' Calling, 'No show tonight, faggots.'

"I leaned over Koogan, told him I was sorry," Zimmer said, shaking his head, looping along Central Park South.

"I was sorry that I'd let him park his car so far away, sorry that I'd followed him blindly out into that street, sorry most of all that I hadn't done a damn thing to help him when they were beating up on him.

"'No you're not,' he said to me, wiping some more blood onto his special concert shirt from his mouth, tearing a bit of the waist off to tie around a gash on his arm."

Zimmer pulled into the taxi lane along Central Park West. They got out of the Bee-atile and sat on the wall that bordered the park, with their backs to the green expanse, looking over to the ornate apartment buildings on the other side of the avenue, the gothic Dakota, for one.

"He said I either wasn't sorry and was just saying that to make him feel better, or I was really *was* sorry, neither of which he wanted to believe of me. He said that even if I'd had the time, that I'd made a decision not to do anything, for pretty good reasons, 'Pretty goddamn good reasons, Z,' and that we were probably both still alive because of my actions, despite his. I told him, 'You did something, at least.'

"All I could do was wonder why I hadn't reacted the same way, since we were supposed to be such kindred spirits, without having to decide, feeling like a puke.

"'Kindred spirits doesn't mean we think the same, Z.'

"I apologized for that, too.

"'No you're not!'

"'What about the Dolls? What about the Challenger?'

"He smiled at me. The son-of-a-bitch actually smiled at me, as he climbed to his feet and reached into the change pocket of his jeans, pulling out two quarters. 'Emergency money. And there's a spare key hidden on the Challenger.'"

Zimmer shook his head, remembering.

"I was still brooding, wondering what the fuck we were going to do with two lousy quarters. 'We can get on a train. Yeah? We can ride all night if we have to. We'll find those assholes.'"

Zimmer looked over at Steph with one eyebrow raised in bewilderment. "And he would have, too. He would have gotten onto a train looking like that, beat, bloody, playing cop, chasing our robbers forever, except we just took the subway back to Van Cortlandt Park, to the Challenger, with a key hidden up in the wheel well, an Esso credit card in the glove compartment, and we left."

Zimmer swung one leg over the wall, straddling it, and peered into the park, to the empty jogging path.

"I remember the mirror image of that trip, too, mostly because it was so excruciatingly long. Because I was sorry, and we both knew it. I'd let him down, let him get the shit beat out of him. And I still think it would've been better if we'd both died back there in that alley, because that was the beginning of the end for us anyway. Only there was nothing I could do about it then, nothing I can do now."

He turned back to face the street. They sat there and watched a New York City traffic cop write out a parking ticket and slip it under the windshield wiper of Abby, utterly uncaring.

"Koogan was important to me. More important than family, more important than wives, lovers, too, I think. Whatever we did, it was because we chose to do it—though that's not quite accurate either. We just did it, no duty, no fulfilling expectations or promises. Preference, pure and simple, a lot like our being here right now," he said, eyeing Steph, eyebrows level. "Which is probably why you're the only person who's ever heard about that little episode."

Zimmer slipped off the wall, started to pace, then leaned against it, on his elbows, looking into the park. "See, we do things, and make decisions whether we know we want to or not, is what he was trying to tell me. Apologizing, in his scheme of things, doesn't mean squat. You're either not that responsible for what happened, which is usually the case; or you can't be absolved that easily, because there's no real going back, no starting over. It's just a big fucking waste of time. But you know what I wonder? If nothing matters, and nothing ever changes, what's the fucking point?"

Steph pulled Zimmer away from the wall, forgetting about research, forgetting about the Dakota, but knowing enough about New York that if they didn't move soon, Abby would be caught in some tow truck's sling again.

In the Bee-atile, cranking the engine and gliding down the avenue with the ticket still flapping on the windshield, Zimmer asked, "Now what?"

Steph reached into his pocket, jamming his feet into the floorboard, scraping his head along the ceiling, pulling out two quarters and flashing them at Zimmer. "Let's do it."

As he might have guessed, that was very nearly the same urging Koogan'd tried on Zimmer after they'd gotten on their first train uptown.

Zimmer said, "I think the price has gone up," offering just that little bit of discouragement, before weaving his way toward the river, thinking he could park near NYU, maybe. They could jump on the Broadway local from there.

"What'd they look like?" Steph asked, once they were settled into bumpy seats, headed downtown.

Zimmer looked over at him in complete shock, confused, and then stunned by the seriousness of the question.

"I don't think I ever knew, or remembered. It's always been their voices that I'll remember forever. 'You look like a real smart boy,' one of them hissed in my ear. 'Use your head, faggot. Keep your mouth shut and I'll let you live a little longer.'

"I probably thanked him."

Steph stood up, both to offer his seat as the train got a little crowded, and to look out the grimy windows. He hung his wrists through the straps directly above Zimmer, hunched over, reading the tiled signs on the station walls as they made their way through dark tunnels, screeching on the curves, as the train turned under Columbus Circle, with the lights blinking off and on; into other dimly lit corridors, platforms where a few blank people waited with their heads bowed into a paperback or the Sunday Times, then shuffled toward a door, not really looking up, just stepping in the direction of the sound as pneumatic doors hissed open for them as they have a hundred thousand times before, no doubt. The numbers of the stations continued decreasing, 59th, to 50th, until Times Square, bright, glitzy, crowded, by comparison.

Zimmer, along with most of the rest of the riders, stood and methodically sifted to the door, out onto the platform, toward a transfer platform or a street level appointment. Steph and Zimmer herded along with one of a few naturally forming crowds, for the escalator, up, when Steph spotted a men's room tucked into the shadows and said, "I'd better do this."

"Why not."

Steph headed for one of two stalls, briefly noticing that the door had been removed, assuming it was part of the charm of the New York City transit system.

Zimmer leaned against one of the sinks along the opposite wall, his head still bowed, still lost in those voices from the past, "Like it was *his* decision. Let you live a little longer, his decision alone."

Steph sat, and took off the ring that Angela'd given him, wondering how such a simple little trinket could really have precipitated all the events it seems to have, turning it over and over in his hands. "Jesus."

"It wasn't his fucking decision. It was mine," Zimmer said, starting to pace. "It was my decision and I made the *wrong* choice."

"Come on, Zimmer."

"The wrong choice, Steph. I shouldn't have kept my mouth

shut, or stood there and done nothing while they hit on Koogan. They might have killed us, though probably not. We weren't *that* young, that green. But who cares? Hell, it's killing me anyway, letting them choose."

"You just reacted."

"Not true. I had a chance to decide. I'm sure of that. Maybe you really think things happen all by themselves, and maybe Koogan did, too, but I don't. I think you have a chance to decide, a split second where you have a chance to ask yourself, Do I really want to do this? Or not. You decide, always. There can't be any excuses, apologizing. Koogan was right about that, at least. So if I was the person I think I am, or was, I should be dead, right?"

"And the rest of the world is supposed to wait around while you make these decisions? If every decision someone makes gets a split second, no matter what else happens to be going on around them at the time, let's see, that's like twenty-six billion splits. How *long* is a split?"

Zimmer shook his head, laughing a little. "Fuck you." In the quiet of his not answering, he heard a *plunk* and looked up to see Steph gazing down between his legs.

"Shit."

"I suppose you think *that's* funny."

"No. I dropped that goddammed ring.

Zimmer laughed again.

"What?"

"*That's* how long a split is."

"Great." Steph sat there and pondering, before finally flushing. "Now what?"

"Let's go."

"Where? The village?"

"No. These trains are depressing me."

"Lear's?" Steph tried. "It's never failed us before."

They rode up the escalator in silence, pausing at the exit turnstiles, before they forfeited their fares.

"No. I *really* think Tripoli's out, now."

"Then where? Where *were* you headed?"

"I don't know. Let's go out for some air, for now. I can't think in here."

They found an exit to street level, such as it was. They stood on a street corner taking in the sights. But on a grey January Sunday morning, all the neon off, beneath the drab skyline rising all around them, New York felt and looked like a whore with all of her make-up scrubbed off.

"It's almost as stuffy out here. Is that because of the buildings?"

"That and the otherwise routine winter weather: grey, damp, depressing."

"Just like Tripoli. The weather never changes."

"That can't be true."

"Seems like it."

"Not down south." Zimmer sat on a curb. "Down in Florida now, along the panhandle, say, Panama City, it's probably sixty-five, seventy, sun shining, warm Gulf breezes rippling the sea oats, mullet running the beach..."

Steph sat next to him. "They got libraries down there?"

"I guess."

"Decent Newspaper?"

"You can always get out of town editions."

Steph stood, brushed off his jeans. "Then let's go."

"To Panama City?"

"Keep it simple. Let's say, Southbound, for now."

Zimmer stared out into the street, at the steam rising from grating along the opposite curb. He couldn't think of any reasons why they shouldn't. "Okay. Let's go get Abby."

"Perfect."

"Near enough," Zimmer said, as they started back down the stairwell into the station.

"87 percent."

"Oh, but wait," he said, searching his pockets. He had thought of one reason. "What about Whomee?"

He pulled out his car keys, some change, and the bundle of plastic sheathing he kept all of his vital papers and licenses in, bound by a fat rubber band.

Zimmer stepped back up to the street level, looking around for a shop, a magazine stand, any business which might be open at that time. Then he pried a notice stapled to the lamppost on the corner. It was a small card, a public invitation to the memorial service they'd had for Lennon three weeks ago.

"Near fucking enough," he said, fishing a stamp out of one of the slips of plastic. "How much is a postcard now?" he asked Steph.

"Eight? Twelve?"

"Less than eighteen?"

"Easy."

Zimmer licked the worn stamp, surprised that its glue still adhered, then spun Steph around to use his back as a writing prop.

"Dear Mr. Boyles," he scribbled in pencil. "Right again. We're southbound, to bask in the sunshine, retiring early. Will send word when we get there, let you know where we can be found. Lear's south. You can winter over, work on your tan. We had to leave Whomee behind though. Maybe he could keep our seats at the bar warm? Regrets and regards to any who care. Z."

The only address he knew to put on it was Lear's, Mountainside Viewway, Tripoli, Pennsylvania.

"The zip's got to be the same as the pink house," Steph reasoned, reciting from what felt like distant memory, "11803 Mountainside Viewway..."

"Think it'll get there?" Zimmer asked, handing him the card to read, as they descended into the station again.

"Bound to," Steph said, looking at the card, that tiny little encapsulation of everything, it seemed—all the spoken, unspoken, misspoken, muted, planned, improvised or imprudent—and slipped it into his back pocket.

Acknowledgements

Thanks to the original lumpers, my brothers, who, whether they realized it or not, have been inspiring me my entire life. And thanks to all you blessed deviants out there. Please keep doing what you're doing. Admittedly, it's a fine line between foolish and dangerous, which shouldn't be taken lightly or ignored, or even flirted with, perhaps. But, as with most thresholds, you can't really know them until they're crossed. In any event, it's damn sure interesting, which is always welcomed, whether funny or frightening, and would be truly missed.

Made in United States
Troutdale, OR
08/06/2024

21790178R00246